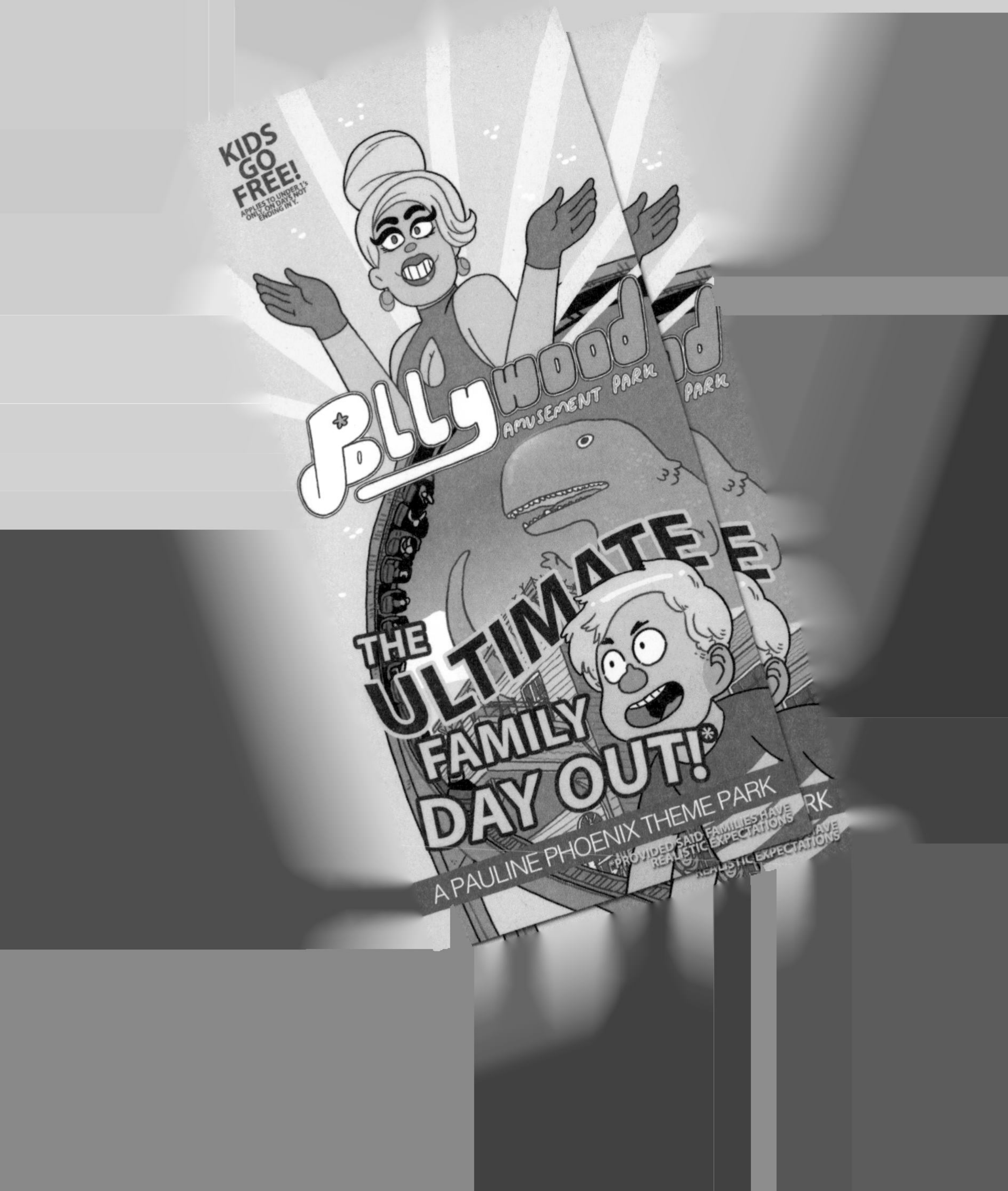
KIDS GO FREE!
APPLIES TO UNDER 1's ONLY ON DAYS NOT ENDING IN Y.
Pollywood
AMUSEMENT PARK
THE ULTIMATE FAMILY DAY OUT!*
A PAULINE PHOENIX THEME PARK
*PROVIDED SAID FAMILIES HAVE REALISTIC EXPECTATIONS

HAMISH STEELE

DEAD ENDIA

- THE WATCHER'S TEST -

NOBROW

LONDON | NEW YORK

PARK MAP

– OPENING TIMES 9AM–8PM –
SOME INDIVIDUAL ATTRACTIONS HAVE SEPARATE OPENING TIMES.
CHECK WEBSITE FOR HOLIDAY OPENING TIMES.

INFO POINT
RESTROOMS
FOOD
FIRST AID

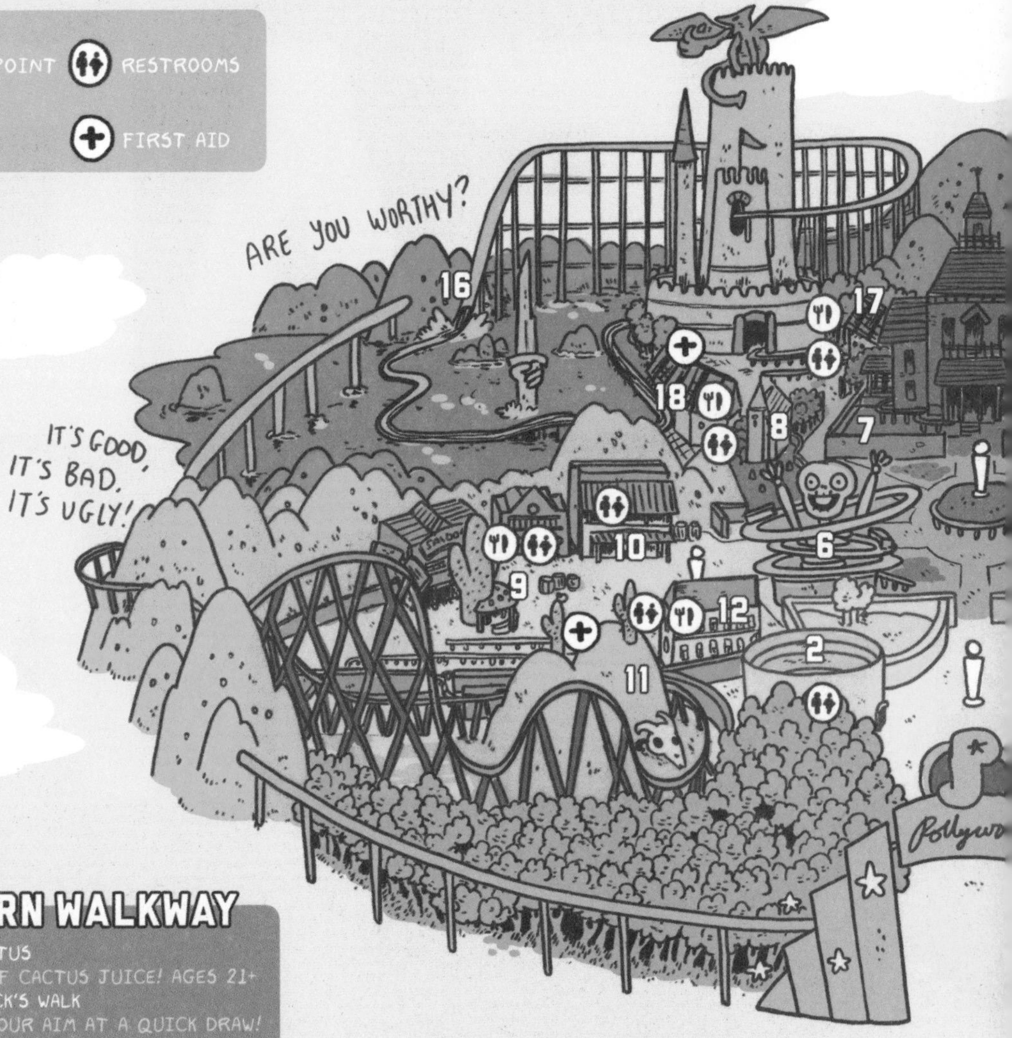

ARE YOU WORTHY?
IT'S GOOD, IT'S BAD, IT'S UGLY!
16
17
18
8
7
6
10
9
12
2
11

WESTERN WALKWAY

9. THE CACTUS
   HOME OF CACTUS JUICE! AGES 21+
10. MURDOCK'S WALK
    TEST YOUR AIM AT A QUICK DRAW!
11. THE RATTLESNAKE
    DARE YOU ENTER THE MINES?
12. SUNSET ARCADE

ANIMAL AVENUE

1. THE REPTILE HOUSE
   MEET PESTO THE KOMODO DRAGON!
2. PENGUIN PARADISE
   DAILY SHOWS AT 11AM AND 3PM!
3. ANIMAL ATTRACTIONS

CAMELOT CREEK

16. SIR LOGS-A-LOT
    THE THIRD LARGEST LOG FLUME IN THE WORLD!
17. MERLIN'S CAFE
18. FAIRY TALE COTTAGE
    OUR EXCLUSIVE HOTEL - PERFECT FOR FAMILIES AND COUPLES

LUNA LOOKOUT

19. THE WHEEL IN SPACE
    THE BEST VIEW OF THE PARK!
20. ROCKETORIUM
    A VERTICAL DROP IN ZERO GRAVITY!
6. MARTIAN INVASION !!
   INTERACTIVE LASER EXPERIENCE!
7. SATURN'S SPINNING SEESAW
   A HORRIFYING ORDEAL!

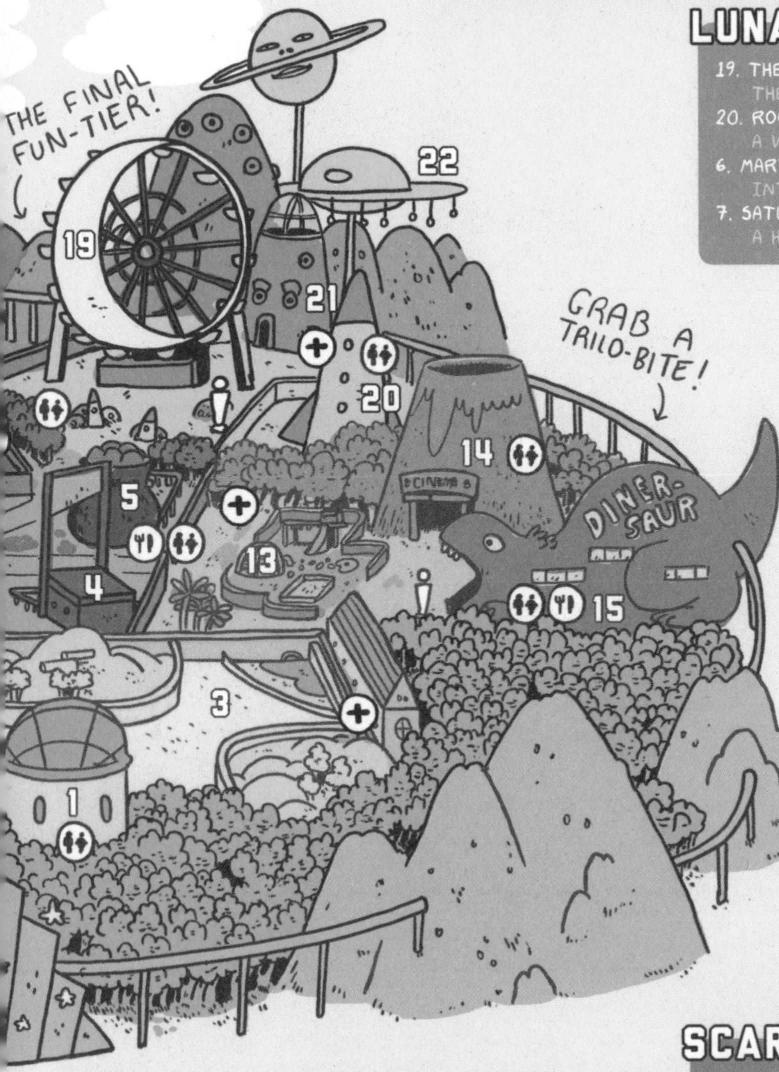

THE FINAL FUN-TIER!
22
19
21
20
GRAB A TRILO-BITE!
14
CINEMA
DINER-SAUR
5
13
4
15
3
1

SCARE SQUARE

4. THE GUILLOTINE
   THE DEATH SLIDE - AGES 13+
5. THE CAULDRON
   THE WORLD'S SCARIEST RESTAURANT!
6. THE RIBCAGE
   ALL AGES RIDE!
7. DEAD END
   GUIDED TOURS EVERY HALF HOUR!
8. THE GIFT SHOP OF THE DEAD

PREHISTORIC PAVILION

13. LITTLE PTERA'S PLAYGROUND
    PERFECT PLACE FOR UNDER-10'S!
14. VOLCANO CINEMA
15. DINO-SAUR
    THE JURASSIC FAMILY RESTAURANT!

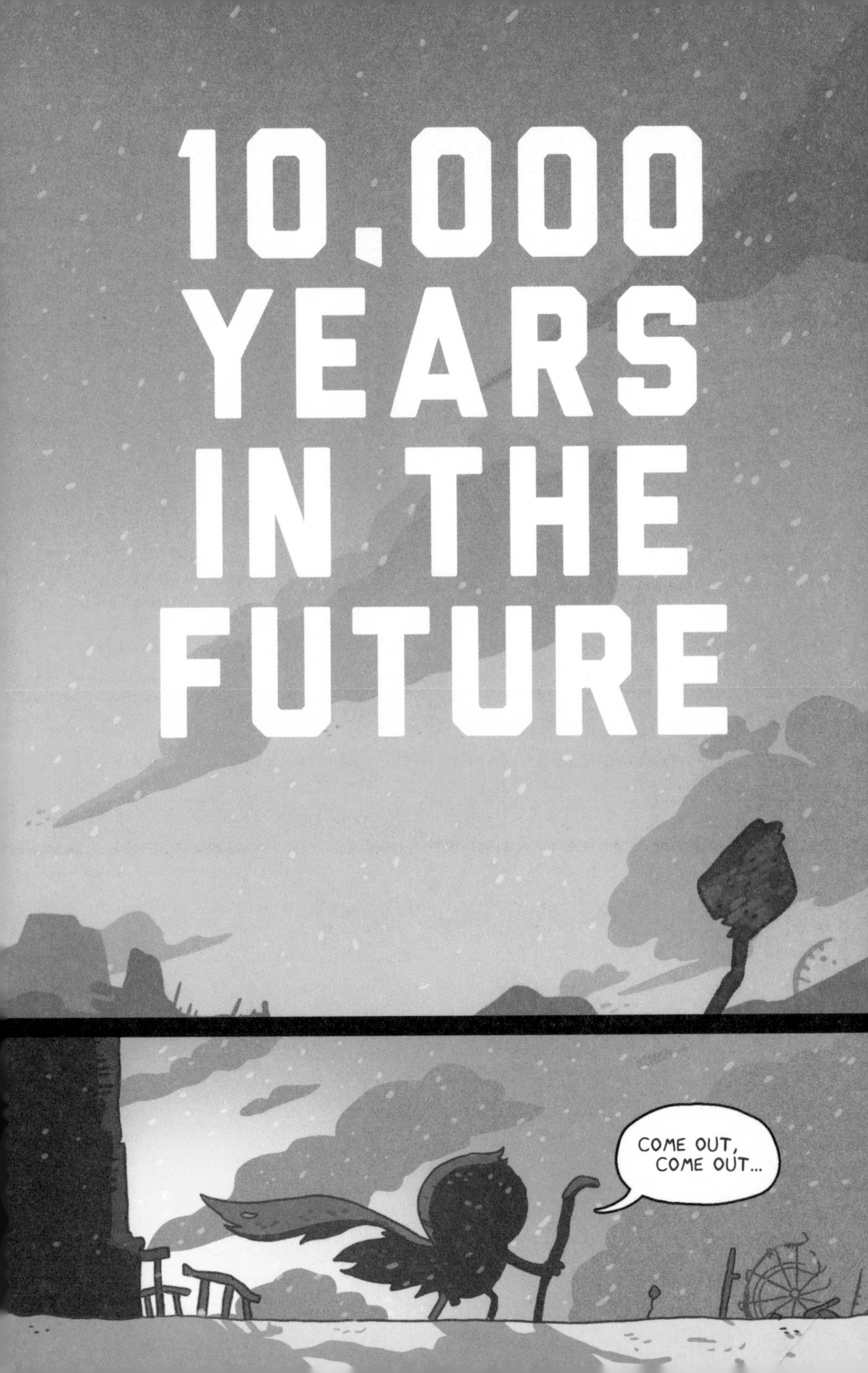
10,000 YEARS IN THE FUTURE
COME OUT, COME OUT...

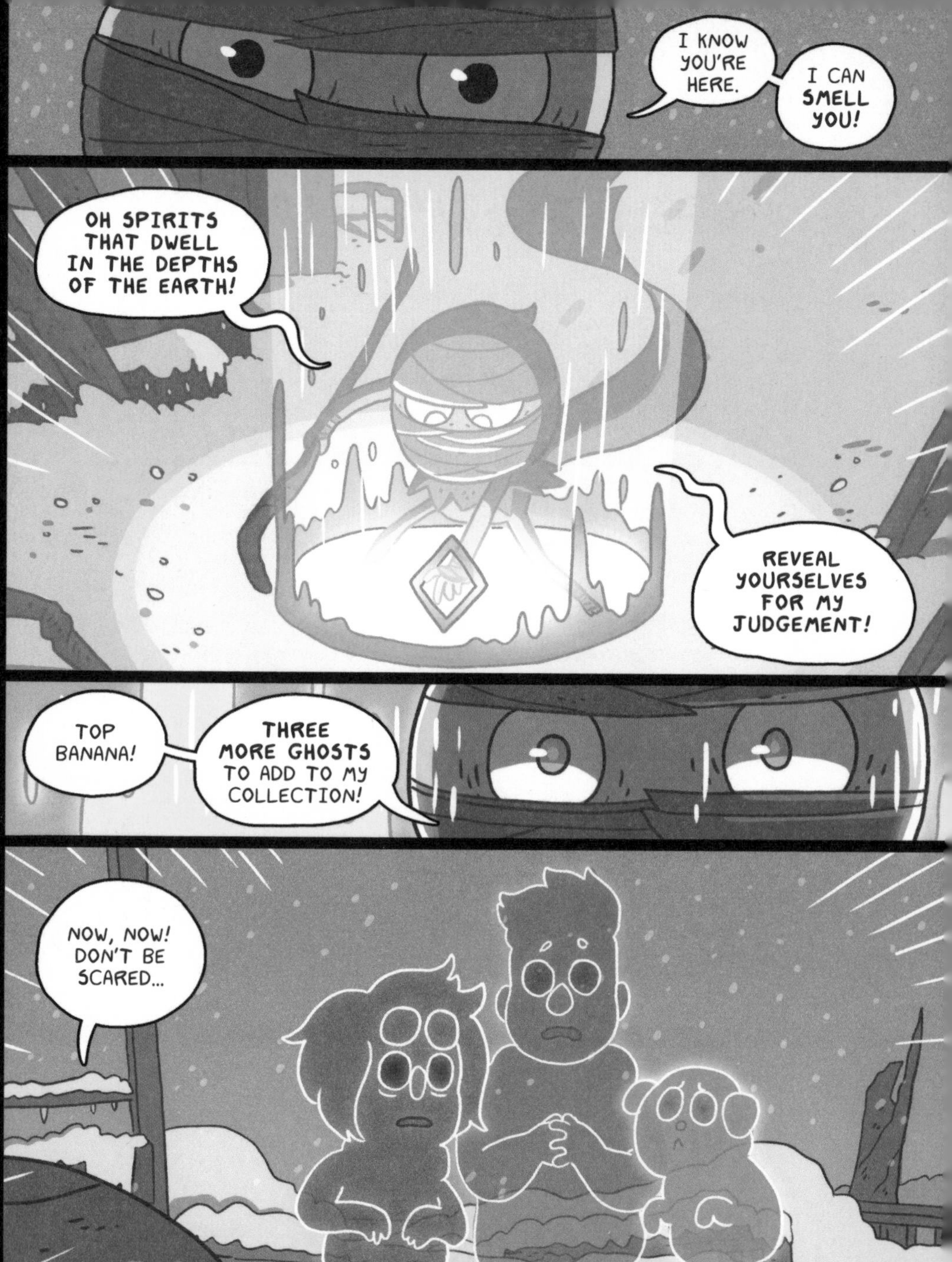
I KNOW YOU'RE HERE.
I CAN SMELL YOU!
OH SPIRITS THAT DWELL IN THE DEPTHS OF THE EARTH!
REVEAL YOURSELVES FOR MY JUDGEMENT!
TOP BANANA!
THREE MORE GHOSTS TO ADD TO MY COLLECTION!
NOW, NOW! DON'T BE SCARED...

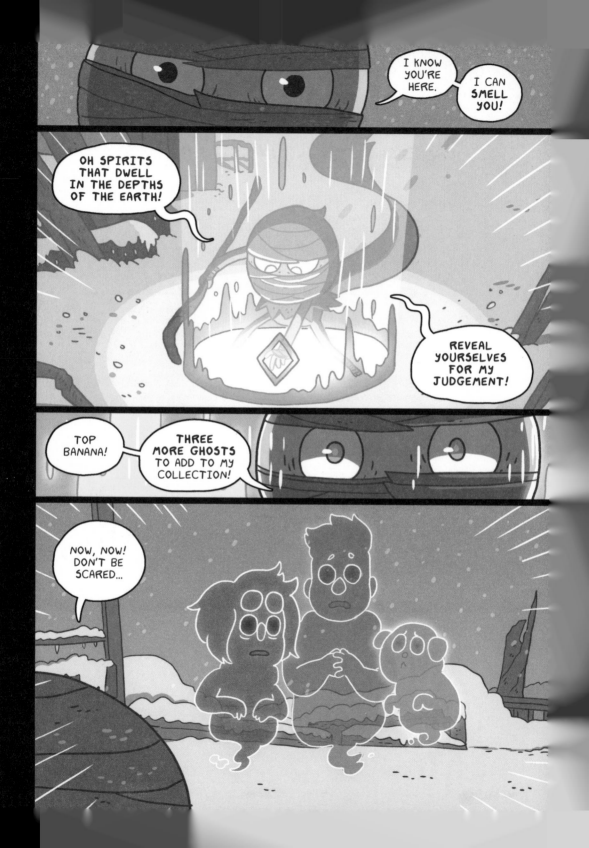

CHAPTER 1

COVER ART BY HAMISH STEELE

HOME AWAY FROM HELL

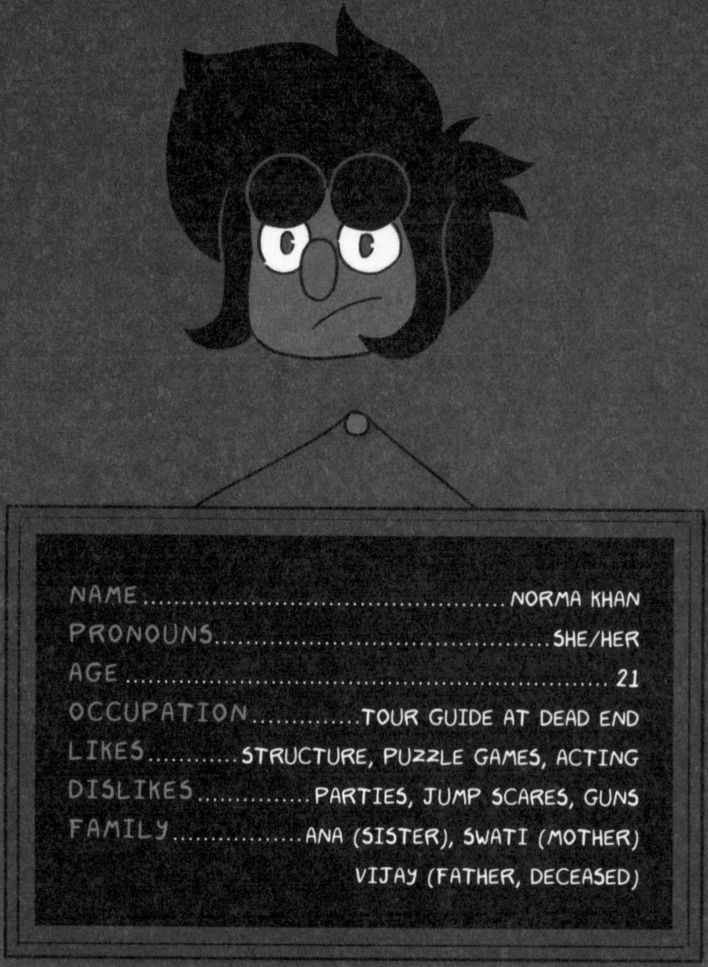

NAME...NORMA KHAN
PRONOUNS...SHE/HER
AGE 21
OCCUPATION.............TOUR GUIDE AT DEAD END
LIKES...........STRUCTURE, PUZZLE GAMES, ACTING
DISLIKES.............PARTIES, JUMP SCARES, GUNS
FAMILY..............ANA (SISTER), SWATI (MOTHER)
                       VIJAY (FATHER, DECEASED)

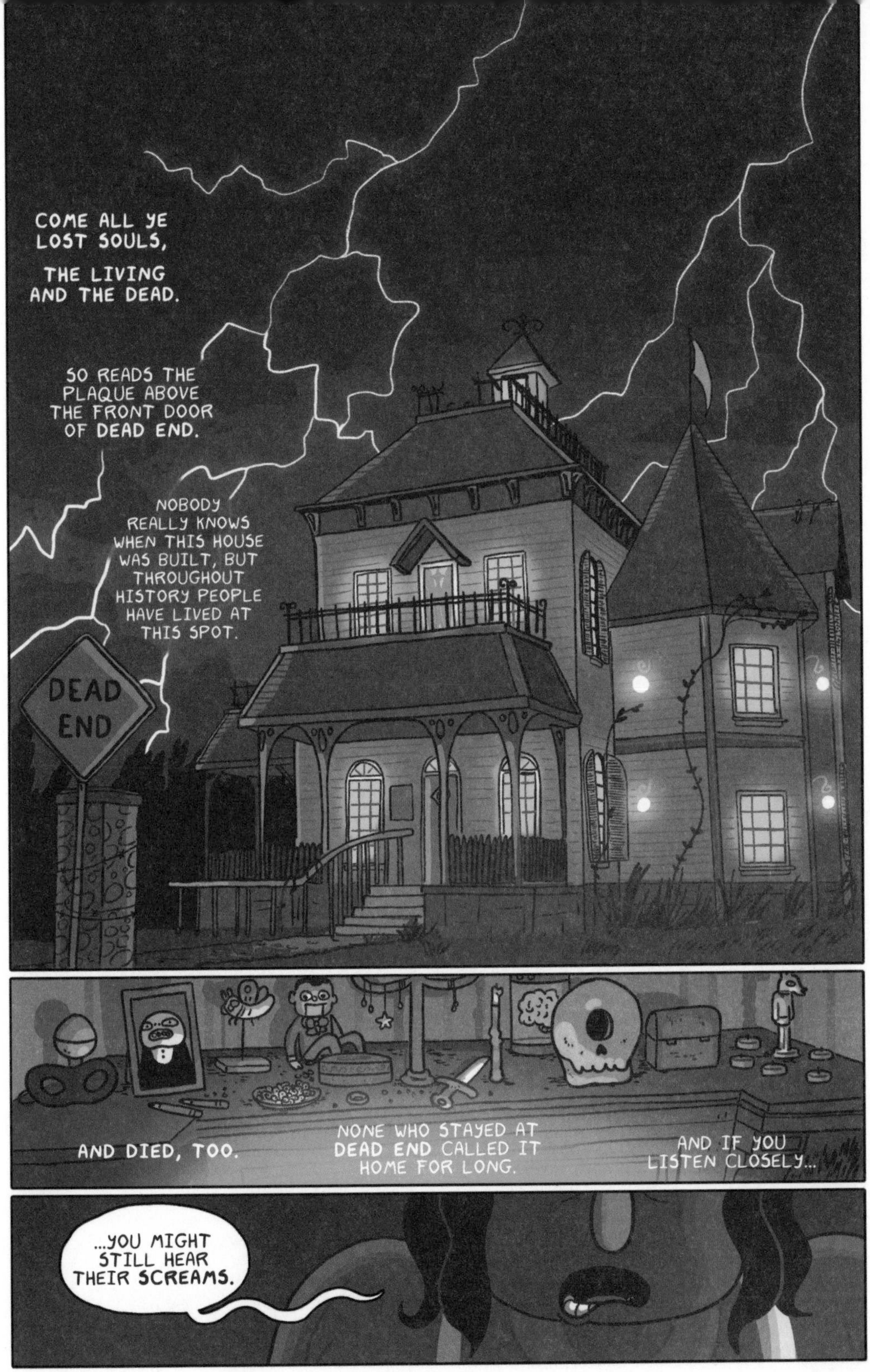
COME ALL YE LOST SOULS,
THE LIVING AND THE DEAD.
SO READS THE PLAQUE ABOVE THE FRONT DOOR OF DEAD END.
NOBODY REALLY KNOWS WHEN THIS HOUSE WAS BUILT, BUT THROUGHOUT HISTORY PEOPLE HAVE LIVED AT THIS SPOT.
DEAD END
AND DIED, TOO.
NONE WHO STAYED AT DEAD END CALLED IT HOME FOR LONG.
AND IF YOU LISTEN CLOSELY...
...YOU MIGHT STILL HEAR THEIR SCREAMS.

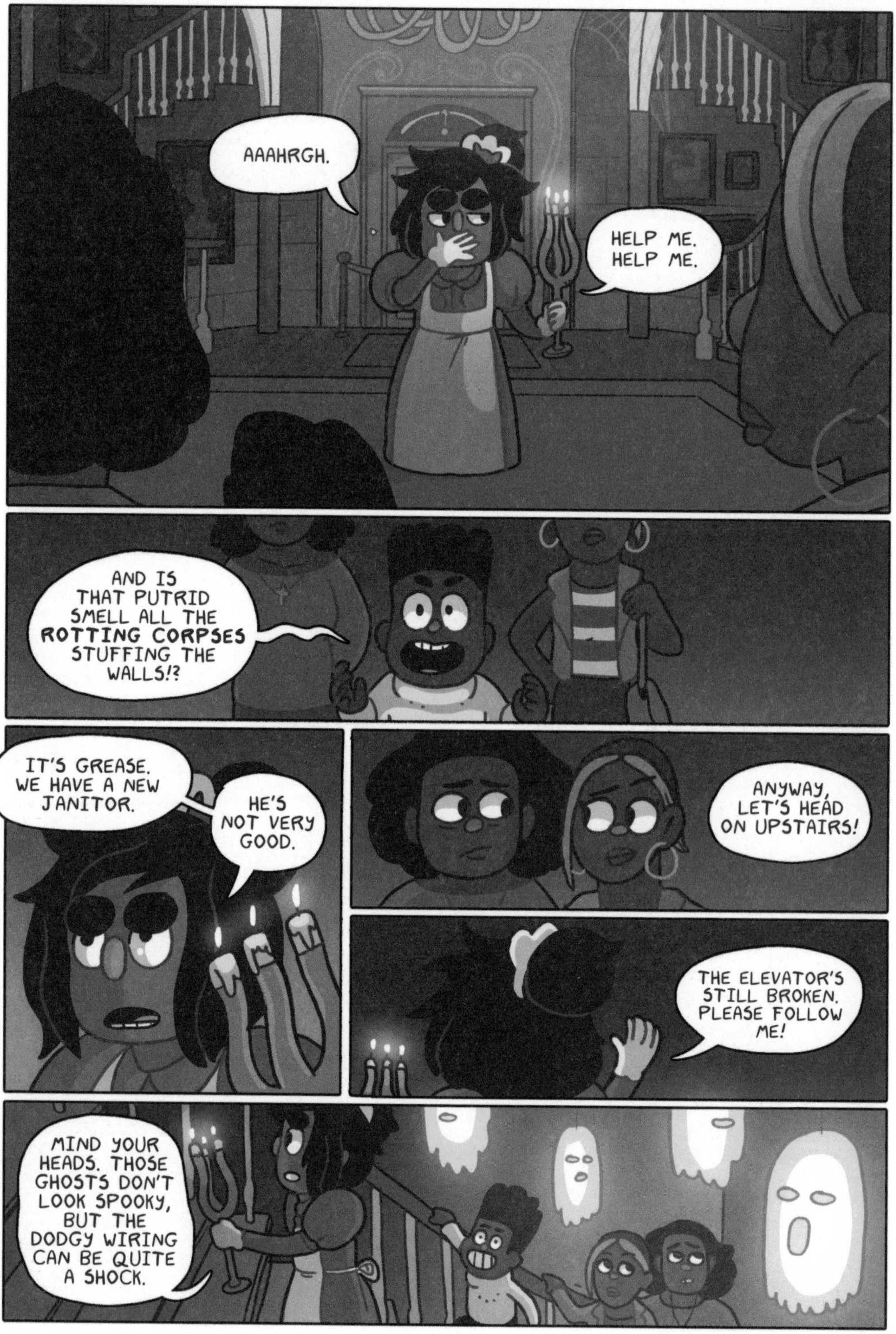
AAAHRGH.
HELP ME. HELP ME.
AND IS THAT PUTRID SMELL ALL THE **ROTTING CORPSES** STUFFING THE WALLS!?
IT'S GREASE. WE HAVE A NEW JANITOR.
HE'S NOT VERY GOOD.
ANYWAY, LET'S HEAD ON UPSTAIRS!
THE ELEVATOR'S STILL BROKEN. PLEASE FOLLOW ME!
MIND YOUR HEADS. THOSE GHOSTS DON'T LOOK SPOOKY, BUT THE DODGY WIRING CAN BE QUITE A SHOCK.

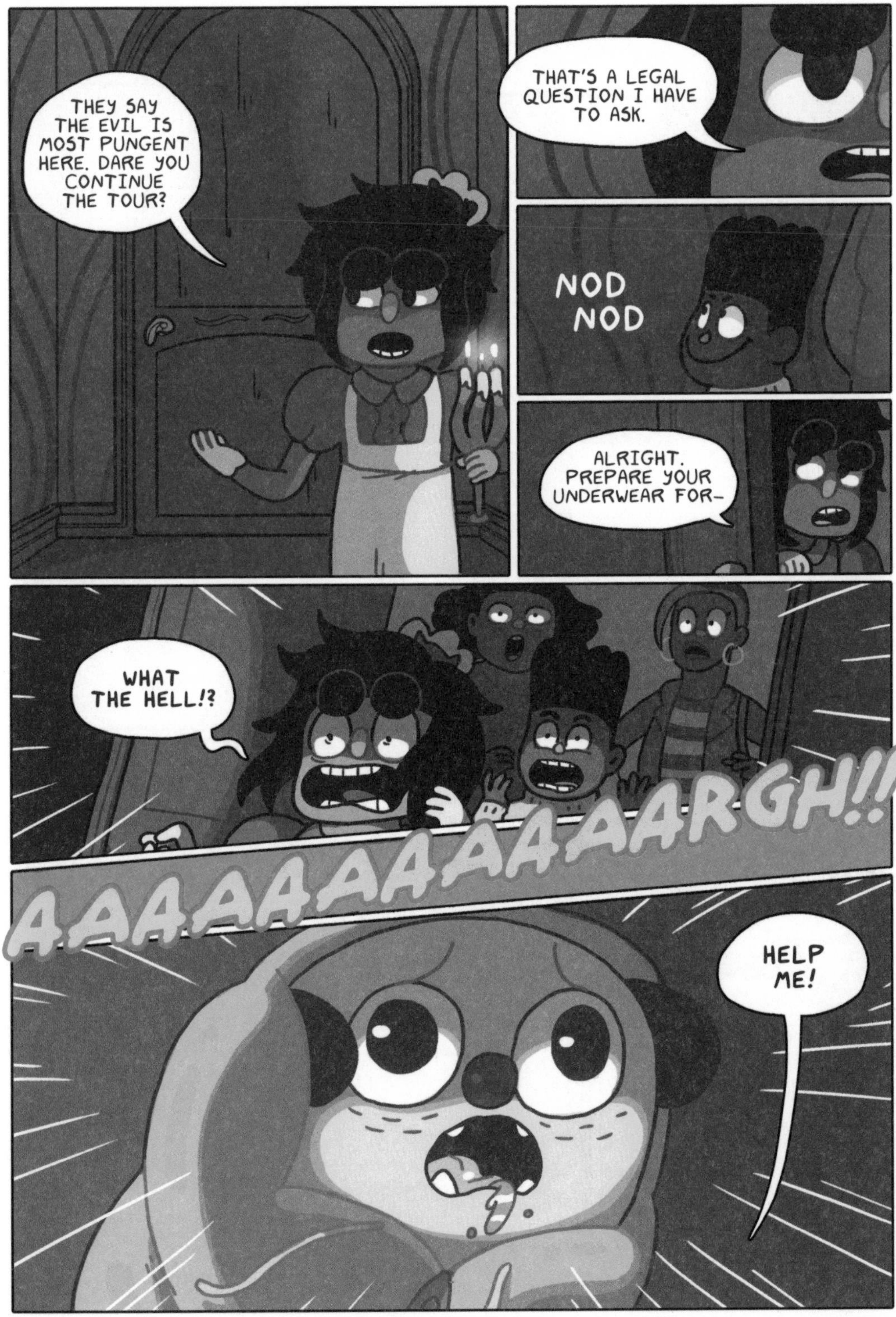
THEY SAY THE EVIL IS MOST PUNGENT HERE. DARE YOU CONTINUE THE TOUR?
THAT'S A LEGAL QUESTION I HAVE TO ASK.
NOD NOD
ALRIGHT. PREPARE YOUR UNDERWEAR FOR-
WHAT THE HELL!?
AAAAAAAAAAAARGH!!
HELP ME!

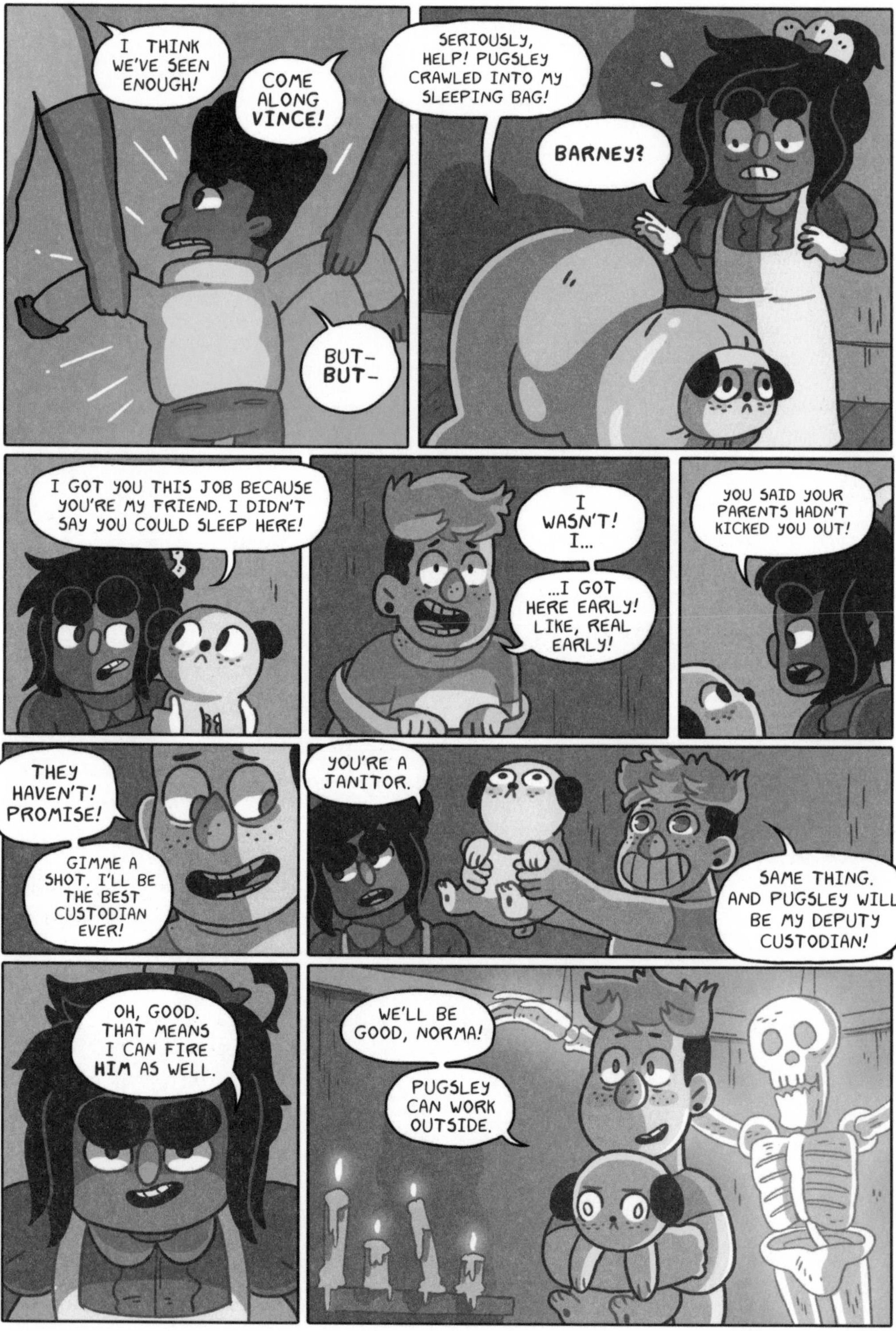
I THINK WE'VE SEEN ENOUGH!
COME ALONG VINCE!
BUT- BUT-
SERIOUSLY, HELP! PUGSLEY CRAWLED INTO MY SLEEPING BAG!
BARNEY?
I GOT YOU THIS JOB BECAUSE YOU'RE MY FRIEND. I DIDN'T SAY YOU COULD SLEEP HERE!
I WASN'T! I...
...I GOT HERE EARLY! LIKE, REAL EARLY!
YOU SAID YOUR PARENTS HADN'T KICKED YOU OUT!
THEY HAVEN'T! PROMISE!
GIMME A SHOT. I'LL BE THE BEST CUSTODIAN EVER!
YOU'RE A JANITOR.
SAME THING. AND PUGSLEY WILL BE MY DEPUTY CUSTODIAN!
OH, GOOD. THAT MEANS I CAN FIRE HIM AS WELL.
WE'LL BE GOOD, NORMA!
PUGSLEY CAN WORK OUTSIDE.

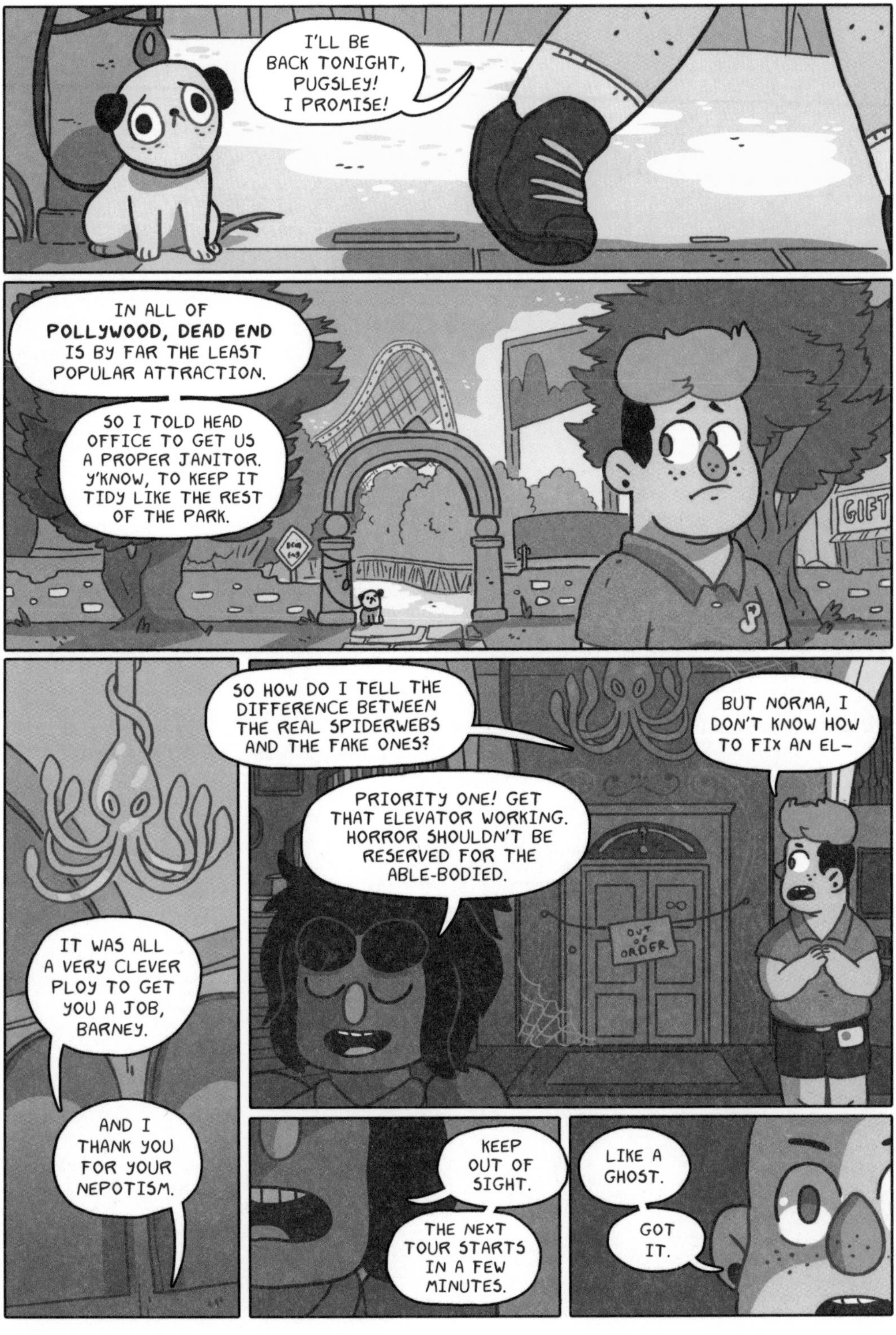
I'LL BE BACK TONIGHT, PUGSLEY! I PROMISE!
IN ALL OF **POLLYWOOD, DEAD END** IS BY FAR THE LEAST POPULAR ATTRACTION.
SO I TOLD HEAD OFFICE TO GET US A PROPER JANITOR. Y'KNOW, TO KEEP IT TIDY LIKE THE REST OF THE PARK.
GIFT
IT WAS ALL A VERY CLEVER PLOY TO GET YOU A JOB, BARNEY.
AND I THANK YOU FOR YOUR NEPOTISM.
SO HOW DO I TELL THE DIFFERENCE BETWEEN THE REAL SPIDERWEBS AND THE FAKE ONES?
PRIORITY ONE! GET THAT ELEVATOR WORKING. HORROR SHOULDN'T BE RESERVED FOR THE ABLE-BODIED.
BUT NORMA, I DON'T KNOW HOW TO FIX AN EL—
OUT OF ORDER
KEEP OUT OF SIGHT.
THE NEXT TOUR STARTS IN A FEW MINUTES.
LIKE A GHOST.
GOT IT.

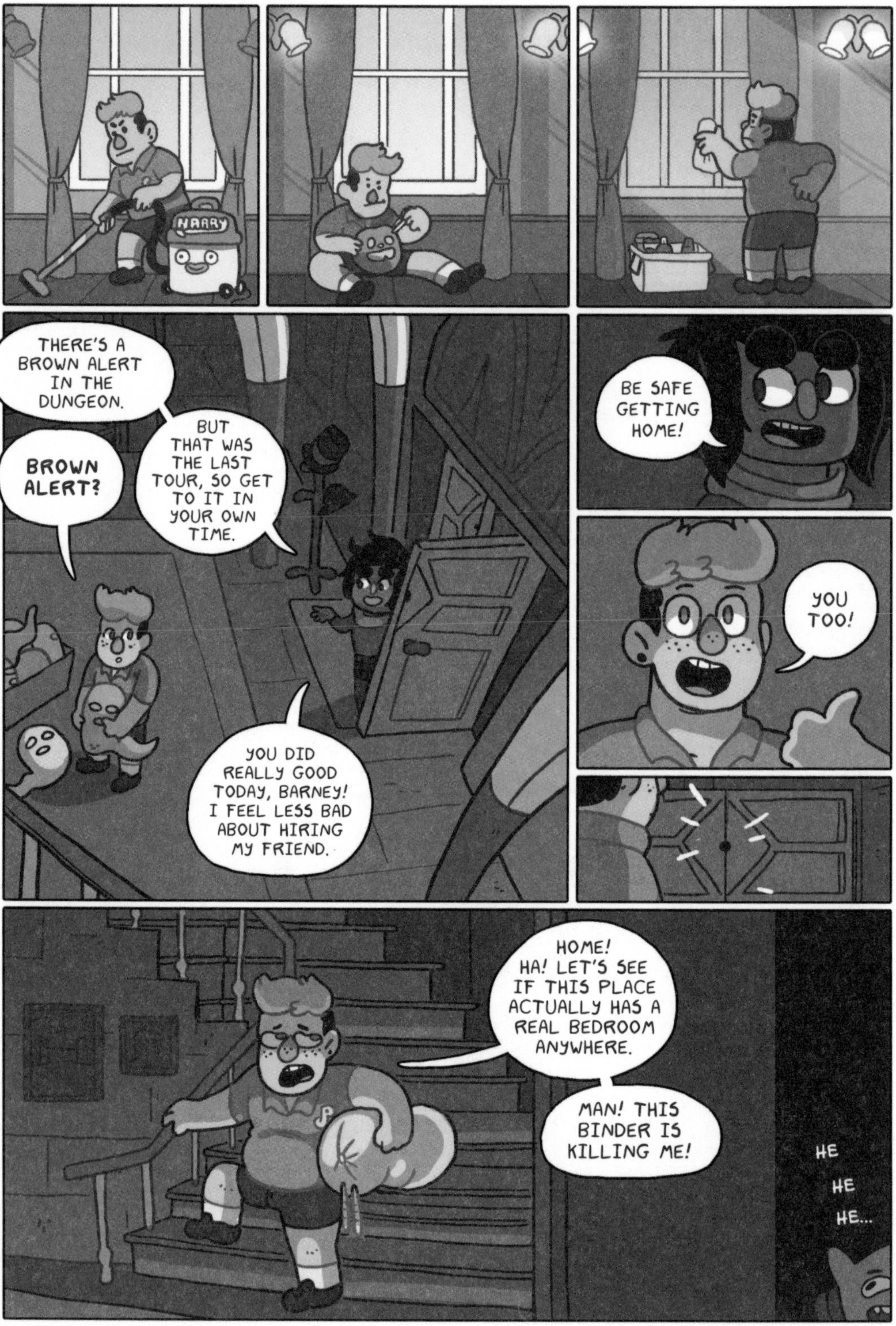
HARRY
THERE'S A BROWN ALERT IN THE DUNGEON.
BUT THAT WAS THE LAST TOUR, SO GET TO IT IN YOUR OWN TIME.
BROWN ALERT?
YOU DID REALLY GOOD TODAY, BARNEY! I FEEL LESS BAD ABOUT HIRING MY FRIEND.
BE SAFE GETTING HOME!
YOU TOO!
HOME! HA! LET'S SEE IF THIS PLACE ACTUALLY HAS A REAL BEDROOM ANYWHERE.
MAN! THIS BINDER IS KILLING ME!
HE
HE
HE...

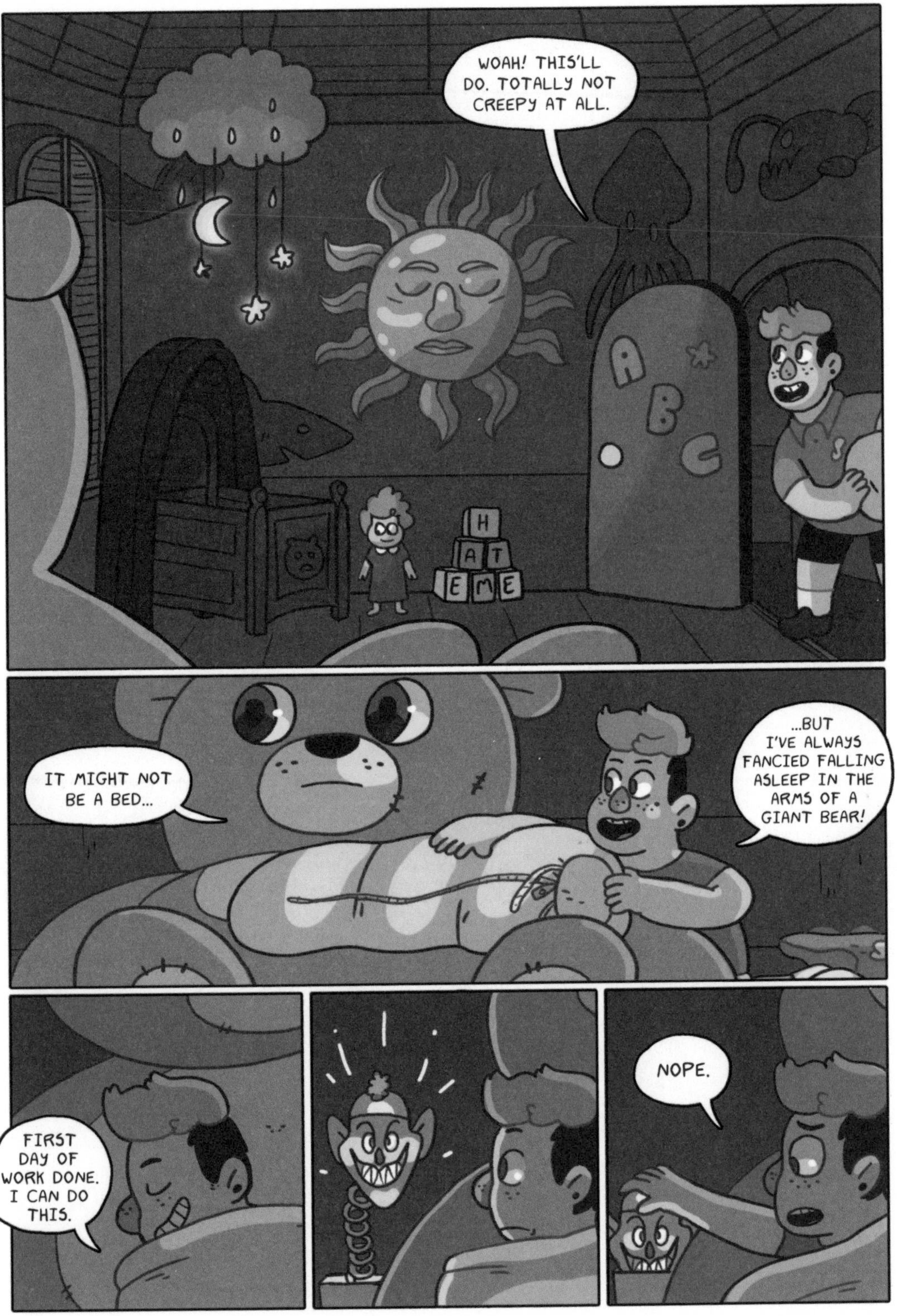
WOAH! THIS'LL DO. TOTALLY NOT CREEPY AT ALL.
H
AT
EME
IT MIGHT NOT BE A BED...
...BUT I'VE ALWAYS FANCIED FALLING ASLEEP IN THE ARMS OF A GIANT BEAR!
FIRST DAY OF WORK DONE. I CAN DO THIS.
NOPE.

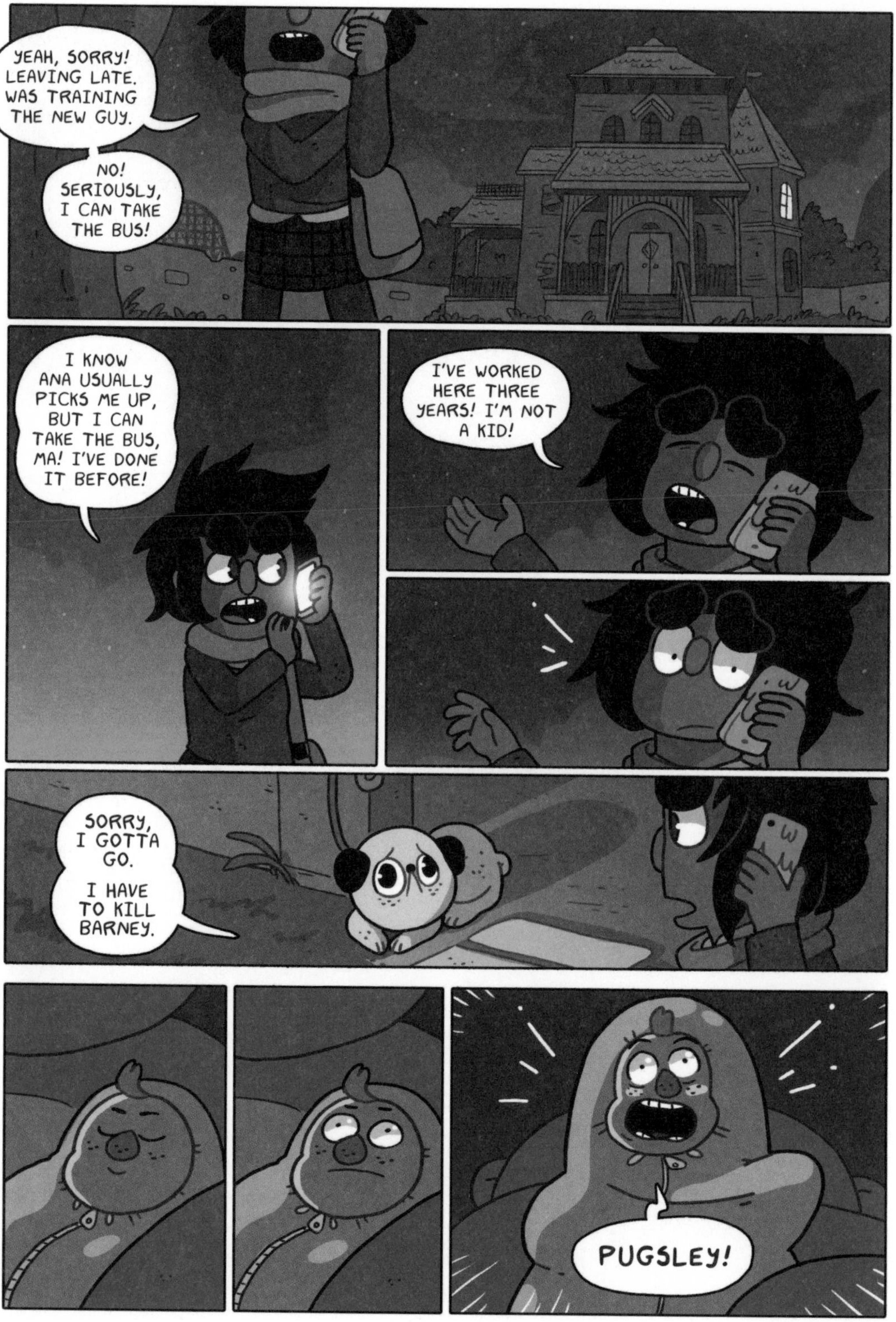
YEAH, SORRY! LEAVING LATE. WAS TRAINING THE NEW GUY.
NO! SERIOUSLY, I CAN TAKE THE BUS!
I KNOW ANA USUALLY PICKS ME UP, BUT I CAN TAKE THE BUS, MA! I'VE DONE IT BEFORE!
I'VE WORKED HERE THREE YEARS! I'M NOT A KID!
SORRY, I GOTTA GO.
I HAVE TO KILL BARNEY.
PUGSLEY!

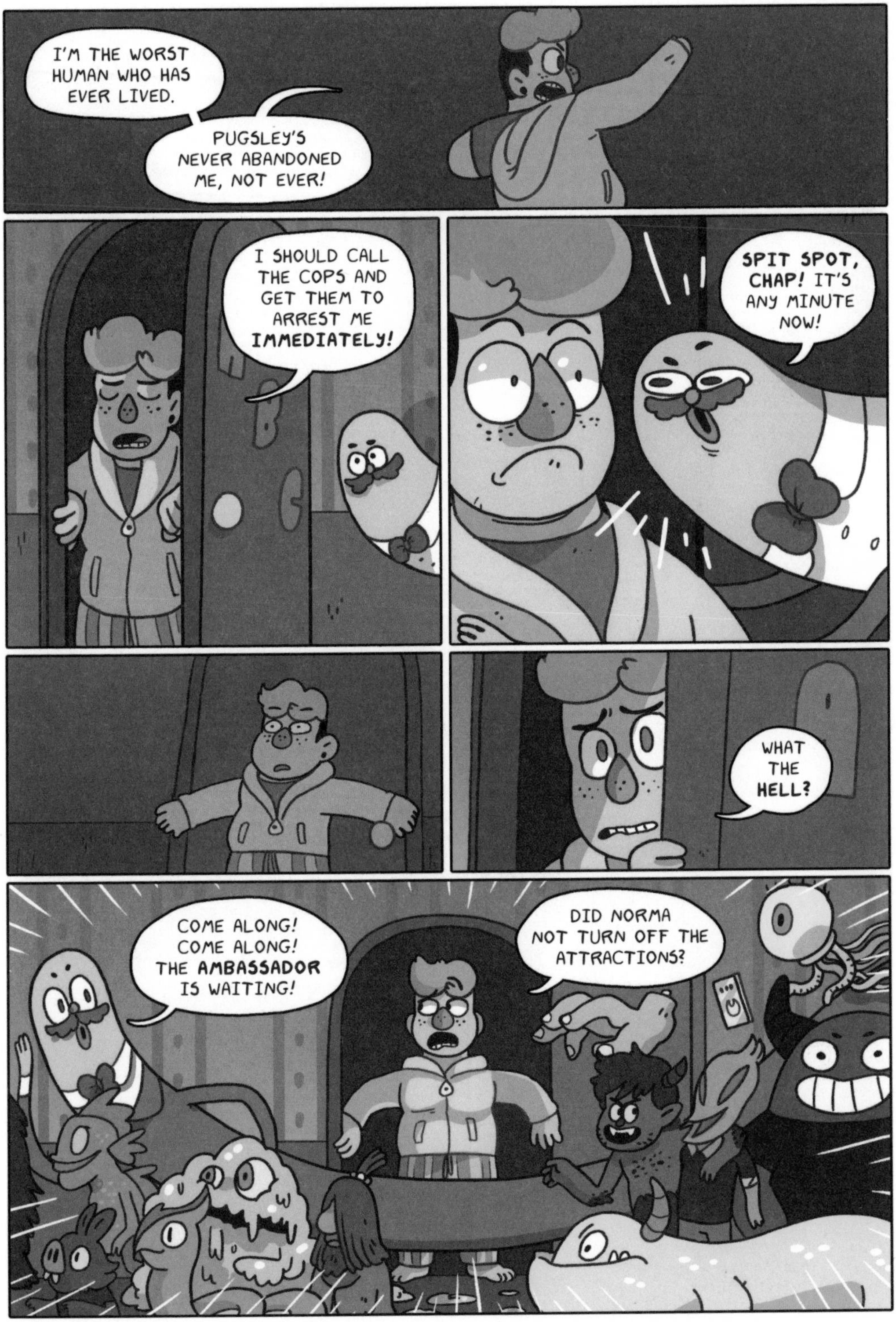
I'M THE WORST HUMAN WHO HAS EVER LIVED.
PUGSLEY'S NEVER ABANDONED ME, NOT EVER!
I SHOULD CALL THE COPS AND GET THEM TO ARREST ME IMMEDIATELY!
SPIT SPOT, CHAP! IT'S ANY MINUTE NOW!
WHAT THE HELL?
COME ALONG! COME ALONG! THE AMBASSADOR IS WAITING!
DID NORMA NOT TURN OFF THE ATTRACTIONS?

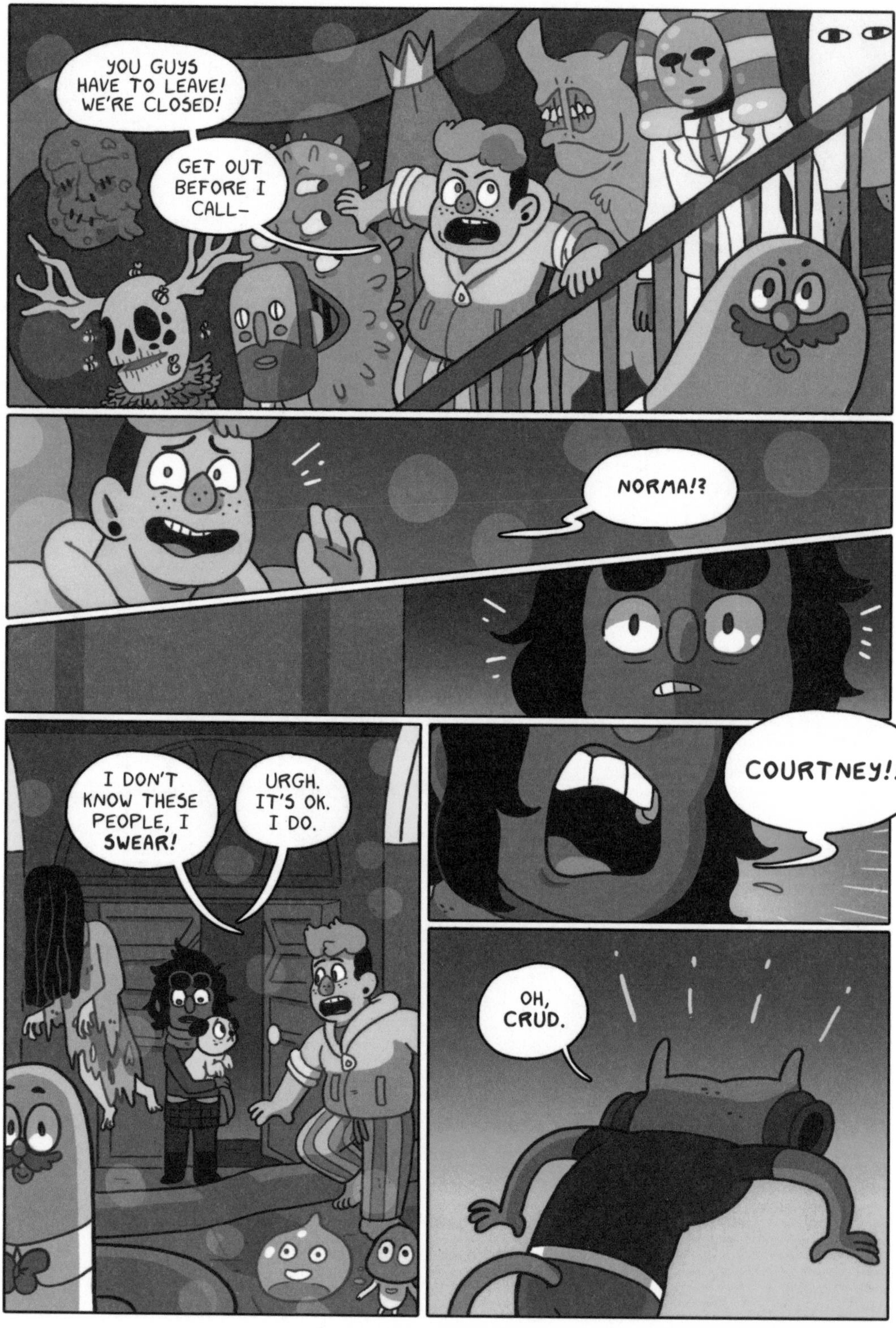
YOU GUYS HAVE TO LEAVE! WE'RE CLOSED!
GET OUT BEFORE I CALL-
NORMA!?
I DON'T KNOW THESE PEOPLE, I SWEAR!
URGH. IT'S OK. I DO.
COURTNEY!!
OH, CRUD.

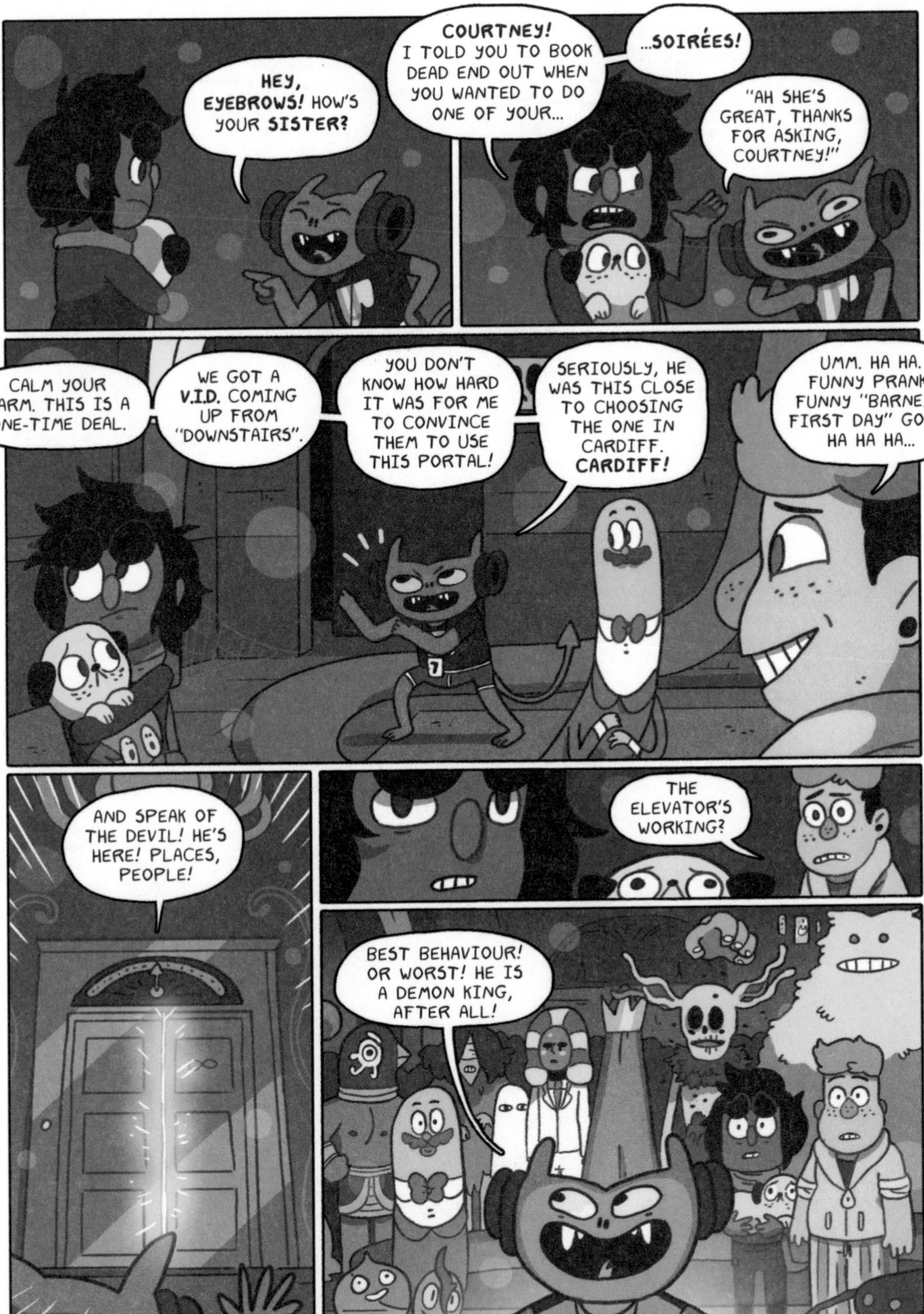
HEY, EYEBROWS! HOW'S YOUR SISTER?
COURTNEY! I TOLD YOU TO BOOK DEAD END OUT WHEN YOU WANTED TO DO ONE OF YOUR...
...SOIRÉES!
"AH SHE'S GREAT, THANKS FOR ASKING, COURTNEY!"
CALM YOUR FARM. THIS IS A ONE-TIME DEAL.
WE GOT A V.I.D. COMING UP FROM "DOWNSTAIRS".
YOU DON'T KNOW HOW HARD IT WAS FOR ME TO CONVINCE THEM TO USE THIS PORTAL!
SERIOUSLY, HE WAS THIS CLOSE TO CHOOSING THE ONE IN CARDIFF. CARDIFF!
UMM. HA HA. FUNNY PRANK! FUNNY "BARNEY'S FIRST DAY" GOOF! HA HA HA...
7
AND SPEAK OF THE DEVIL! HE'S HERE! PLACES, PEOPLE!
THE ELEVATOR'S WORKING?
BEST BEHAVIOUR! OR WORST! HE IS A DEMON KING, AFTER ALL!

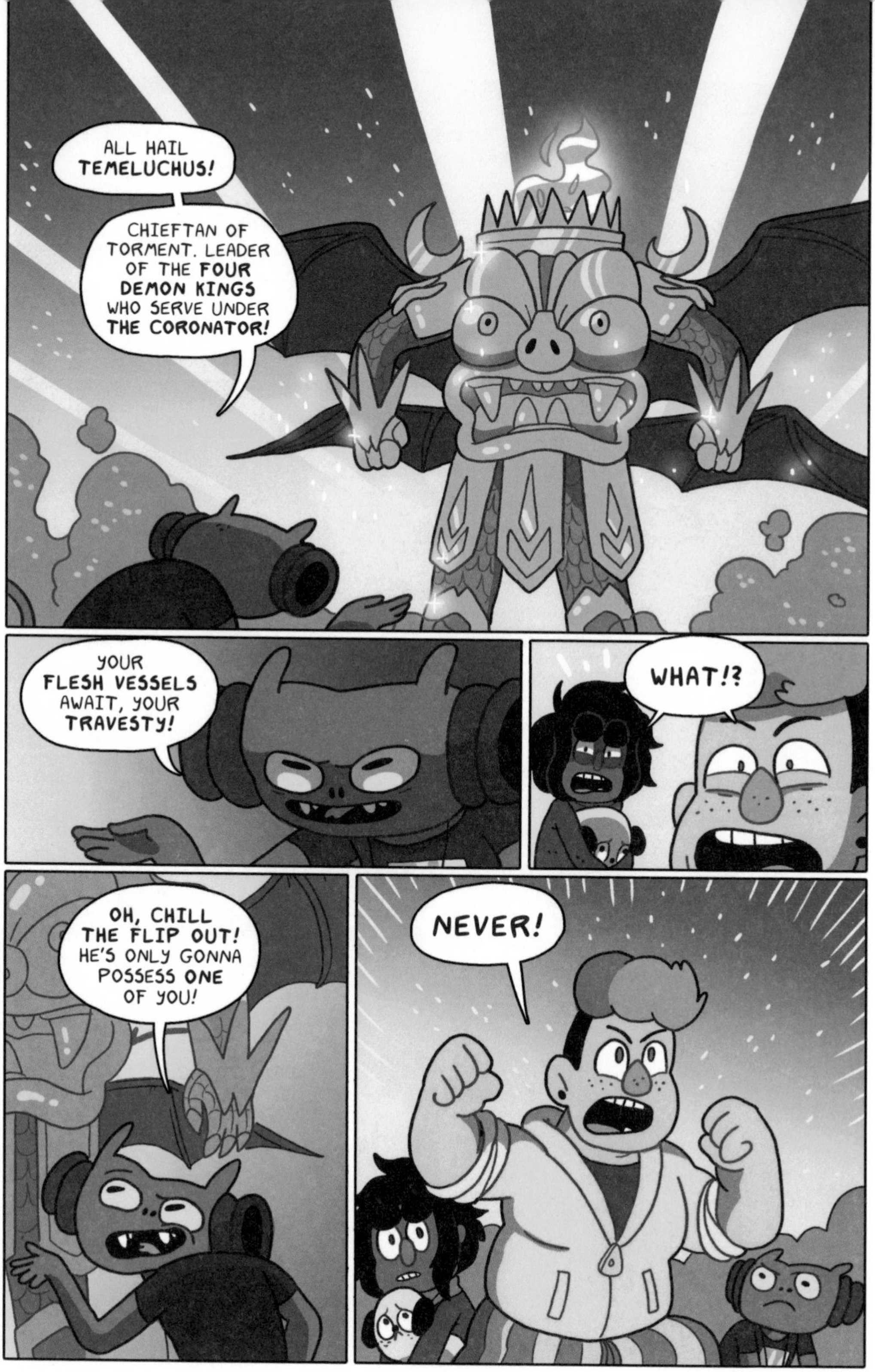
ALL HAIL TEMELUCHUS!
CHIEFTAN OF TORMENT. LEADER OF THE FOUR DEMON KINGS WHO SERVE UNDER THE CORONATOR!
YOUR FLESH VESSELS AWAIT, YOUR TRAVESTY!
WHAT!?
OH, CHILL THE FLIP OUT! HE'S ONLY GONNA POSSESS ONE OF YOU!
NEVER!

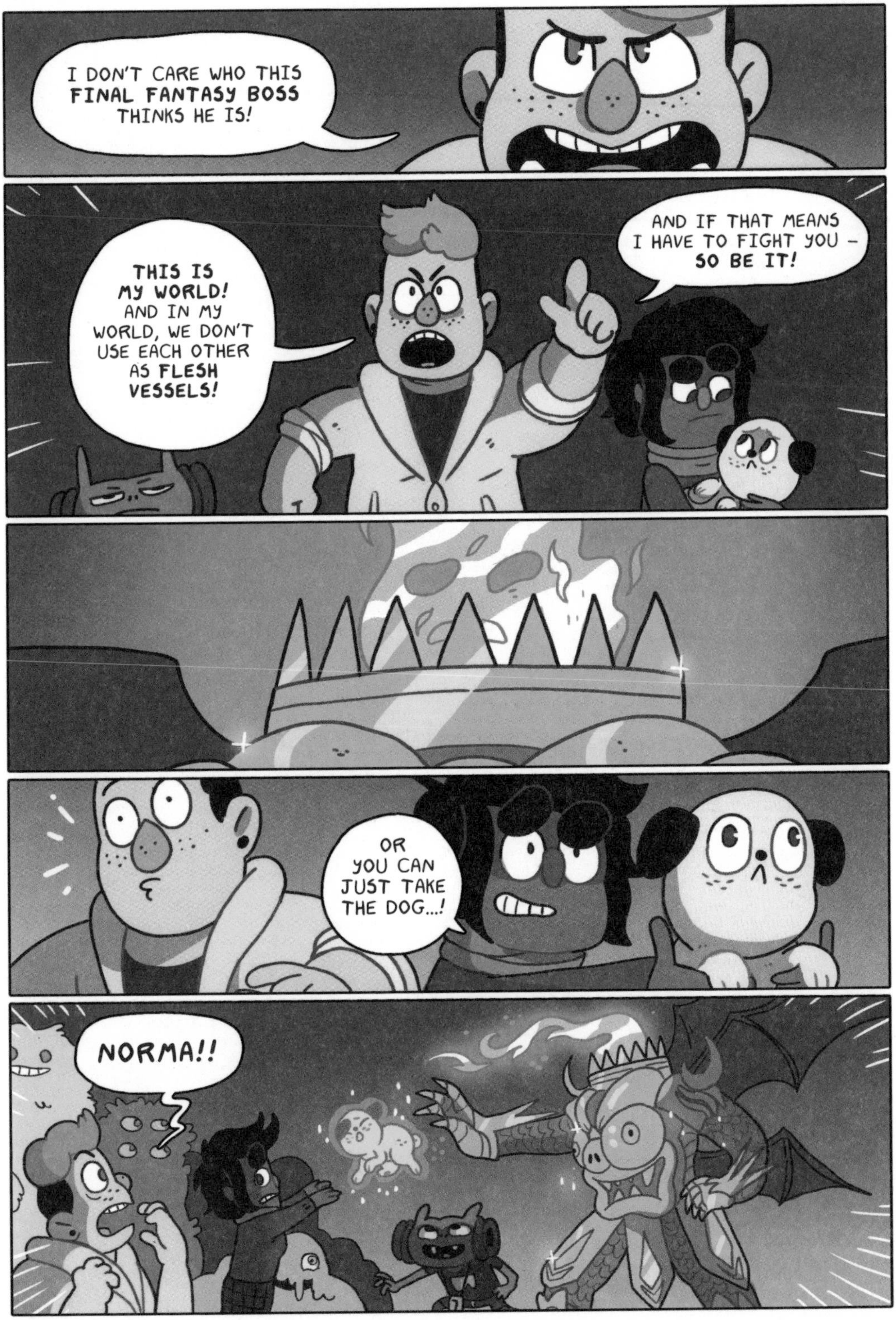
I DON'T CARE WHO THIS FINAL FANTASY BOSS THINKS HE IS!
THIS IS MY WORLD! AND IN MY WORLD, WE DON'T USE EACH OTHER AS FLESH VESSELS!
AND IF THAT MEANS I HAVE TO FIGHT YOU – SO BE IT!
OR YOU CAN JUST TAKE THE DOG...!
NORMA!!

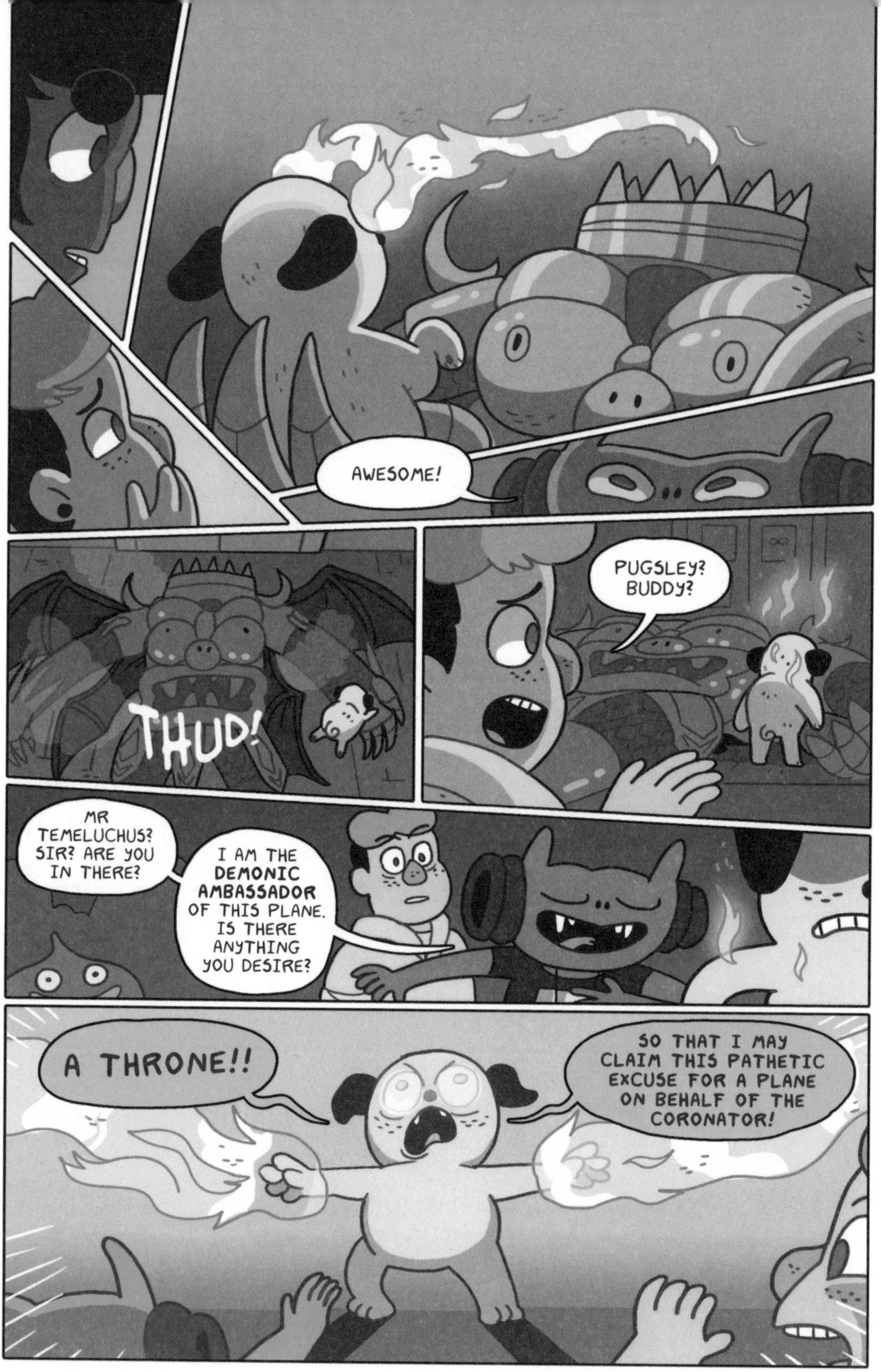

AWESOME!
THUD!
PUGSLEY? BUDDY?
MR TEMELUCHUS? SIR? ARE YOU IN THERE?
I AM THE DEMONIC AMBASSADOR OF THIS PLANE. IS THERE ANYTHING YOU DESIRE?
A THRONE!!
SO THAT I MAY CLAIM THIS PATHETIC EXCUSE FOR A PLANE ON BEHALF OF THE CORONATOR!

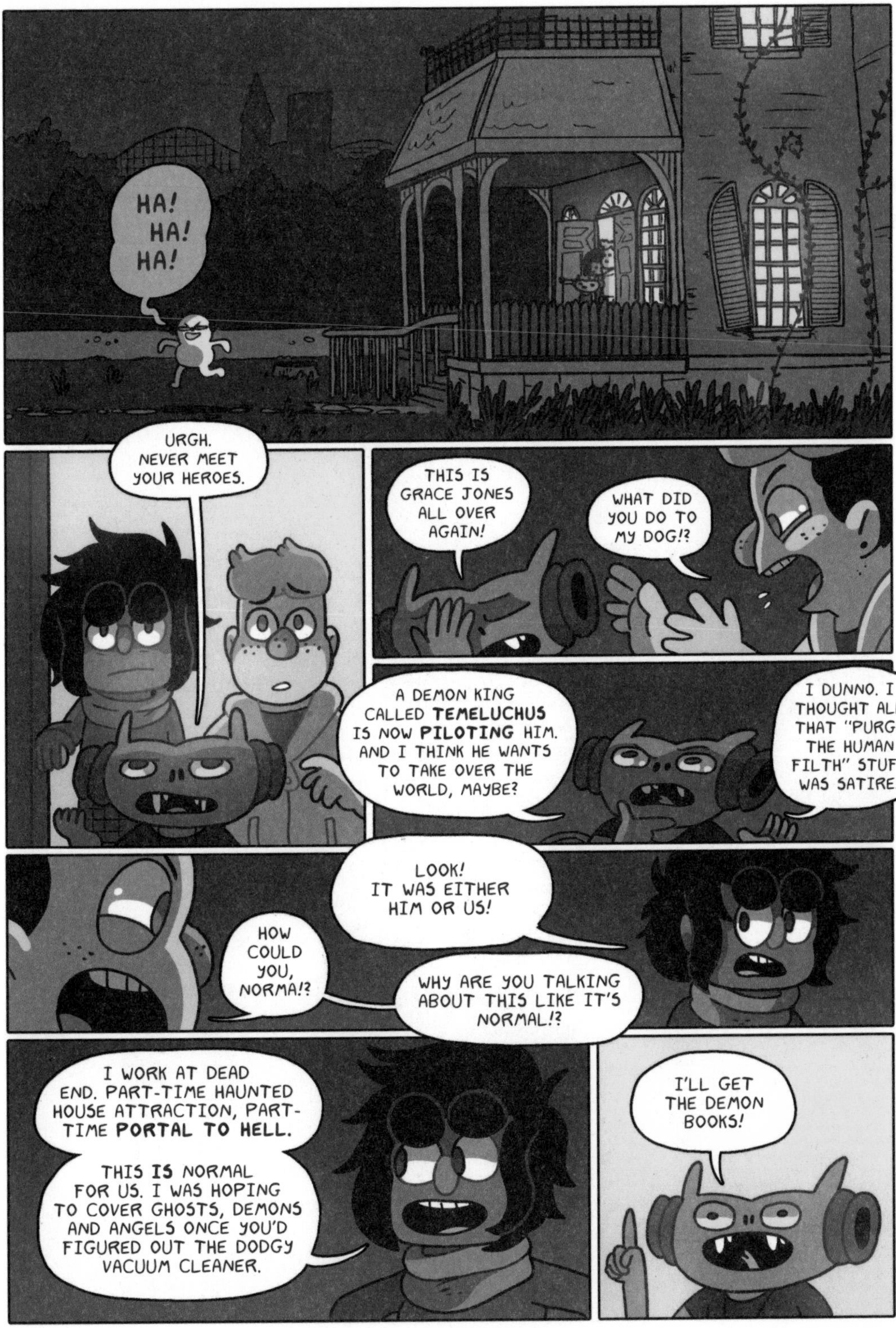

HA! HA! HA!
URGH. NEVER MEET YOUR HEROES.
THIS IS GRACE JONES ALL OVER AGAIN!
WHAT DID YOU DO TO MY DOG!?
A DEMON KING CALLED **TEMELUCHUS** IS NOW **PILOTING** HIM. AND I THINK HE WANTS TO TAKE OVER THE WORLD, MAYBE?
I DUNNO. I THOUGHT ALL THAT "PURGE THE HUMAN FILTH" STUFF WAS SATIRE!
HOW COULD YOU, NORMA!?
LOOK! IT WAS EITHER HIM OR US!
WHY ARE YOU TALKING ABOUT THIS LIKE IT'S NORMAL!?
I WORK AT DEAD END. PART-TIME HAUNTED HOUSE ATTRACTION, PART-TIME **PORTAL TO HELL.**
THIS **IS** NORMAL FOR US. I WAS HOPING TO COVER GHOSTS, DEMONS AND ANGELS ONCE YOU'D FIGURED OUT THE DODGY VACUUM CLEANER.
I'LL GET THE DEMON BOOKS!

THERE'S NO TIME! THAT THING HAS PUGSLEY!

AND HE'S ALL THE FAMILY I'VE GOT!

BARNEY! WAIT! I'M SORRY!

YOU DON'T UNDERSTAND! HE'S NOT JUST A DOG! HE'S MY FAMILY!

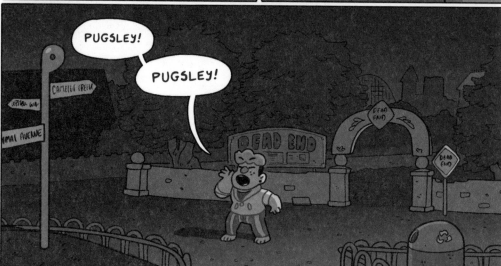

PUGSLEY!

PUGSLEY!

BUT THIS ISN'T PUGSLEY! THIS IS A DEMON KING... WHAT DOES HE WANT?

A THRONE!

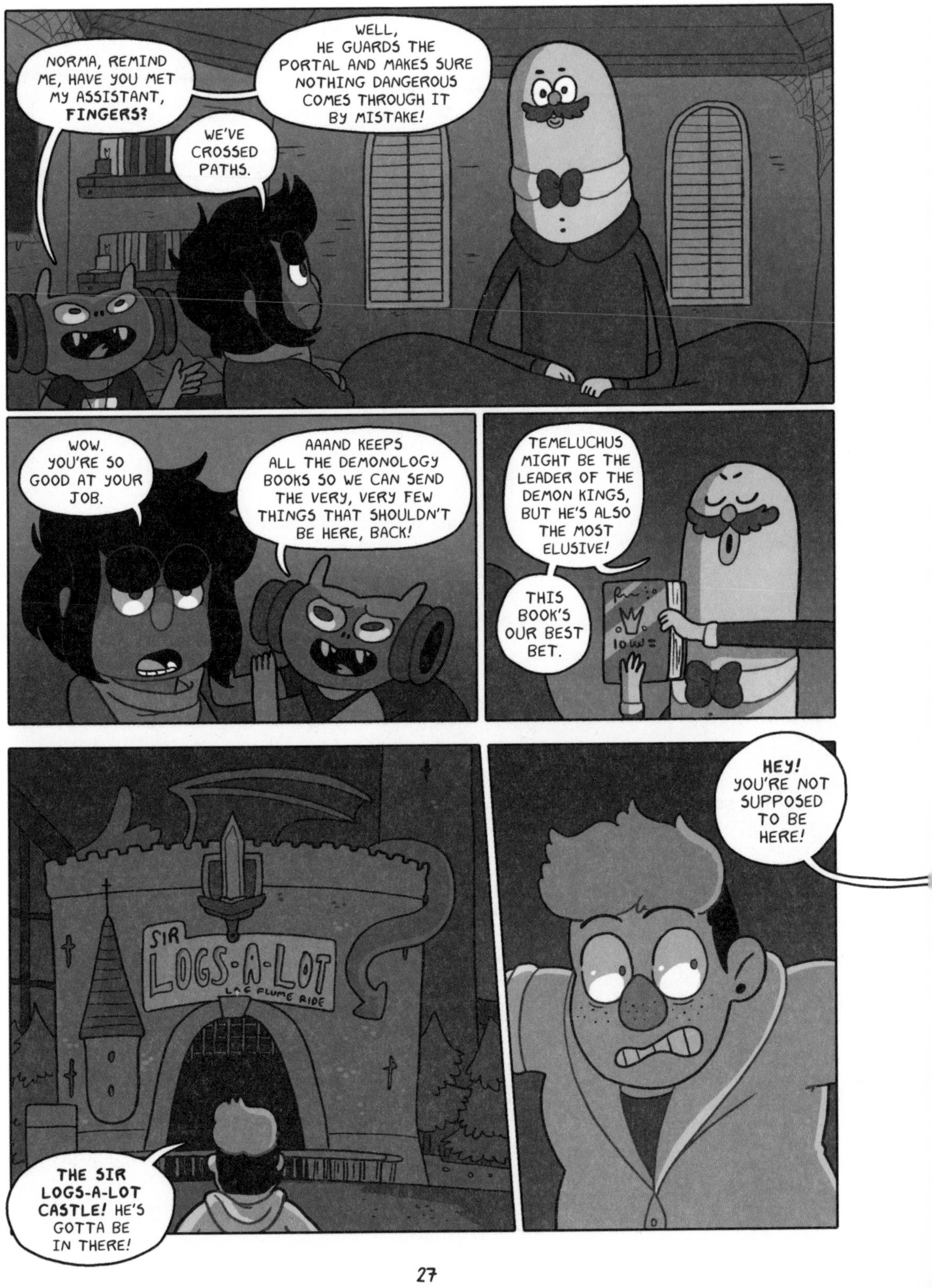
NORMA, REMIND ME, HAVE YOU MET MY ASSISTANT, FINGERS?
WELL, HE GUARDS THE PORTAL AND MAKES SURE NOTHING DANGEROUS COMES THROUGH IT BY MISTAKE!
WE'VE CROSSED PATHS.
WOW. YOU'RE SO GOOD AT YOUR JOB.
AAAND KEEPS ALL THE DEMONOLOGY BOOKS SO WE CAN SEND THE VERY, VERY FEW THINGS THAT SHOULDN'T BE HERE, BACK!
TEMELUCHUS MIGHT BE THE LEADER OF THE DEMON KINGS, BUT HE'S ALSO THE MOST ELUSIVE!
THIS BOOK'S OUR BEST BET.
SIR LOGS-A-LOT
THE SIR LOGS-A-LOT CASTLE! HE'S GOTTA BE IN THERE!
HEY! YOU'RE NOT SUPPOSED TO BE HERE!

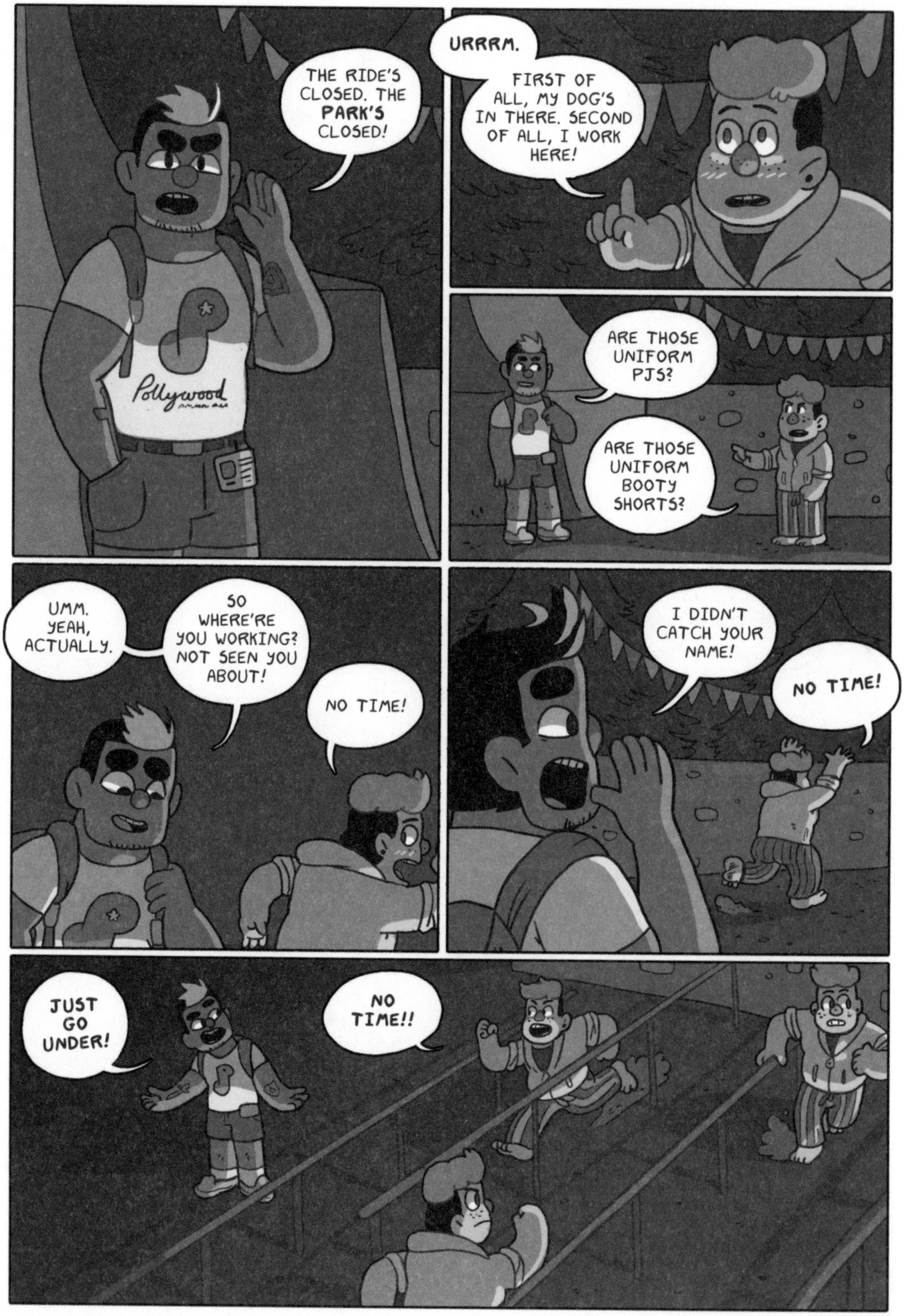
THE RIDE'S CLOSED. THE PARK'S CLOSED!
URRRM.
FIRST OF ALL, MY DOG'S IN THERE. SECOND OF ALL, I WORK HERE!
Pollywood
ARE THOSE UNIFORM PJS?
ARE THOSE UNIFORM BOOTY SHORTS?
UMM. YEAH, ACTUALLY.
SO WHERE'RE YOU WORKING? NOT SEEN YOU ABOUT!
NO TIME!
I DIDN'T CATCH YOUR NAME!
NO TIME!
JUST GO UNDER!
NO TIME!!

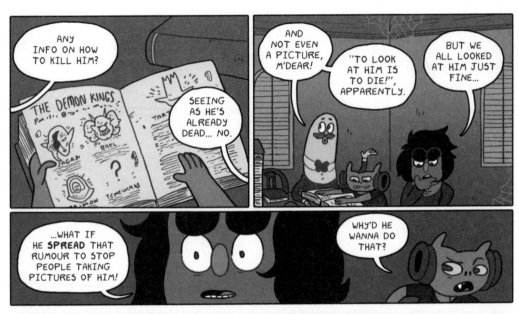

ANY INFO ON HOW TO KILL HIM?

THE DEMON KINGS

SEEING AS HE'S ALREADY DEAD... NO.

AND NOT EVEN A PICTURE, M'DEAR!

"TO LOOK AT HIM IS TO DIE!", APPARENTLY.

BUT WE ALL LOOKED AT HIM JUST FINE...

...WHAT IF HE **SPREAD** THAT RUMOUR TO STOP PEOPLE TAKING PICTURES OF HIM!

WHY'D HE WANNA DO THAT?

HA HA! YOU'VE FOUND ME. BRAVO!

BUT SURELY YOU DON'T INTEND TO TRY AND STOP ME?

YOU LOOK LIKE A WALKING PILLOW!

GET A PHOTO IN KING ARTHUR THRONE!

YEAH!? WELL YOU LOOK LIKE A BIG... UGLY...

...URGH! I CAN'T DO IT. YOU'RE A BEAUTIFUL ANGEL, PUGSLEY!

DO NOT CALL ME THAT WORD!!

YOU SHALL BECOME MY FIRST VICTIM!

29

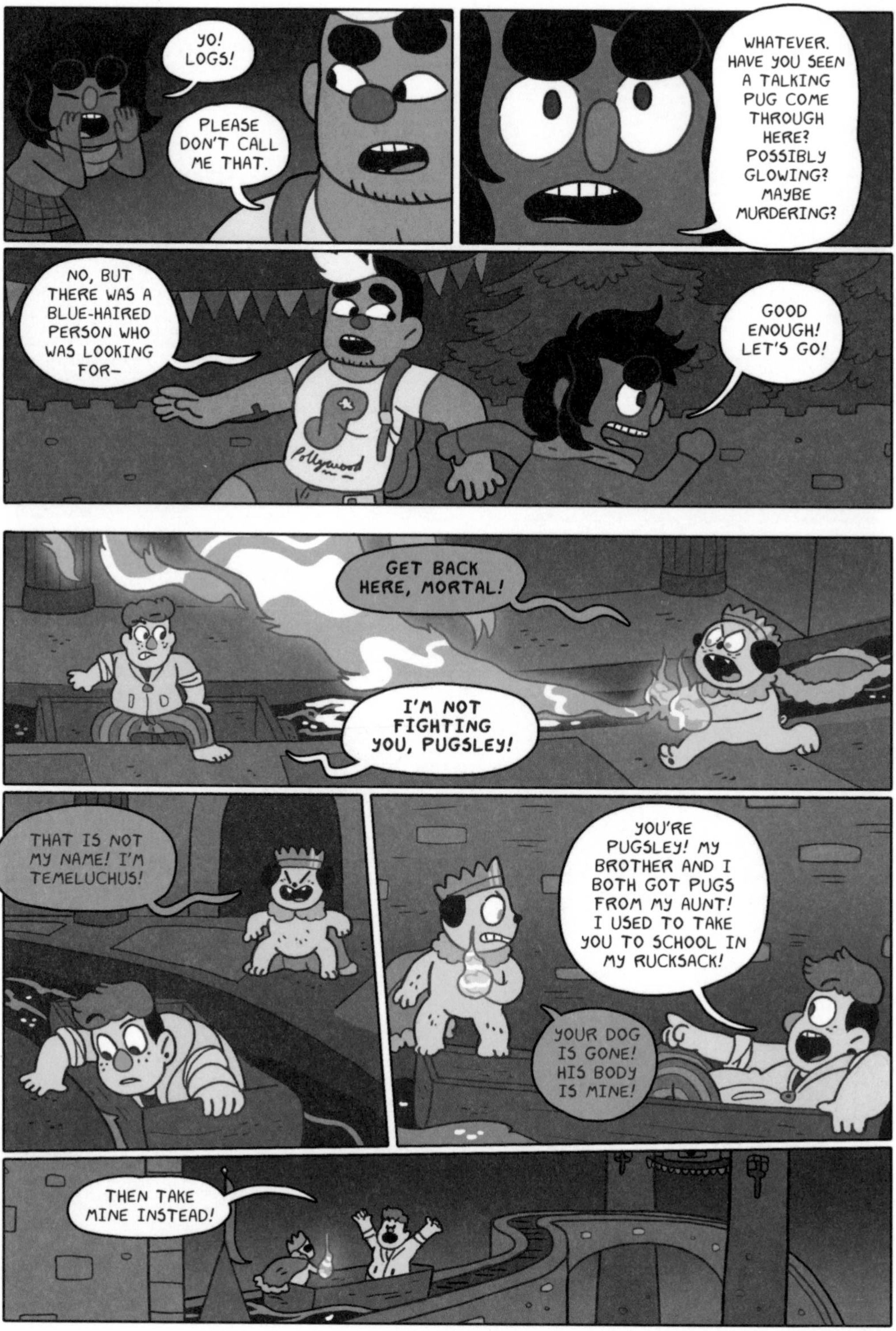

YO! LOGS!
PLEASE DON'T CALL ME THAT.
WHATEVER. HAVE YOU SEEN A TALKING PUG COME THROUGH HERE? POSSIBLY GLOWING? MAYBE MURDERING?
NO, BUT THERE WAS A BLUE-HAIRED PERSON WHO WAS LOOKING FOR–
GOOD ENOUGH! LET'S GO!
Pollywood
GET BACK HERE, MORTAL!
I'M NOT FIGHTING YOU, PUGSLEY!
THAT IS NOT MY NAME! I'M TEMELUCHUS!
YOU'RE PUGSLEY! MY BROTHER AND I BOTH GOT PUGS FROM MY AUNT! I USED TO TAKE YOU TO SCHOOL IN MY RUCKSACK!
YOUR DOG IS GONE! HIS BODY IS MINE!
THEN TAKE MINE INSTEAD!

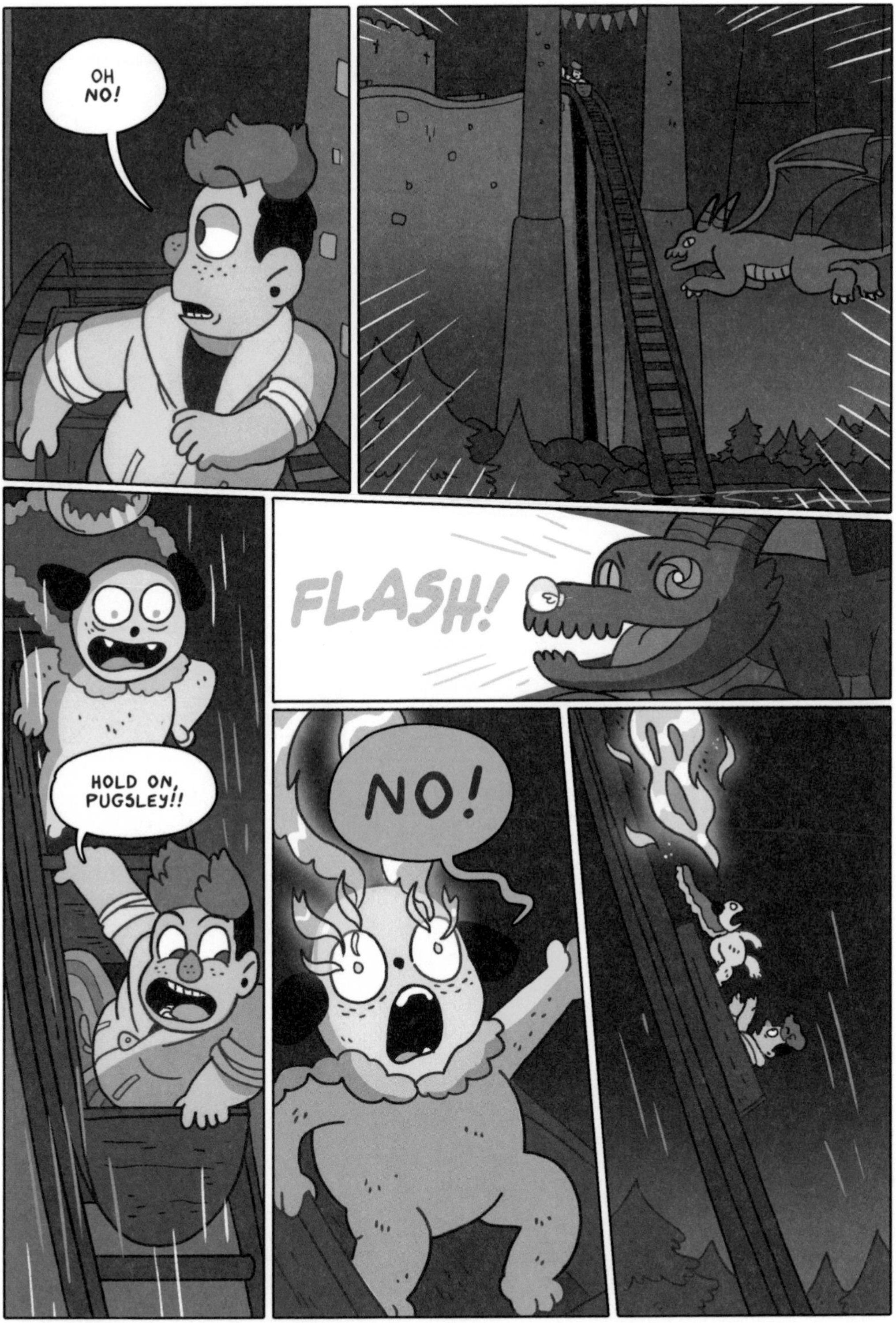
OH NO!
FLASH!
HOLD ON, PUGSLEY!!
NO!

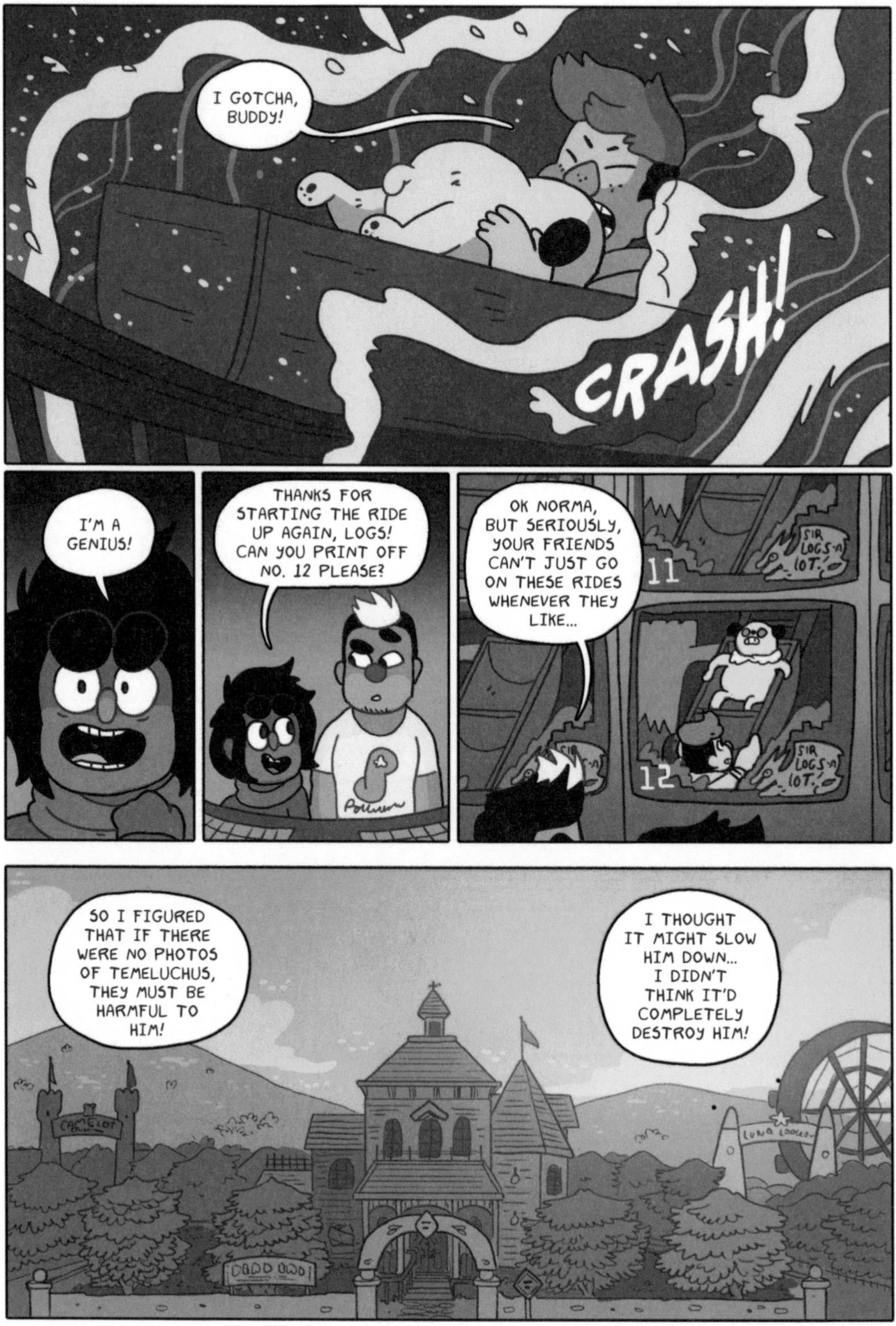
I GOTCHA, BUDDY!
CRASH!
I'M A GENIUS!
THANKS FOR STARTING THE RIDE UP AGAIN, LOGS! CAN YOU PRINT OFF NO. 12 PLEASE?
OK NORMA, BUT SERIOUSLY, YOUR FRIENDS CAN'T JUST GO ON THESE RIDES WHENEVER THEY LIKE...
SIR LOGS-A LOT!
11
12
SO I FIGURED THAT IF THERE WERE NO PHOTOS OF TEMELUCHUS, THEY MUST BE HARMFUL TO HIM!
I THOUGHT IT MIGHT SLOW HIM DOWN... I DIDN'T THINK IT'D COMPLETELY DESTROY HIM!

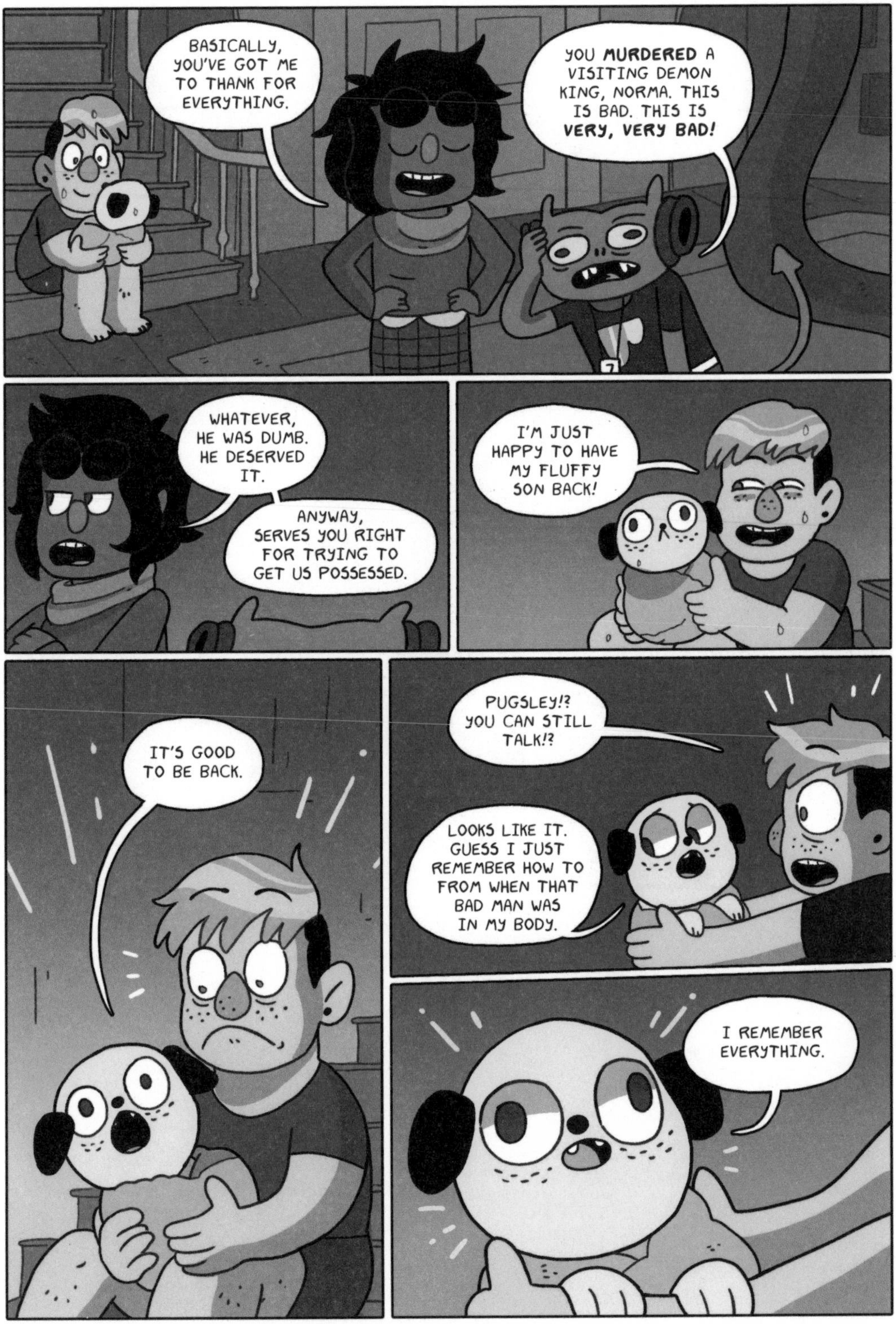
BASICALLY, YOU'VE GOT ME TO THANK FOR EVERYTHING.
YOU **MURDERED** A VISITING DEMON KING, NORMA. THIS IS BAD. THIS IS **VERY, VERY BAD!**
WHATEVER, HE WAS DUMB. HE DESERVED IT.
ANYWAY, SERVES YOU RIGHT FOR TRYING TO GET US POSSESSED.
I'M JUST HAPPY TO HAVE MY FLUFFY SON BACK!
IT'S GOOD TO BE BACK.
PUGSLEY!? YOU CAN STILL TALK!?
LOOKS LIKE IT. GUESS I JUST REMEMBER HOW TO FROM WHEN THAT BAD MAN WAS IN MY BODY.
I REMEMBER EVERYTHING.

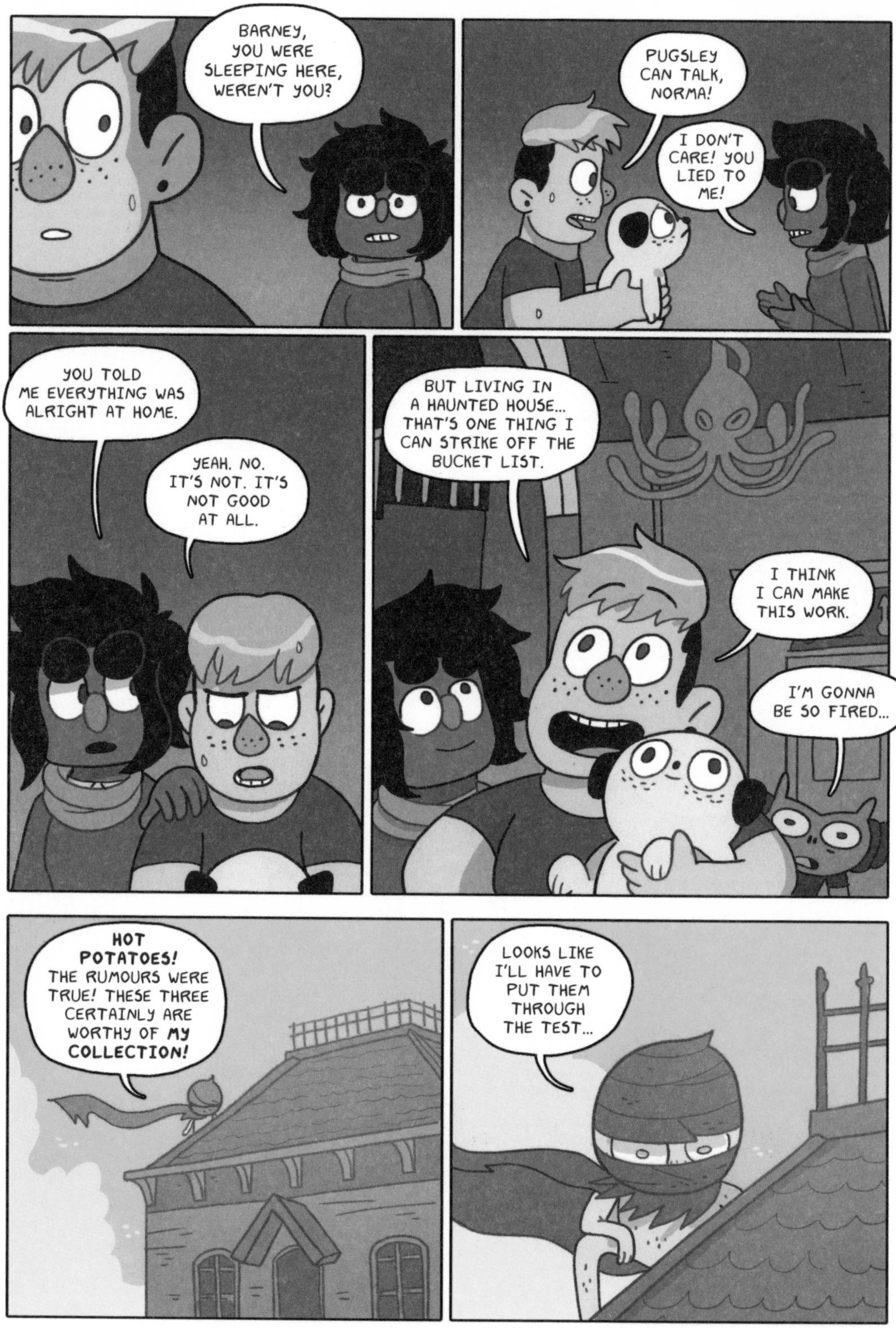
BARNEY, YOU WERE SLEEPING HERE, WEREN'T YOU?
PUGSLEY CAN TALK, NORMA!
I DON'T CARE! YOU LIED TO ME!
YOU TOLD ME EVERYTHING WAS ALRIGHT AT HOME.
YEAH. NO. IT'S NOT. IT'S NOT GOOD AT ALL.
BUT LIVING IN A HAUNTED HOUSE... THAT'S ONE THING I CAN STRIKE OFF THE BUCKET LIST.
I THINK I CAN MAKE THIS WORK.
I'M GONNA BE SO FIRED...
HOT POTATOES! THE RUMOURS WERE TRUE! THESE THREE CERTAINLY ARE WORTHY OF MY COLLECTION!
LOOKS LIKE I'LL HAVE TO PUT THEM THROUGH THE TEST...

CHAPTER 2

COVER ART BY CERI GIDDENS

AN ECHO FROM HEAVEN

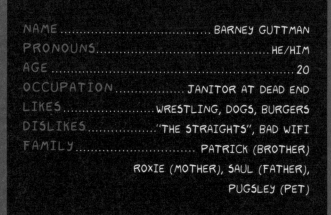

NAME......................................BARNEY GUTTMAN
PRONOUNS..................................HE/HIM
AGE 20
OCCUPATION..................JANITOR AT DEAD END
LIKES.......................WRESTLING, DOGS, BURGERS
DISLIKES................."THE STRAIGHTS", BAD WIFI
FAMILY.............................PATRICK (BROTHER)
ROXIE (MOTHER), SAUL (FATHER),
PUGSLEY (PET)

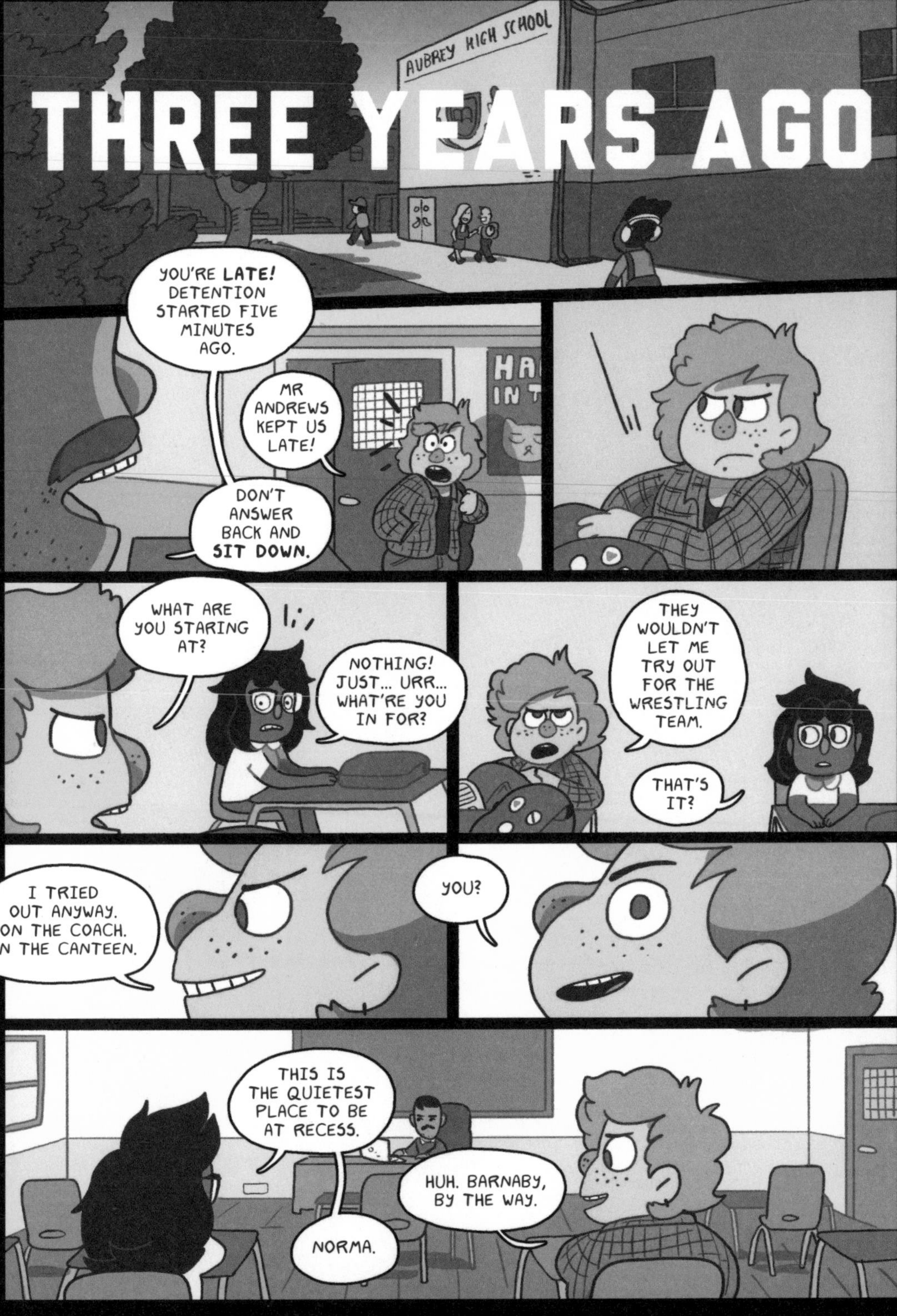
AUBREY HIGH SCHOOL
THREE YEARS AGO
YOU'RE LATE! DETENTION STARTED FIVE MINUTES AGO.
MR ANDREWS KEPT US LATE!
DON'T ANSWER BACK AND SIT DOWN.
WHAT ARE YOU STARING AT?
NOTHING! JUST... URR... WHAT'RE YOU IN FOR?
THEY WOULDN'T LET ME TRY OUT FOR THE WRESTLING TEAM.
THAT'S IT?
I TRIED OUT ANYWAY. ON THE COACH. IN THE CANTEEN.
YOU?
THIS IS THE QUIETEST PLACE TO BE AT RECESS.
HUH. BARNABY, BY THE WAY.
NORMA.

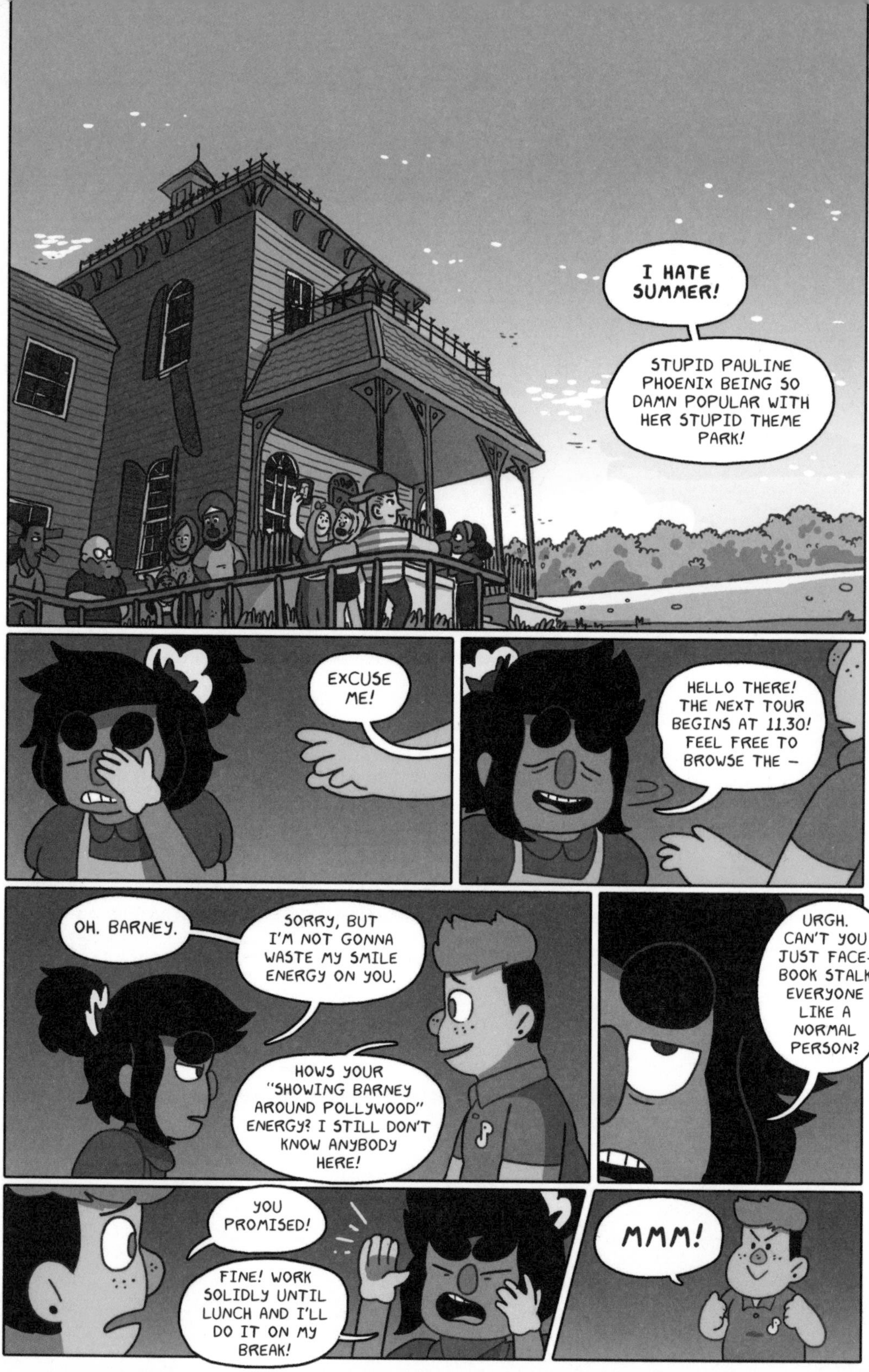
I HATE SUMMER!
STUPID PAULINE PHOENIX BEING SO DAMN POPULAR WITH HER STUPID THEME PARK!
EXCUSE ME!
HELLO THERE! THE NEXT TOUR BEGINS AT 11.30! FEEL FREE TO BROWSE THE –
OH. BARNEY.
SORRY, BUT I'M NOT GONNA WASTE MY SMILE ENERGY ON YOU.
HOWS YOUR "SHOWING BARNEY AROUND POLLYWOOD" ENERGY? I STILL DON'T KNOW ANYBODY HERE!
URGH. CAN'T YOU JUST FACE-BOOK STALK EVERYONE LIKE A NORMAL PERSON?
YOU PROMISED!
FINE! WORK SOLIDLY UNTIL LUNCH AND I'LL DO IT ON MY BREAK!
MMM!

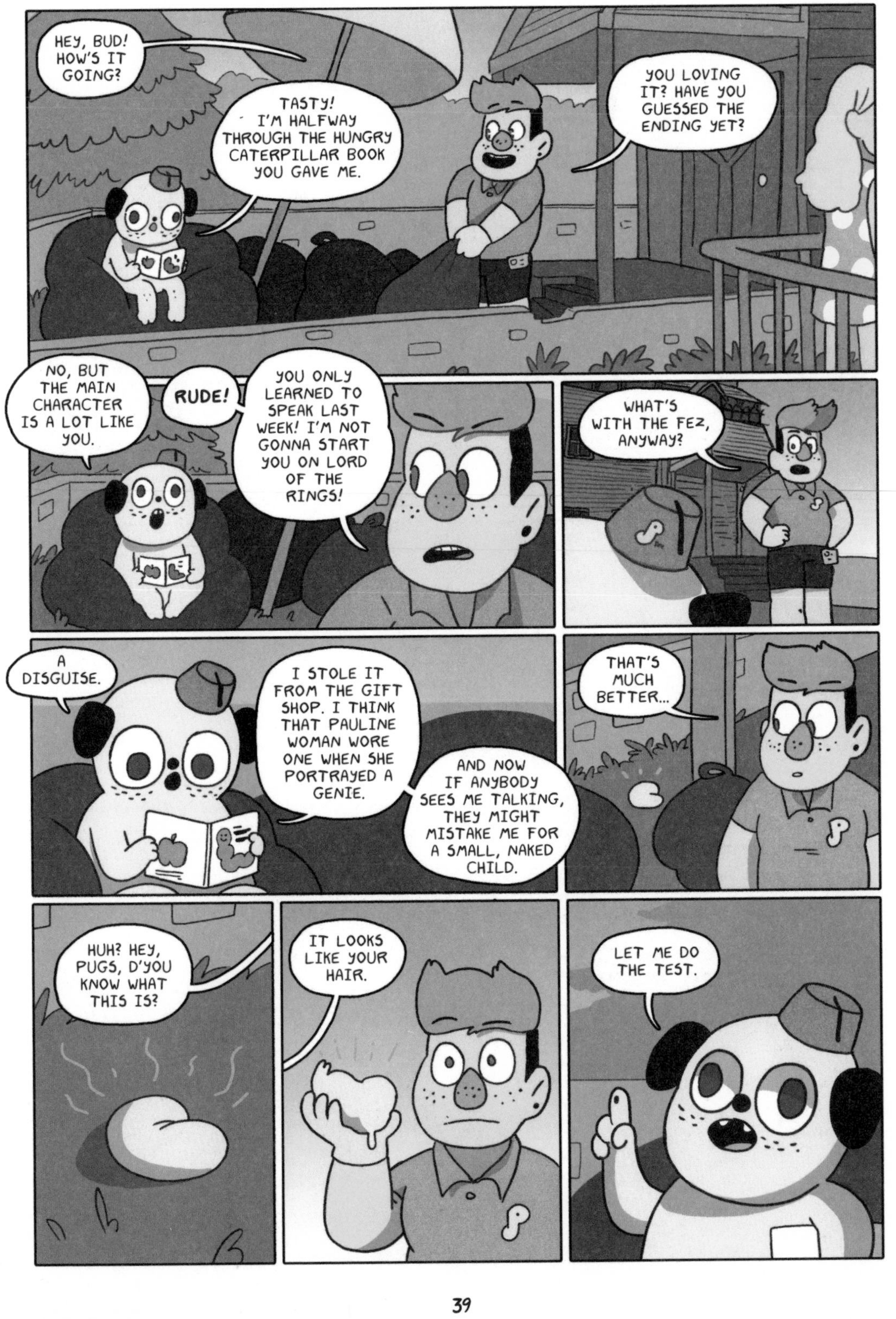
HEY, BUD! HOW'S IT GOING?
TASTY! I'M HALFWAY THROUGH THE HUNGRY CATERPILLAR BOOK YOU GAVE ME.
YOU LOVING IT? HAVE YOU GUESSED THE ENDING YET?
NO, BUT THE MAIN CHARACTER IS A LOT LIKE YOU.
RUDE!
YOU ONLY LEARNED TO SPEAK LAST WEEK! I'M NOT GONNA START YOU ON LORD OF THE RINGS!
WHAT'S WITH THE FEZ, ANYWAY?
A DISGUISE.
I STOLE IT FROM THE GIFT SHOP. I THINK THAT PAULINE WOMAN WORE ONE WHEN SHE PORTRAYED A GENIE.
AND NOW IF ANYBODY SEES ME TALKING, THEY MIGHT MISTAKE ME FOR A SMALL, NAKED CHILD.
THAT'S MUCH BETTER...
HUH? HEY, PUGS, D'YOU KNOW WHAT THIS IS?
IT LOOKS LIKE YOUR HAIR.
LET ME DO THE TEST.

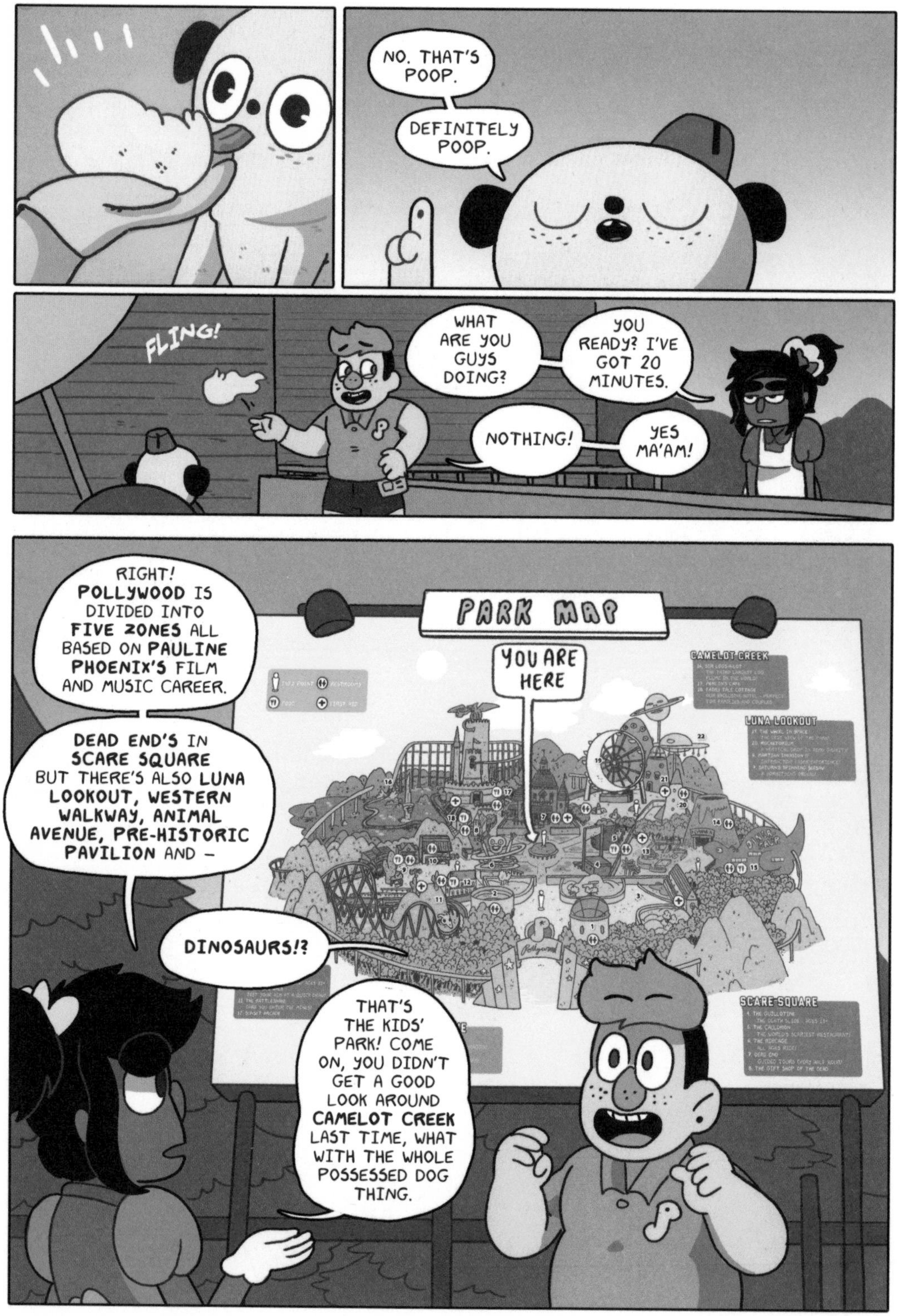
NO. THAT'S POOP.
DEFINITELY POOP.
FLING!
WHAT ARE YOU GUYS DOING?
YOU READY? I'VE GOT 20 MINUTES.
NOTHING!
YES MA'AM!
RIGHT! POLLYWOOD IS DIVIDED INTO FIVE ZONES ALL BASED ON PAULINE PHOENIX'S FILM AND MUSIC CAREER.
DEAD END'S IN SCARE SQUARE BUT THERE'S ALSO LUNA LOOKOUT, WESTERN WALKWAY, ANIMAL AVENUE, PRE-HISTORIC PAVILION AND –
PARK MAP
YOU ARE HERE
CAMELOT CREEK
LUNA LOOKOUT
SCARE SQUARE
DINOSAURS!?
THAT'S THE KIDS' PARK! COME ON, YOU DIDN'T GET A GOOD LOOK AROUND CAMELOT CREEK LAST TIME, WHAT WITH THE WHOLE POSSESSED DOG THING.

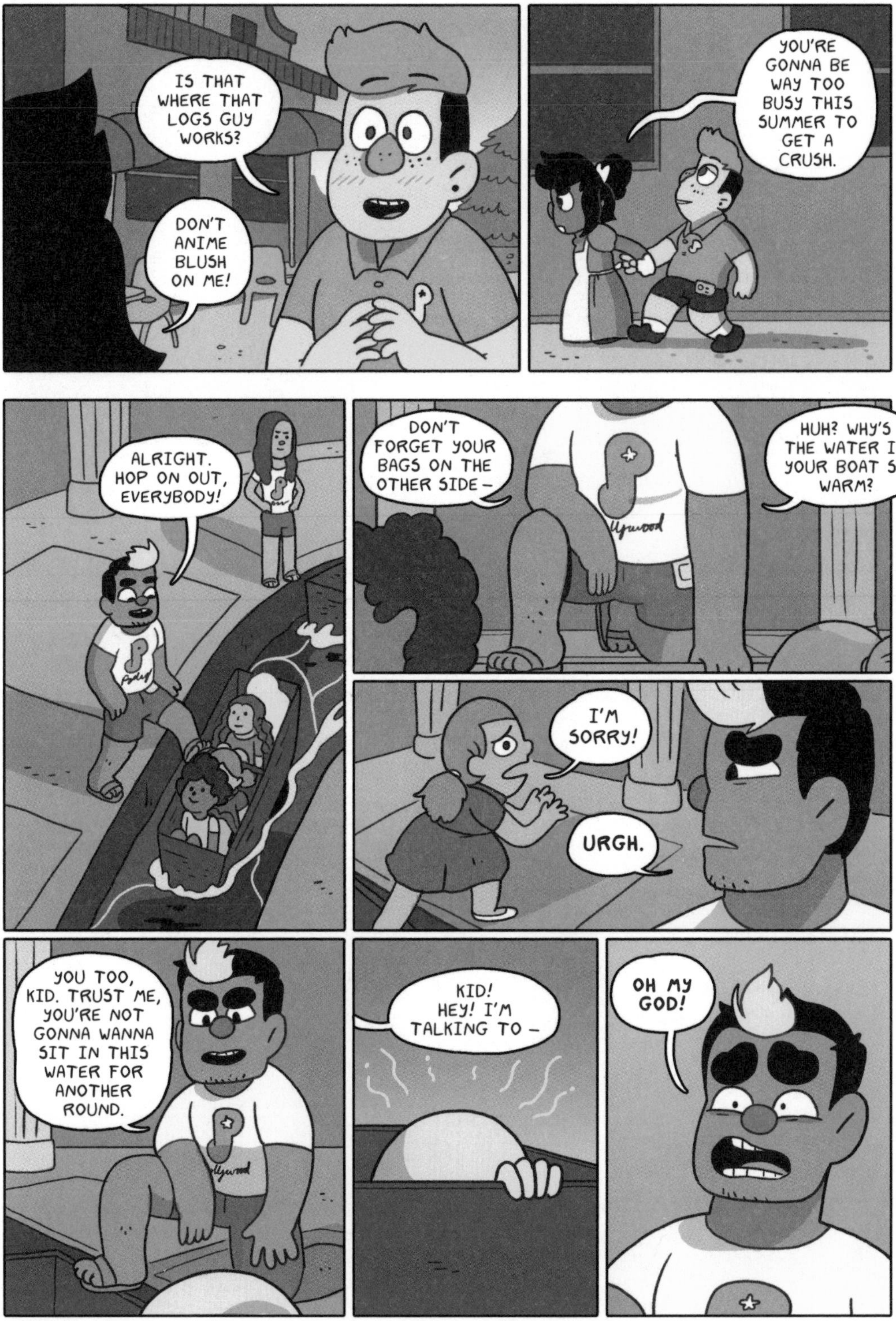
IS THAT WHERE THAT LOGS GUY WORKS?
DON'T ANIME BLUSH ON ME!
YOU'RE GONNA BE WAY TOO BUSY THIS SUMMER TO GET A CRUSH.
ALRIGHT. HOP ON OUT, EVERYBODY!
DON'T FORGET YOUR BAGS ON THE OTHER SIDE –
HUH? WHY'S THE WATER IN YOUR BOAT SO WARM?
I'M SORRY!
URGH.
YOU TOO, KID. TRUST ME, YOU'RE NOT GONNA WANNA SIT IN THIS WATER FOR ANOTHER ROUND.
KID! HEY! I'M TALKING TO –
OH MY GOD!

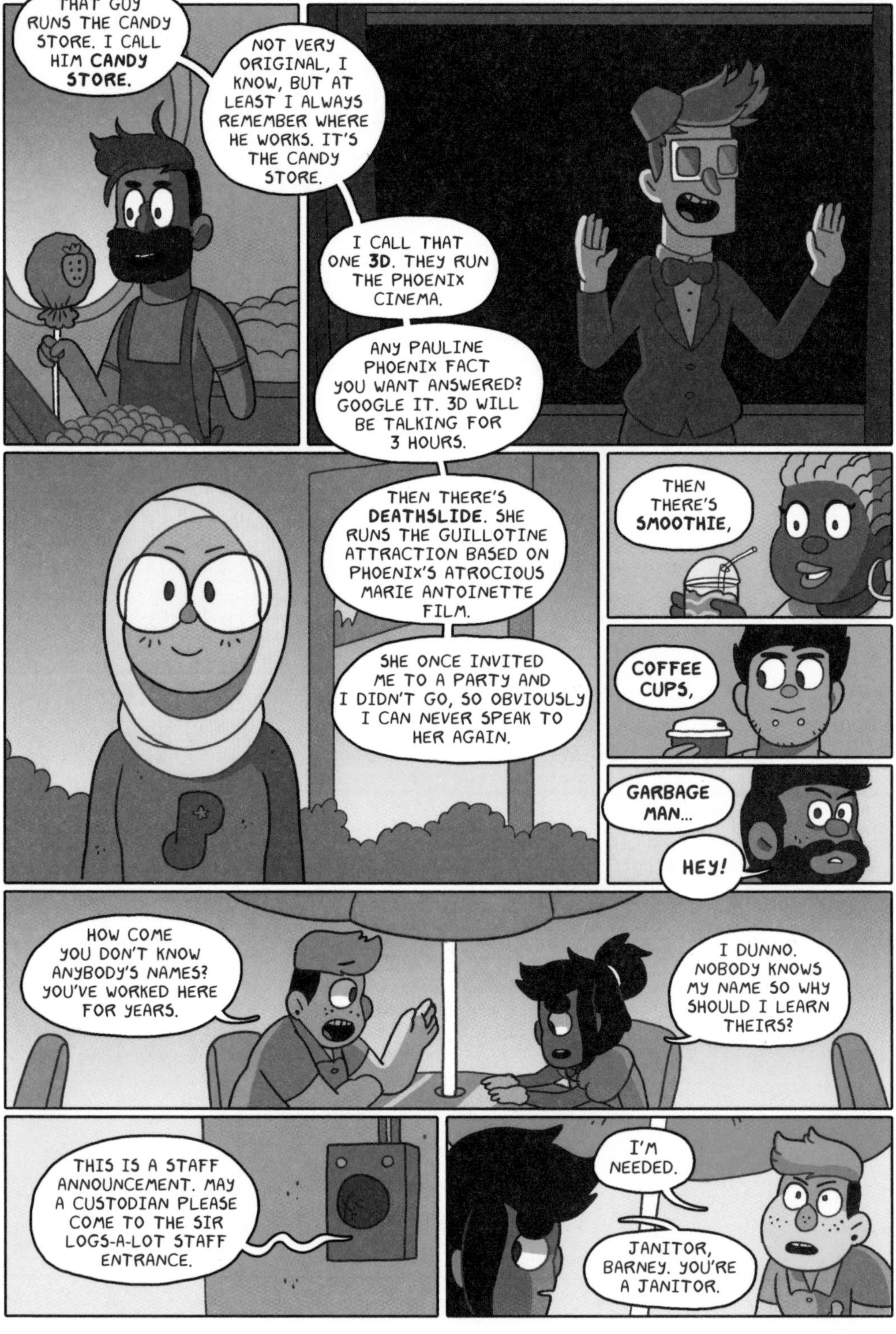
THAT GUY RUNS THE CANDY STORE. I CALL HIM CANDY STORE.
NOT VERY ORIGINAL, I KNOW, BUT AT LEAST I ALWAYS REMEMBER WHERE HE WORKS. IT'S THE CANDY STORE.
I CALL THAT ONE 3D. THEY RUN THE PHOENIX CINEMA.
ANY PAULINE PHOENIX FACT YOU WANT ANSWERED? GOOGLE IT. 3D WILL BE TALKING FOR 3 HOURS.
THEN THERE'S DEATHSLIDE. SHE RUNS THE GUILLOTINE ATTRACTION BASED ON PHOENIX'S ATROCIOUS MARIE ANTOINETTE FILM.
SHE ONCE INVITED ME TO A PARTY AND I DIDN'T GO, SO OBVIOUSLY I CAN NEVER SPEAK TO HER AGAIN.
THEN THERE'S SMOOTHIE,
COFFEE CUPS,
GARBAGE MAN...
HEY!
HOW COME YOU DON'T KNOW ANYBODY'S NAMES? YOU'VE WORKED HERE FOR YEARS.
I DUNNO. NOBODY KNOWS MY NAME SO WHY SHOULD I LEARN THEIRS?
THIS IS A STAFF ANNOUNCEMENT. MAY A CUSTODIAN PLEASE COME TO THE SIR LOGS-A-LOT STAFF ENTRANCE.
I'M NEEDED.
JANITOR, BARNEY. YOU'RE A JANITOR.

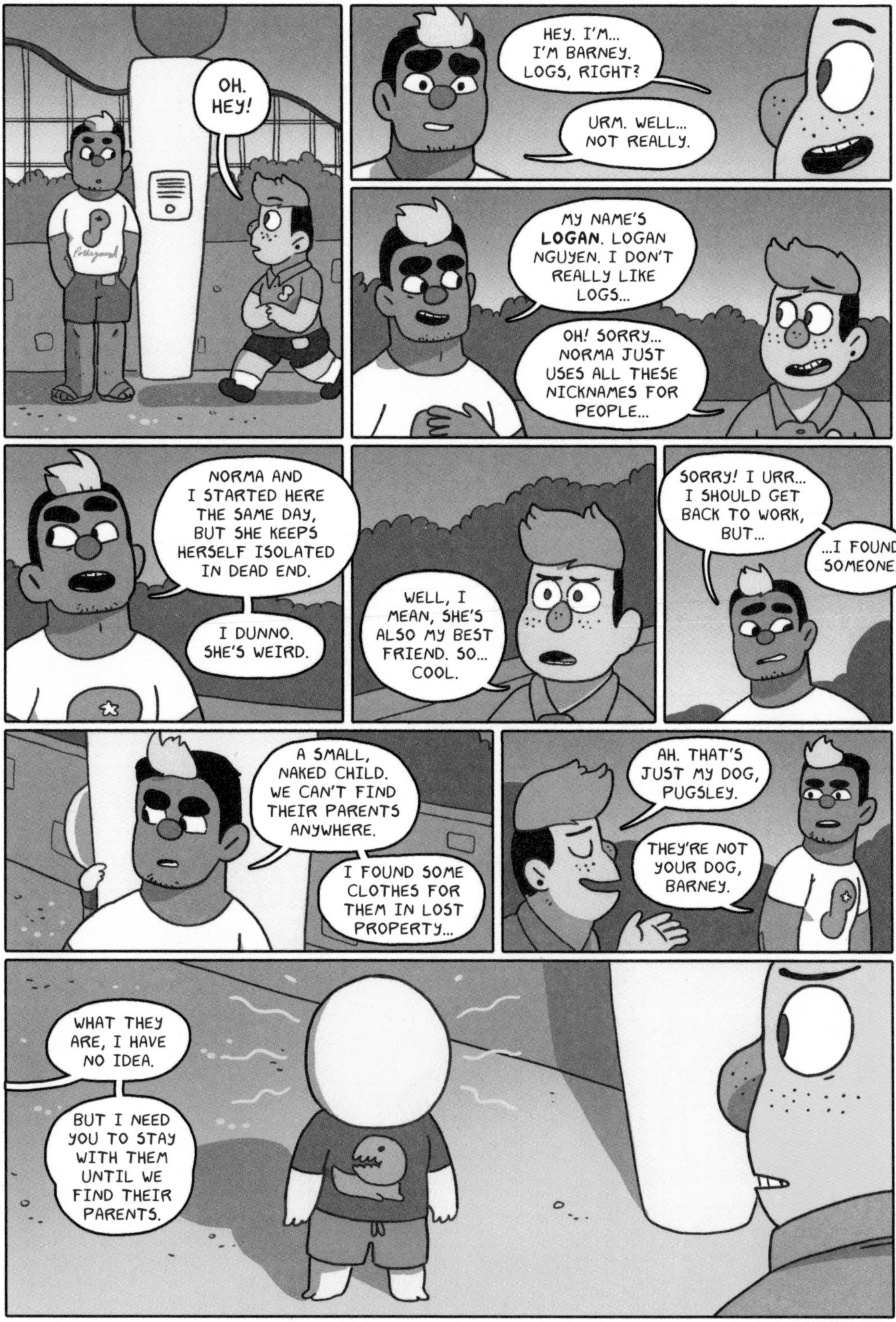

OH. HEY!
HEY. I'M... I'M BARNEY. LOGS, RIGHT?
URM. WELL... NOT REALLY.
MY NAME'S **LOGAN**. LOGAN NGUYEN. I DON'T REALLY LIKE LOGS...
OH! SORRY... NORMA JUST USES ALL THESE NICKNAMES FOR PEOPLE...
NORMA AND I STARTED HERE THE SAME DAY, BUT SHE KEEPS HERSELF ISOLATED IN DEAD END.
I DUNNO. SHE'S WEIRD.
WELL, I MEAN, SHE'S ALSO MY BEST FRIEND. SO... COOL.
SORRY! I URR... I SHOULD GET BACK TO WORK, BUT...
...I FOUND SOMEONE.
A SMALL, NAKED CHILD. WE CAN'T FIND THEIR PARENTS ANYWHERE.
I FOUND SOME CLOTHES FOR THEM IN LOST PROPERTY...
AH. THAT'S JUST MY DOG, PUGSLEY.
THEY'RE NOT YOUR DOG, BARNEY.
WHAT THEY ARE, I HAVE NO IDEA.
BUT I NEED YOU TO STAY WITH THEM UNTIL WE FIND THEIR PARENTS.

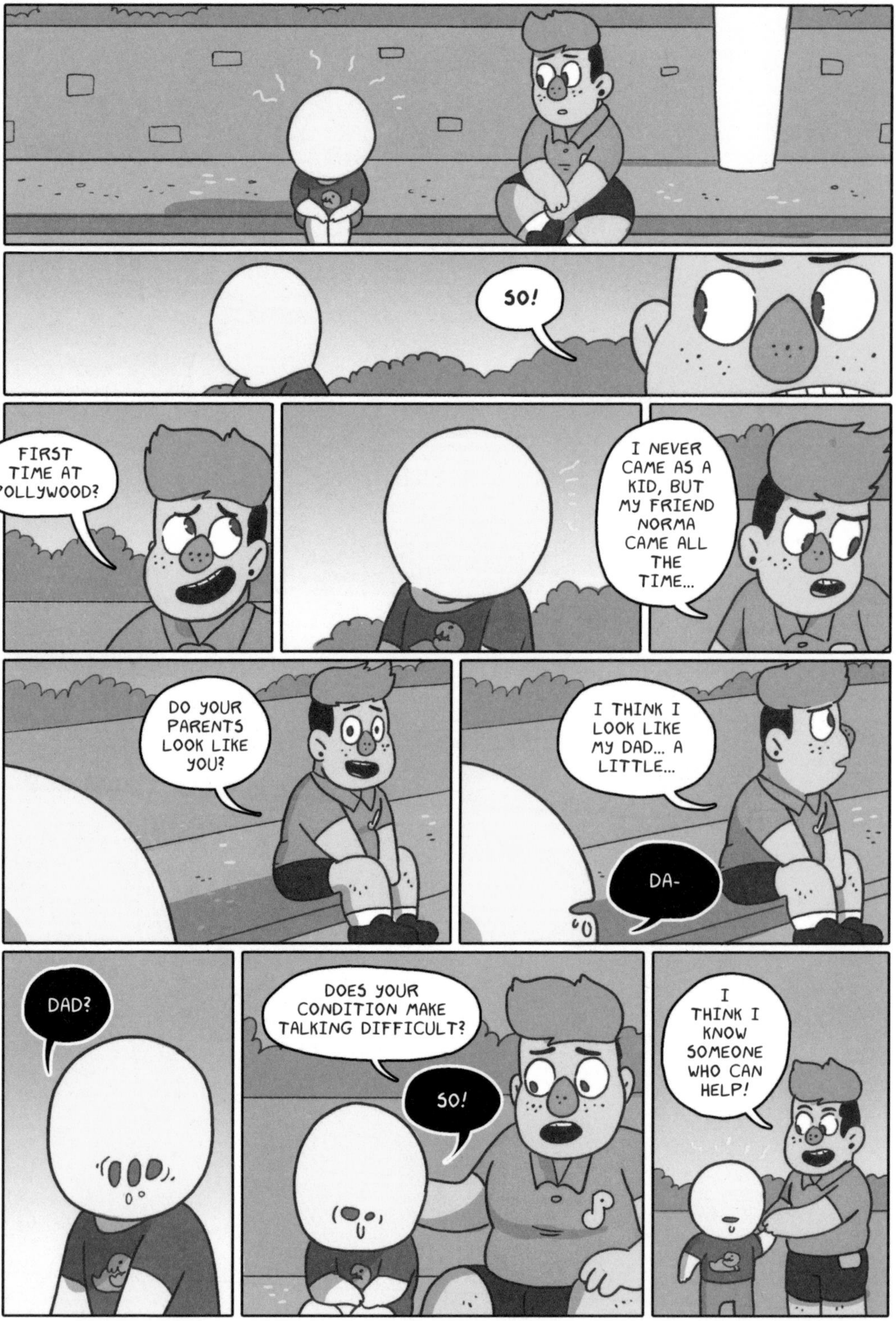
SO!
FIRST TIME AT POLLYWOOD?
I NEVER CAME AS A KID, BUT MY FRIEND NORMA CAME ALL THE TIME...
DO YOUR PARENTS LOOK LIKE YOU?
I THINK I LOOK LIKE MY DAD... A LITTLE...
DA-
DAD?
DOES YOUR CONDITION MAKE TALKING DIFFICULT?
SO!
I THINK I KNOW SOMEONE WHO CAN HELP!

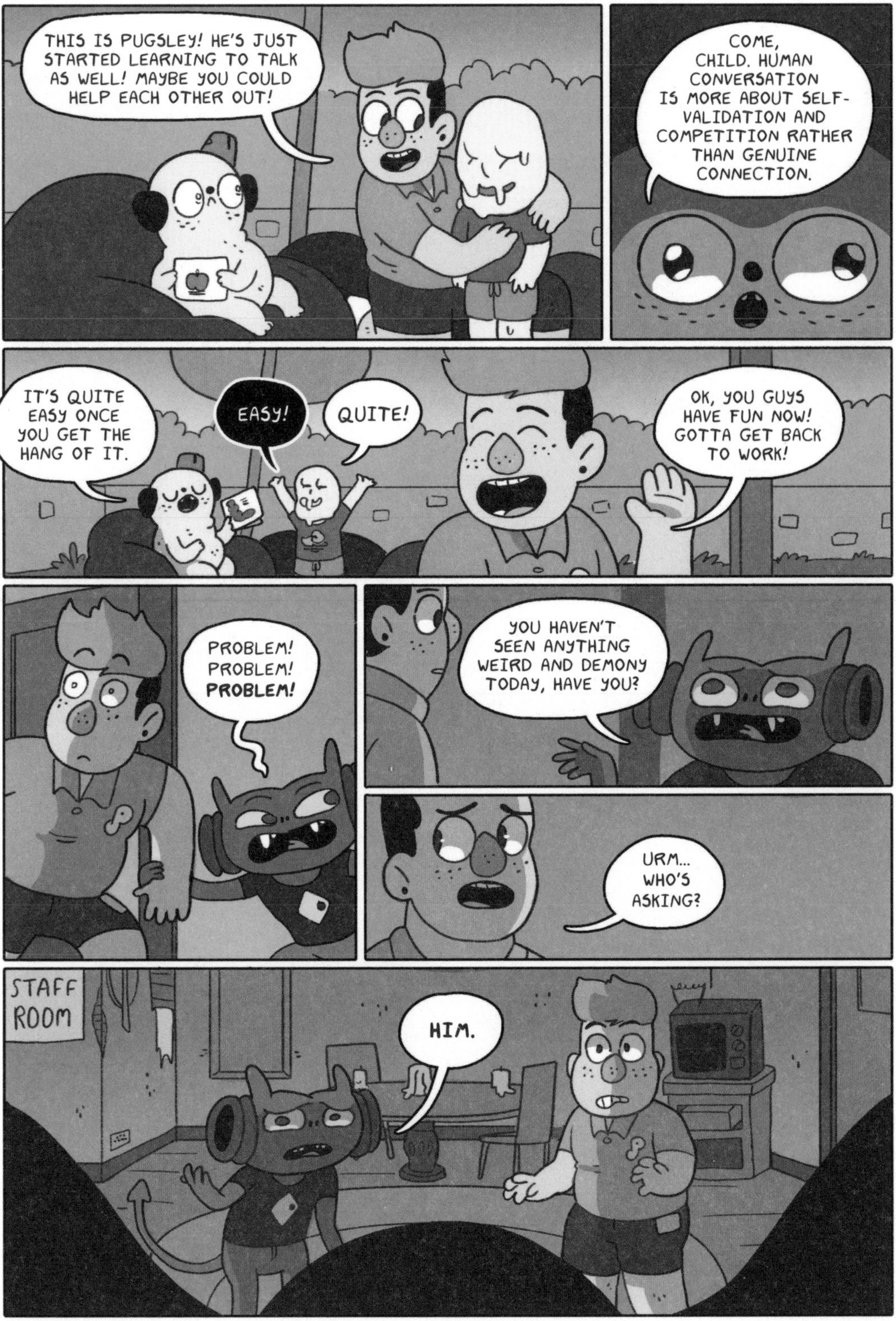
THIS IS PUGSLEY! HE'S JUST STARTED LEARNING TO TALK AS WELL! MAYBE YOU COULD HELP EACH OTHER OUT!
COME, CHILD. HUMAN CONVERSATION IS MORE ABOUT SELF-VALIDATION AND COMPETITION RATHER THAN GENUINE CONNECTION.
IT'S QUITE EASY ONCE YOU GET THE HANG OF IT.
EASY!
QUITE!
OK, YOU GUYS HAVE FUN NOW! GOTTA GET BACK TO WORK!
PROBLEM! PROBLEM! PROBLEM!
YOU HAVEN'T SEEN ANYTHING WEIRD AND DEMONY TODAY, HAVE YOU?
URM... WHO'S ASKING?
STAFF ROOM
HIM.

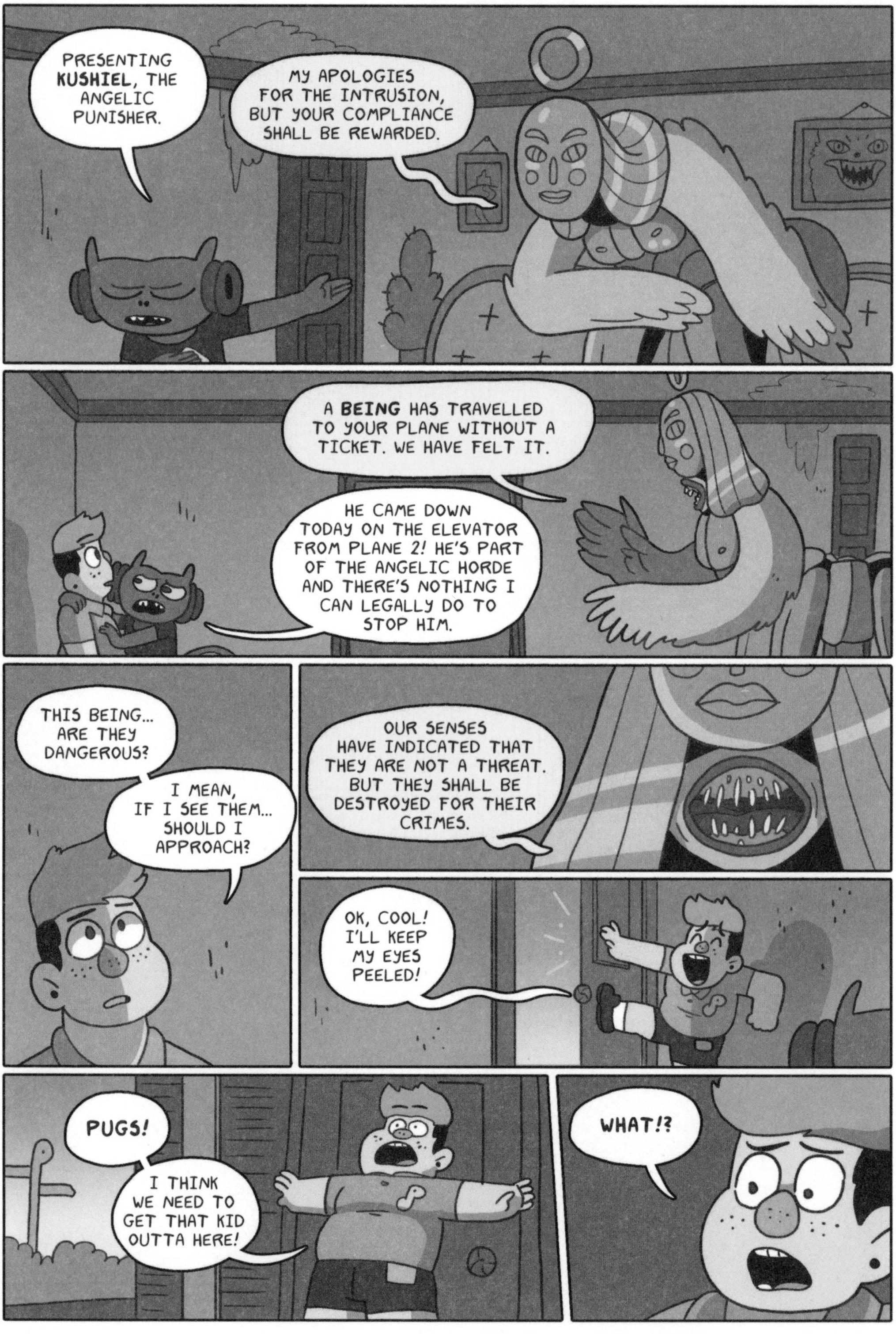
PRESENTING **KUSHIEL**, THE ANGELIC PUNISHER.
MY APOLOGIES FOR THE INTRUSION, BUT YOUR COMPLIANCE SHALL BE REWARDED.
A **BEING** HAS TRAVELLED TO YOUR PLANE WITHOUT A TICKET. WE HAVE FELT IT.
HE CAME DOWN TODAY ON THE ELEVATOR FROM PLANE 2! HE'S PART OF THE ANGELIC HORDE AND THERE'S NOTHING I CAN LEGALLY DO TO STOP HIM.
THIS BEING... ARE THEY DANGEROUS?
I MEAN, IF I SEE THEM... SHOULD I APPROACH?
OUR SENSES HAVE INDICATED THAT THEY ARE NOT A THREAT. BUT THEY SHALL BE DESTROYED FOR THEIR CRIMES.
OK, COOL! I'LL KEEP MY EYES PEELED!
PUGS!
I THINK WE NEED TO GET THAT KID OUTTA HERE!
WHAT!?

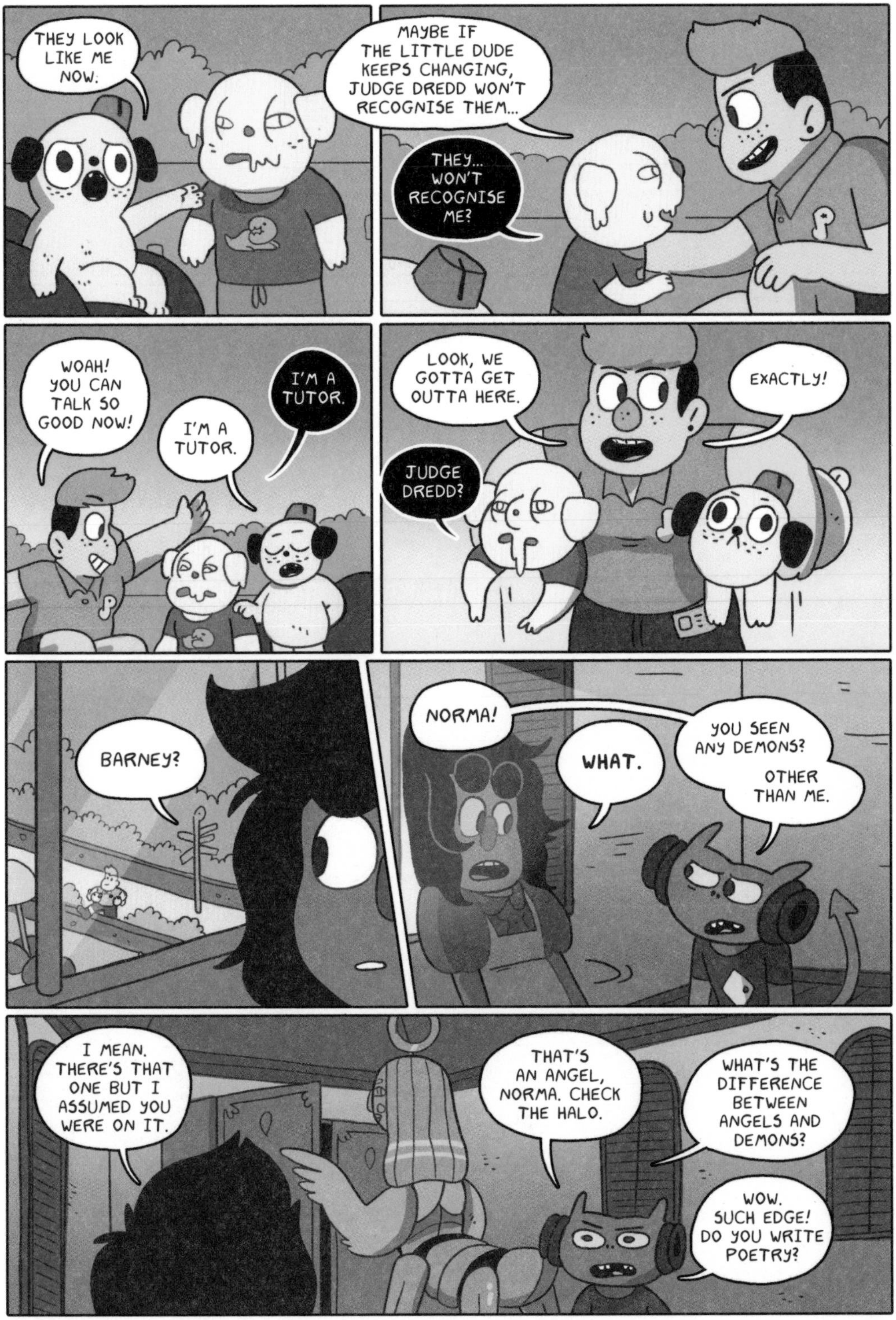
THEY LOOK LIKE ME NOW.
MAYBE IF THE LITTLE DUDE KEEPS CHANGING, JUDGE DREDD WON'T RECOGNISE THEM...
THEY... WON'T RECOGNISE ME?
WOAH! YOU CAN TALK SO GOOD NOW!
I'M A TUTOR.
I'M A TUTOR.
LOOK, WE GOTTA GET OUTTA HERE.
JUDGE DREDD?
EXACTLY!
BARNEY?
NORMA!
WHAT.
YOU SEEN ANY DEMONS?
OTHER THAN ME.
I MEAN. THERE'S THAT ONE BUT I ASSUMED YOU WERE ON IT.
THAT'S AN ANGEL, NORMA. CHECK THE HALO.
WHAT'S THE DIFFERENCE BETWEEN ANGELS AND DEMONS?
WOW. SUCH EDGE! DO YOU WRITE POETRY?

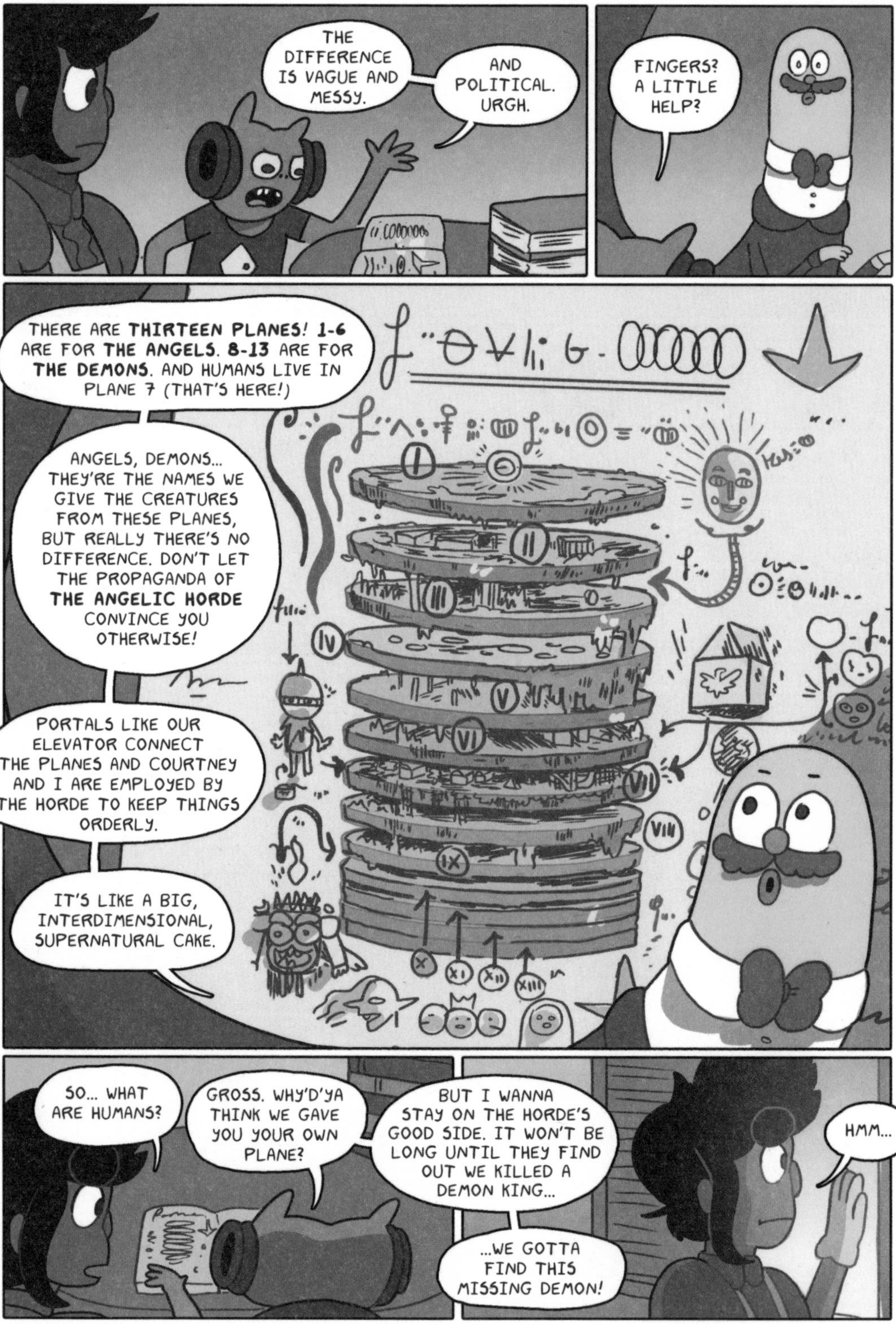
THE DIFFERENCE IS VAGUE AND MESSY.
AND POLITICAL. URGH.
FINGERS? A LITTLE HELP?
THERE ARE **THIRTEEN PLANES! 1-6** ARE FOR **THE ANGELS. 8-13** ARE FOR **THE DEMONS**. AND HUMANS LIVE IN PLANE 7 (THAT'S HERE!)
ANGELS, DEMONS... THEY'RE THE NAMES WE GIVE THE CREATURES FROM THESE PLANES, BUT REALLY THERE'S NO DIFFERENCE. DON'T LET THE PROPAGANDA OF **THE ANGELIC HORDE** CONVINCE YOU OTHERWISE!
PORTALS LIKE OUR ELEVATOR CONNECT THE PLANES AND COURTNEY AND I ARE EMPLOYED BY THE HORDE TO KEEP THINGS ORDERLY.
IT'S LIKE A BIG, INTERDIMENSIONAL, SUPERNATURAL CAKE.
SO... WHAT ARE HUMANS?
GROSS. WHY'D'YA THINK WE GAVE YOU YOUR OWN PLANE?
BUT I WANNA STAY ON THE HORDE'S GOOD SIDE. IT WON'T BE LONG UNTIL THEY FIND OUT WE KILLED A DEMON KING...
...WE GOTTA FIND THIS MISSING DEMON!
HMM...

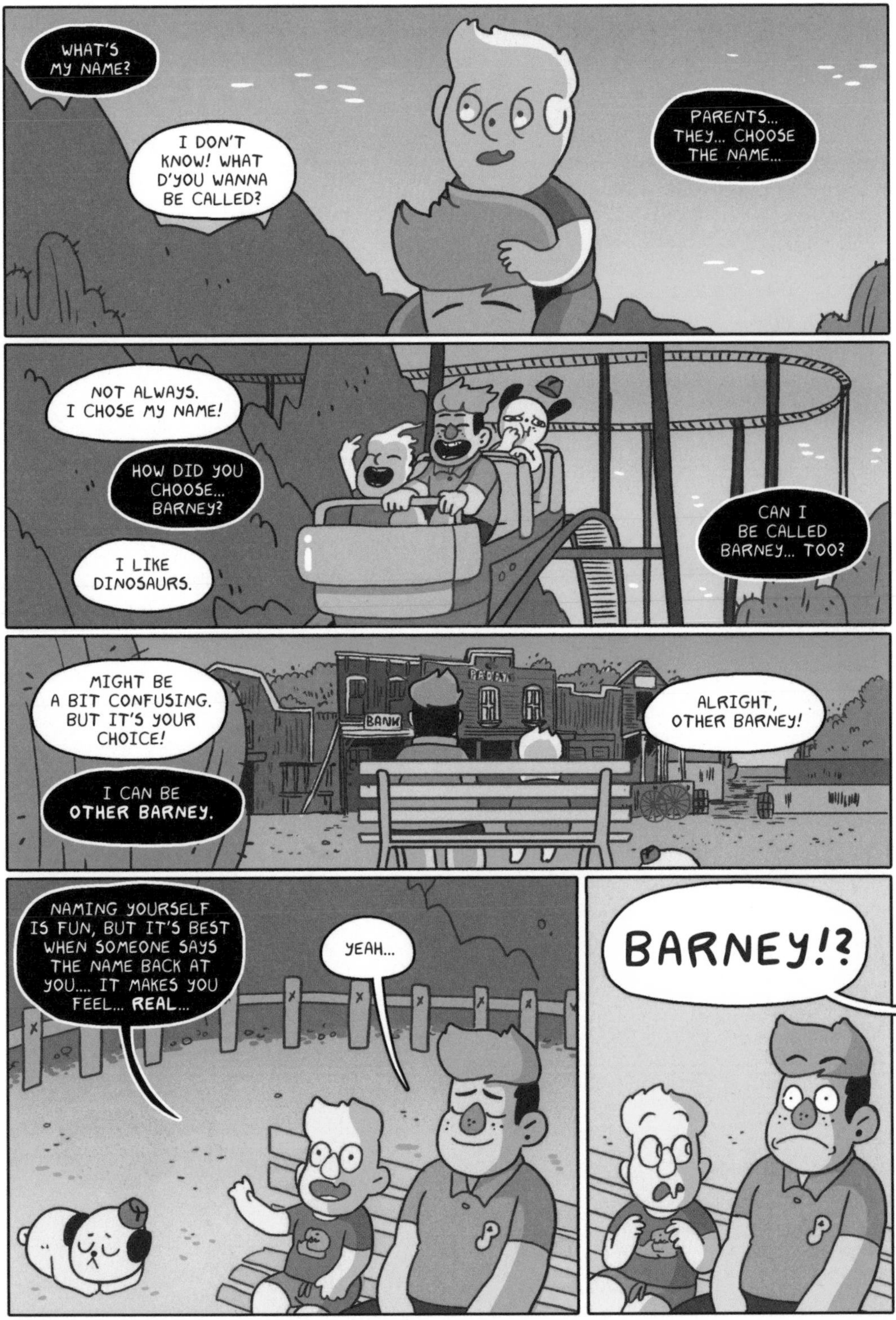

WHAT'S MY NAME?
I DON'T KNOW! WHAT D'YOU WANNA BE CALLED?
PARENTS... THEY... CHOOSE THE NAME...
NOT ALWAYS. I CHOSE MY NAME!
HOW DID YOU CHOOSE... BARNEY?
I LIKE DINOSAURS.
CAN I BE CALLED BARNEY... TOO?
MIGHT BE A BIT CONFUSING. BUT IT'S YOUR CHOICE!
BANK
I CAN BE **OTHER BARNEY.**
ALRIGHT, OTHER BARNEY!
NAMING YOURSELF IS FUN, BUT IT'S BEST WHEN SOMEONE SAYS THE NAME BACK AT YOU.... IT MAKES YOU FEEL... **REAL**...
YEAH...
BARNEY!?

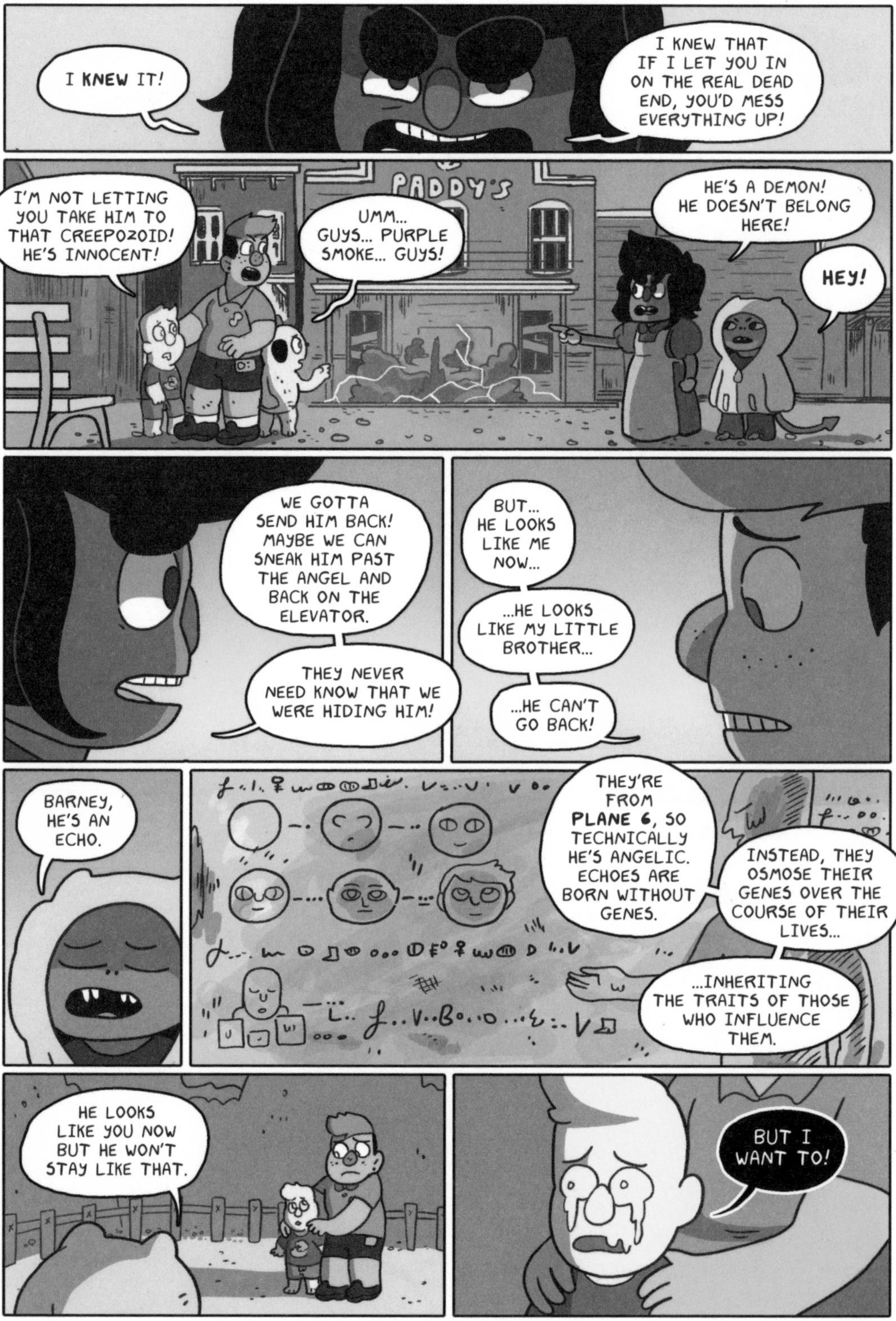
I KNEW IT!
I KNEW THAT IF I LET YOU IN ON THE REAL DEAD END, YOU'D MESS EVERYTHING UP!
PADDY'S
I'M NOT LETTING YOU TAKE HIM TO THAT CREEPOZOID! HE'S INNOCENT!
UMM... GUYS... PURPLE SMOKE... GUYS!
HE'S A DEMON! HE DOESN'T BELONG HERE!
HEY!
WE GOTTA SEND HIM BACK! MAYBE WE CAN SNEAK HIM PAST THE ANGEL AND BACK ON THE ELEVATOR.
THEY NEVER NEED KNOW THAT WE WERE HIDING HIM!
BUT... HE LOOKS LIKE ME NOW...
...HE LOOKS LIKE MY LITTLE BROTHER...
...HE CAN'T GO BACK!
BARNEY, HE'S AN ECHO.
THEY'RE FROM PLANE 6, SO TECHNICALLY HE'S ANGELIC. ECHOES ARE BORN WITHOUT GENES.
INSTEAD, THEY OSMOSE THEIR GENES OVER THE COURSE OF THEIR LIVES...
...INHERITING THE TRAITS OF THOSE WHO INFLUENCE THEM.
HE LOOKS LIKE YOU NOW BUT HE WON'T STAY LIKE THAT.
BUT I WANT TO!

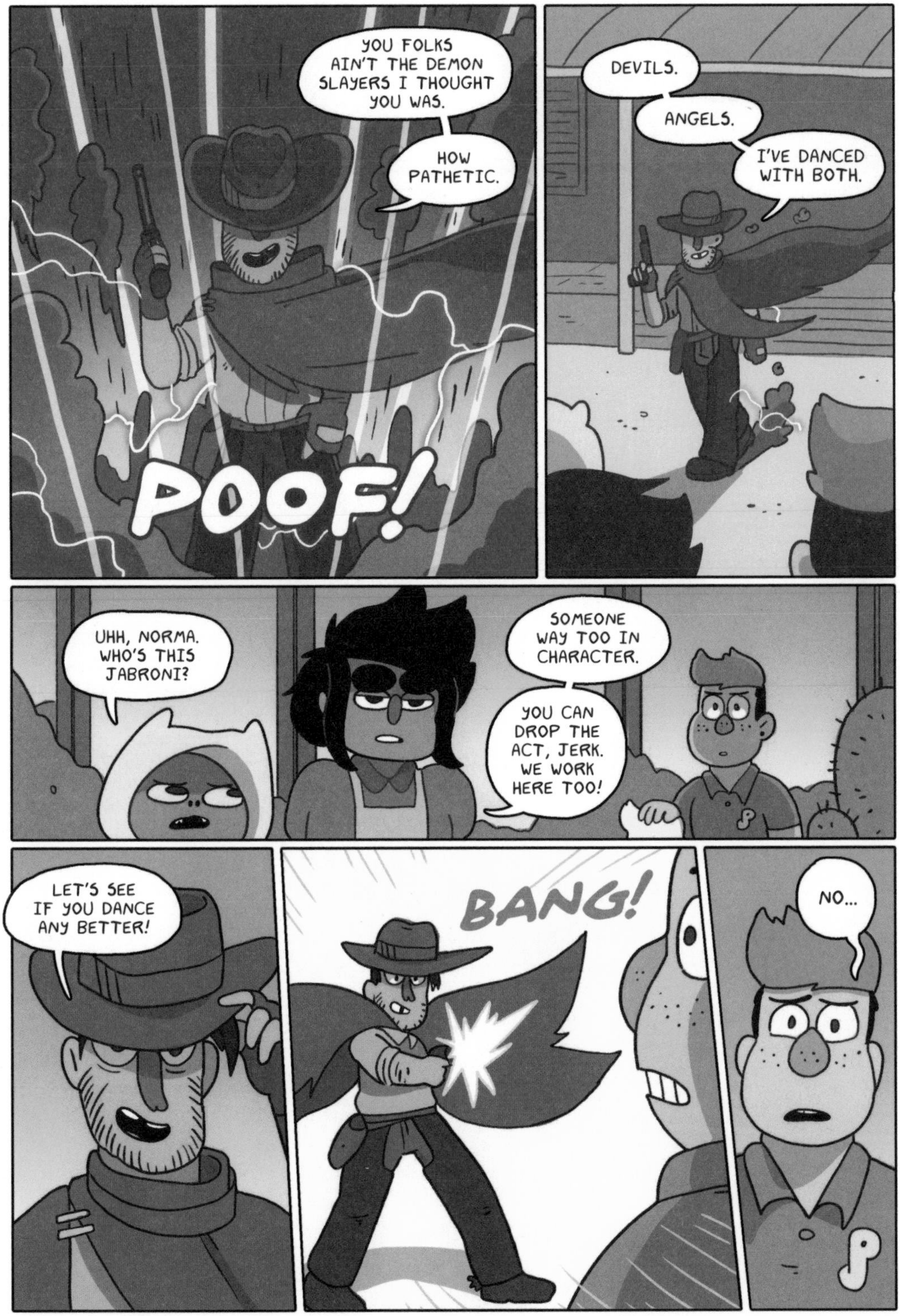
YOU FOLKS AIN'T THE DEMON SLAYERS I THOUGHT YOU WAS.
HOW PATHETIC.
POOF!
DEVILS.
ANGELS.
I'VE DANCED WITH BOTH.
UHH, NORMA. WHO'S THIS JABRONI?
SOMEONE WAY TOO IN CHARACTER.
YOU CAN DROP THE ACT, JERK. WE WORK HERE TOO!
LET'S SEE IF YOU DANCE ANY BETTER!
BANG!
NO...

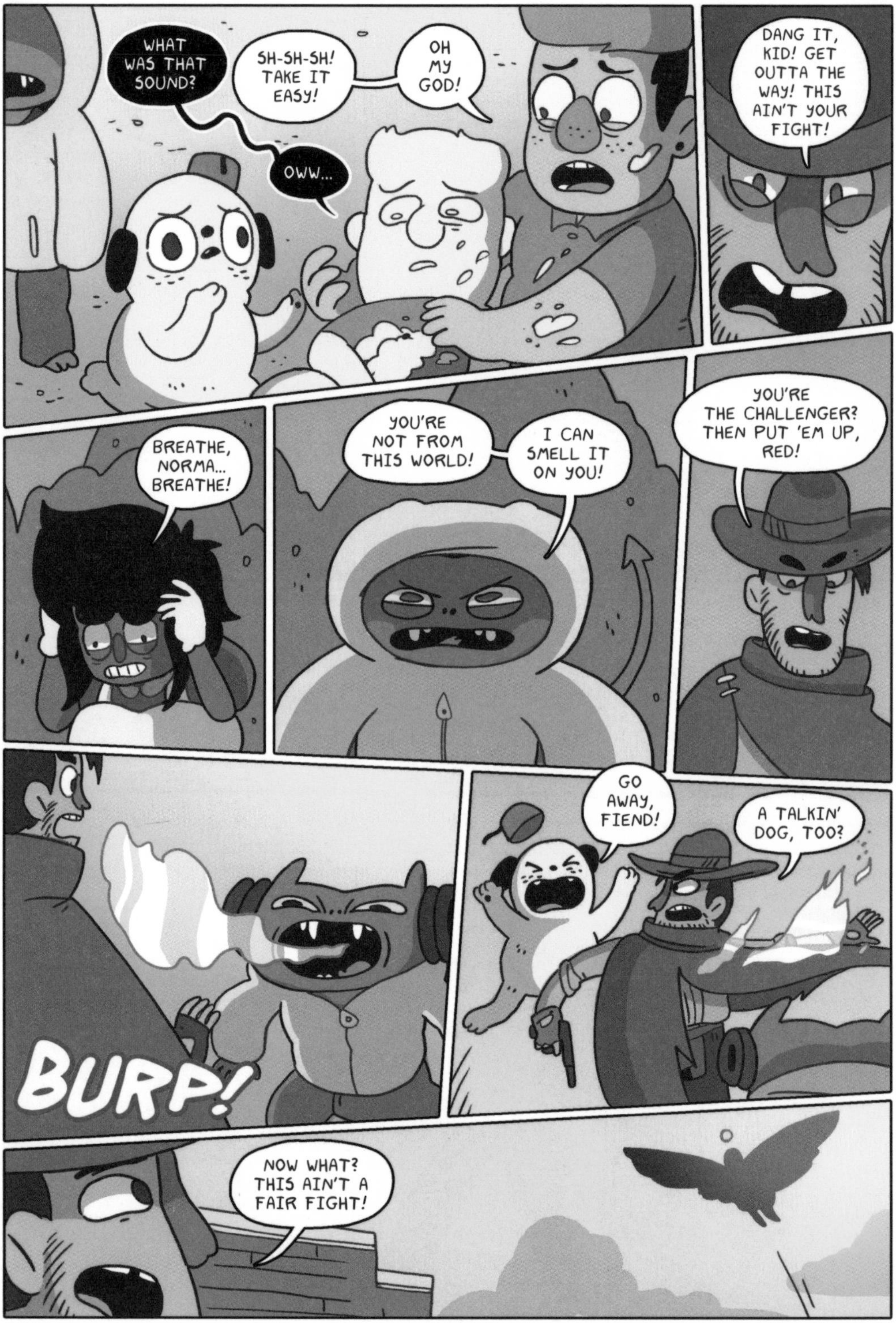
WHAT WAS THAT SOUND?
SH-SH-SH! TAKE IT EASY!
OH MY GOD!
OWW...
DANG IT, KID! GET OUTTA THE WAY! THIS AIN'T YOUR FIGHT!
BREATHE, NORMA... BREATHE!
YOU'RE NOT FROM THIS WORLD!
I CAN SMELL IT ON YOU!
YOU'RE THE CHALLENGER? THEN PUT 'EM UP, RED!
BURP!
GO AWAY, FIEND!
A TALKIN' DOG, TOO?
NOW WHAT? THIS AIN'T A FAIR FIGHT!

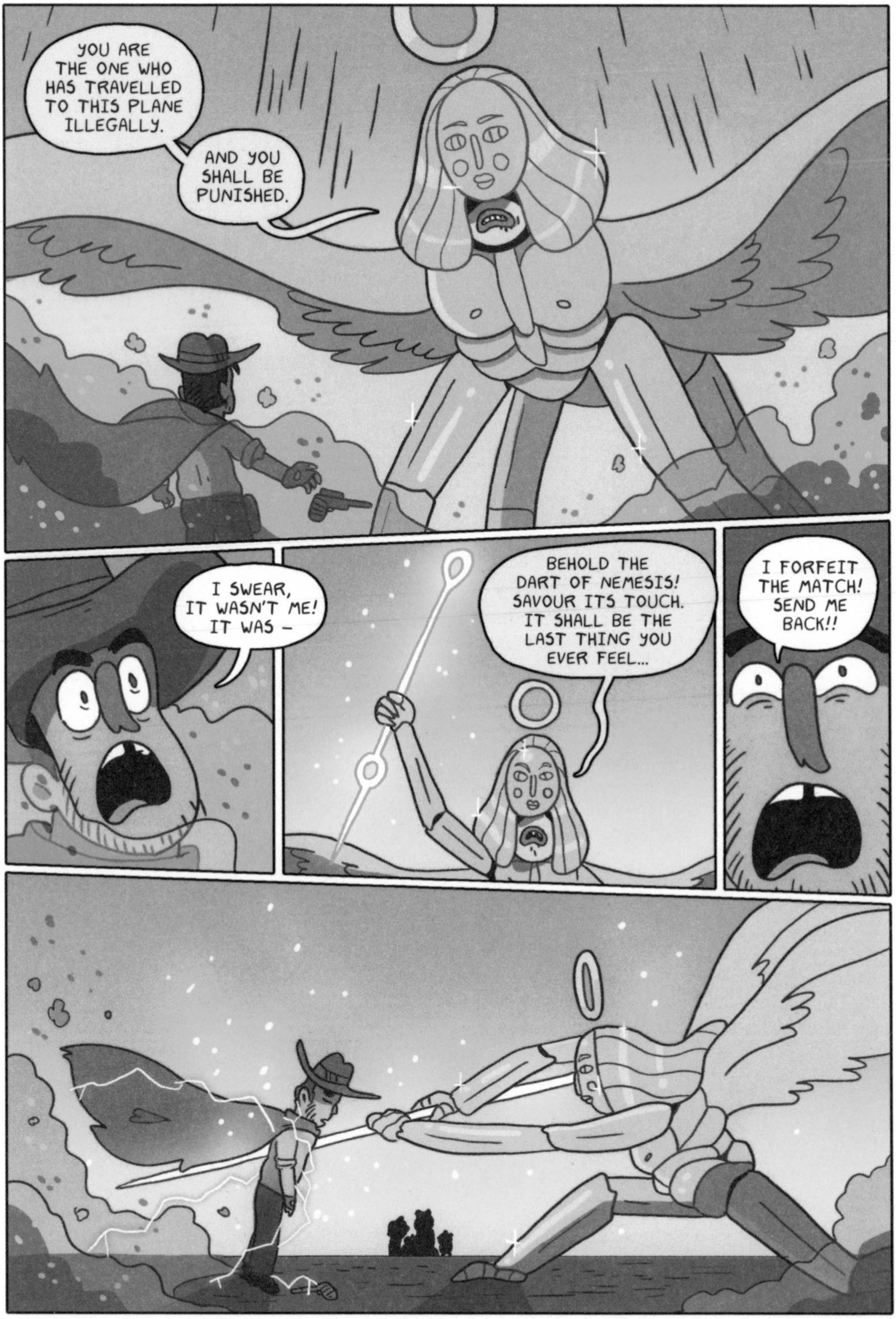
YOU ARE THE ONE WHO HAS TRAVELLED TO THIS PLANE ILLEGALLY.
AND YOU SHALL BE PUNISHED.
I SWEAR, IT WASN'T ME! IT WAS –
BEHOLD THE DART OF NEMESIS! SAVOUR ITS TOUCH. IT SHALL BE THE LAST THING YOU EVER FEEL...
I FORFEIT THE MATCH! SEND ME BACK!!

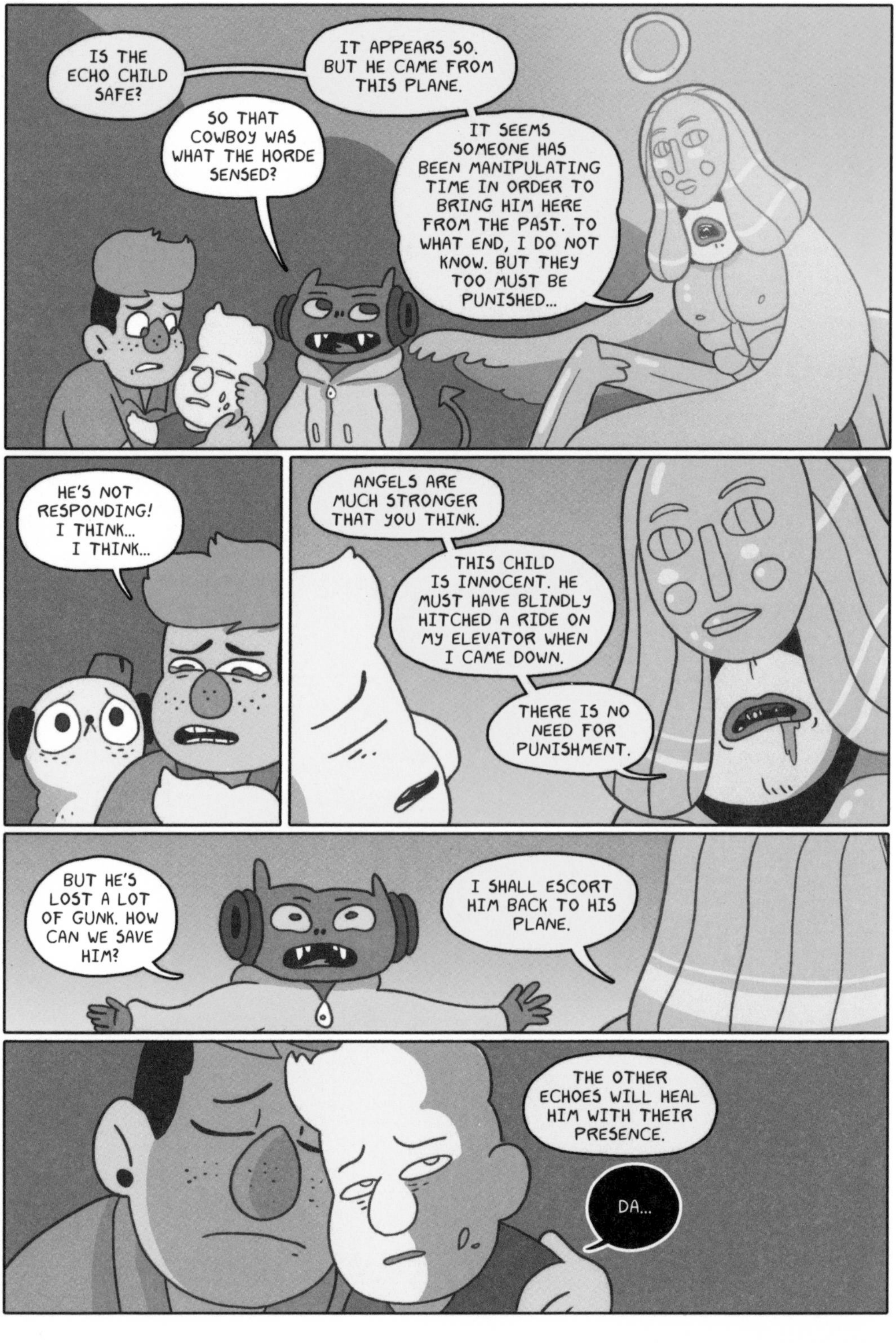
IS THE ECHO CHILD SAFE?
IT APPEARS SO. BUT HE CAME FROM THIS PLANE.
SO THAT COWBOY WAS WHAT THE HORDE SENSED?
IT SEEMS SOMEONE HAS BEEN MANIPULATING TIME IN ORDER TO BRING HIM HERE FROM THE PAST. TO WHAT END, I DO NOT KNOW. BUT THEY TOO MUST BE PUNISHED...
HE'S NOT RESPONDING! I THINK... I THINK...
ANGELS ARE MUCH STRONGER THAT YOU THINK.
THIS CHILD IS INNOCENT. HE MUST HAVE BLINDLY HITCHED A RIDE ON MY ELEVATOR WHEN I CAME DOWN.
THERE IS NO NEED FOR PUNISHMENT.
BUT HE'S LOST A LOT OF GUNK. HOW CAN WE SAVE HIM?
I SHALL ESCORT HIM BACK TO HIS PLANE.
THE OTHER ECHOES WILL HEAL HIM WITH THEIR PRESENCE.
DA...

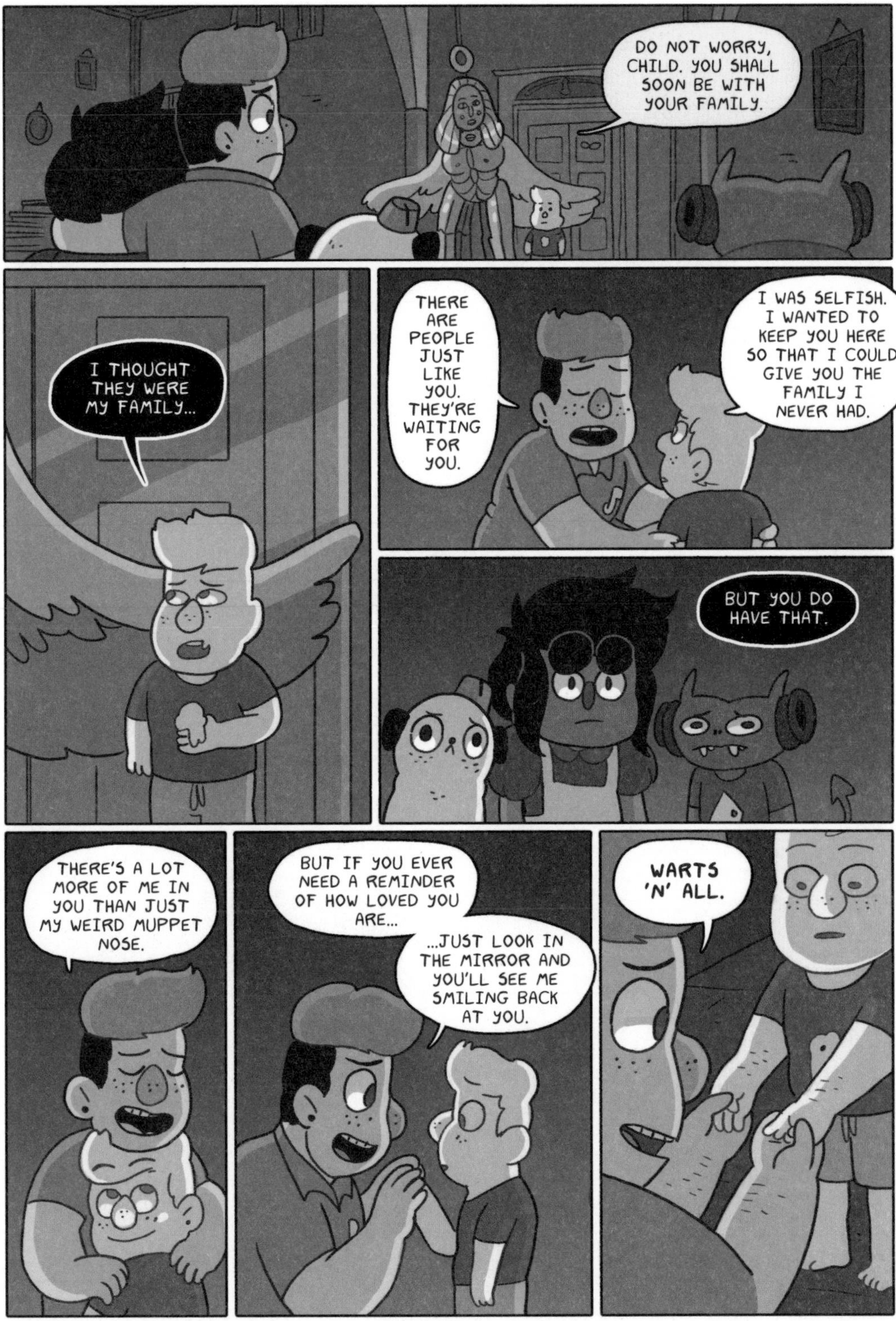
DO NOT WORRY, CHILD. YOU SHALL SOON BE WITH YOUR FAMILY.
I THOUGHT THEY WERE MY FAMILY...
THERE ARE PEOPLE JUST LIKE YOU. THEY'RE WAITING FOR YOU.
I WAS SELFISH. I WANTED TO KEEP YOU HERE SO THAT I COULD GIVE YOU THE FAMILY I NEVER HAD.
BUT YOU DO HAVE THAT.
THERE'S A LOT MORE OF ME IN YOU THAN JUST MY WEIRD MUPPET NOSE.
BUT IF YOU EVER NEED A REMINDER OF HOW LOVED YOU ARE...
...JUST LOOK IN THE MIRROR AND YOU'LL SEE ME SMILING BACK AT YOU.
WARTS 'N' ALL.

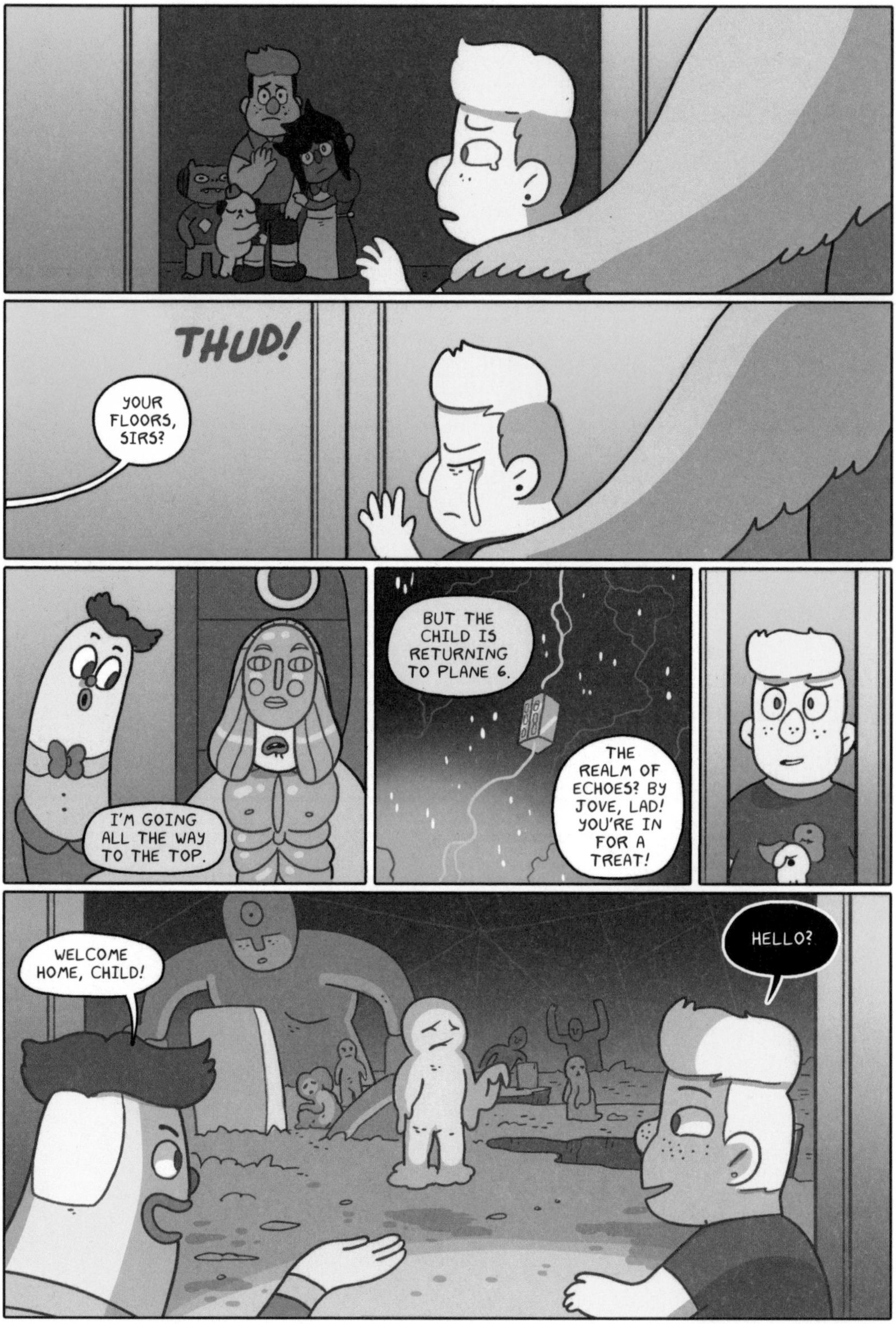
THUD!
YOUR FLOORS, SIRS?
I'M GOING ALL THE WAY TO THE TOP.
BUT THE CHILD IS RETURNING TO PLANE 6.
THE REALM OF ECHOES? BY JOVE, LAD! YOU'RE IN FOR A TREAT!
WELCOME HOME, CHILD!
HELLO?

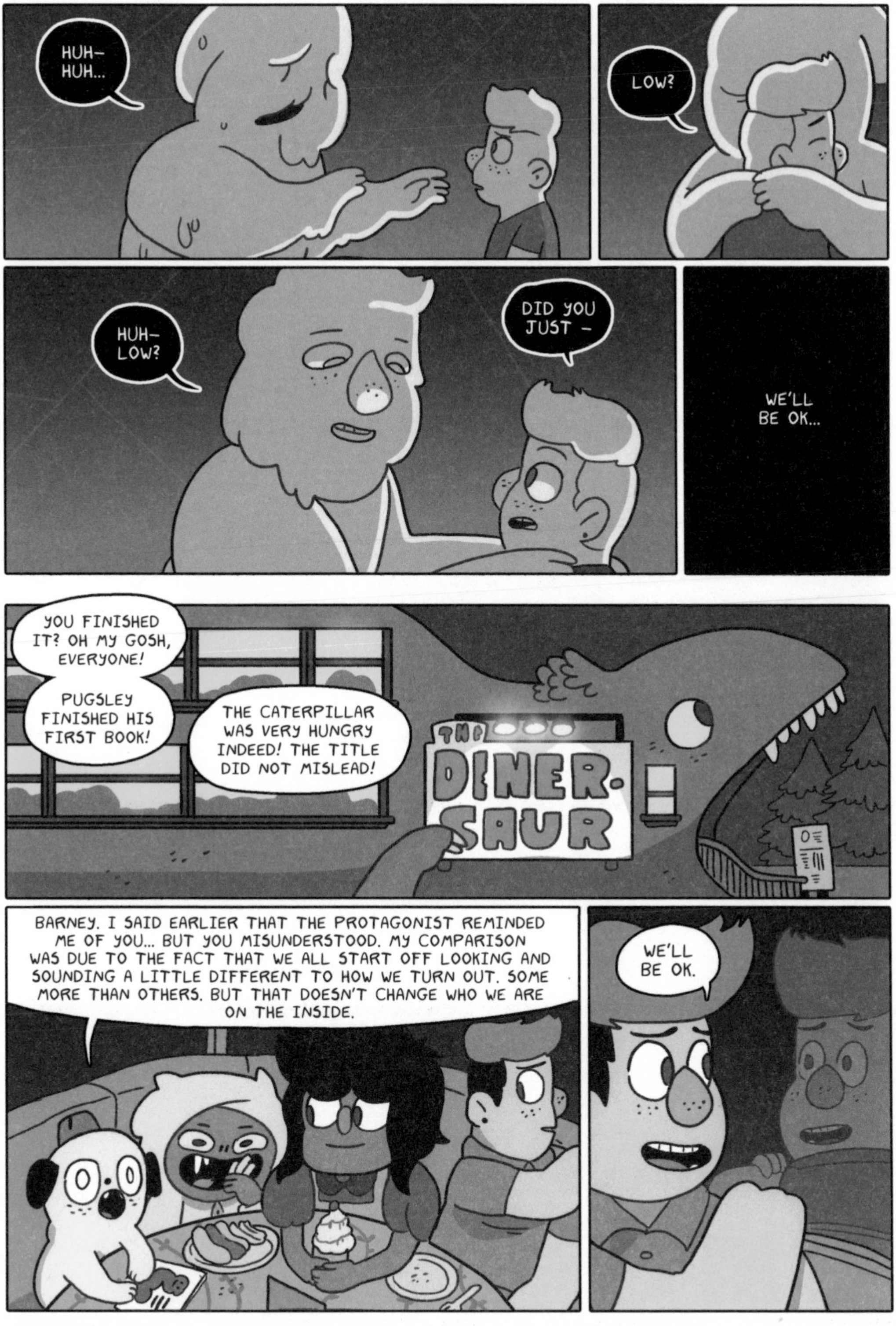
HUH-
HUH...
LOW?
HUH-
LOW?
DID YOU
JUST -
WE'LL
BE OK...
YOU FINISHED IT? OH MY GOSH, EVERYONE!
PUGSLEY FINISHED HIS FIRST BOOK!
THE CATERPILLAR WAS VERY HUNGRY INDEED! THE TITLE DID NOT MISLEAD!
THE DINER-SAUR
BARNEY. I SAID EARLIER THAT THE PROTAGONIST REMINDED ME OF YOU... BUT YOU MISUNDERSTOOD. MY COMPARISON WAS DUE TO THE FACT THAT WE ALL START OFF LOOKING AND SOUNDING A LITTLE DIFFERENT TO HOW WE TURN OUT. SOME MORE THAN OTHERS. BUT THAT DOESN'T CHANGE WHO WE ARE ON THE INSIDE.
WE'LL
BE OK.

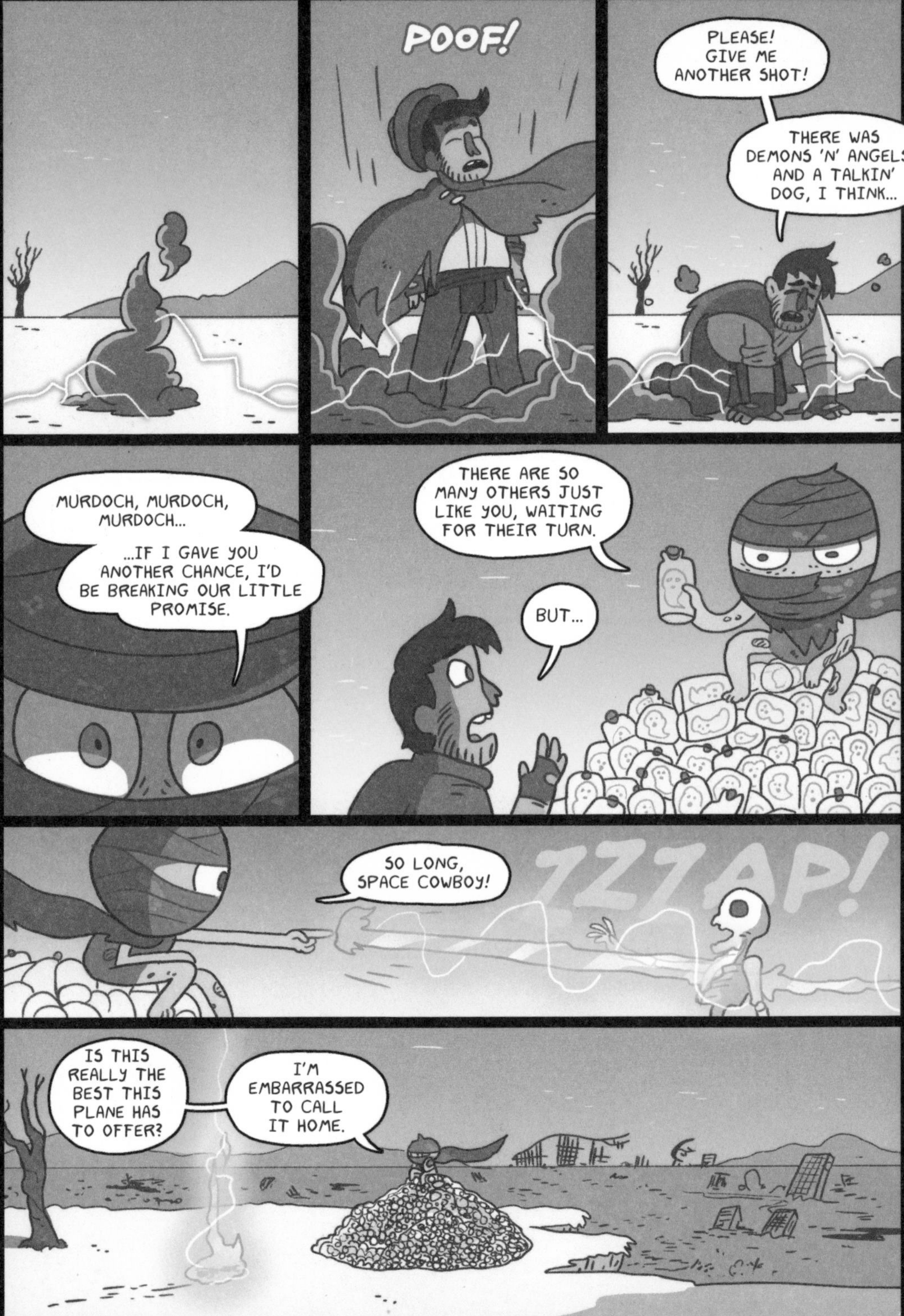
POOF!
PLEASE! GIVE ME ANOTHER SHOT!
THERE WAS DEMONS 'N' ANGELS... AND A TALKIN' DOG, I THINK...
MURDOCH, MURDOCH, MURDOCH...
...IF I GAVE YOU ANOTHER CHANCE, I'D BE BREAKING OUR LITTLE PROMISE.
THERE ARE SO MANY OTHERS JUST LIKE YOU, WAITING FOR THEIR TURN.
BUT...
SO LONG, SPACE COWBOY!
ZZZAP!
IS THIS REALLY THE BEST THIS PLANE HAS TO OFFER?
I'M EMBARRASSED TO CALL IT HOME.

CHAPTER 3

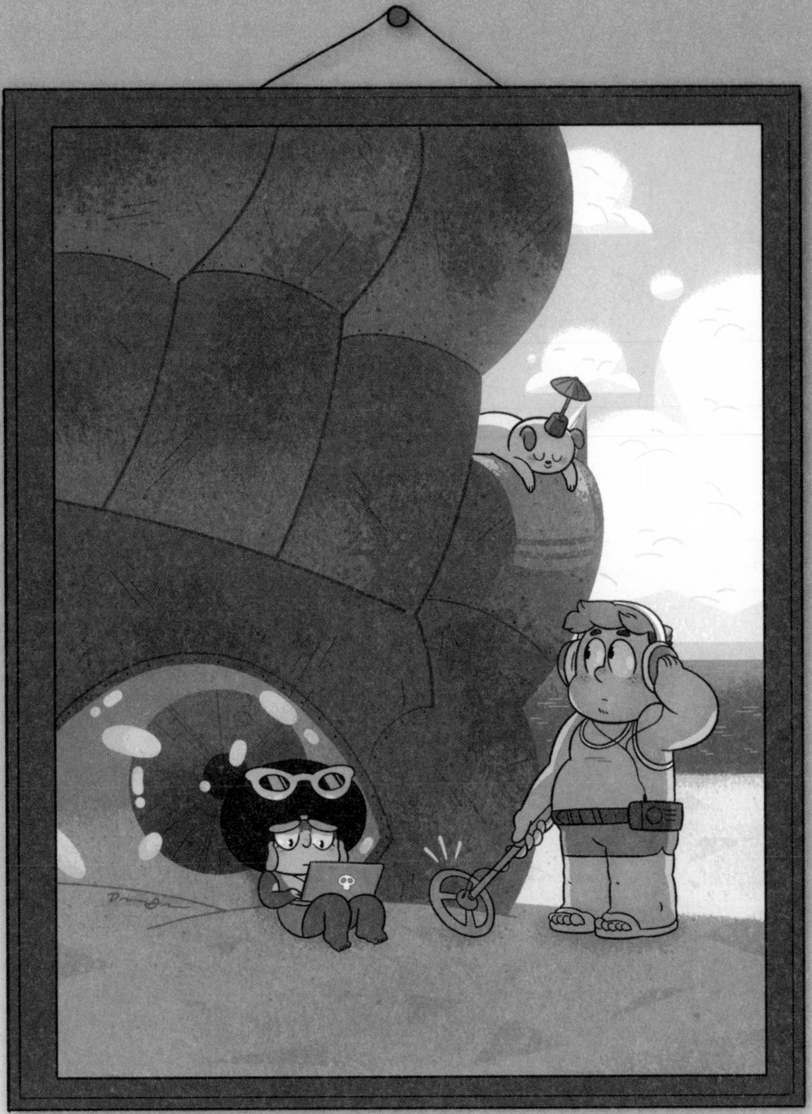

COVER ART BY DREW GREEN

THE SKULL OF FEAR

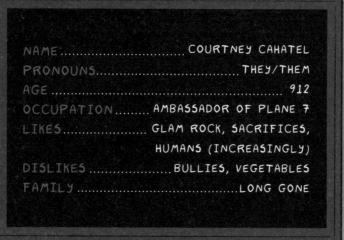

NAME..................................COURTNEY CAHATEL

PRONOUNS.......................................THEY/THEM

AGE 912

OCCUPATION.........AMBASSADOR OF PLANE 7

LIKES.....................GLAM ROCK, SACRIFICES,

HUMANS (INCREASINGLY)

DISLIKES ....BULLIES, VEGETABLES

FAMILY ....LONG GONE

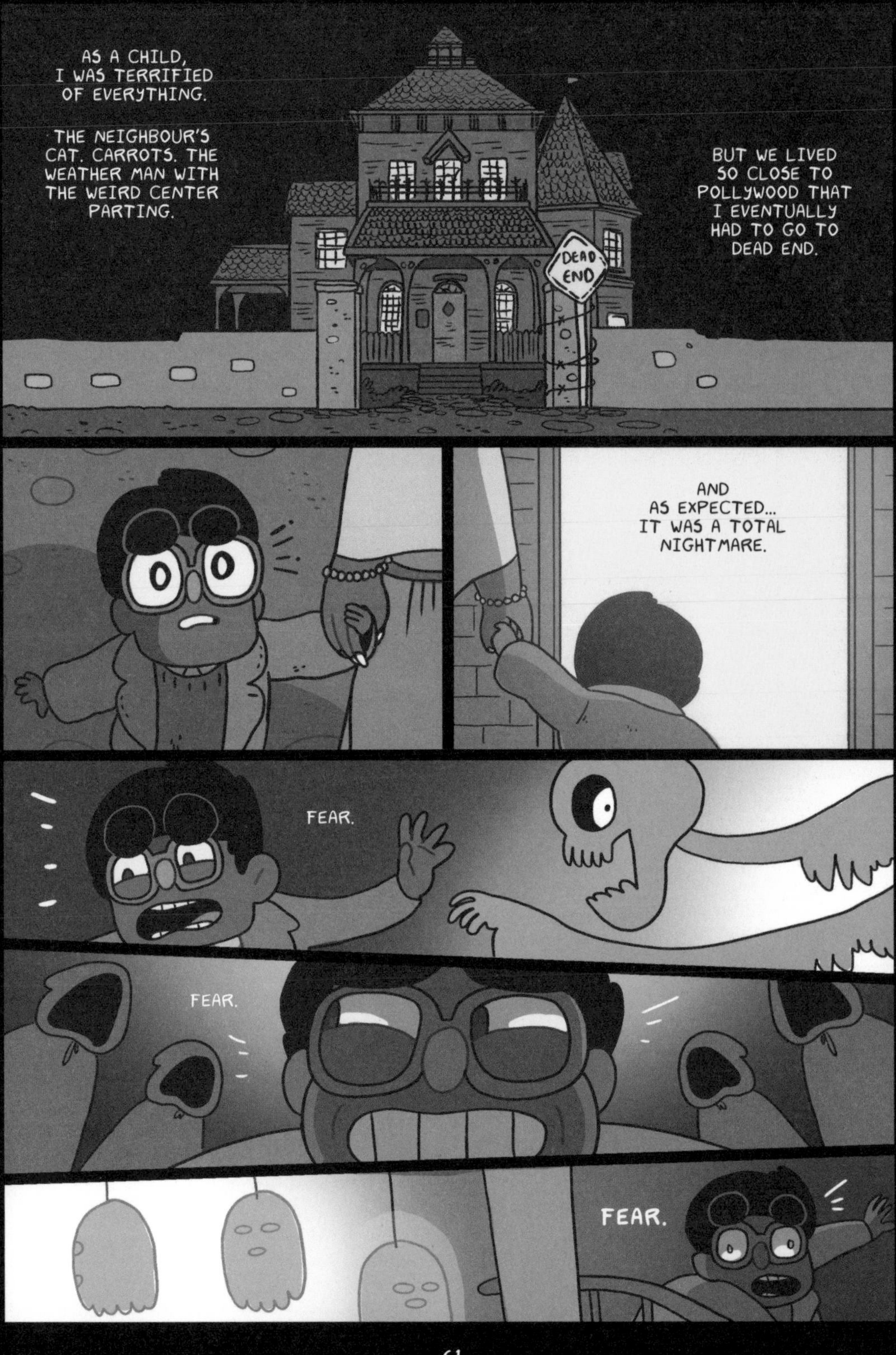
AS A CHILD, I WAS TERRIFIED OF EVERYTHING.
THE NEIGHBOUR'S CAT. CARROTS. THE WEATHER MAN WITH THE WEIRD CENTER PARTING.
DEAD END
BUT WE LIVED SO CLOSE TO POLLYWOOD THAT I EVENTUALLY HAD TO GO TO DEAD END.
AND AS EXPECTED... IT WAS A TOTAL NIGHTMARE.
FEAR.
FEAR.
FEAR.

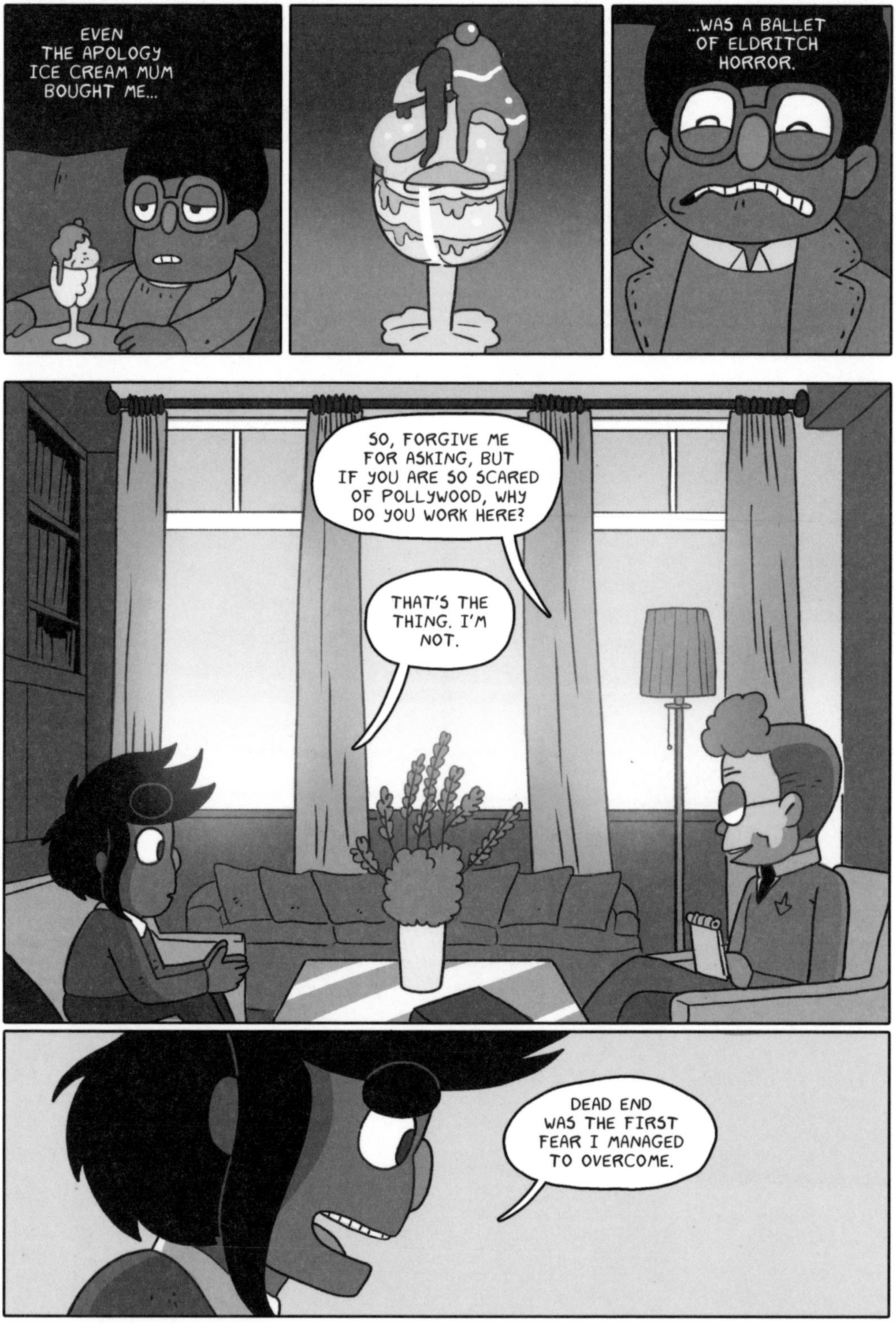
EVEN THE APOLOGY ICE CREAM MUM BOUGHT ME...
...WAS A BALLET OF ELDRITCH HORROR.
SO, FORGIVE ME FOR ASKING, BUT IF YOU ARE SO SCARED OF POLLYWOOD, WHY DO YOU WORK HERE?
THAT'S THE THING. I'M NOT.
DEAD END WAS THE FIRST FEAR I MANAGED TO OVERCOME.

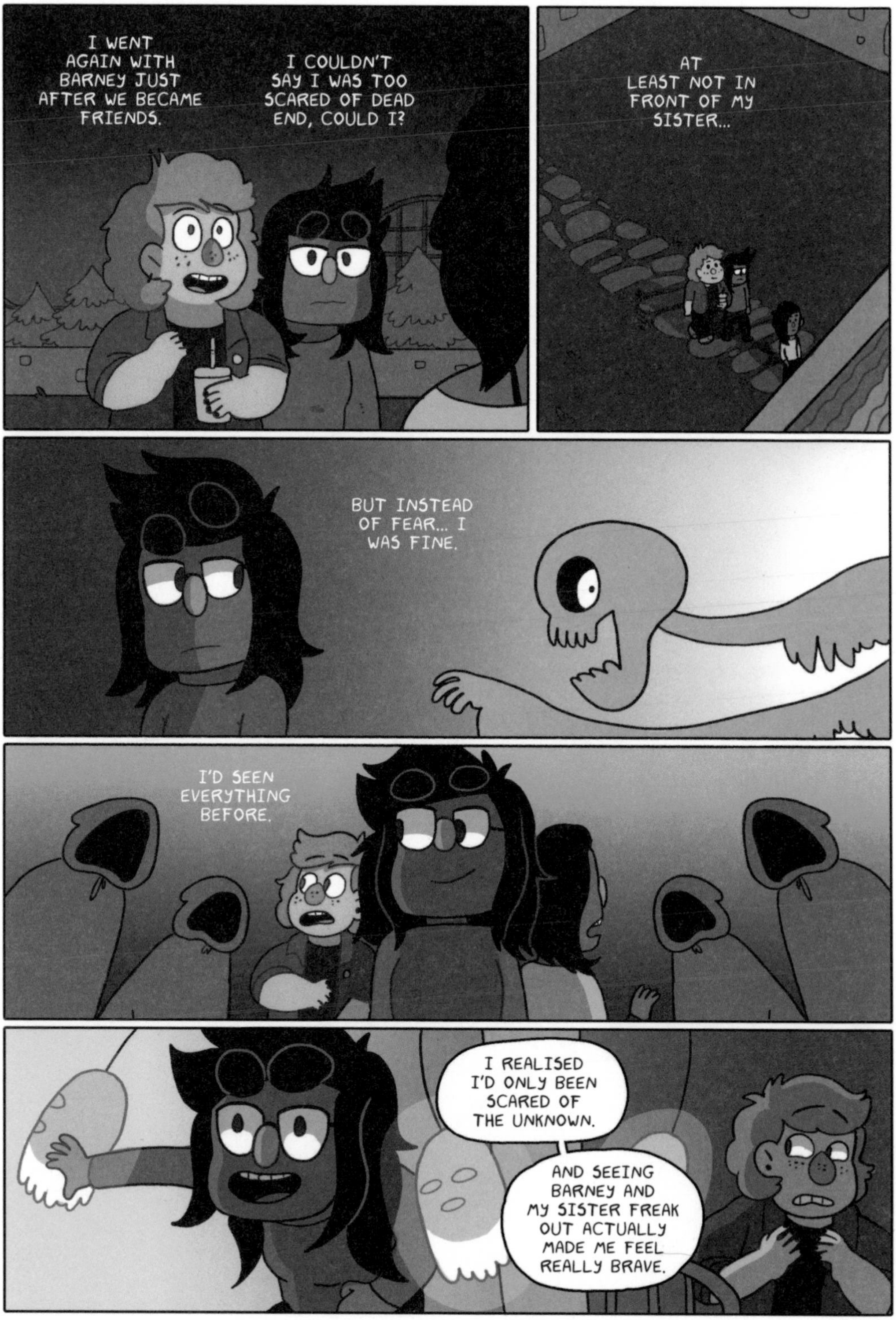
I WENT AGAIN WITH BARNEY JUST AFTER WE BECAME FRIENDS.
I COULDN'T SAY I WAS TOO SCARED OF DEAD END, COULD I?
AT LEAST NOT IN FRONT OF MY SISTER...
BUT INSTEAD OF FEAR... I WAS FINE.
I'D SEEN EVERYTHING BEFORE.
I REALISED I'D ONLY BEEN SCARED OF THE UNKNOWN.
AND SEEING BARNEY AND MY SISTER FREAK OUT ACTUALLY MADE ME FEEL REALLY BRAVE.

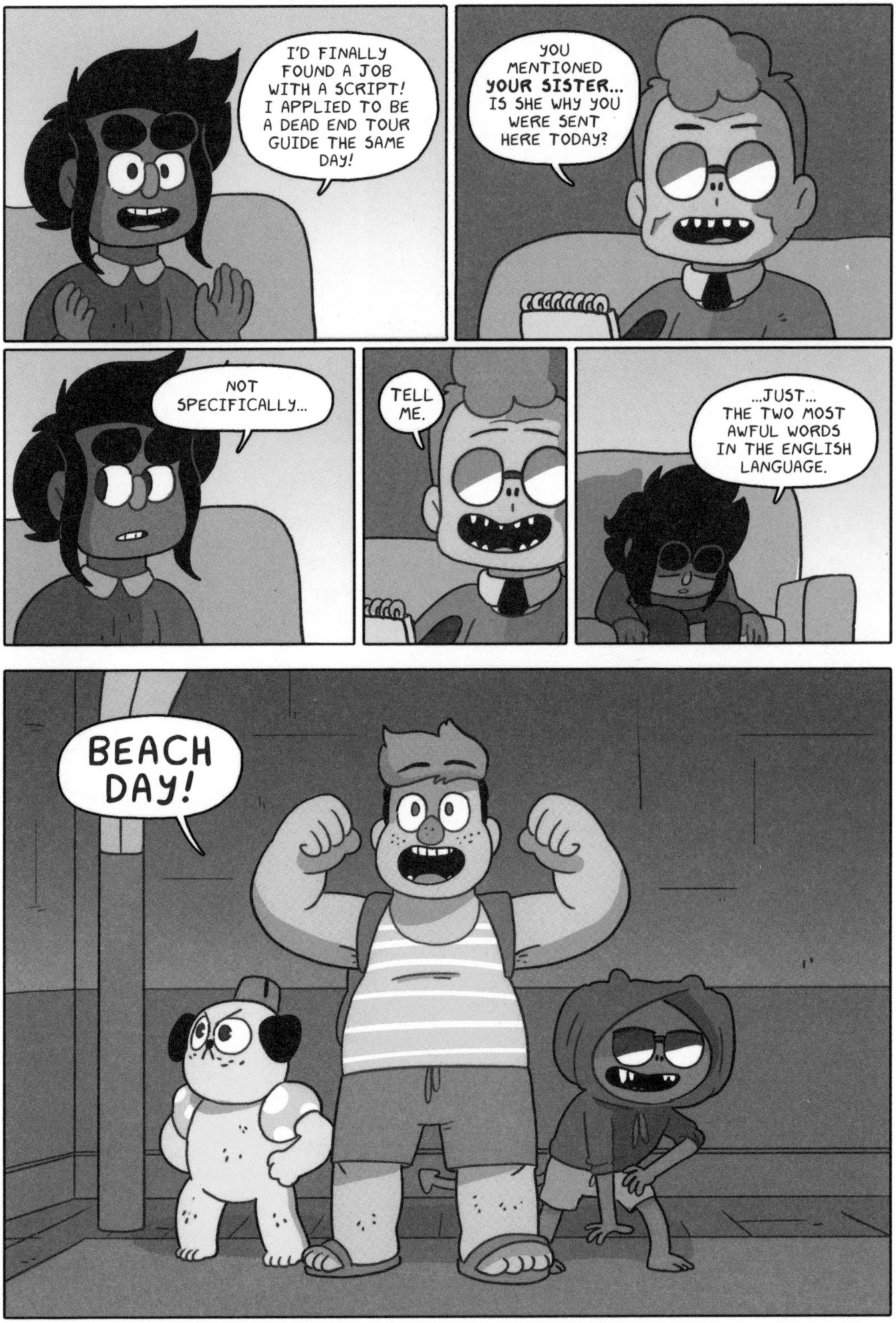
I'D FINALLY FOUND A JOB WITH A SCRIPT! I APPLIED TO BE A DEAD END TOUR GUIDE THE SAME DAY!
YOU MENTIONED **YOUR SISTER...** IS SHE WHY YOU WERE SENT HERE TODAY?
NOT SPECIFICALLY...
TELL ME.
...JUST... THE TWO MOST AWFUL WORDS IN THE ENGLISH LANGUAGE.
BEACH DAY!

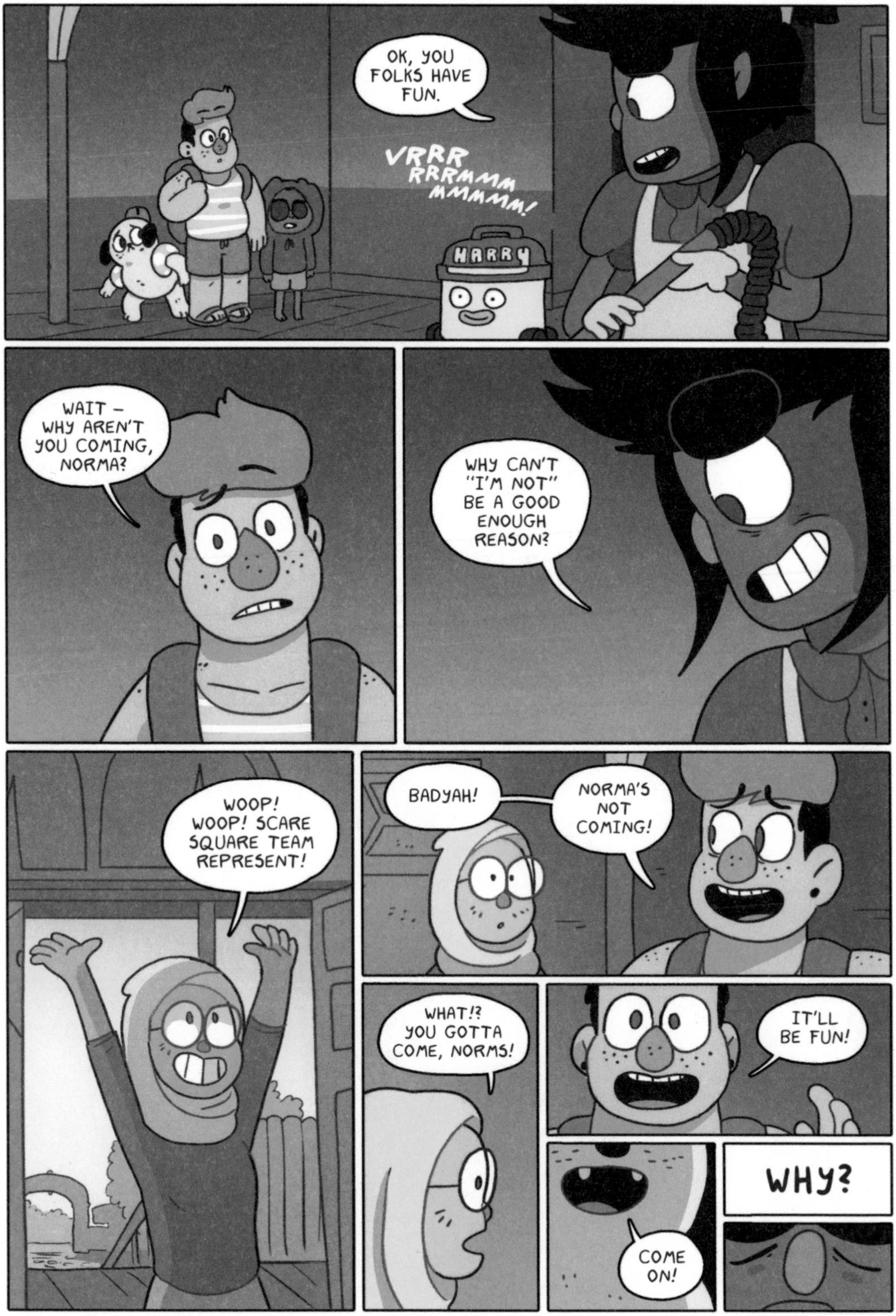
OK, YOU FOLKS HAVE FUN.
VRRR RRRMMM MMMMM!
HARRY
WAIT – WHY AREN'T YOU COMING, NORMA?
WHY CAN'T "I'M NOT" BE A GOOD ENOUGH REASON?
WOOP! WOOP! SCARE SQUARE TEAM REPRESENT!
BADYAH!
NORMA'S NOT COMING!
WHAT!? YOU GOTTA COME, NORMS!
IT'LL BE FUN!
COME ON!
WHY?

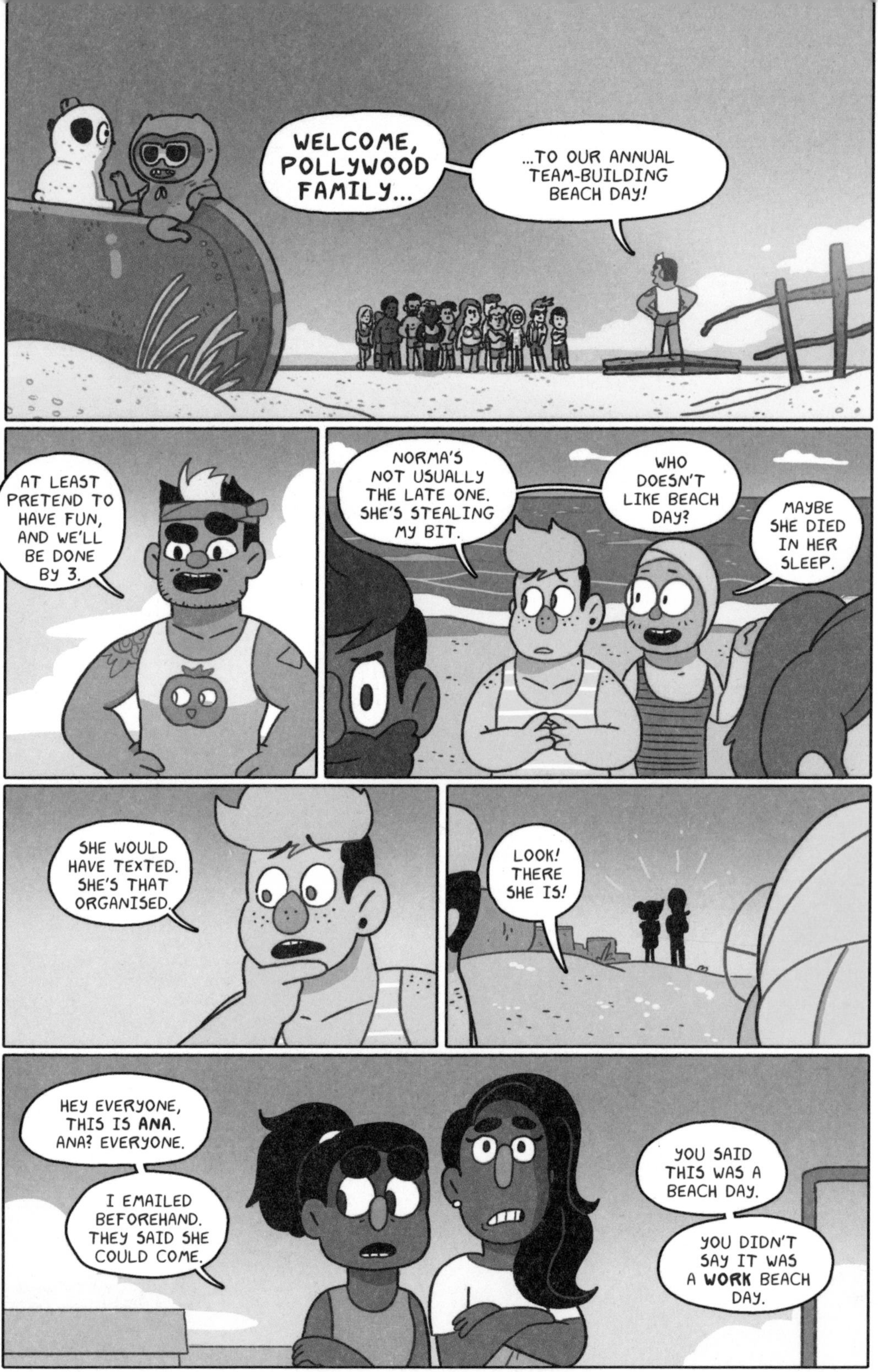
WELCOME, POLLYWOOD FAMILY...
...TO OUR ANNUAL TEAM-BUILDING BEACH DAY!
AT LEAST PRETEND TO HAVE FUN, AND WE'LL BE DONE BY 3.
NORMA'S NOT USUALLY THE LATE ONE. SHE'S STEALING MY BIT.
WHO DOESN'T LIKE BEACH DAY?
MAYBE SHE DIED IN HER SLEEP.
SHE WOULD HAVE TEXTED. SHE'S THAT ORGANISED.
LOOK! THERE SHE IS!
HEY EVERYONE, THIS IS **ANA**. ANA? EVERYONE.
I EMAILED BEFOREHAND. THEY SAID SHE COULD COME.
YOU SAID THIS WAS A BEACH DAY.
YOU DIDN'T SAY IT WAS A **WORK** BEACH DAY.

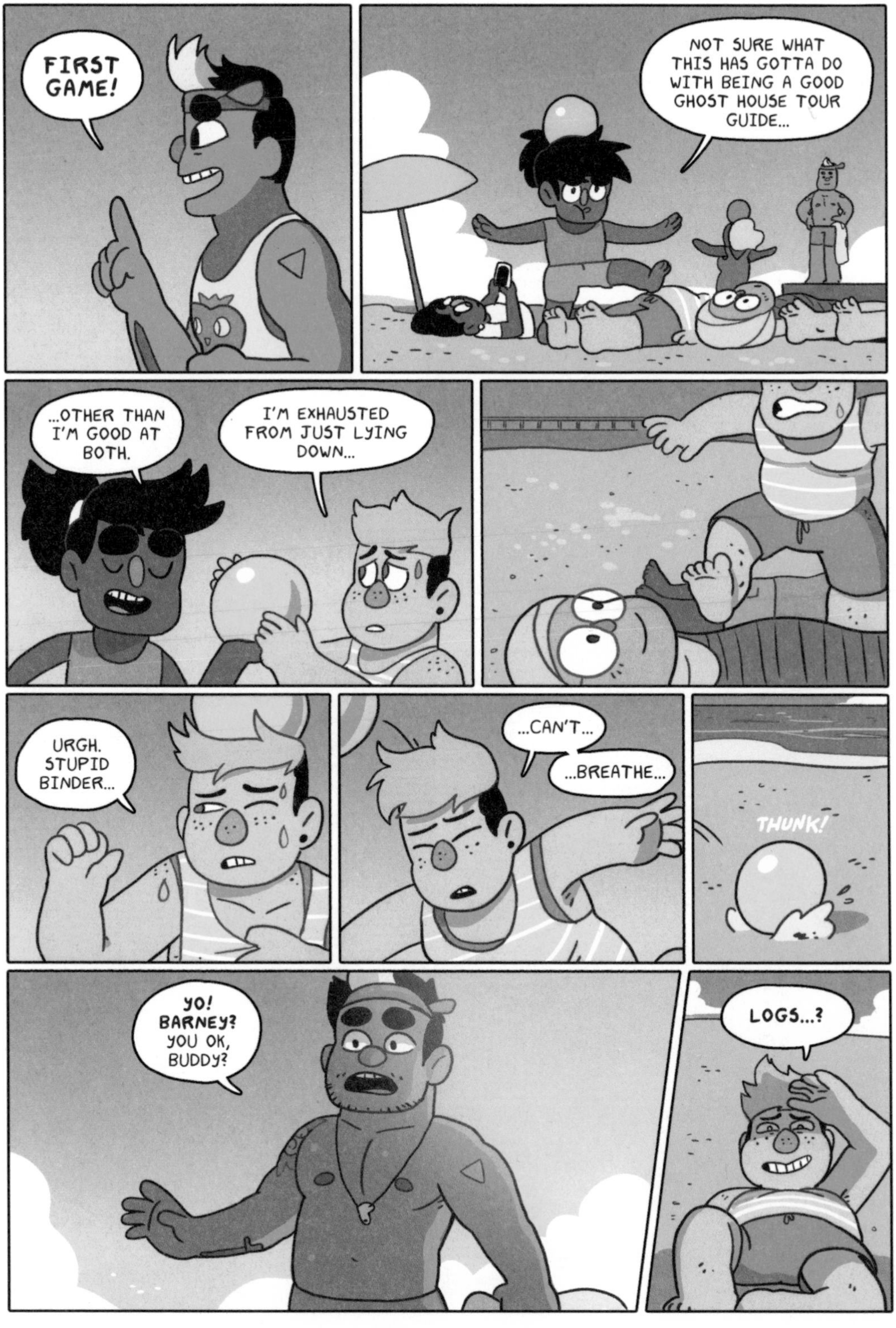
FIRST GAME!
NOT SURE WHAT THIS HAS GOTTA DO WITH BEING A GOOD GHOST HOUSE TOUR GUIDE...
...OTHER THAN I'M GOOD AT BOTH.
I'M EXHAUSTED FROM JUST LYING DOWN...
URGH. STUPID BINDER...
...CAN'T...
...BREATHE...
THUNK!
YO! BARNEY? YOU OK, BUDDY?
LOGS...?

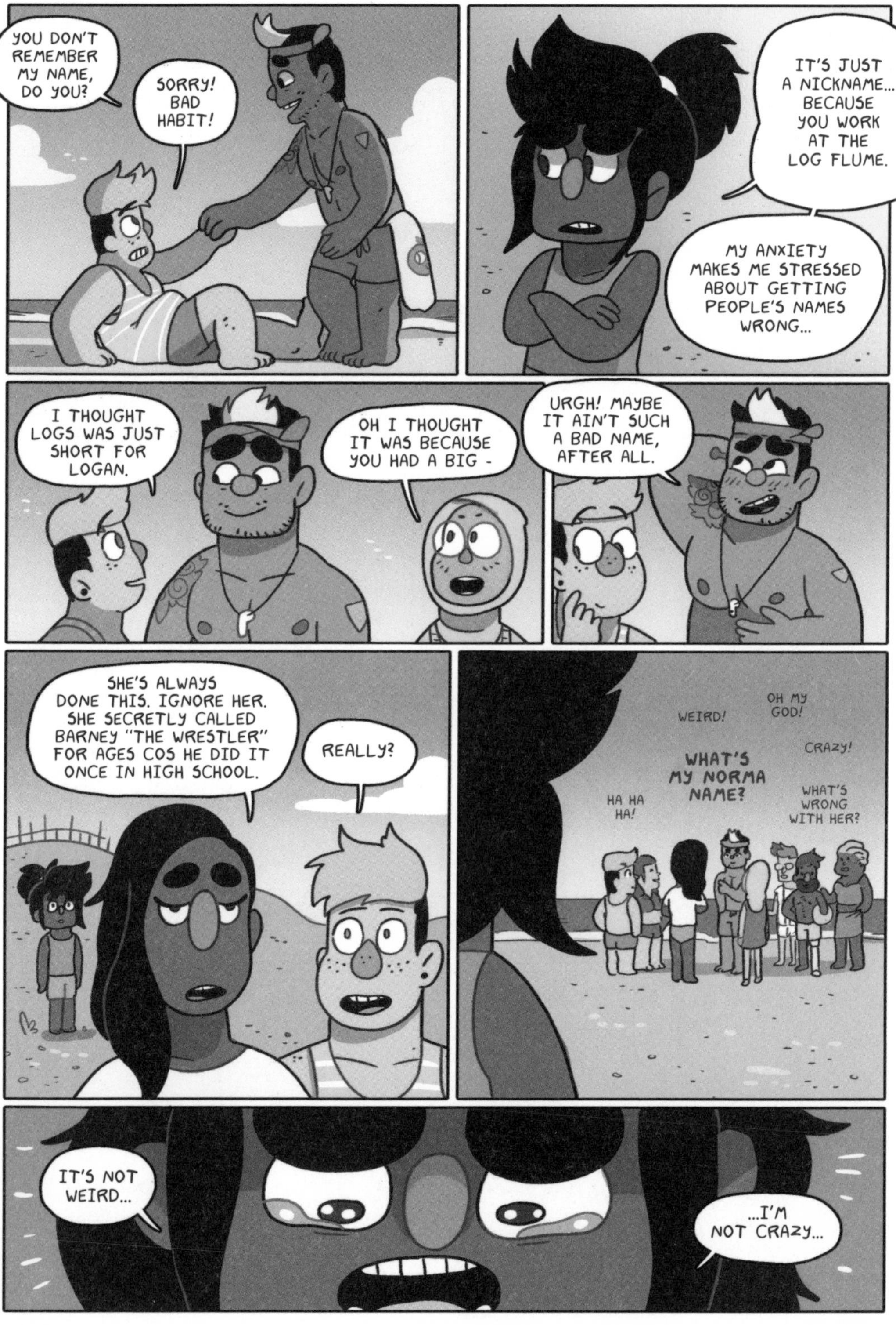
YOU DON'T REMEMBER MY NAME, DO YOU?
SORRY! BAD HABIT!
IT'S JUST A NICKNAME... BECAUSE YOU WORK AT THE LOG FLUME.
MY ANXIETY MAKES ME STRESSED ABOUT GETTING PEOPLE'S NAMES WRONG...
I THOUGHT LOGS WAS JUST SHORT FOR LOGAN.
OH I THOUGHT IT WAS BECAUSE YOU HAD A BIG -
URGH! MAYBE IT AIN'T SUCH A BAD NAME, AFTER ALL.
SHE'S ALWAYS DONE THIS. IGNORE HER. SHE SECRETLY CALLED BARNEY "THE WRESTLER" FOR AGES COS HE DID IT ONCE IN HIGH SCHOOL.
REALLY?
WEIRD!
OH MY GOD!
CRAZY!
WHAT'S MY NORMA NAME?
HA HA HA!
WHAT'S WRONG WITH HER?
IT'S NOT WEIRD...
...I'M NOT CRAZY...

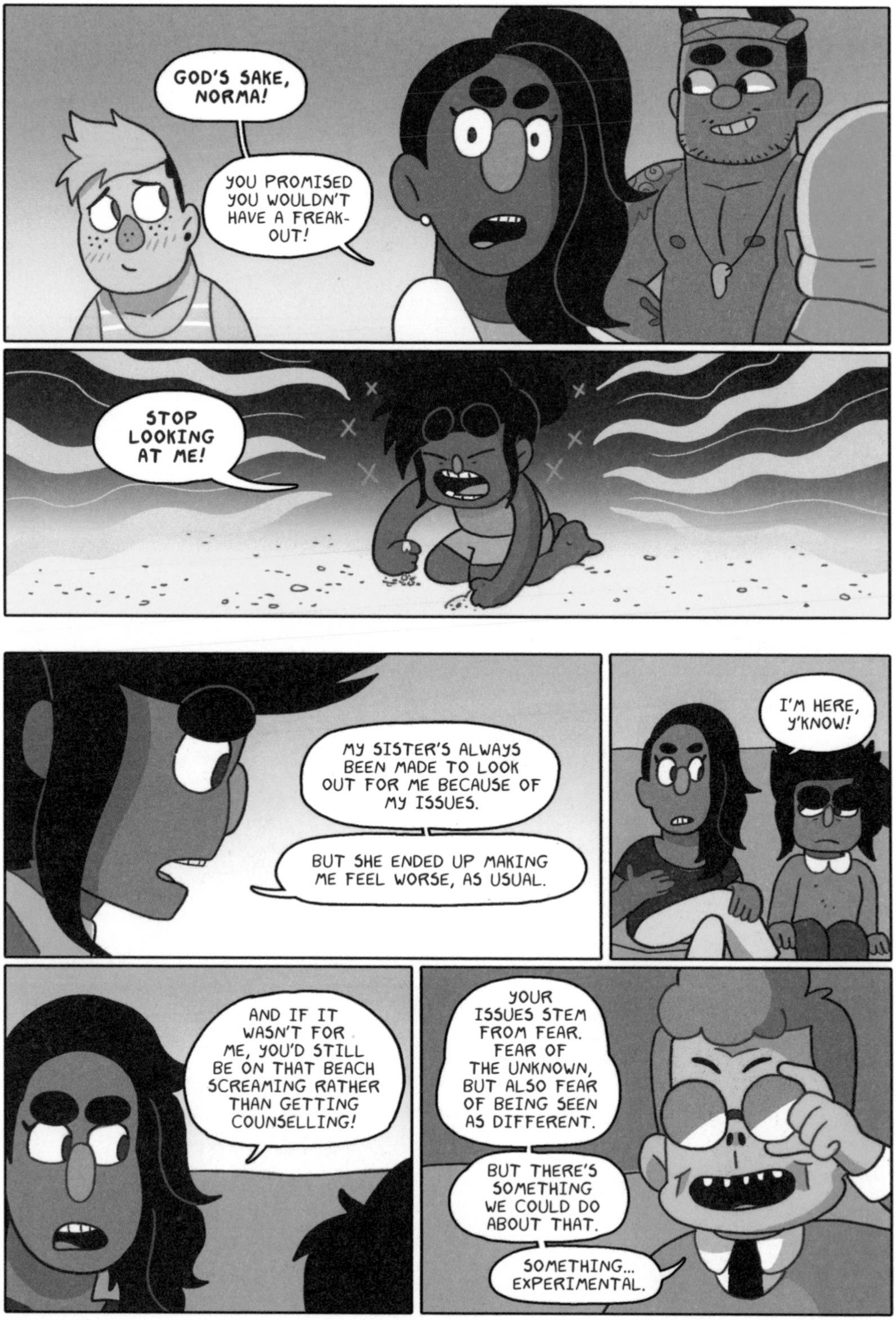
GOD'S SAKE, NORMA!
YOU PROMISED YOU WOULDN'T HAVE A FREAK-OUT!
STOP LOOKING AT ME!
MY SISTER'S ALWAYS BEEN MADE TO LOOK OUT FOR ME BECAUSE OF MY ISSUES.
BUT SHE ENDED UP MAKING ME FEEL WORSE, AS USUAL.
I'M HERE, Y'KNOW!
AND IF IT WASN'T FOR ME, YOU'D STILL BE ON THAT BEACH SCREAMING RATHER THAN GETTING COUNSELLING!
YOUR ISSUES STEM FROM FEAR. FEAR OF THE UNKNOWN, BUT ALSO FEAR OF BEING SEEN AS DIFFERENT.
BUT THERE'S SOMETHING WE COULD DO ABOUT THAT.
SOMETHING... EXPERIMENTAL.

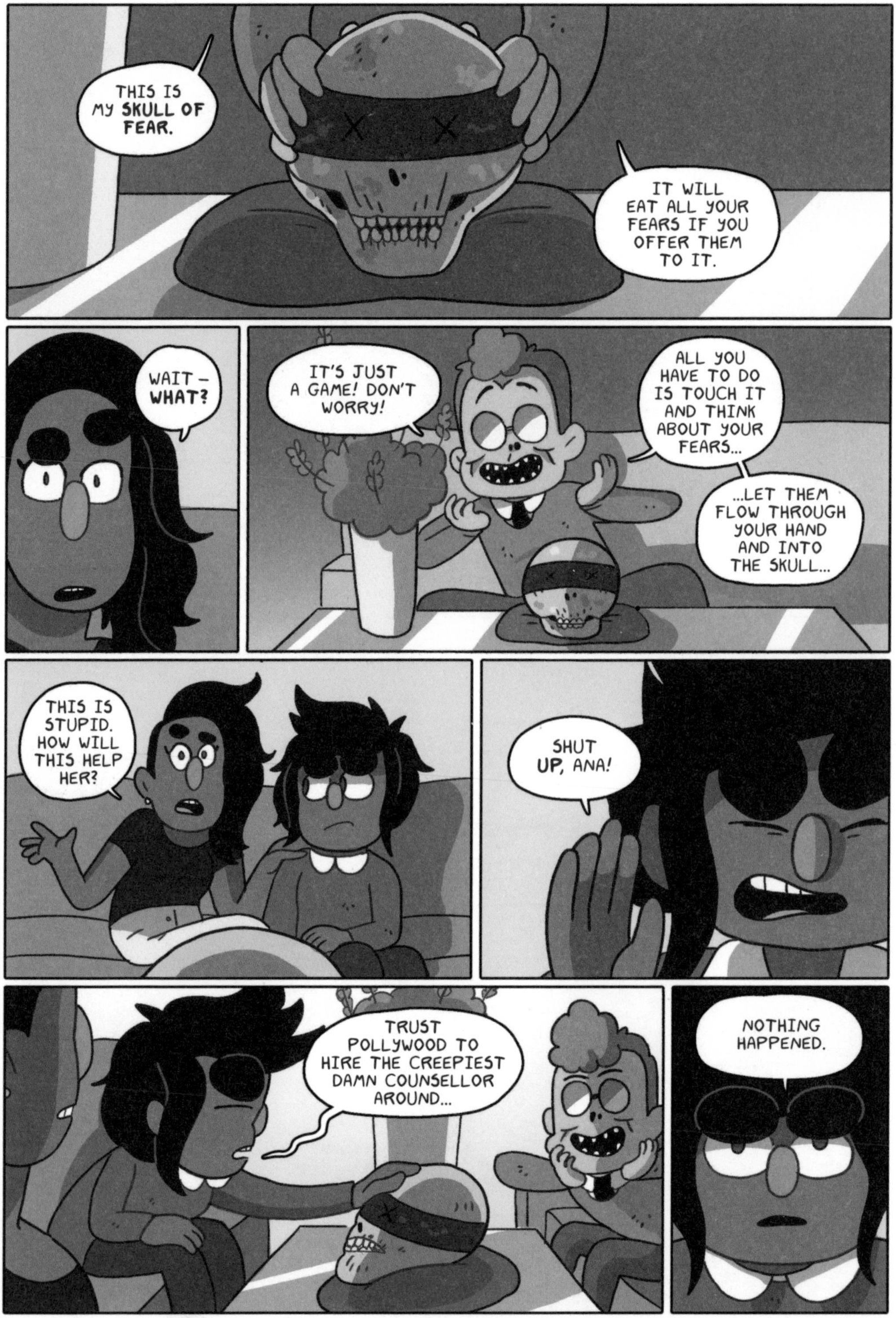
THIS IS MY **SKULL OF FEAR.**
IT WILL EAT ALL YOUR FEARS IF YOU OFFER THEM TO IT.
WAIT – **WHAT?**
IT'S JUST A GAME! DON'T WORRY!
ALL YOU HAVE TO DO IS TOUCH IT AND THINK ABOUT YOUR FEARS...
...LET THEM FLOW THROUGH YOUR HAND AND INTO THE SKULL...
THIS IS STUPID. HOW WILL THIS HELP HER?
SHUT **UP,** ANA!
TRUST POLLYWOOD TO HIRE THE CREEPIEST DAMN COUNSELLOR AROUND...
NOTHING HAPPENED.

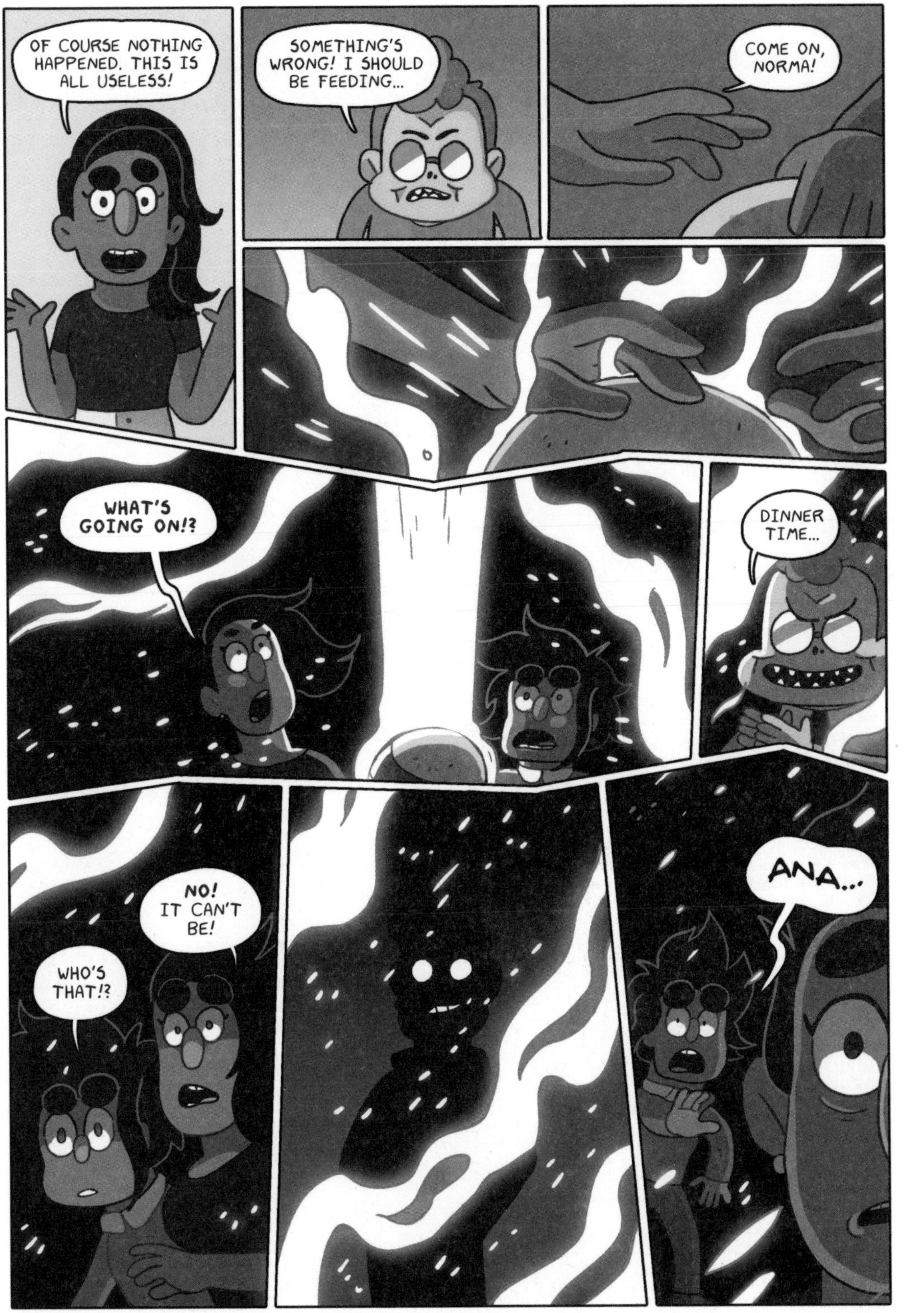
OF COURSE NOTHING HAPPENED. THIS IS ALL USELESS!
SOMETHING'S WRONG! I SHOULD BE FEEDING...
COME ON, NORMA!
WHAT'S GOING ON!?
DINNER TIME...
NO! IT CAN'T BE!
WHO'S THAT!?
ANA...

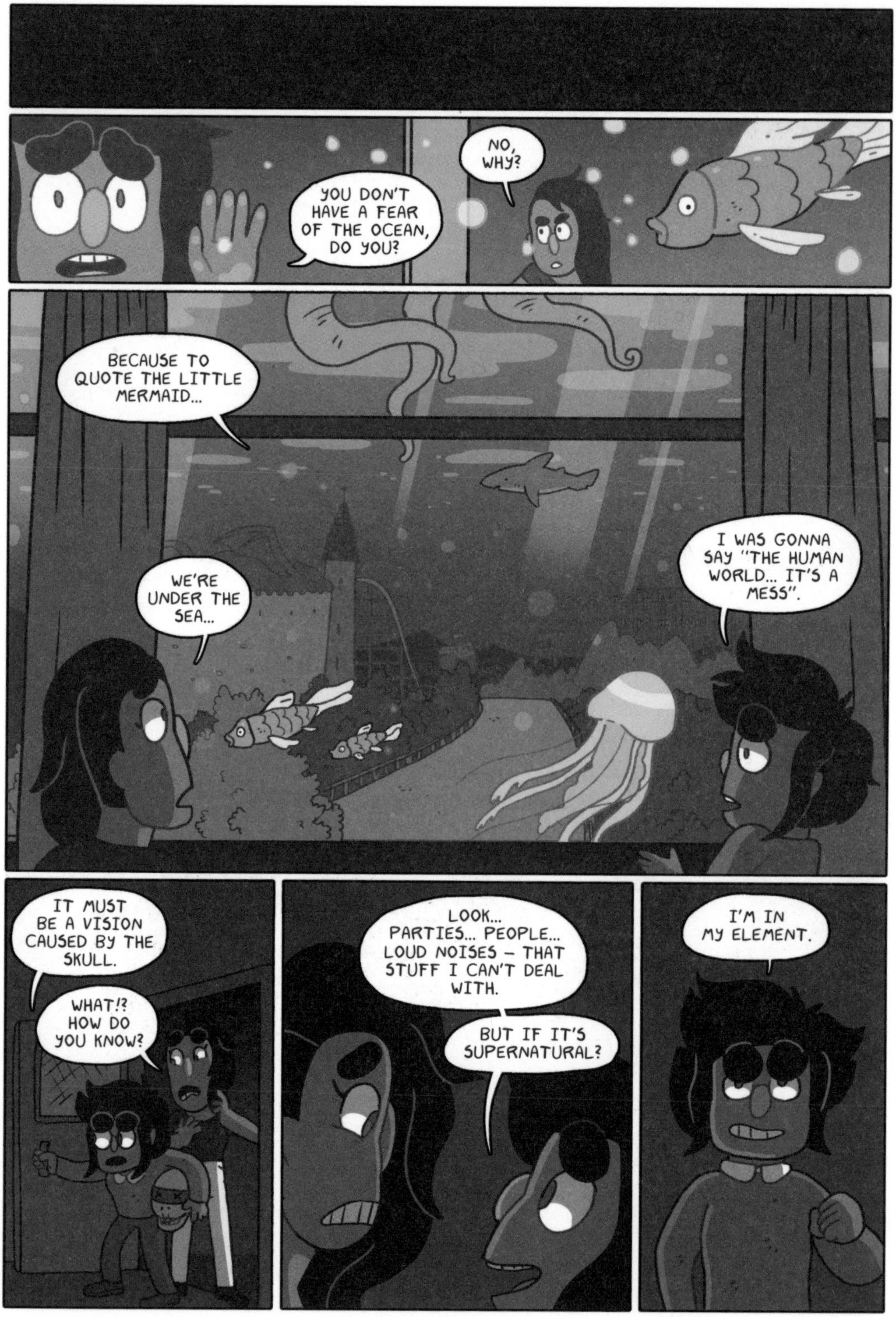
YOU DON'T HAVE A FEAR OF THE OCEAN, DO YOU?
NO, WHY?
BECAUSE TO QUOTE THE LITTLE MERMAID...
WE'RE UNDER THE SEA...
I WAS GONNA SAY "THE HUMAN WORLD... IT'S A MESS".
IT MUST BE A VISION CAUSED BY THE SKULL.
WHAT!? HOW DO YOU KNOW?
LOOK... PARTIES... PEOPLE... LOUD NOISES – THAT STUFF I CAN'T DEAL WITH.
BUT IF IT'S SUPERNATURAL?
I'M IN MY ELEMENT.

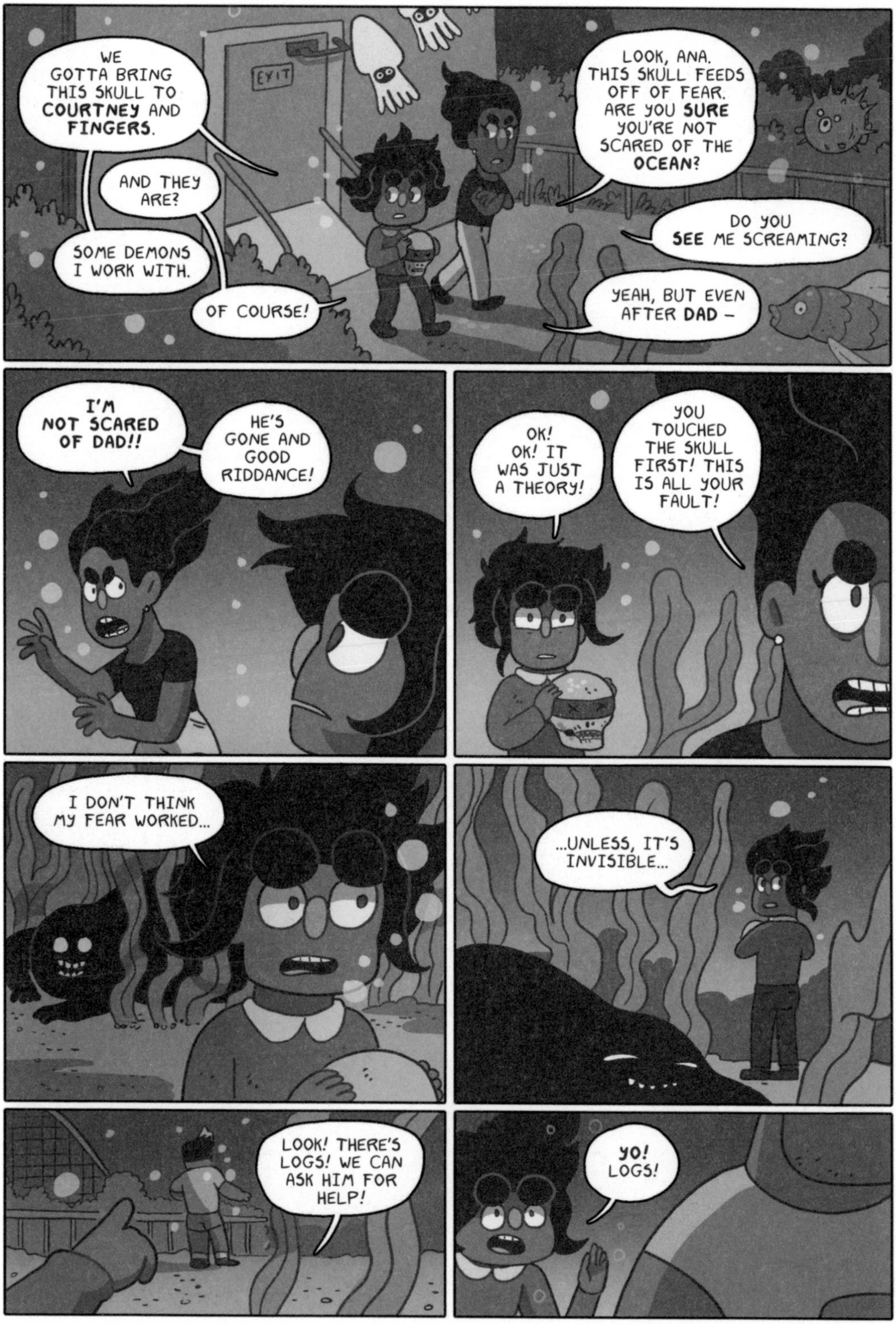
WE GOTTA BRING THIS SKULL TO **COURTNEY** AND **FINGERS**.
AND THEY ARE?
SOME DEMONS I WORK WITH.
OF COURSE!
LOOK, ANA. THIS SKULL FEEDS OFF OF FEAR. ARE YOU **SURE** YOU'RE NOT SCARED OF THE **OCEAN**?
DO YOU **SEE** ME SCREAMING?
YEAH, BUT EVEN AFTER **DAD** –
I'M NOT SCARED OF DAD!!
HE'S GONE AND GOOD RIDDANCE!
OK! OK! IT WAS JUST A THEORY!
YOU TOUCHED THE SKULL FIRST! THIS IS ALL YOUR FAULT!
I DON'T THINK MY FEAR WORKED...
...UNLESS, IT'S INVISIBLE...
LOOK! THERE'S LOGS! WE CAN ASK HIM FOR HELP!
YO! LOGS!

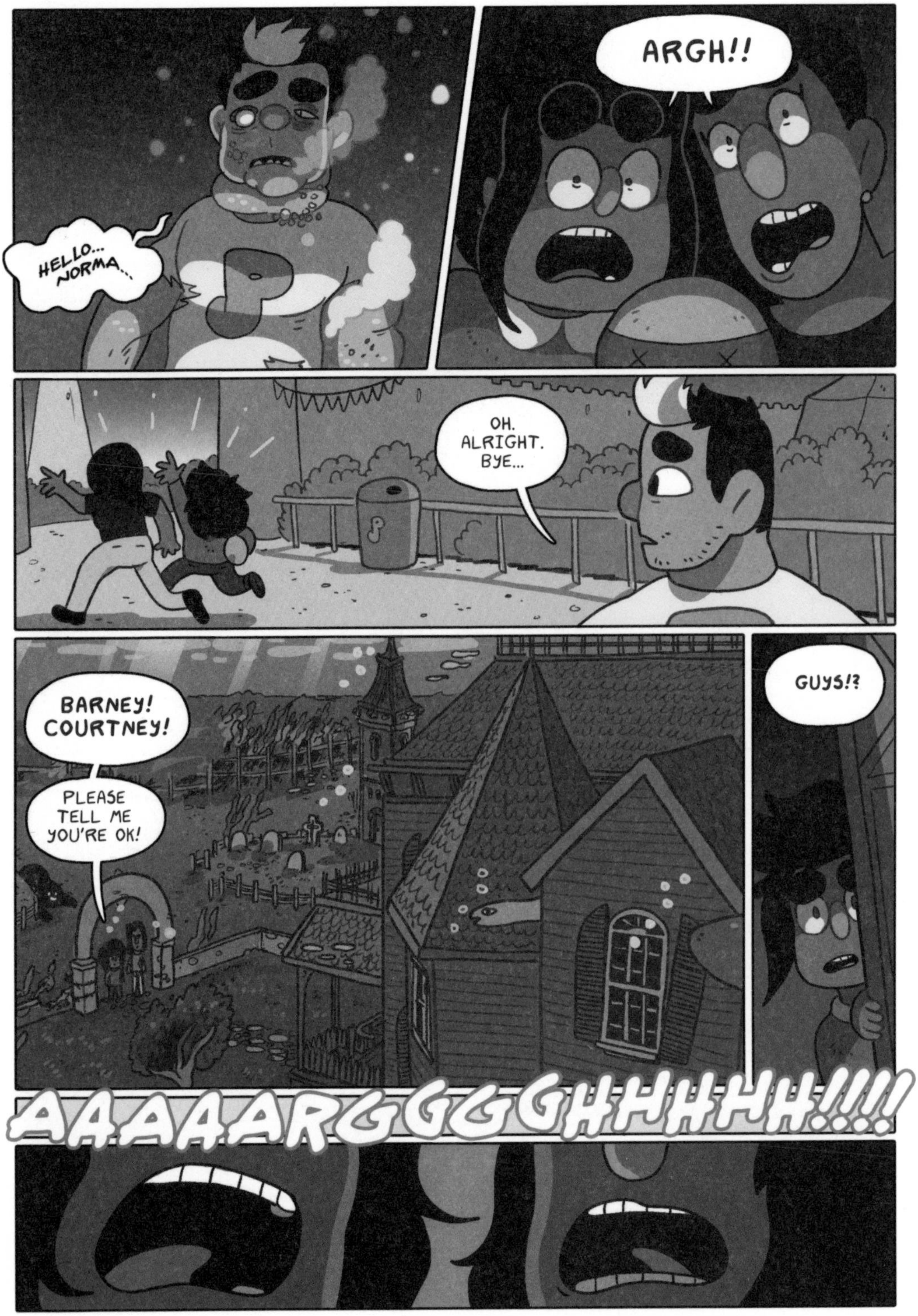
HELLO... NORMA...
ARGH!!
OH. ALRIGHT. BYE...
BARNEY! COURTNEY!
PLEASE TELL ME YOU'RE OK!
GUYS!?
AAAAARGGGGHHHHH!!!!

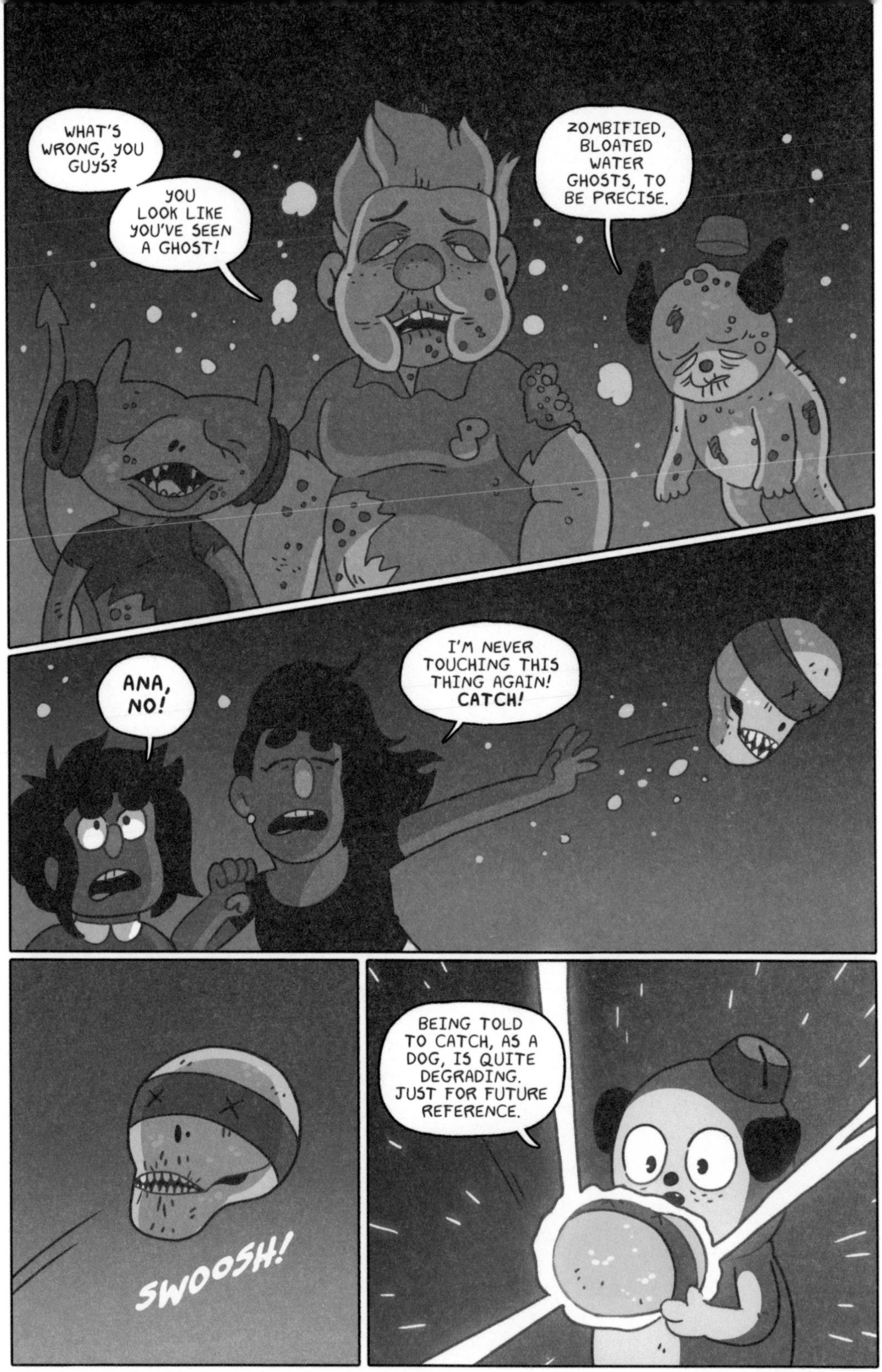
WHAT'S WRONG, YOU GUYS?
YOU LOOK LIKE YOU'VE SEEN A GHOST!
ZOMBIFIED, BLOATED WATER GHOSTS, TO BE PRECISE.
ANA, NO!
I'M NEVER TOUCHING THIS THING AGAIN! CATCH!
SWOOSH!
BEING TOLD TO CATCH, AS A DOG, IS QUITE DEGRADING. JUST FOR FUTURE REFERENCE.

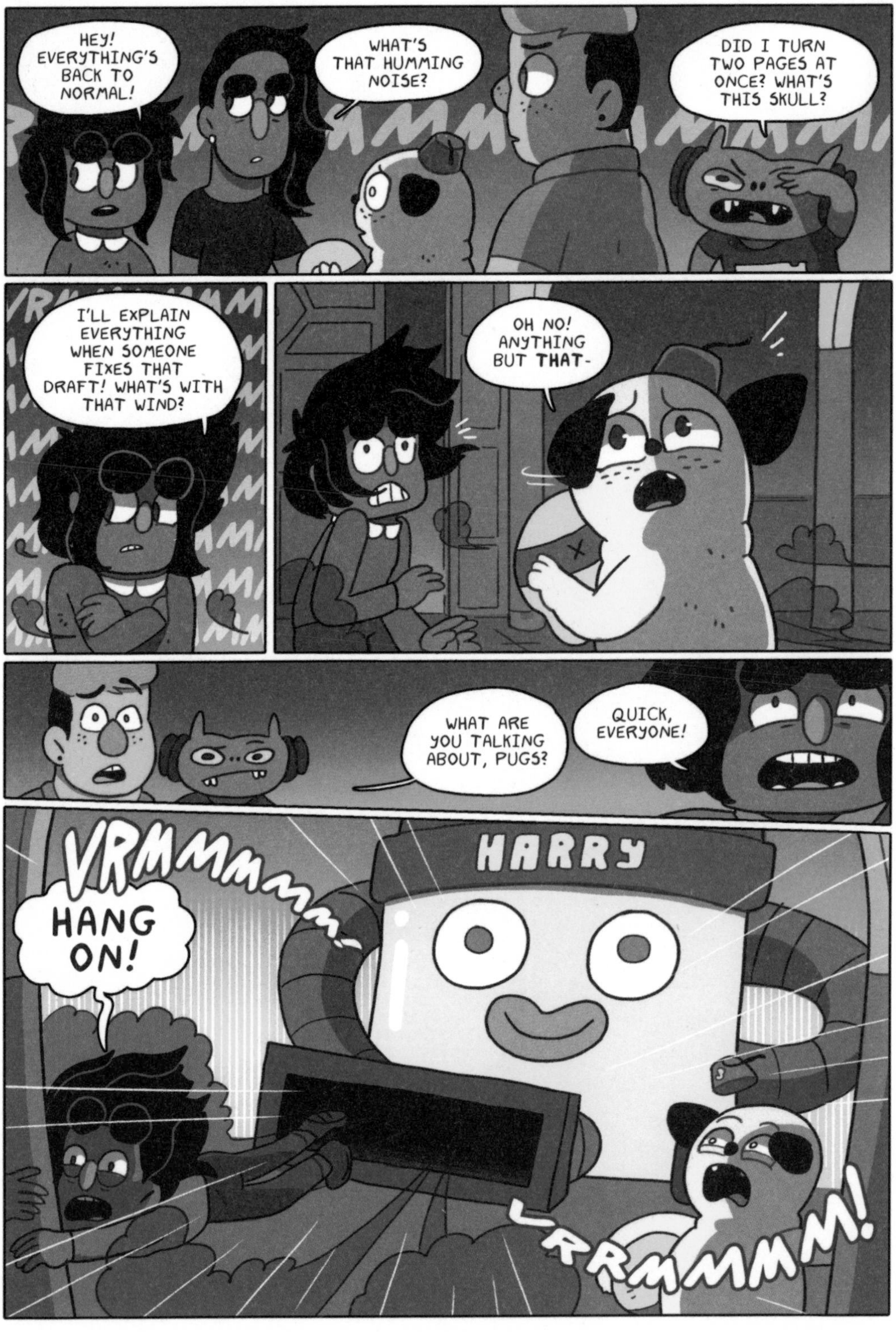
HEY! EVERYTHING'S BACK TO NORMAL!
WHAT'S THAT HUMMING NOISE?
DID I TURN TWO PAGES AT ONCE? WHAT'S THIS SKULL?
I'LL EXPLAIN EVERYTHING WHEN SOMEONE FIXES THAT DRAFT! WHAT'S WITH THAT WIND?
OH NO! ANYTHING BUT THAT-
WHAT ARE YOU TALKING ABOUT, PUGS?
QUICK, EVERYONE!
HARRY
VRMMMMM-
HANG ON!
LRRMMMM!

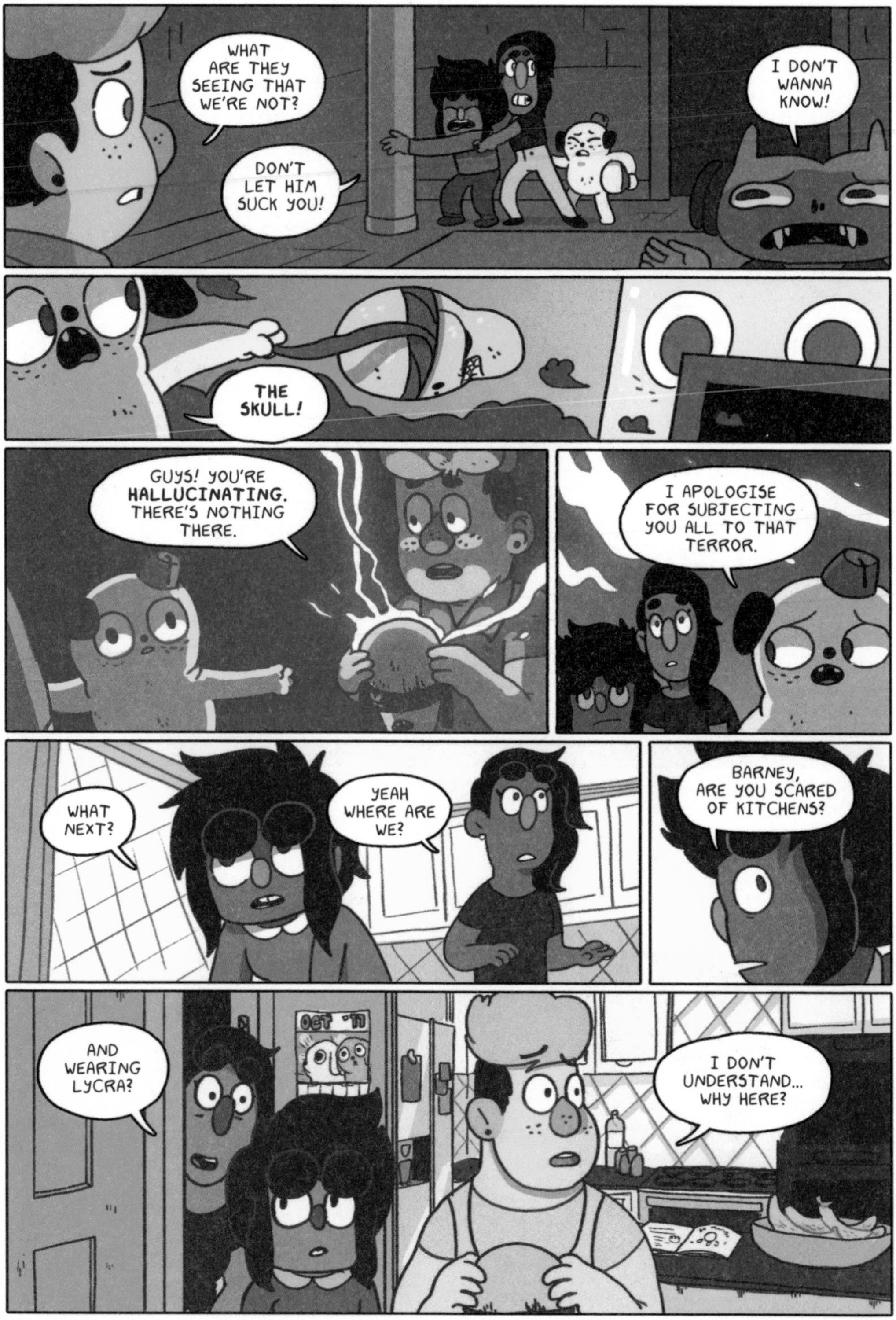

WHAT ARE THEY SEEING THAT WE'RE NOT?
DON'T LET HIM SUCK YOU!
I DON'T WANNA KNOW!
THE SKULL!
GUYS! YOU'RE HALLUCINATING. THERE'S NOTHING THERE.
I APOLOGISE FOR SUBJECTING YOU ALL TO THAT TERROR.
WHAT NEXT?
YEAH WHERE ARE WE?
BARNEY, ARE YOU SCARED OF KITCHENS?
AND WEARING LYCRA?
I DON'T UNDERSTAND... WHY HERE?
OCT '77

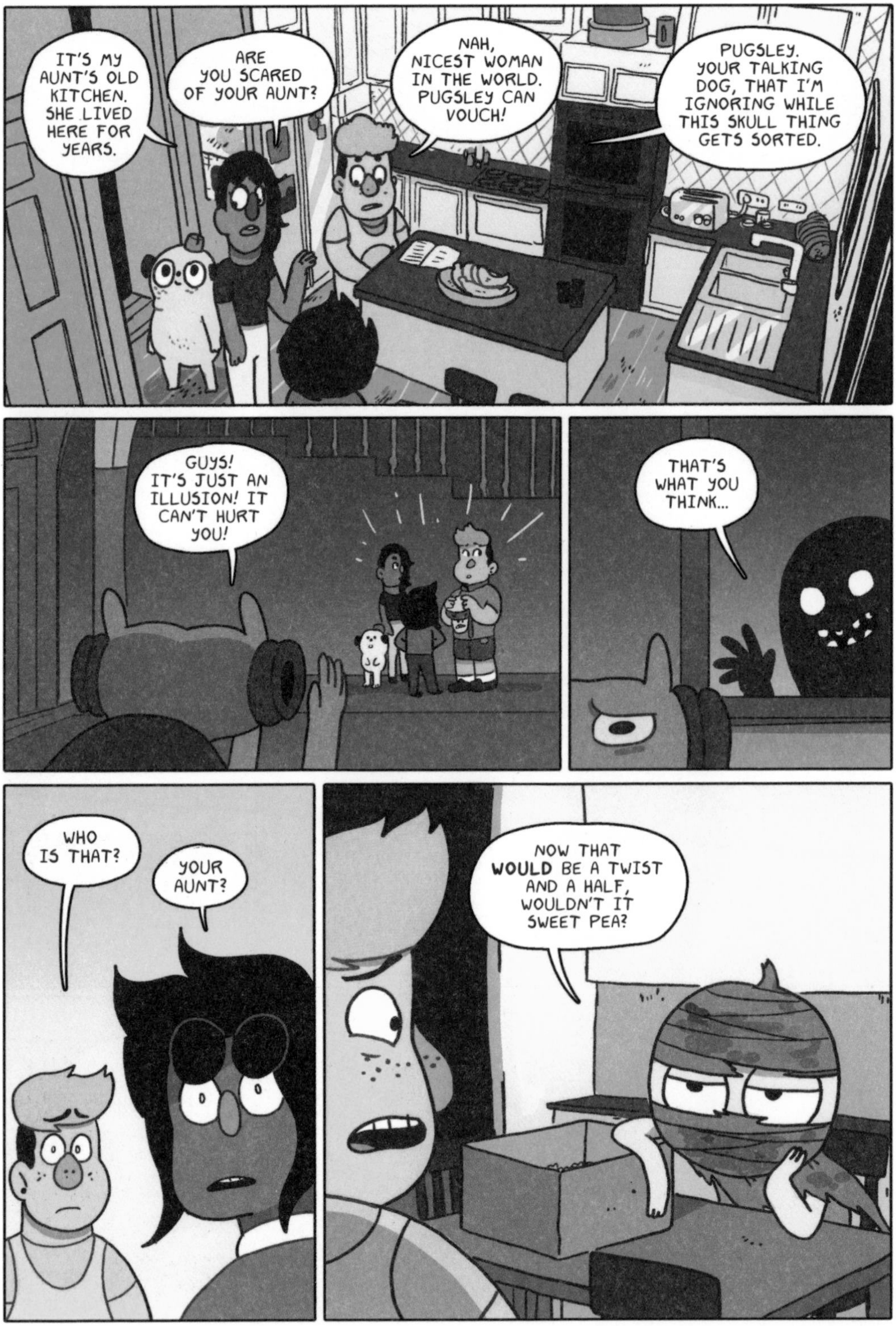
IT'S MY AUNT'S OLD KITCHEN. SHE LIVED HERE FOR YEARS.
ARE YOU SCARED OF YOUR AUNT?
NAH, NICEST WOMAN IN THE WORLD. PUGSLEY CAN VOUCH!
PUGSLEY. YOUR TALKING DOG, THAT I'M IGNORING WHILE THIS SKULL THING GETS SORTED.
GUYS! IT'S JUST AN ILLUSION! IT CAN'T HURT YOU!
THAT'S WHAT YOU THINK...
WHO IS THAT?
YOUR AUNT?
NOW THAT **WOULD** BE A TWIST AND A HALF, WOULDN'T IT SWEET PEA?

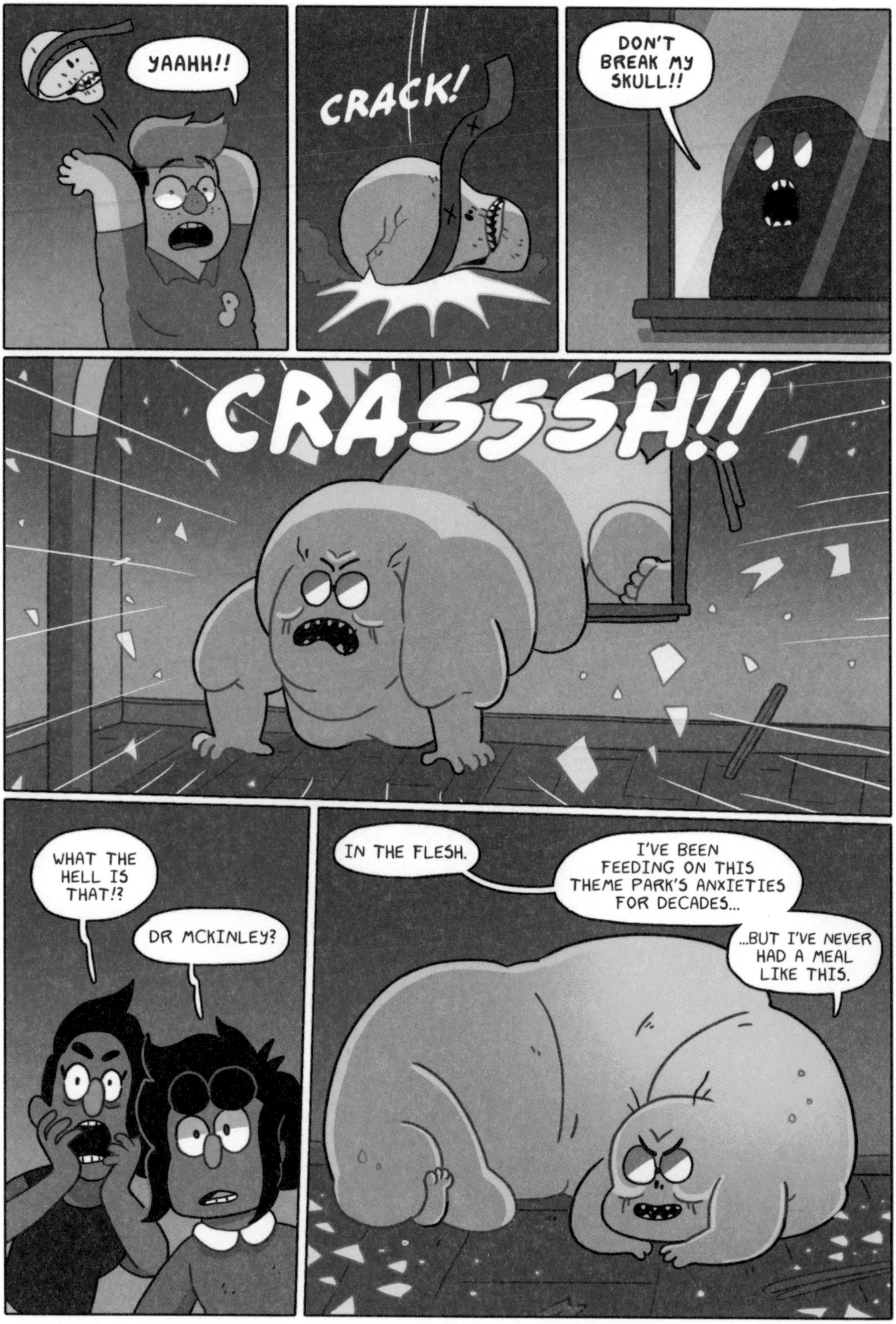
YAAHH!!
CRACK!
DON'T BREAK MY SKULL!!
CRASSSH!!
WHAT THE HELL IS THAT!?
DR MCKINLEY?
IN THE FLESH.
I'VE BEEN FEEDING ON THIS THEME PARK'S ANXIETIES FOR DECADES...
...BUT I'VE NEVER HAD A MEAL LIKE THIS.

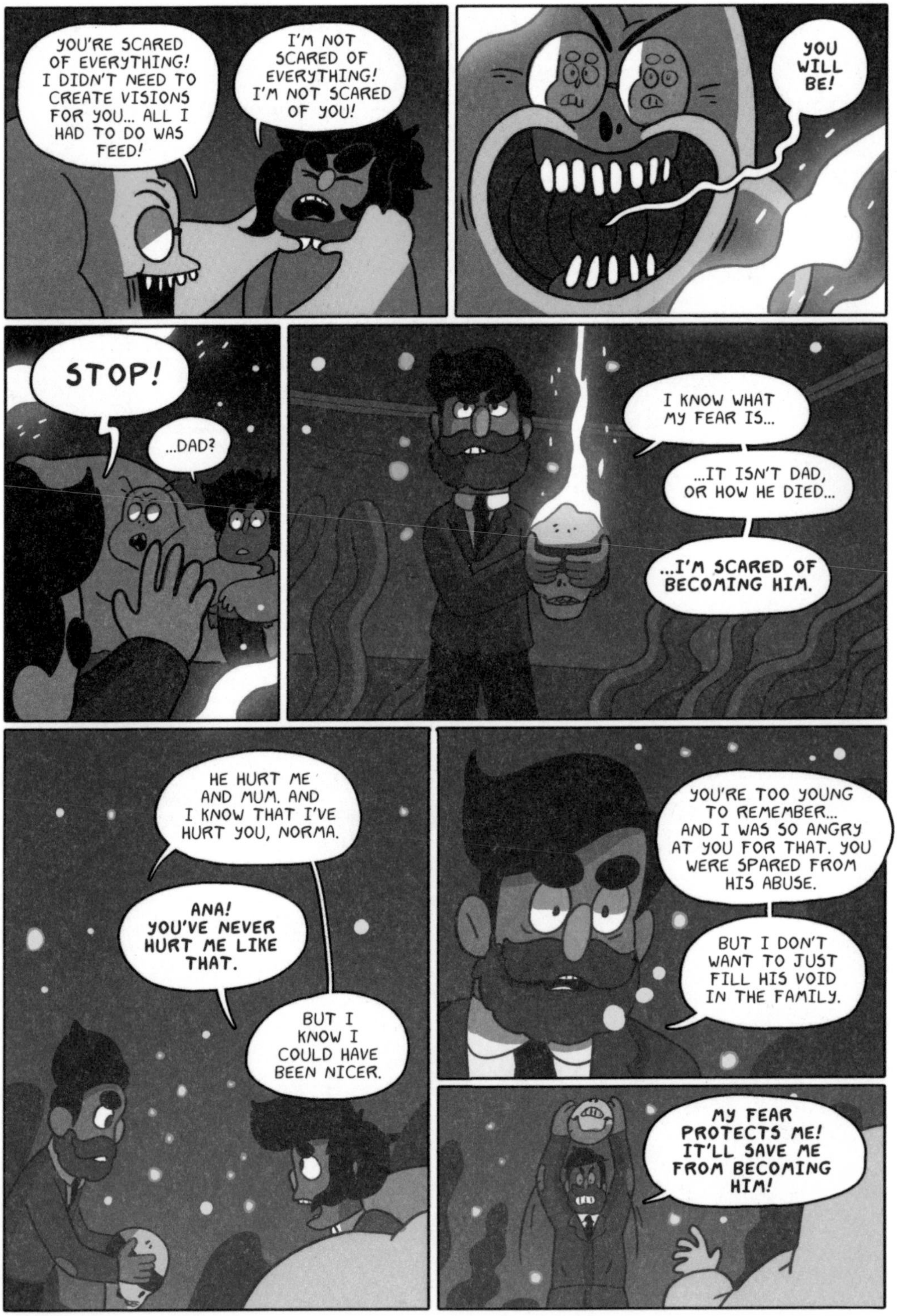
YOU'RE SCARED OF EVERYTHING! I DIDN'T NEED TO CREATE VISIONS FOR YOU... ALL I HAD TO DO WAS FEED!
I'M NOT SCARED OF EVERYTHING! I'M NOT SCARED OF YOU!
YOU WILL BE!
STOP!
...DAD?
I KNOW WHAT MY FEAR IS...
...IT ISN'T DAD, OR HOW HE DIED...
...I'M SCARED OF BECOMING HIM.
HE HURT ME AND MUM. AND I KNOW THAT I'VE HURT YOU, NORMA.
ANA! YOU'VE NEVER HURT ME LIKE THAT.
BUT I KNOW I COULD HAVE BEEN NICER.
YOU'RE TOO YOUNG TO REMEMBER... AND I WAS SO ANGRY AT YOU FOR THAT. YOU WERE SPARED FROM HIS ABUSE.
BUT I DON'T WANT TO JUST FILL HIS VOID IN THE FAMILY.
MY FEAR PROTECTS ME! IT'LL SAVE ME FROM BECOMING HIM!

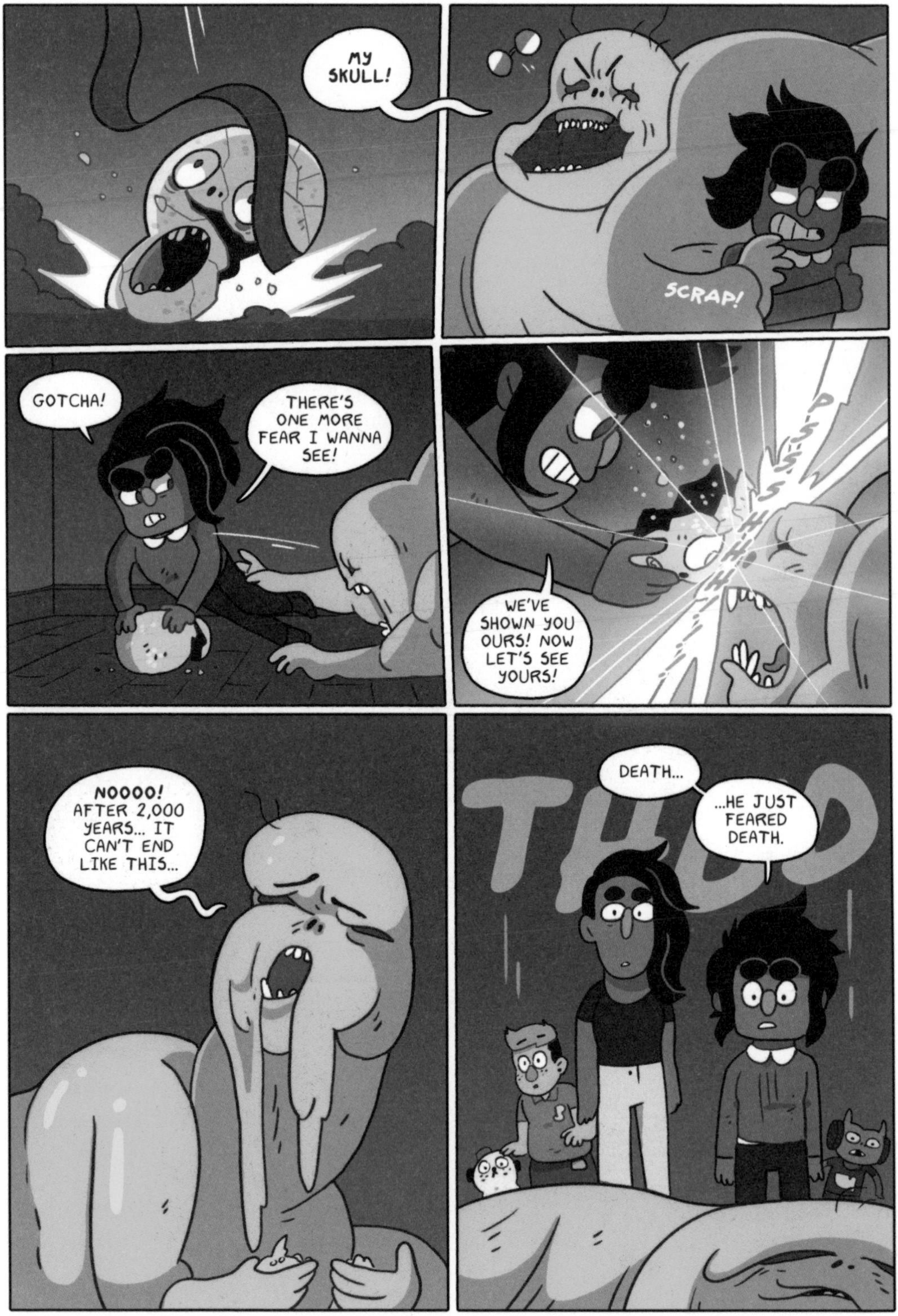
MY SKULL!
SCRAP!
GOTCHA!
THERE'S ONE MORE FEAR I WANNA SEE!
WE'VE SHOWN YOU OURS! NOW LET'S SEE YOURS!
NOOOO! AFTER 2,000 YEARS... IT CAN'T END LIKE THIS...
DEATH...
...HE JUST FEARED DEATH.

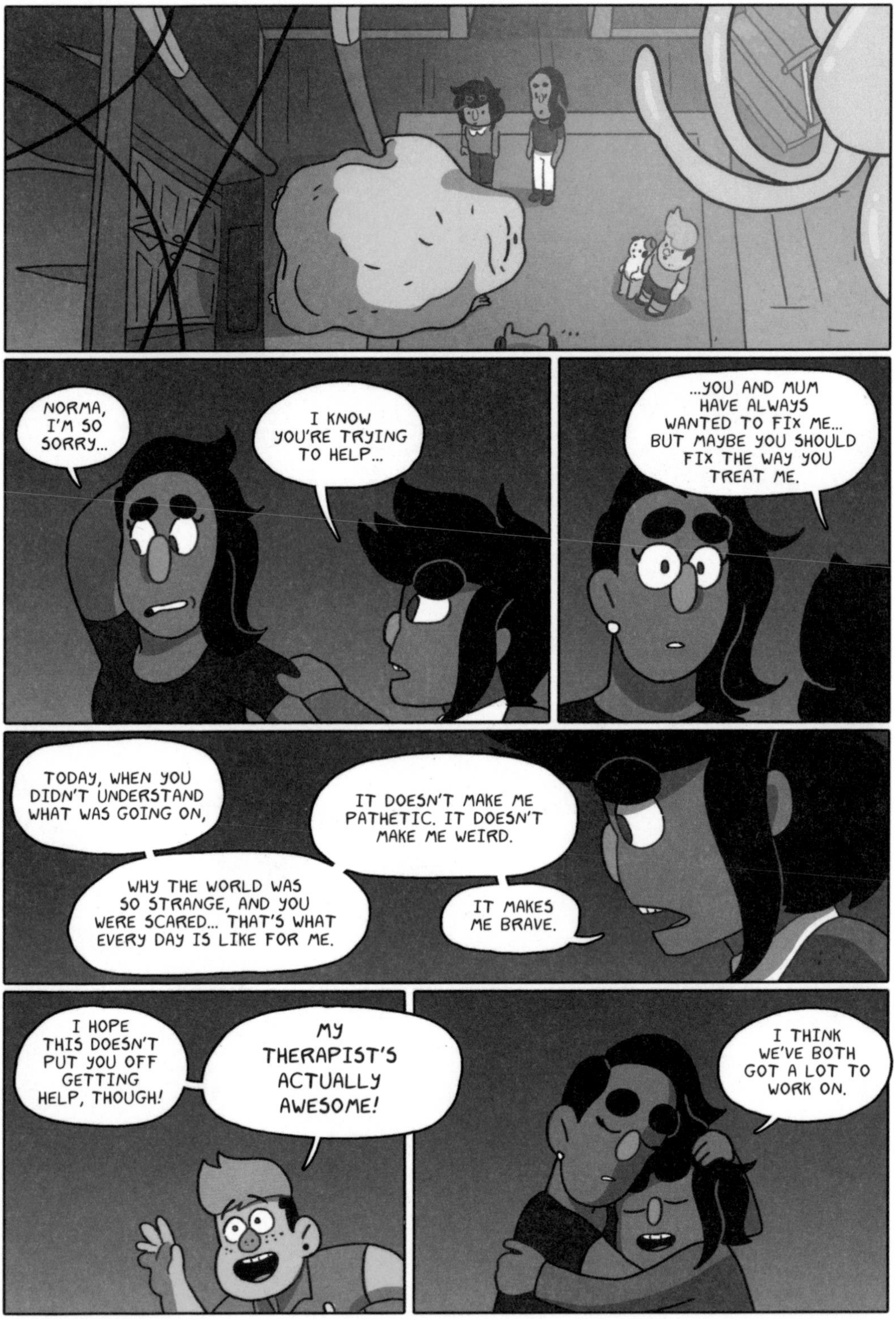
NORMA, I'M SO SORRY...
I KNOW YOU'RE TRYING TO HELP...
...YOU AND MUM HAVE ALWAYS WANTED TO FIX ME... BUT MAYBE YOU SHOULD FIX THE WAY YOU TREAT ME.
TODAY, WHEN YOU DIDN'T UNDERSTAND WHAT WAS GOING ON,
WHY THE WORLD WAS SO STRANGE, AND YOU WERE SCARED... THAT'S WHAT EVERY DAY IS LIKE FOR ME.
IT DOESN'T MAKE ME PATHETIC. IT DOESN'T MAKE ME WEIRD.
IT MAKES ME BRAVE.
I HOPE THIS DOESN'T PUT YOU OFF GETTING HELP, THOUGH!
MY THERAPIST'S ACTUALLY AWESOME!
I THINK WE'VE BOTH GOT A LOT TO WORK ON.

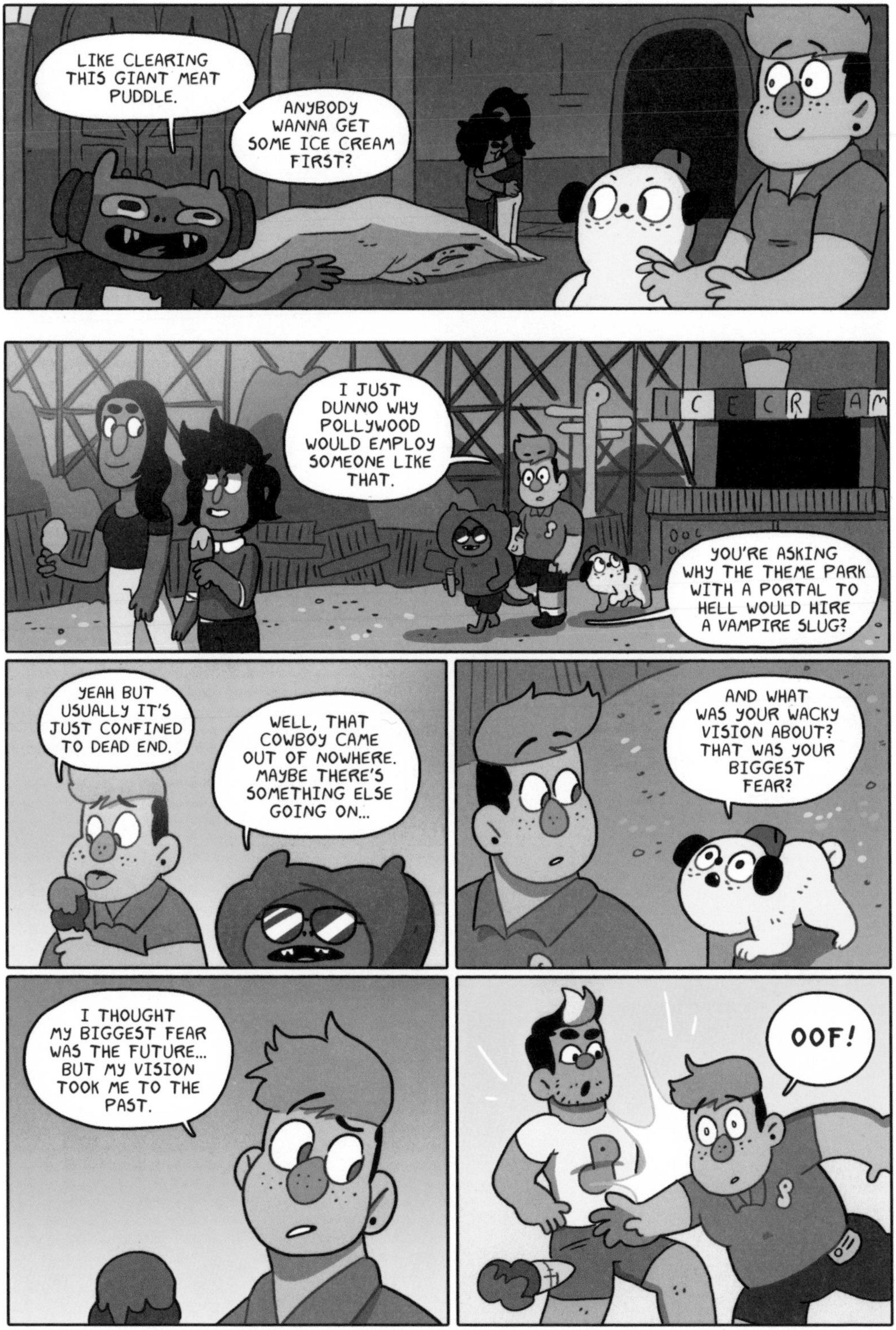
LIKE CLEARING THIS GIANT MEAT PUDDLE.
ANYBODY WANNA GET SOME ICE CREAM FIRST?
ICE CREAM
I JUST DUNNO WHY POLLYWOOD WOULD EMPLOY SOMEONE LIKE THAT.
YOU'RE ASKING WHY THE THEME PARK WITH A PORTAL TO HELL WOULD HIRE A VAMPIRE SLUG?
YEAH BUT USUALLY IT'S JUST CONFINED TO DEAD END.
WELL, THAT COWBOY CAME OUT OF NOWHERE. MAYBE THERE'S SOMETHING ELSE GOING ON...
AND WHAT WAS YOUR WACKY VISION ABOUT? THAT WAS YOUR BIGGEST FEAR?
I THOUGHT MY BIGGEST FEAR WAS THE FUTURE... BUT MY VISION TOOK ME TO THE PAST.
OOF!

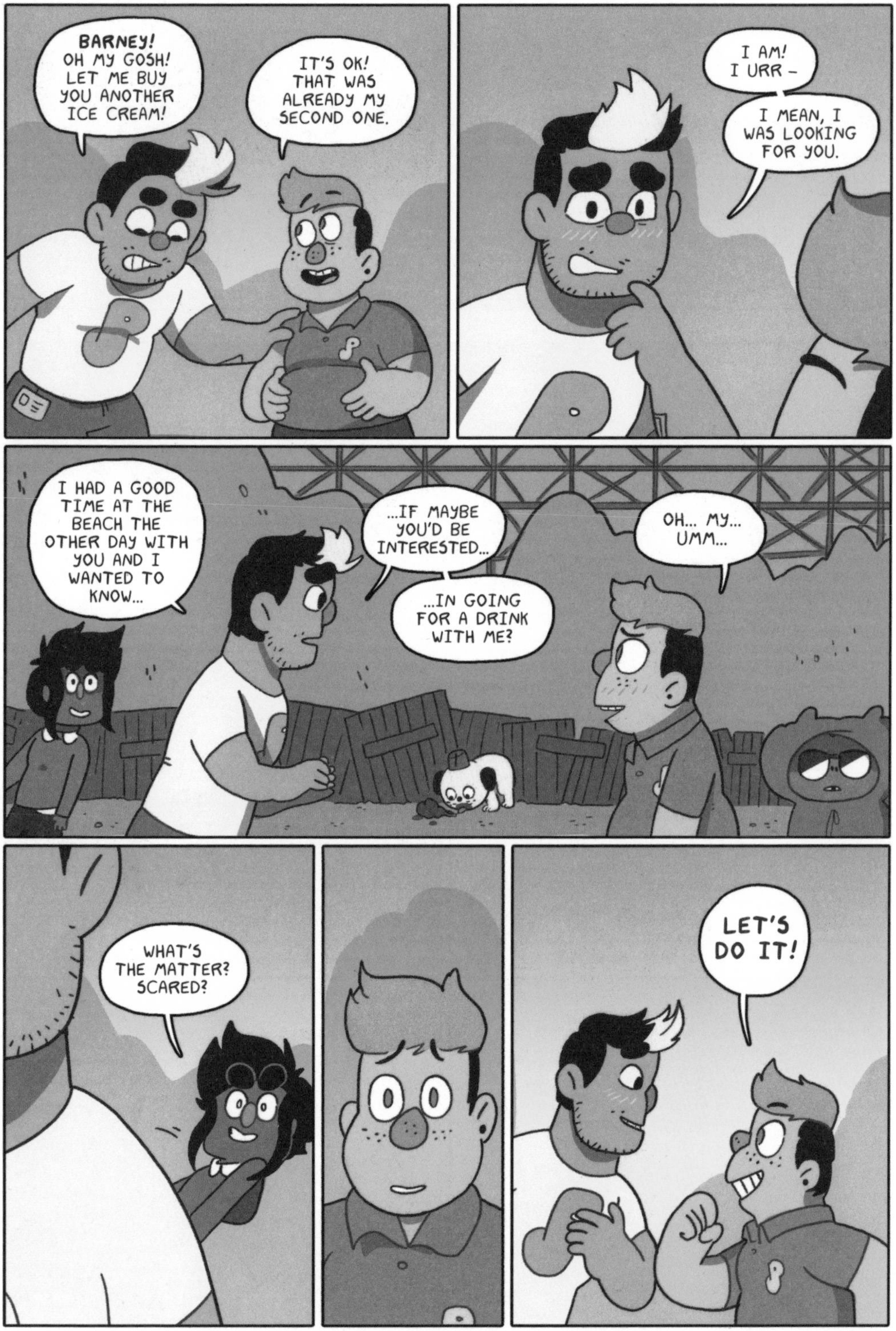
BARNEY! OH MY GOSH! LET ME BUY YOU ANOTHER ICE CREAM!
IT'S OK! THAT WAS ALREADY MY SECOND ONE.
I AM! I URR –
I MEAN, I WAS LOOKING FOR YOU.
I HAD A GOOD TIME AT THE BEACH THE OTHER DAY WITH YOU AND I WANTED TO KNOW...
...IF MAYBE YOU'D BE INTERESTED...
...IN GOING FOR A DRINK WITH ME?
OH... MY... UMM...
WHAT'S THE MATTER? SCARED?
LET'S DO IT!

CHAPTER 4

COVER ART BY JONNY CLAPHAM

EVERY DAY HAS ITS DOG

```
NAME...........................LOGAN "LOGS" NGUYEN
PRONOUNS...............................HE/HIM
AGE ................................................23
OCCUPATION............LOG FLUME OPERATOR
LIKES.....SWIMMING, VLOGGING, TV BINGING
DISLIKES........THE SHOWRUNNERS OF ALL HIS
                         FAVOURITE TV SHOWS
FAMILY .................... ELIZABETH (SISTER),
          WENDY (SISTER), PHUONG (MOTHER)
```

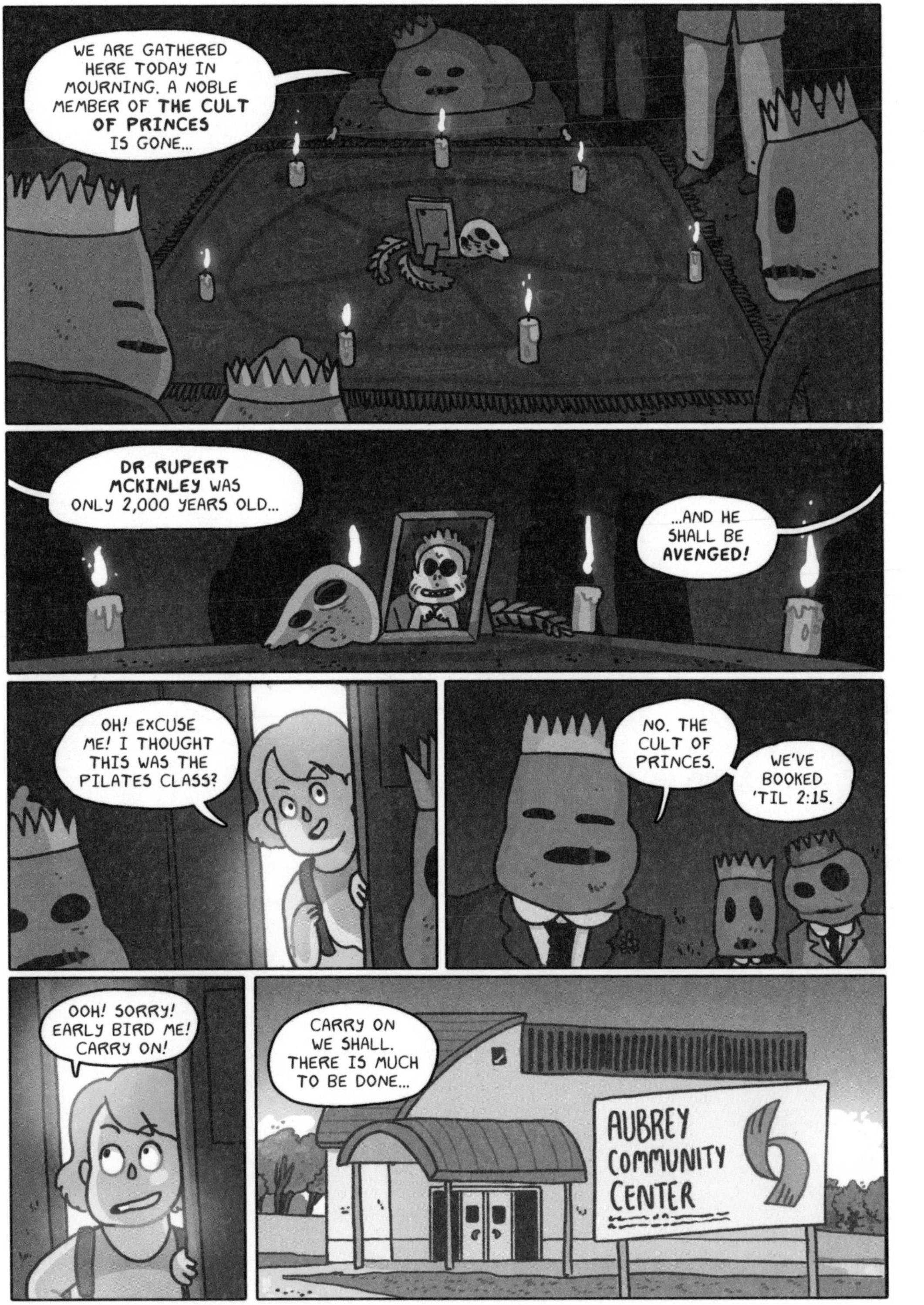
WE ARE GATHERED HERE TODAY IN MOURNING. A NOBLE MEMBER OF THE CULT OF PRINCES IS GONE...
DR RUPERT MCKINLEY WAS ONLY 2,000 YEARS OLD...
...AND HE SHALL BE AVENGED!
OH! EXCUSE ME! I THOUGHT THIS WAS THE PILATES CLASS?
NO. THE CULT OF PRINCES.
WE'VE BOOKED 'TIL 2:15.
OOH! SORRY! EARLY BIRD ME! CARRY ON!
CARRY ON WE SHALL. THERE IS MUCH TO BE DONE...
AUBREY COMMUNITY CENTER

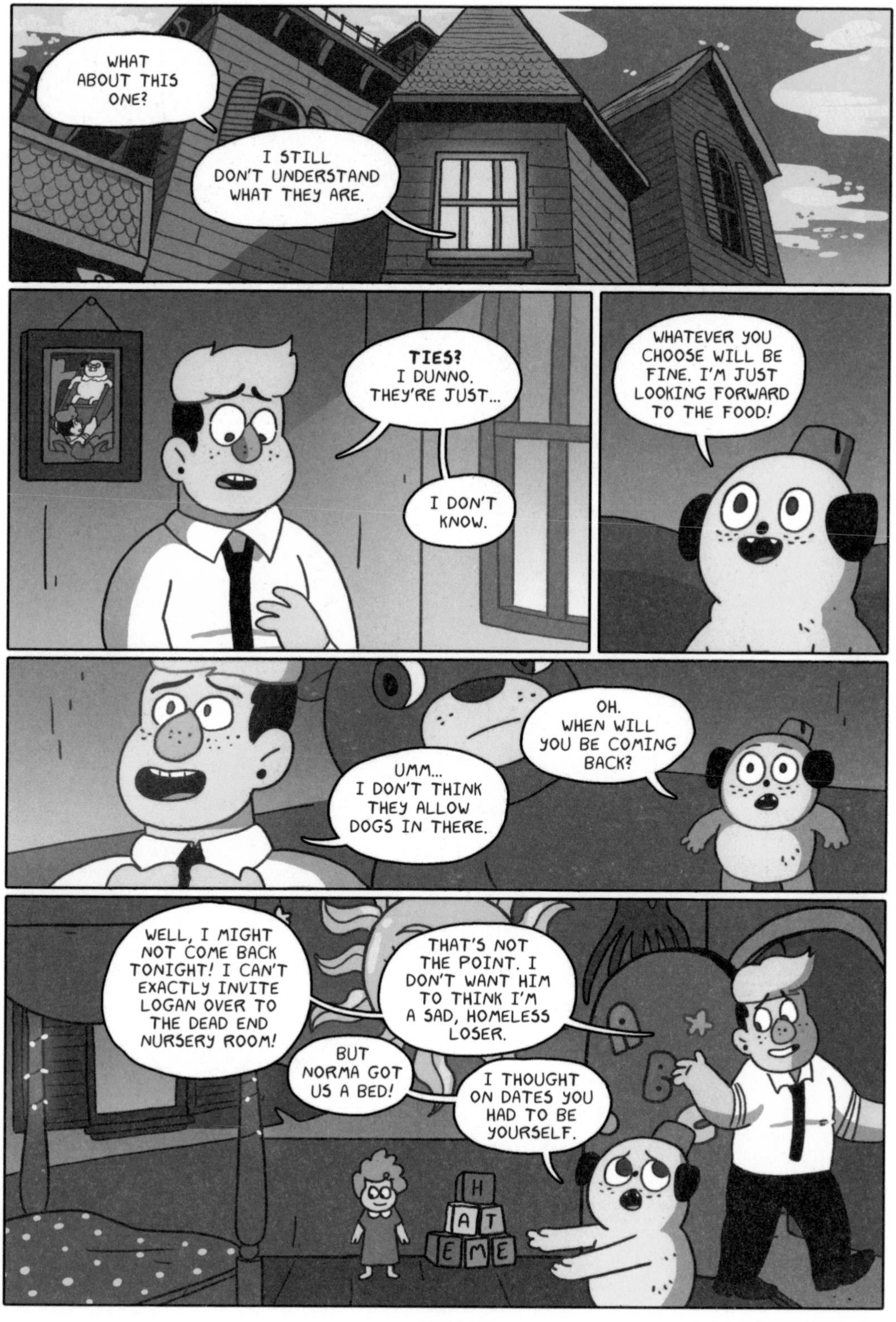
WHAT ABOUT THIS ONE?
I STILL DON'T UNDERSTAND WHAT THEY ARE.
TIES? I DUNNO. THEY'RE JUST...
I DON'T KNOW.
WHATEVER YOU CHOOSE WILL BE FINE. I'M JUST LOOKING FORWARD TO THE FOOD!
UMM... I DON'T THINK THEY ALLOW DOGS IN THERE.
OH. WHEN WILL YOU BE COMING BACK?
WELL, I MIGHT NOT COME BACK TONIGHT! I CAN'T EXACTLY INVITE LOGAN OVER TO THE DEAD END NURSERY ROOM!
BUT NORMA GOT US A BED!
THAT'S NOT THE POINT. I DON'T WANT HIM TO THINK I'M A SAD, HOMELESS LOSER.
I THOUGHT ON DATES YOU HAD TO BE YOURSELF.

I'LL SEE YOU TONIGHT THEN!

WE'RE GONNA DRINK OUR BODY WEIGHT IN ICED TEA AND GET WEIRD.

HOW DO I NOT HAVE AN EXCUSE?

THIS IS THE WORST!

YOU CAN SAY NO!

OKAY?

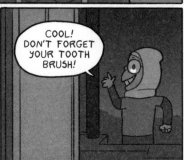

COOL! DON'T FORGET YOUR TOOTH BRUSH!

BARNEY IS WEARING A TIE TO A PLACE AND I CAN'T GO.

CAN WE HANG OUT?

PUGSLEY! IF YOU'D ASKED ME THAT A MINUTE AGO, I'D HAVE HAD AN EXCUSE!

NOW... I HAVE "PLANS".

ARE THEY PLANS A DOG CAN ATTEND?

SORRY. SHE'S ALLERGIC. AND I HATE THAT I ALREADY KNOW A FACT ABOUT HER.

89

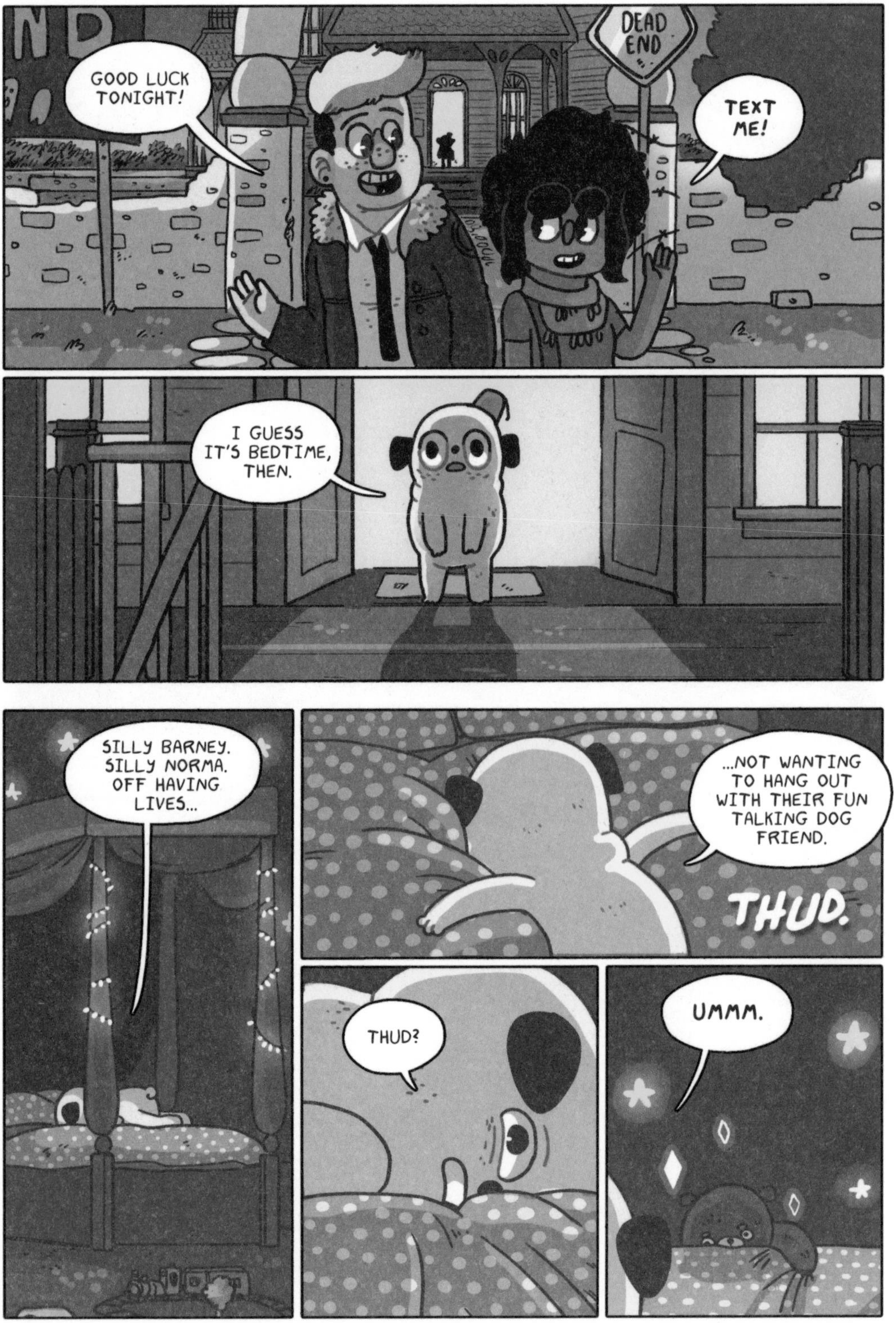
DEAD END
GOOD LUCK TONIGHT!
TEXT ME!
I GUESS IT'S BEDTIME, THEN.
SILLY BARNEY. SILLY NORMA. OFF HAVING LIVES...
...NOT WANTING TO HANG OUT WITH THEIR FUN TALKING DOG FRIEND.
THUD.
THUD?
UMMM.

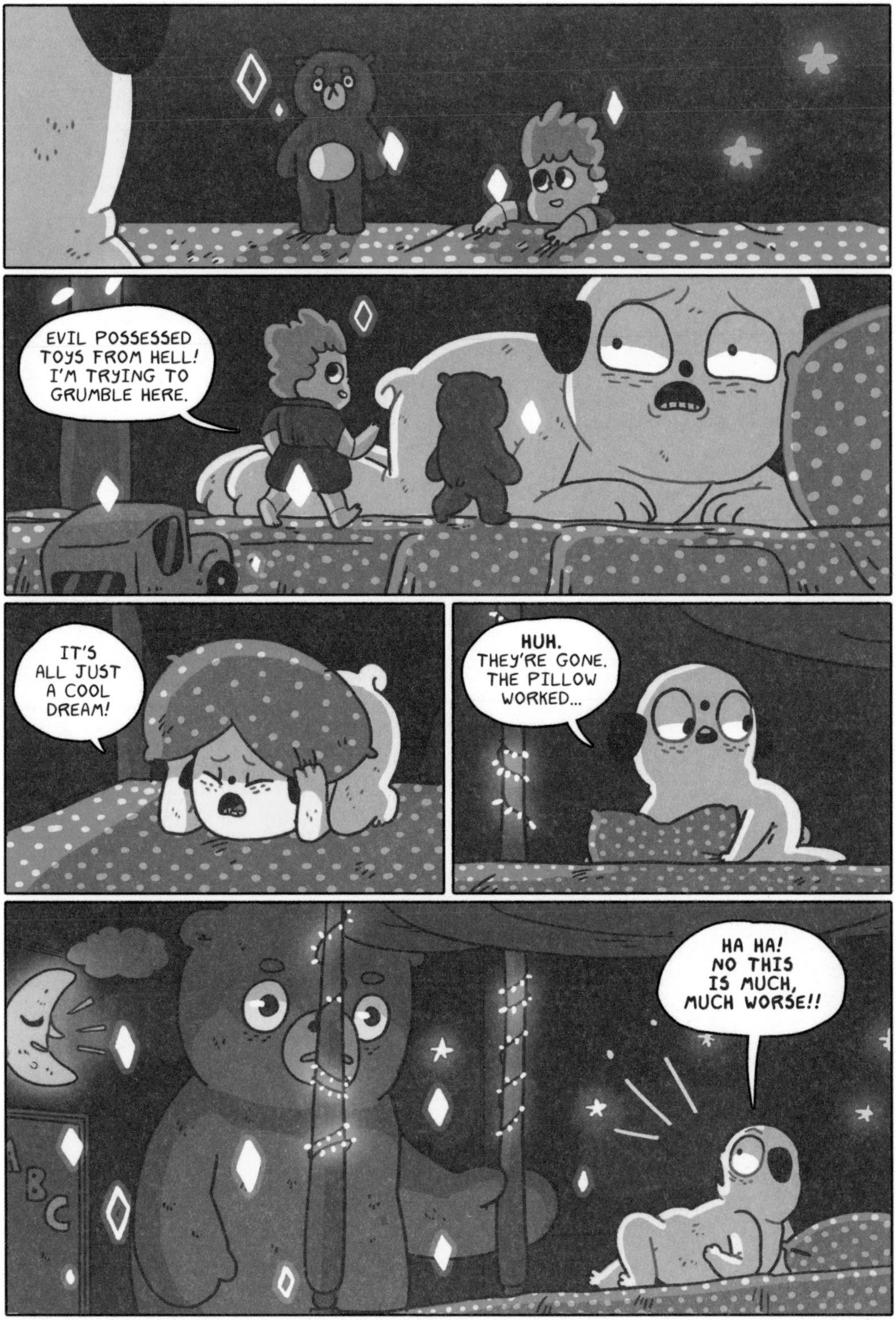
EVIL POSSESSED TOYS FROM HELL! I'M TRYING TO GRUMBLE HERE.
IT'S ALL JUST A COOL DREAM!
HUH. THEY'RE GONE. THE PILLOW WORKED...
HA HA! NO THIS IS MUCH, MUCH WORSE!!

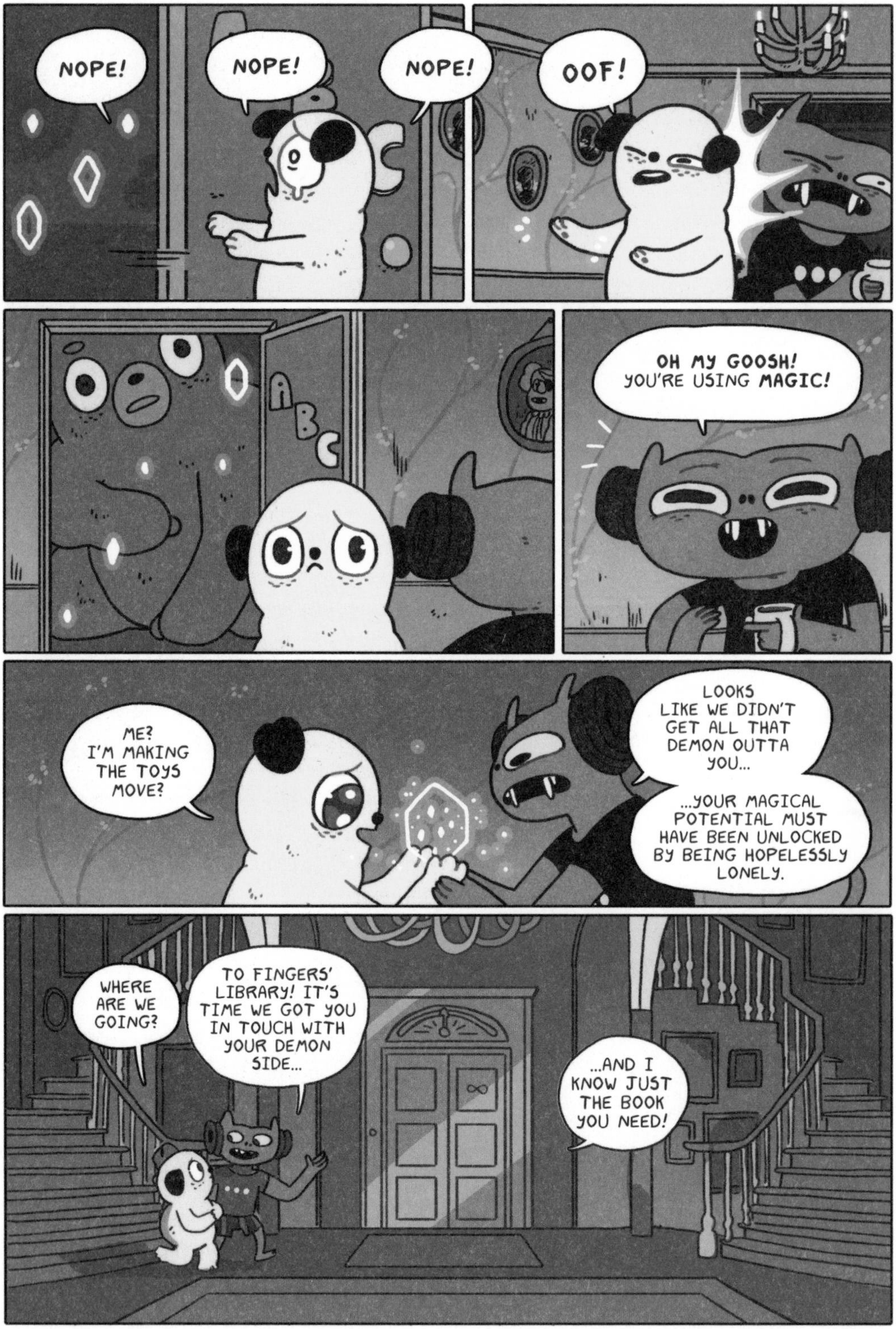
NOPE!
NOPE!
NOPE!
OOF!
A B C
OH MY GOOSH! YOU'RE USING MAGIC!
ME? I'M MAKING THE TOYS MOVE?
LOOKS LIKE WE DIDN'T GET ALL THAT DEMON OUTTA YOU...
...YOUR MAGICAL POTENTIAL MUST HAVE BEEN UNLOCKED BY BEING HOPELESSLY LONELY.
WHERE ARE WE GOING?
TO FINGERS' LIBRARY! IT'S TIME WE GOT YOU IN TOUCH WITH YOUR DEMON SIDE...
...AND I KNOW JUST THE BOOK YOU NEED!

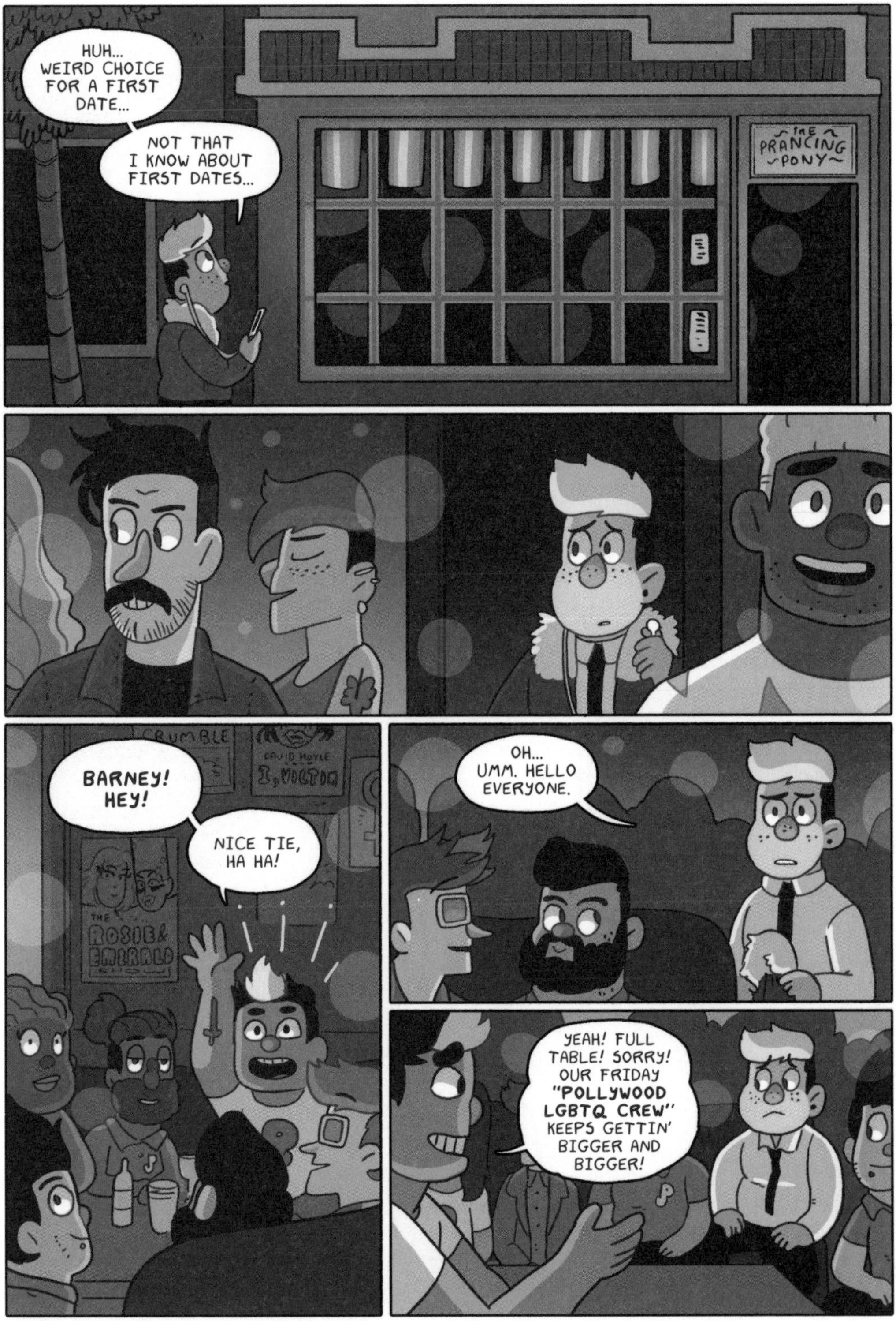
HUH... WEIRD CHOICE FOR A FIRST DATE...
NOT THAT I KNOW ABOUT FIRST DATES...
THE PRANCING PONY
BARNEY! HEY!
NICE TIE, HA HA!
OH... UMM. HELLO EVERYONE.
YEAH! FULL TABLE! SORRY! OUR FRIDAY "POLLYWOOD LGBTQ CREW" KEEPS GETTIN' BIGGER AND BIGGER!

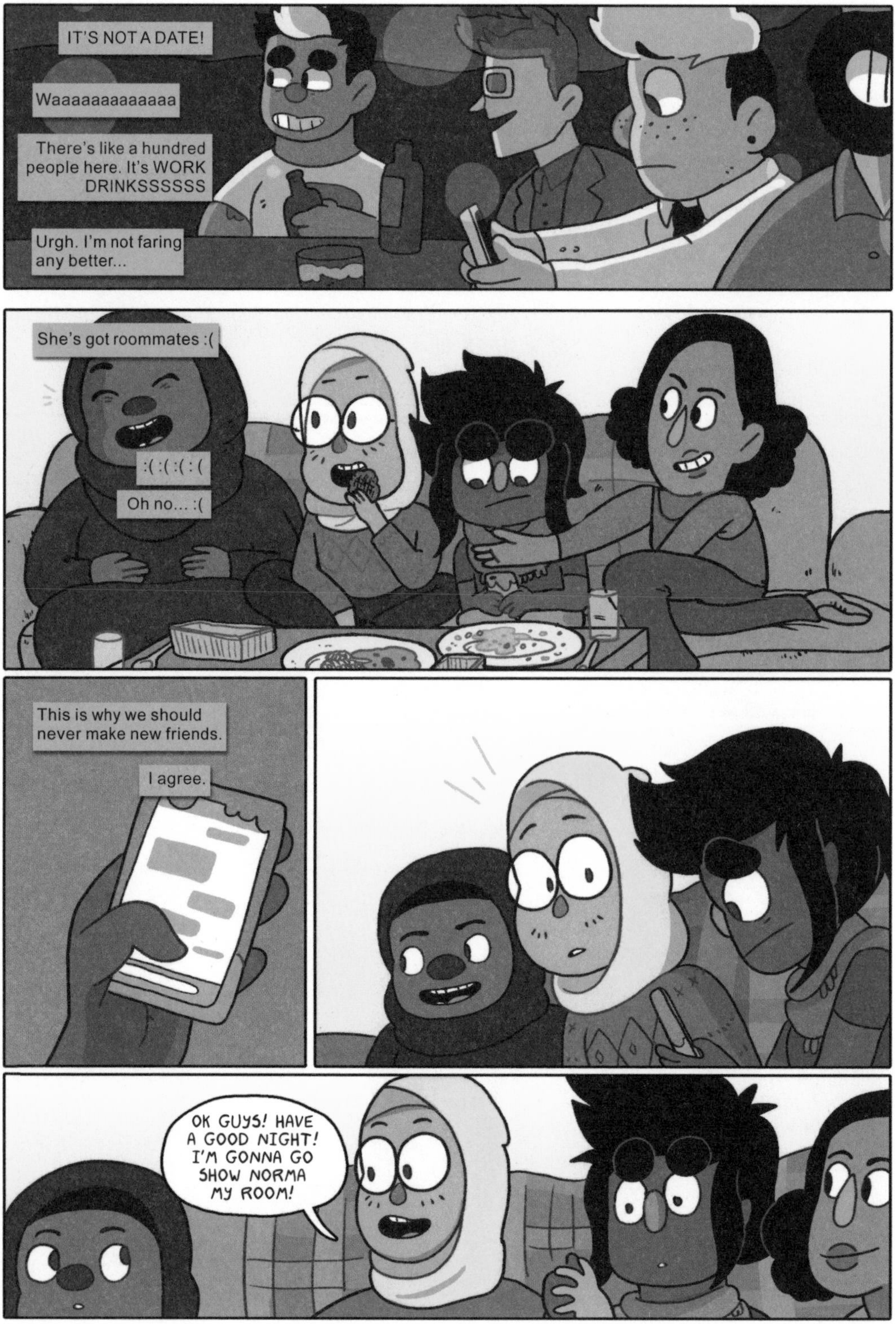
IT'S NOT A DATE!
Waaaaaaaaaaaaa
There's like a hundred people here. It's WORK DRINKSSSSSS
Urgh. I'm not faring any better...
She's got roommates :(
:(:(:(:(
Oh no... :(
This is why we should never make new friends.
I agree.
OK GUYS! HAVE A GOOD NIGHT! I'M GONNA GO SHOW NORMA MY ROOM!

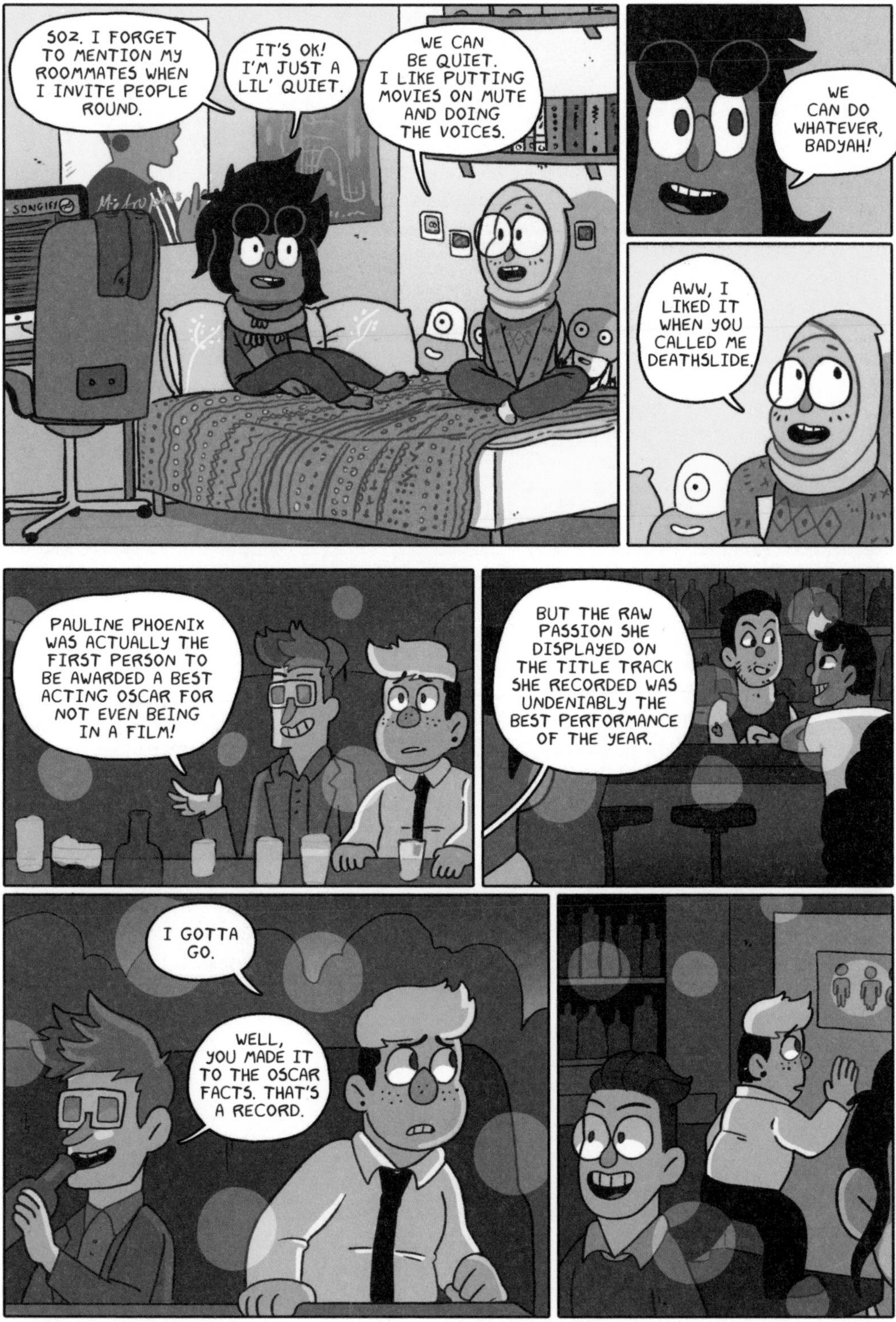
SOZ. I FORGET TO MENTION MY ROOMMATES WHEN I INVITE PEOPLE ROUND.
IT'S OK! I'M JUST A LIL' QUIET.
WE CAN BE QUIET. I LIKE PUTTING MOVIES ON MUTE AND DOING THE VOICES.
WE CAN DO WHATEVER, BADYAH!
AWW, I LIKED IT WHEN YOU CALLED ME DEATHSLIDE.
PAULINE PHOENIX WAS ACTUALLY THE FIRST PERSON TO BE AWARDED A BEST ACTING OSCAR FOR NOT EVEN BEING IN A FILM!
BUT THE RAW PASSION SHE DISPLAYED ON THE TITLE TRACK SHE RECORDED WAS UNDENIABLY THE BEST PERFORMANCE OF THE YEAR.
I GOTTA GO.
WELL, YOU MADE IT TO THE OSCAR FACTS. THAT'S A RECORD.

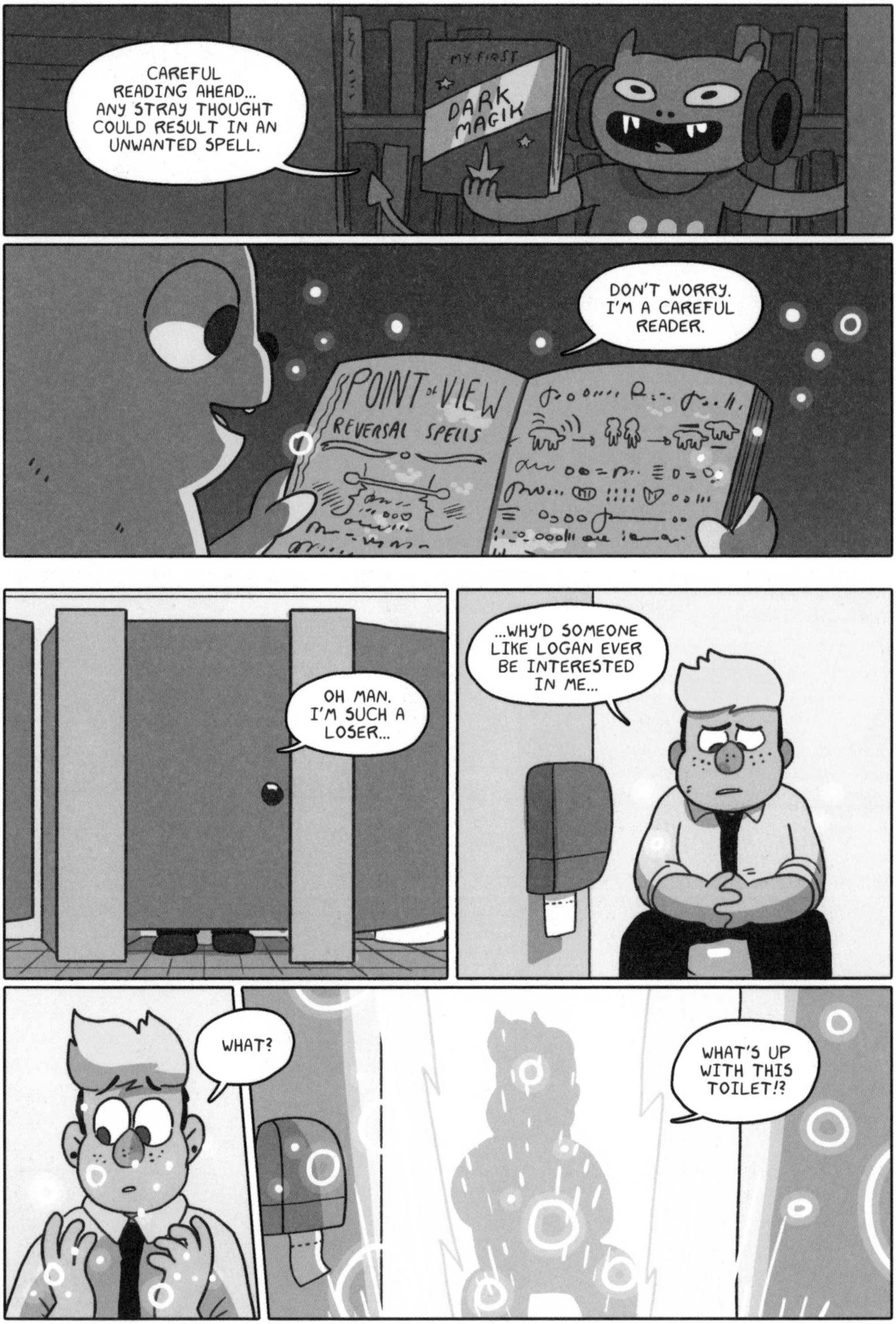
CAREFUL READING AHEAD... ANY STRAY THOUGHT COULD RESULT IN AN UNWANTED SPELL.
MY FIRST DARK MAGIK
DON'T WORRY. I'M A CAREFUL READER.
POINT OF VIEW REVERSAL SPELLS
OH MAN. I'M SUCH A LOSER...
...WHY'D SOMEONE LIKE LOGAN EVER BE INTERESTED IN ME...
WHAT?
WHAT'S UP WITH THIS TOILET!?

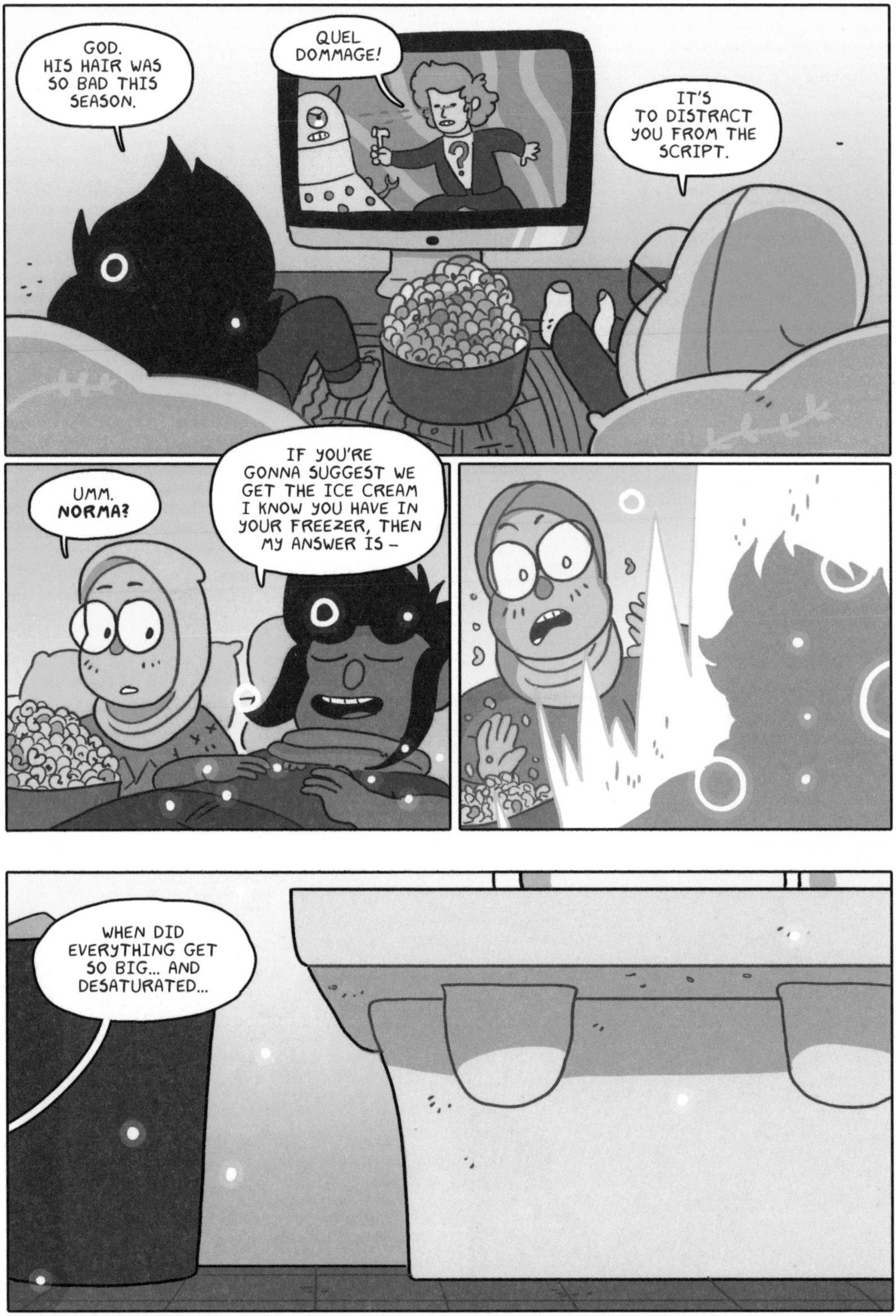
GOD. HIS HAIR WAS SO BAD THIS SEASON.
QUEL DOMMAGE!
IT'S TO DISTRACT YOU FROM THE SCRIPT.
UMM. **NORMA?**
IF YOU'RE GONNA SUGGEST WE GET THE ICE CREAM I KNOW YOU HAVE IN YOUR FREEZER, THEN MY ANSWER IS –
WHEN DID EVERYTHING GET SO BIG... AND DESATURATED...

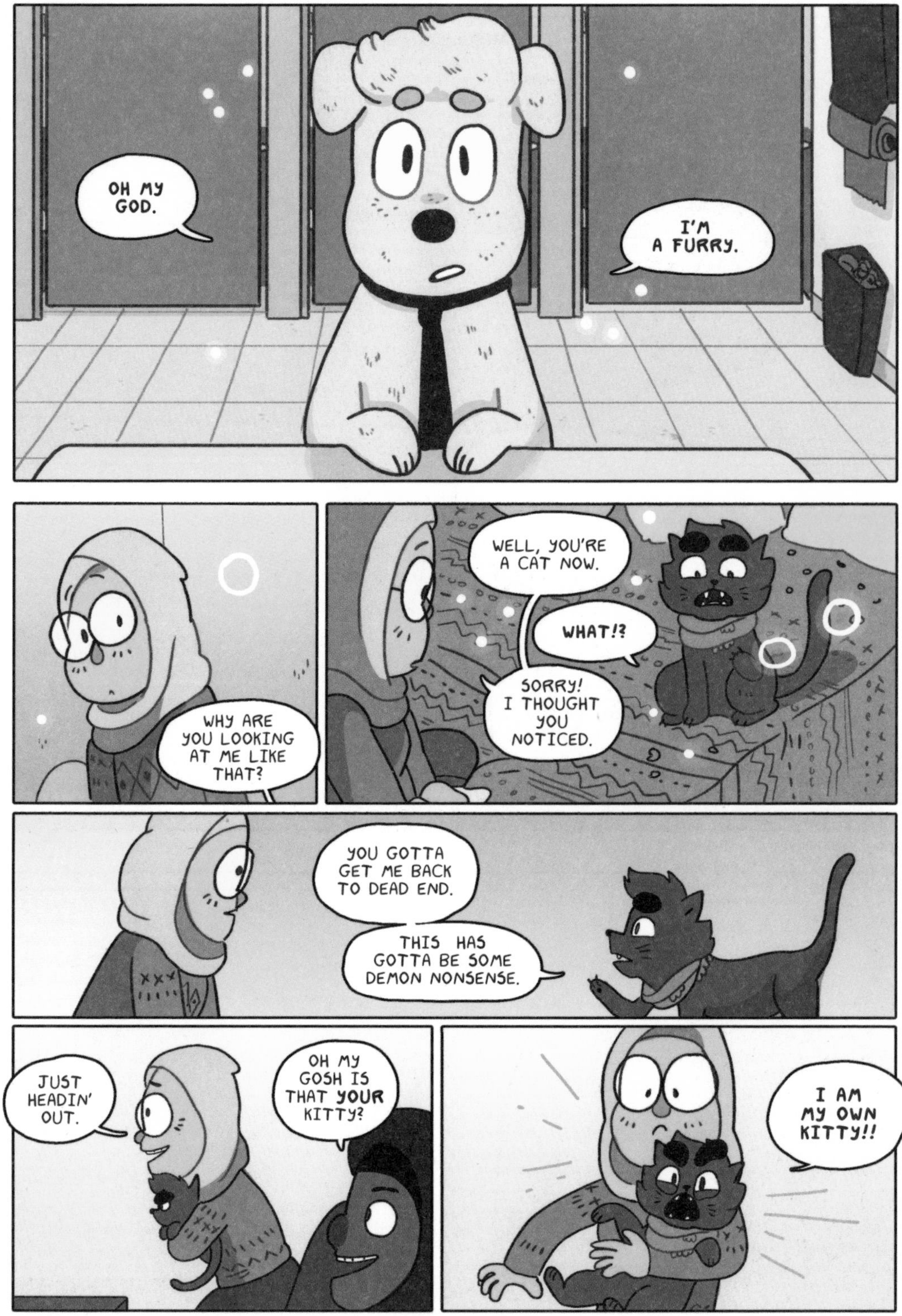
OH MY GOD.
I'M A FURRY.
WHY ARE YOU LOOKING AT ME LIKE THAT?
WELL, YOU'RE A CAT NOW.
WHAT!?
SORRY! I THOUGHT YOU NOTICED.
YOU GOTTA GET ME BACK TO DEAD END.
THIS HAS GOTTA BE SOME DEMON NONSENSE.
JUST HEADIN' OUT.
OH MY GOSH IS THAT **YOUR** KITTY?
I AM MY OWN KITTY!!

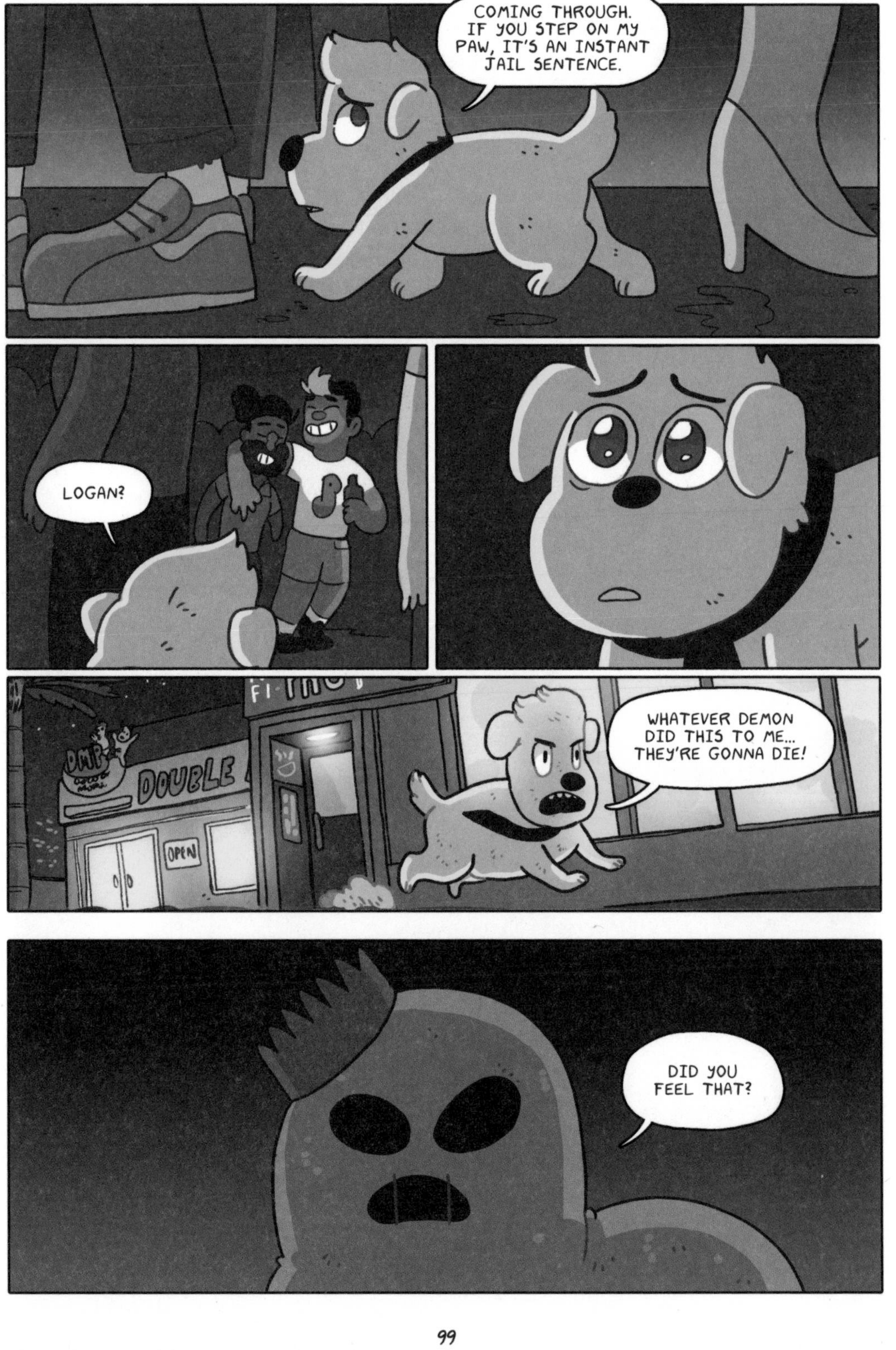
COMING THROUGH. IF YOU STEP ON MY PAW, IT'S AN INSTANT JAIL SENTENCE.
LOGAN?
DOUBLE
OPEN
WHATEVER DEMON DID THIS TO ME... THEY'RE GONNA DIE!
DID YOU FEEL THAT?

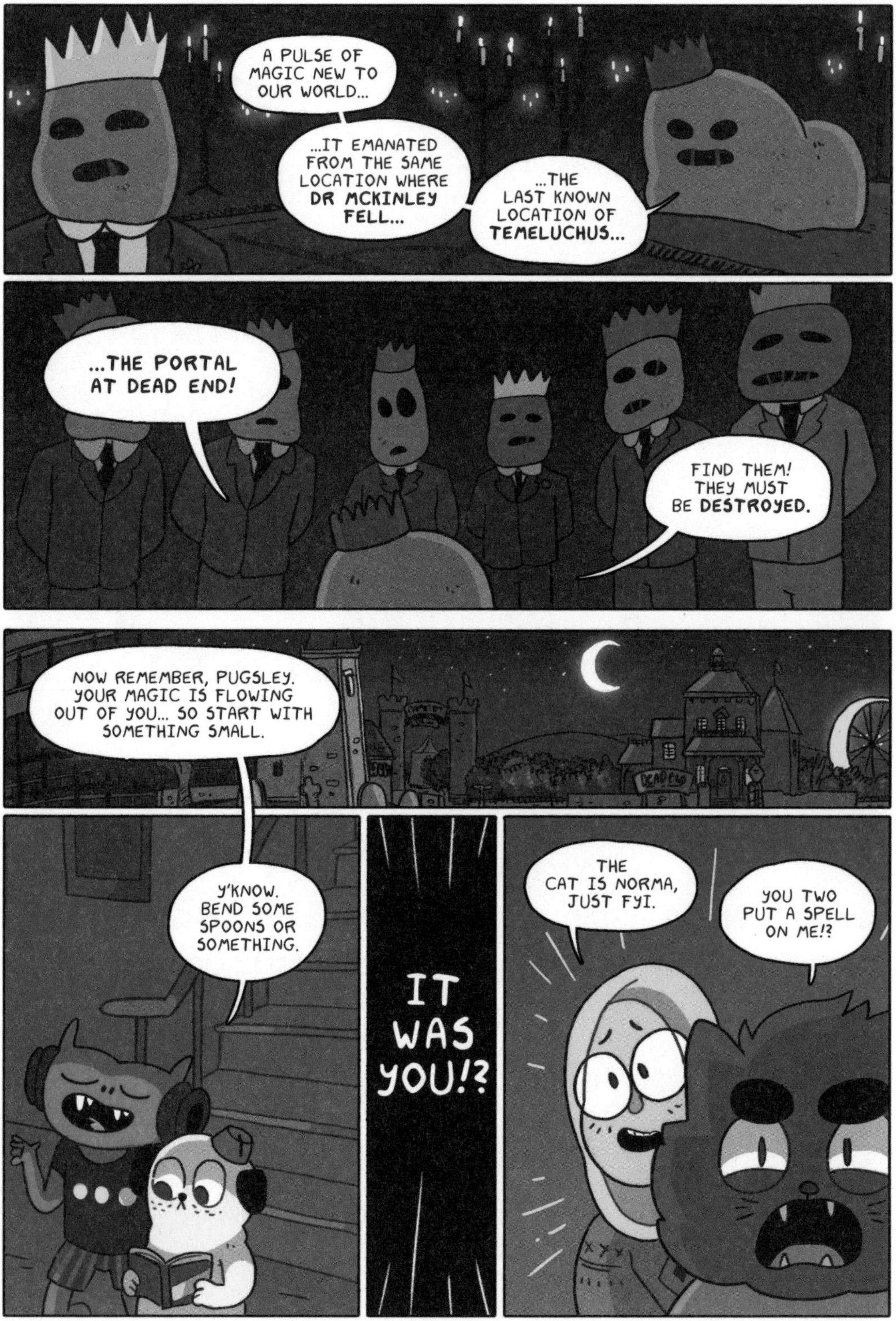
A PULSE OF MAGIC NEW TO OUR WORLD...
...IT EMANATED FROM THE SAME LOCATION WHERE DR MCKINLEY FELL...
...THE LAST KNOWN LOCATION OF TEMELUCHUS...
...THE PORTAL AT DEAD END!
FIND THEM! THEY MUST BE DESTROYED.
NOW REMEMBER, PUGSLEY. YOUR MAGIC IS FLOWING OUT OF YOU... SO START WITH SOMETHING SMALL.
Y'KNOW. BEND SOME SPOONS OR SOMETHING.
IT WAS YOU!?
THE CAT IS NORMA, JUST FYI.
YOU TWO PUT A SPELL ON ME!?

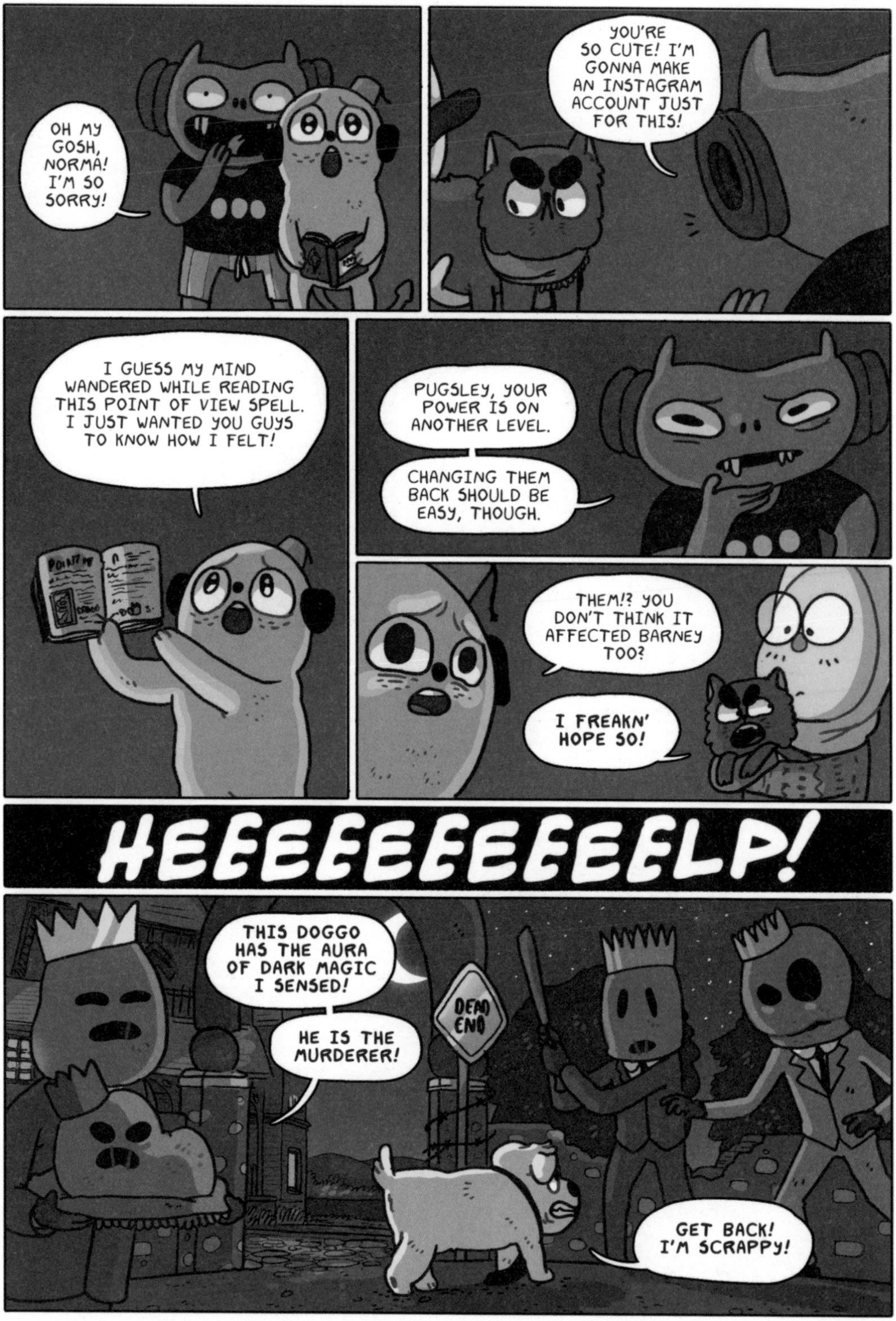
OH MY GOSH, NORMA! I'M SO SORRY!
YOU'RE SO CUTE! I'M GONNA MAKE AN INSTAGRAM ACCOUNT JUST FOR THIS!
I GUESS MY MIND WANDERED WHILE READING THIS POINT OF VIEW SPELL. I JUST WANTED YOU GUYS TO KNOW HOW I FELT!
PUGSLEY, YOUR POWER IS ON ANOTHER LEVEL.
CHANGING THEM BACK SHOULD BE EASY, THOUGH.
THEM!? YOU DON'T THINK IT AFFECTED BARNEY TOO?
I FREAKN' HOPE SO!
HEEEEEEEEEEELP!
THIS DOGGO HAS THE AURA OF DARK MAGIC I SENSED!
HE IS THE MURDERER!
DEAD END
GET BACK! I'M SCRAPPY!

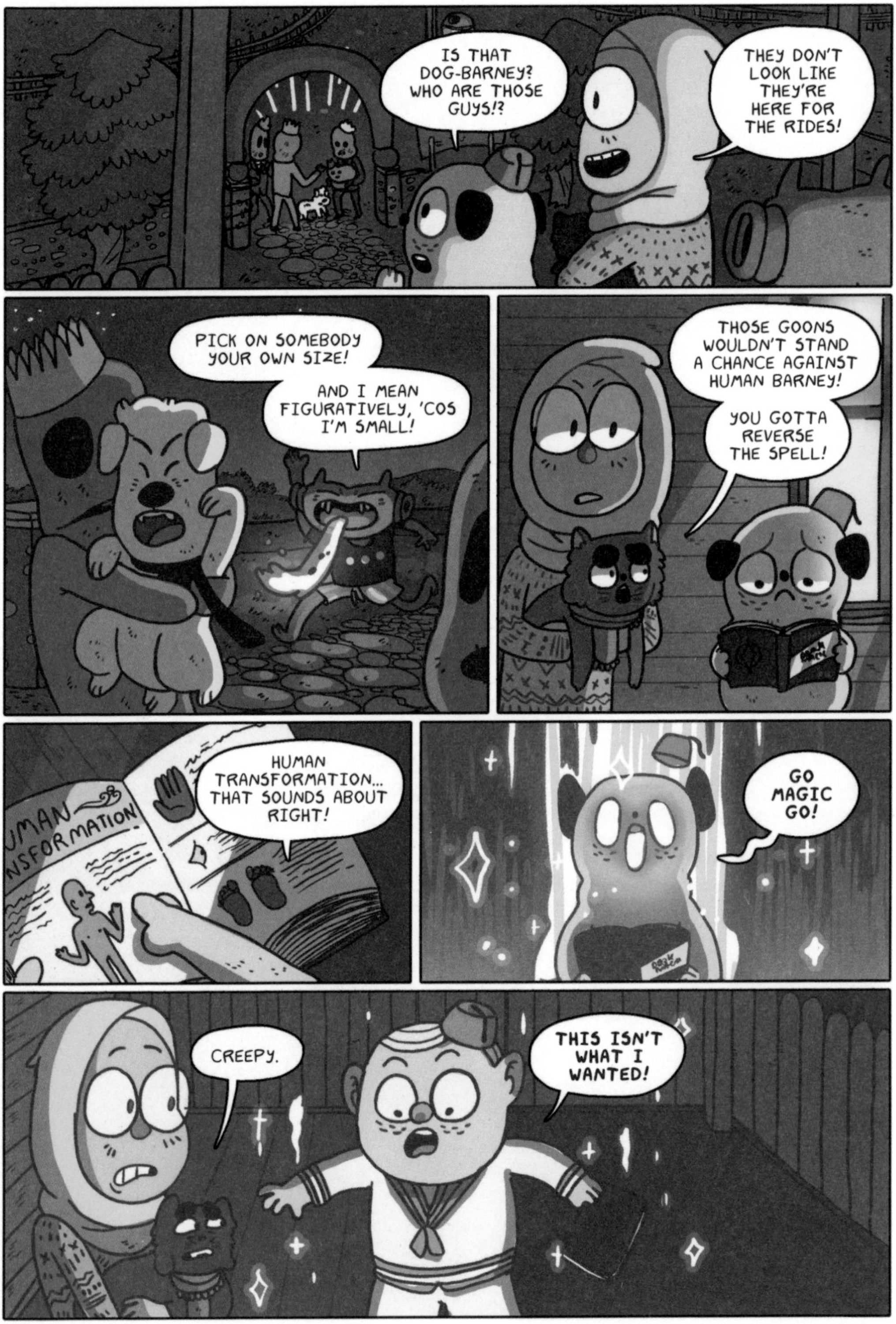
IS THAT DOG-BARNEY? WHO ARE THOSE GUYS!?
THEY DON'T LOOK LIKE THEY'RE HERE FOR THE RIDES!
PICK ON SOMEBODY YOUR OWN SIZE!
AND I MEAN FIGURATIVELY, 'COS I'M SMALL!
THOSE GOONS WOULDN'T STAND A CHANCE AGAINST HUMAN BARNEY!
YOU GOTTA REVERSE THE SPELL!
HUMAN TRANSFORMATION... THAT SOUNDS ABOUT RIGHT!
GO MAGIC GO!
CREEPY.
THIS ISN'T WHAT I WANTED!

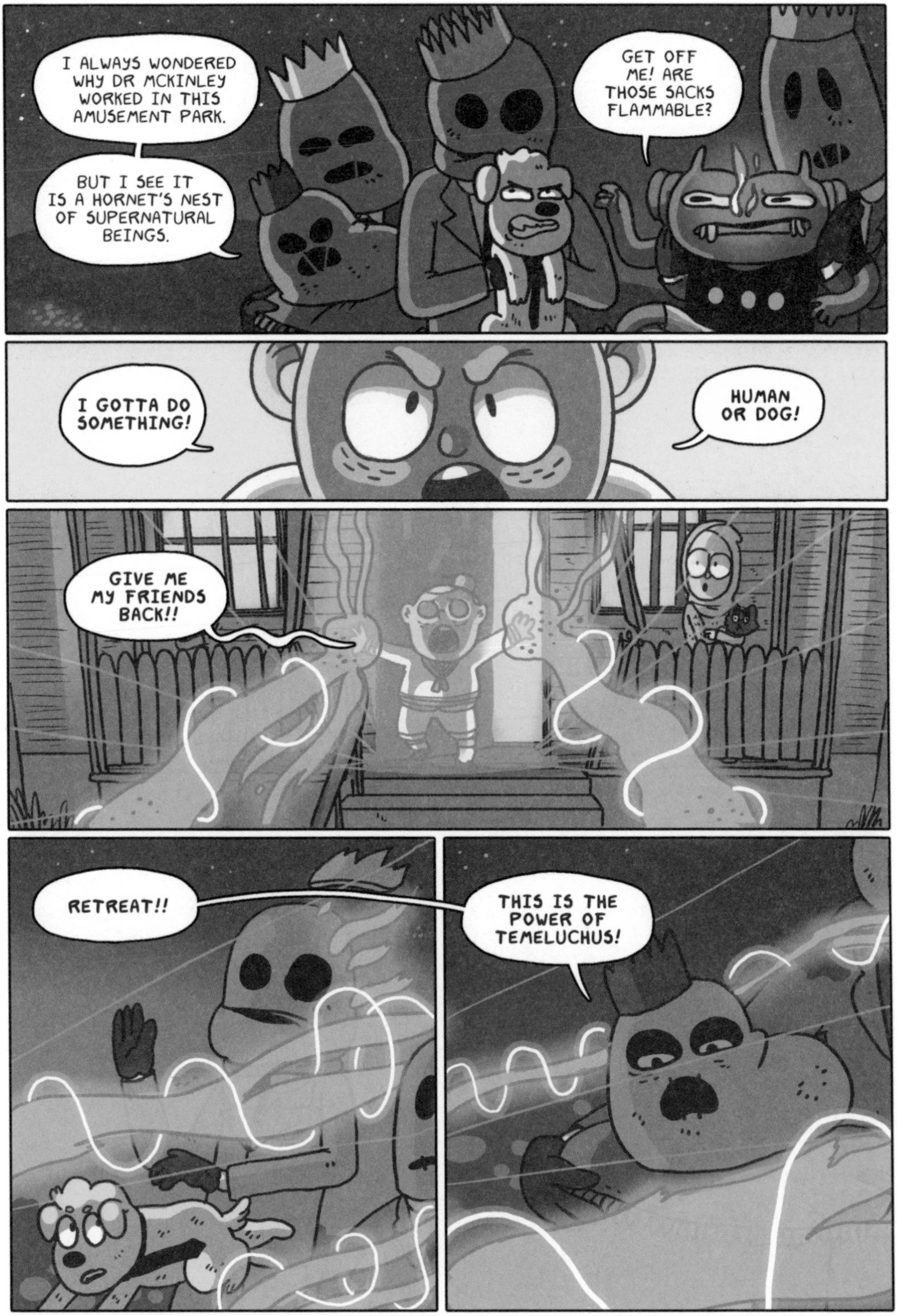
I ALWAYS WONDERED WHY DR MCKINLEY WORKED IN THIS AMUSEMENT PARK.
BUT I SEE IT IS A HORNET'S NEST OF SUPERNATURAL BEINGS.
GET OFF ME! ARE THOSE SACKS FLAMMABLE?
I GOTTA DO SOMETHING!
HUMAN OR DOG!
GIVE ME MY FRIENDS BACK!!
RETREAT!!
THIS IS THE POWER OF TEMELUCHUS!

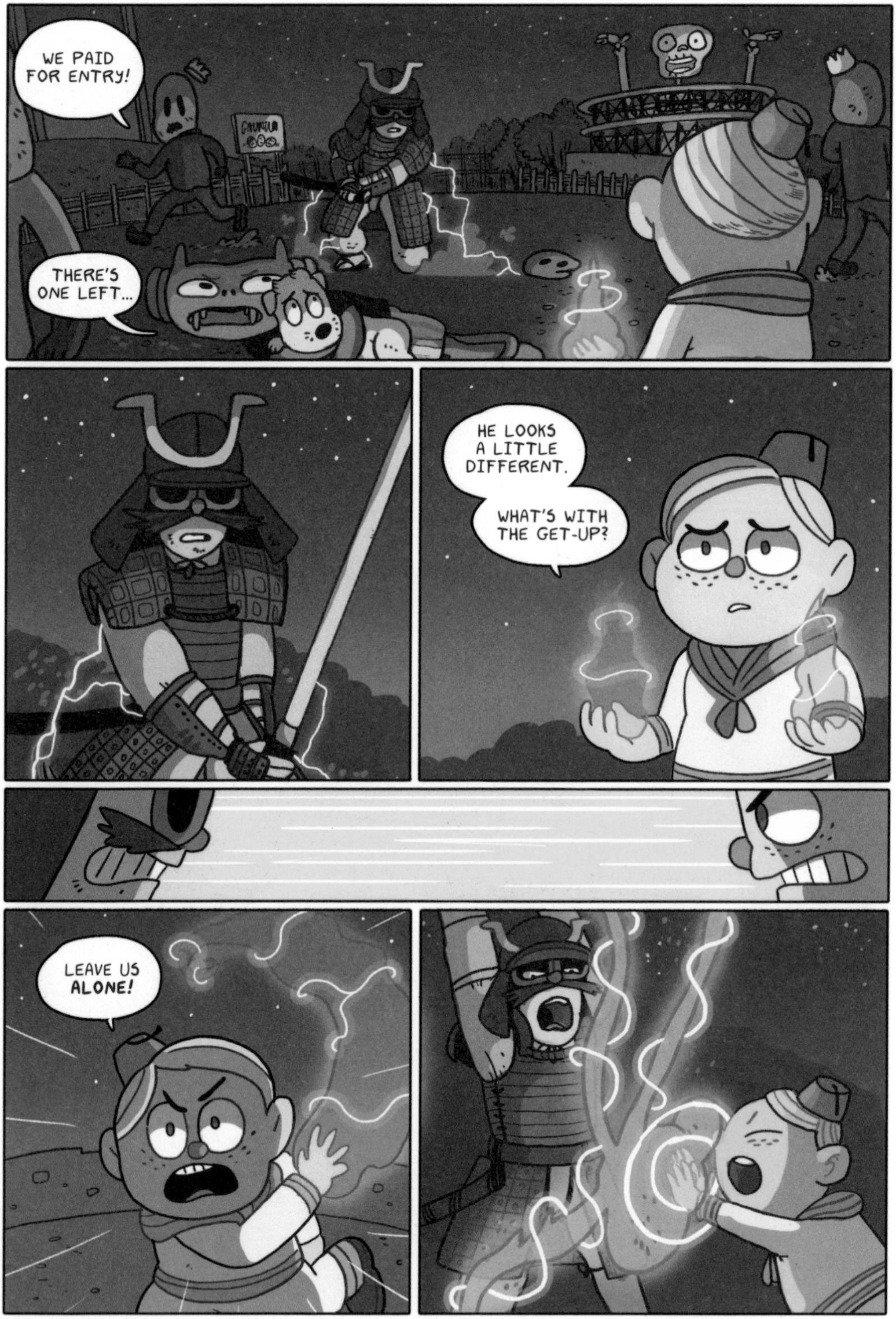
WE PAID FOR ENTRY!
THERE'S ONE LEFT...
HE LOOKS A LITTLE DIFFERENT.
WHAT'S WITH THE GET-UP?
LEAVE US ALONE!

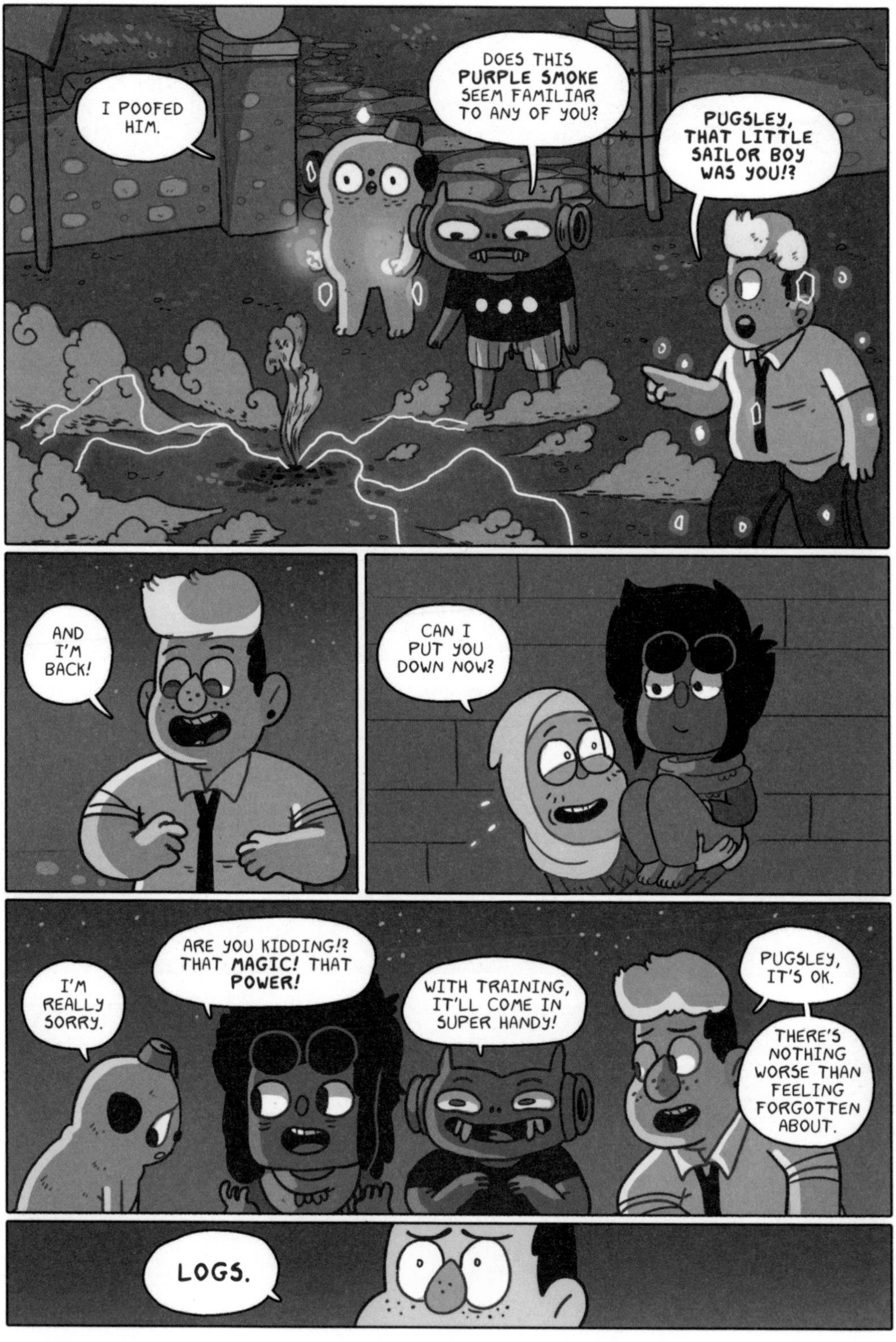
I POOFED HIM.
DOES THIS **PURPLE SMOKE** SEEM FAMILIAR TO ANY OF YOU?
PUGSLEY, THAT LITTLE SAILOR BOY WAS YOU!?
AND I'M BACK!
CAN I PUT YOU DOWN NOW?
I'M REALLY SORRY.
ARE YOU KIDDING!? THAT **MAGIC!** THAT **POWER!**
WITH TRAINING, IT'LL COME IN SUPER HANDY!
PUGSLEY, IT'S OK.
THERE'S NOTHING WORSE THAN FEELING FORGOTTEN ABOUT.
LOGS.

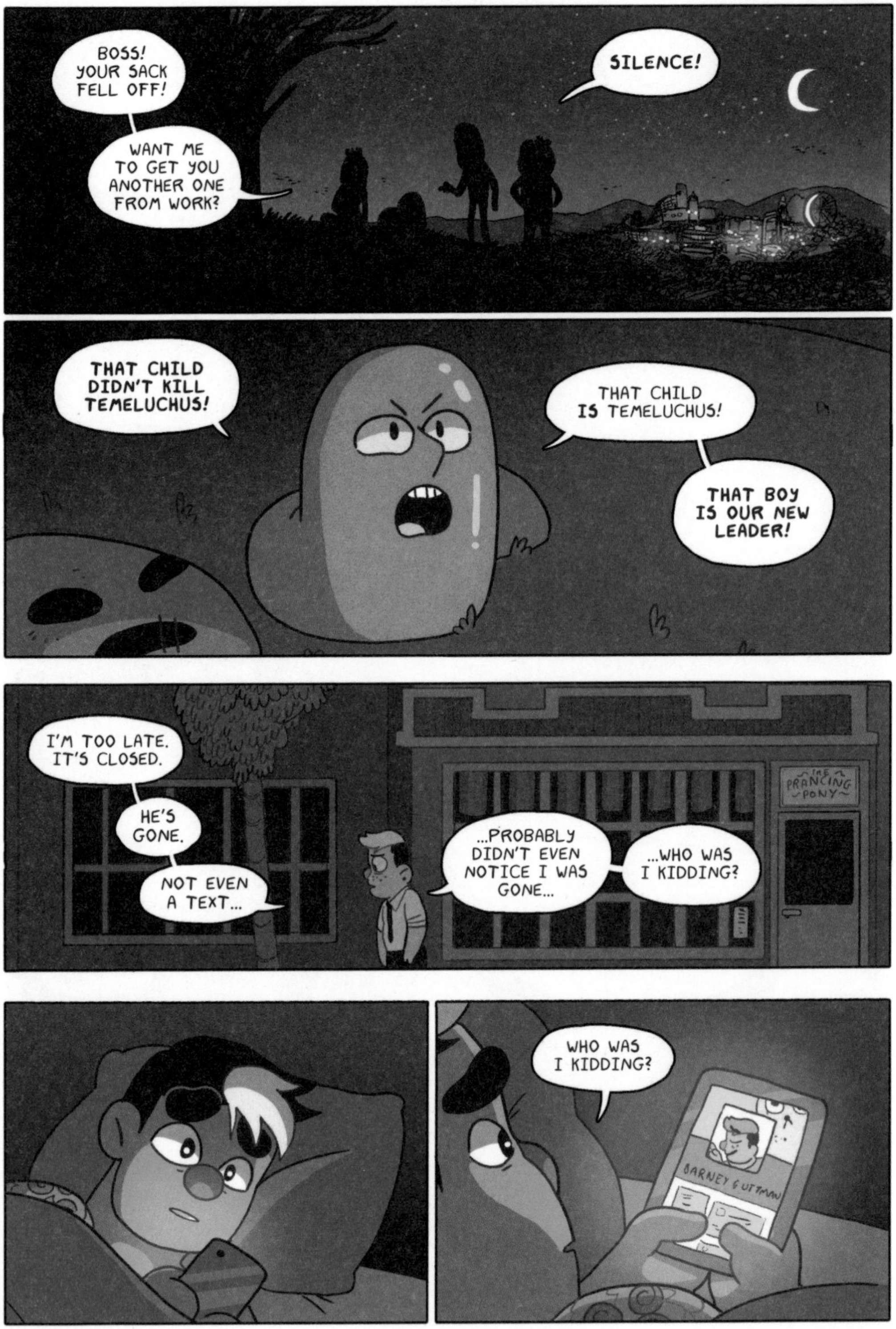

BOSS! YOUR SACK FELL OFF!
WANT ME TO GET YOU ANOTHER ONE FROM WORK?
SILENCE!
THAT CHILD DIDN'T KILL TEMELUCHUS!
THAT CHILD IS TEMELUCHUS!
THAT BOY IS OUR NEW LEADER!
I'M TOO LATE. IT'S CLOSED.
HE'S GONE.
NOT EVEN A TEXT...
THE PRANCING PONY
...PROBABLY DIDN'T EVEN NOTICE I WAS GONE...
...WHO WAS I KIDDING?
WHO WAS I KIDDING?

CHAPTER 5

COVER ART BY LYDIA BUTZ

THE PARTY POOPER

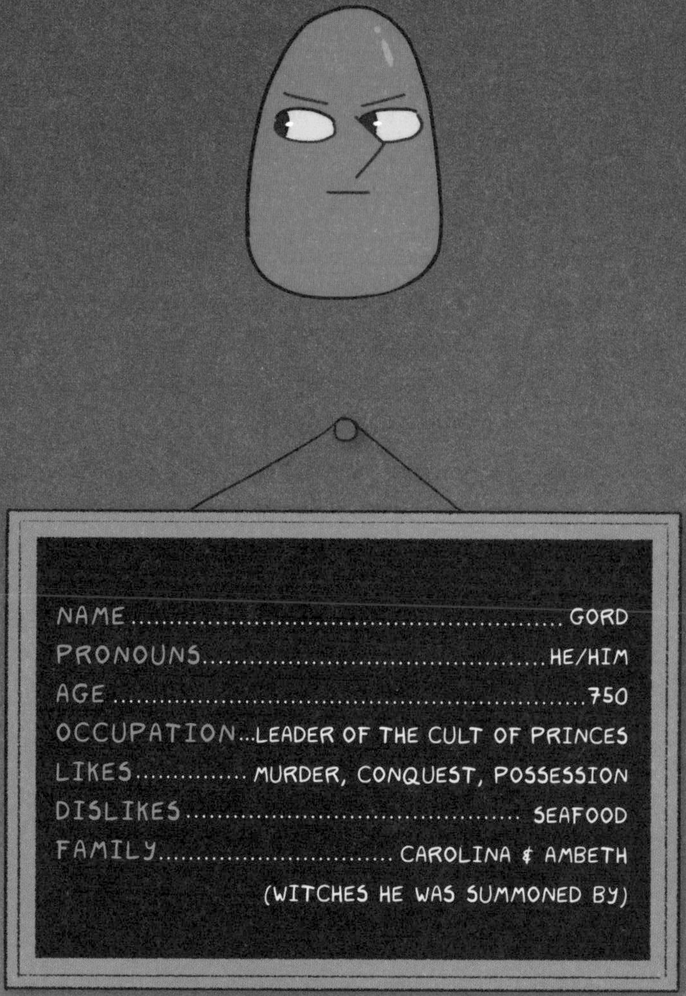

```
NAME .......................................................... GORD
PRONOUNS........................................HE/HIM
AGE ...................................................750
OCCUPATION...LEADER OF THE CULT OF PRINCES
LIKES.............. MURDER, CONQUEST, POSSESSION
DISLIKES........................................ SEAFOOD
FAMILY............................. CAROLINA & AMBETH
           (WITCHES HE WAS SUMMONED BY)
```

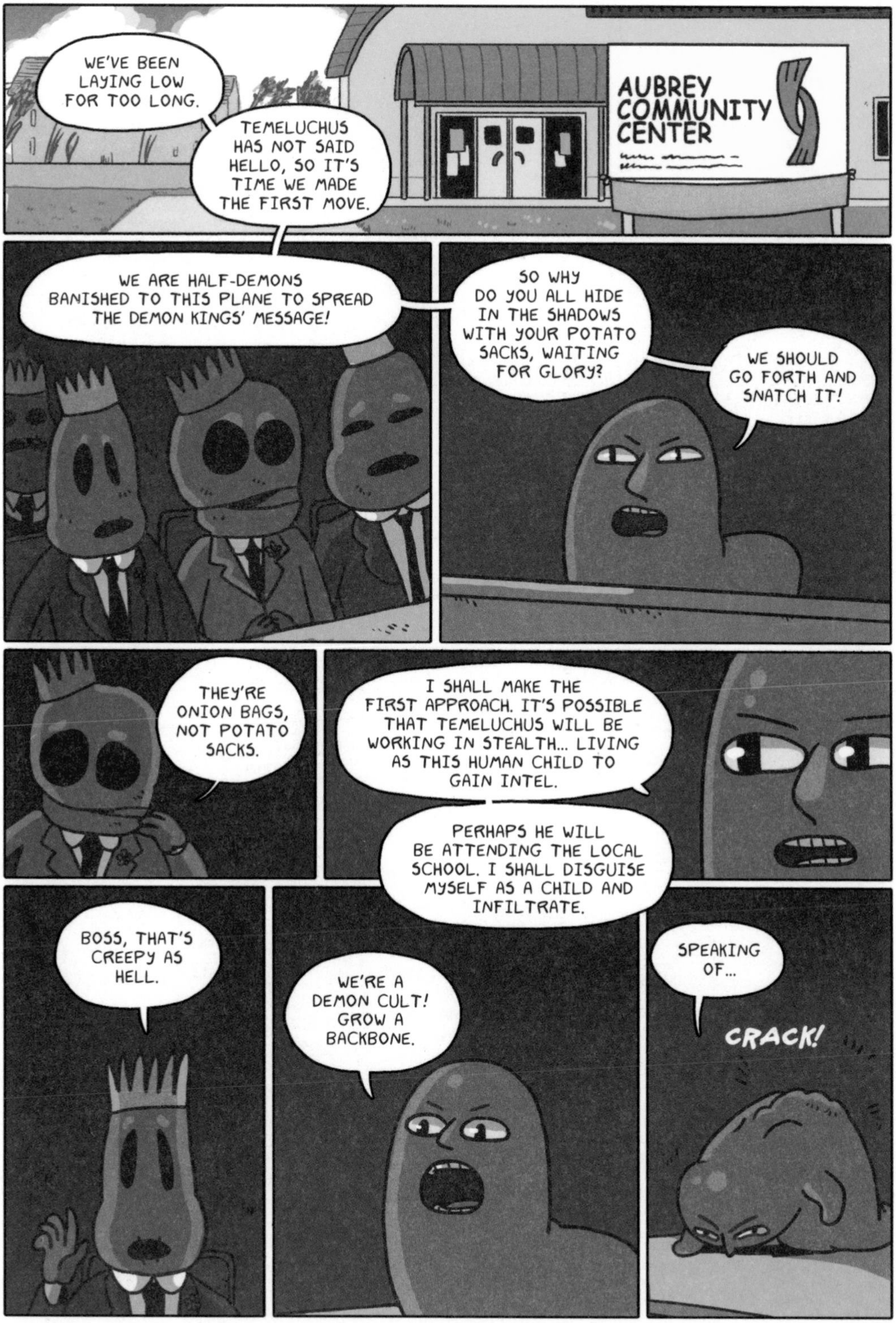
WE'VE BEEN LAYING LOW FOR TOO LONG.
TEMELUCHUS HAS NOT SAID HELLO, SO IT'S TIME WE MADE THE FIRST MOVE.
AUBREY COMMUNITY CENTER
WE ARE HALF-DEMONS BANISHED TO THIS PLANE TO SPREAD THE DEMON KINGS' MESSAGE!
SO WHY DO YOU ALL HIDE IN THE SHADOWS WITH YOUR POTATO SACKS, WAITING FOR GLORY?
WE SHOULD GO FORTH AND SNATCH IT!
THEY'RE ONION BAGS, NOT POTATO SACKS.
I SHALL MAKE THE FIRST APPROACH. IT'S POSSIBLE THAT TEMELUCHUS WILL BE WORKING IN STEALTH... LIVING AS THIS HUMAN CHILD TO GAIN INTEL.
PERHAPS HE WILL BE ATTENDING THE LOCAL SCHOOL. I SHALL DISGUISE MYSELF AS A CHILD AND INFILTRATE.
BOSS, THAT'S CREEPY AS HELL.
WE'RE A DEMON CULT! GROW A BACKBONE.
SPEAKING OF...
CRACK!

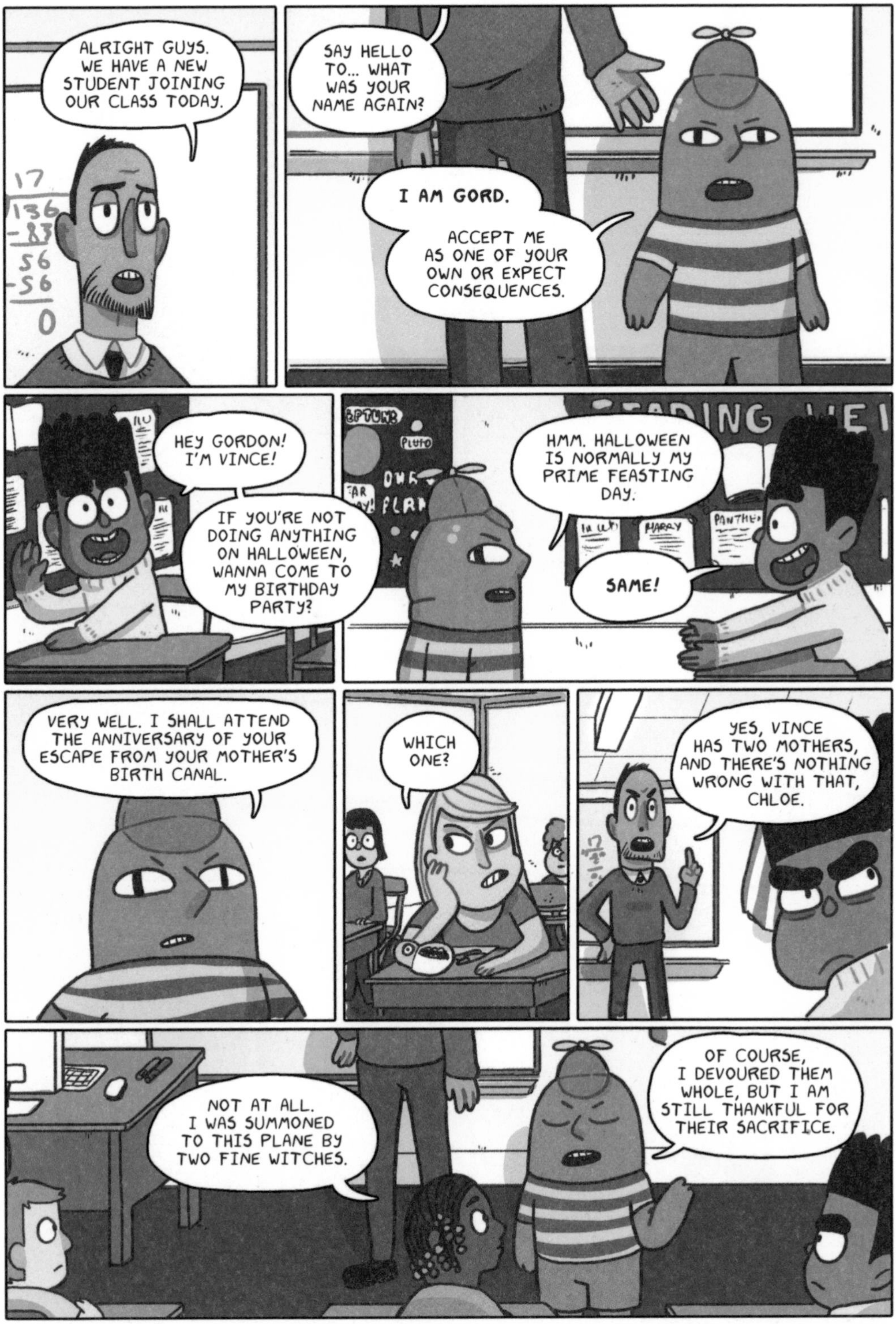
ALRIGHT GUYS. WE HAVE A NEW STUDENT JOINING OUR CLASS TODAY.
SAY HELLO TO... WHAT WAS YOUR NAME AGAIN?
I AM GORD.
ACCEPT ME AS ONE OF YOUR OWN OR EXPECT CONSEQUENCES.
HEY GORDON! I'M VINCE!
IF YOU'RE NOT DOING ANYTHING ON HALLOWEEN, WANNA COME TO MY BIRTHDAY PARTY?
HMM. HALLOWEEN IS NORMALLY MY PRIME FEASTING DAY.
SAME!
VERY WELL. I SHALL ATTEND THE ANNIVERSARY OF YOUR ESCAPE FROM YOUR MOTHER'S BIRTH CANAL.
WHICH ONE?
YES, VINCE HAS TWO MOTHERS, AND THERE'S NOTHING WRONG WITH THAT, CHLOE.
NOT AT ALL. I WAS SUMMONED TO THIS PLANE BY TWO FINE WITCHES.
OF COURSE, I DEVOURED THEM WHOLE, BUT I AM STILL THANKFUL FOR THEIR SACRIFICE.

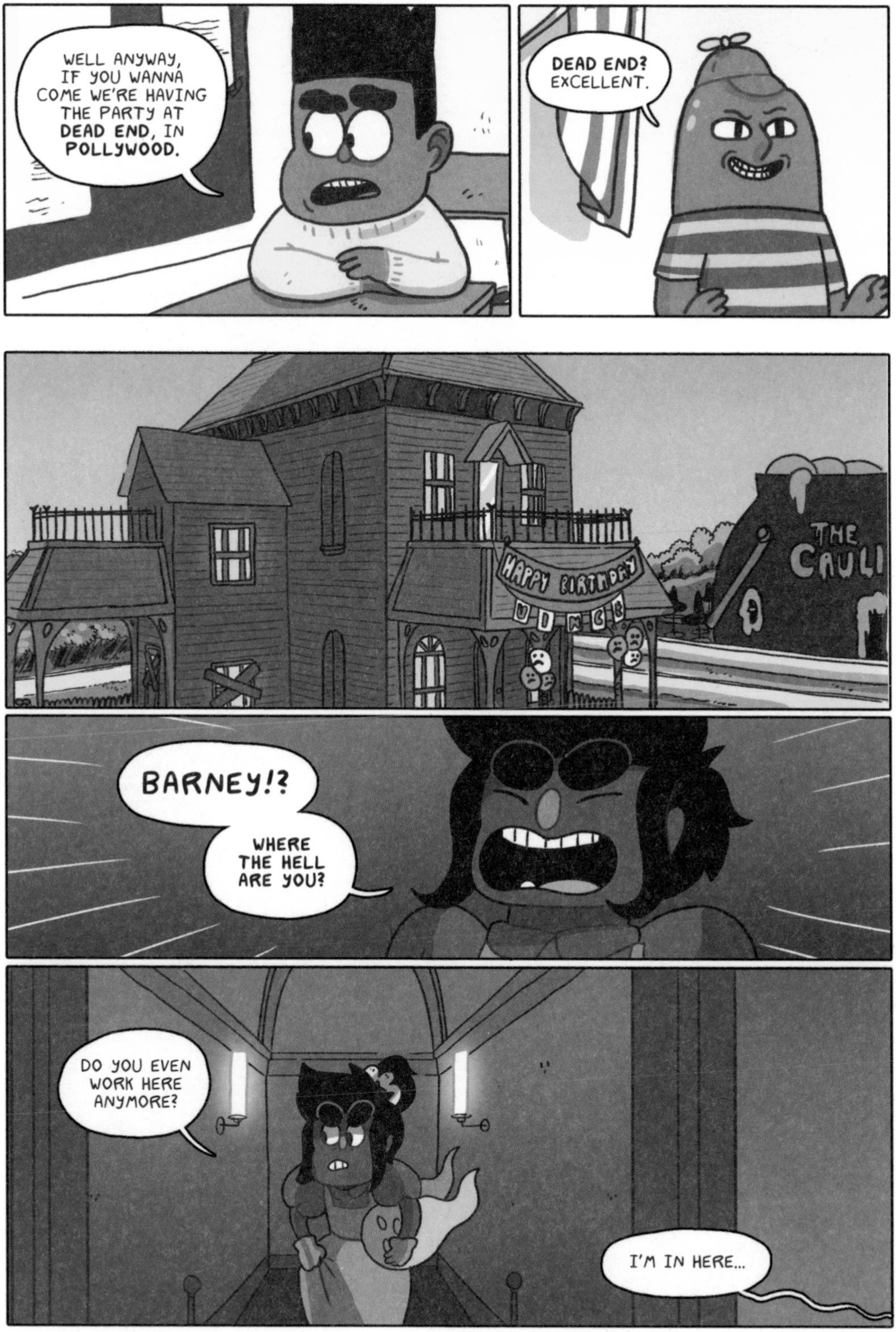
WELL ANYWAY, IF YOU WANNA COME WE'RE HAVING THE PARTY AT DEAD END, IN POLLYWOOD.
DEAD END? EXCELLENT.
HAPPY BIRTHDAY
THE CAULI
BARNEY!?
WHERE THE HELL ARE YOU?
DO YOU EVEN WORK HERE ANYMORE?
I'M IN HERE...

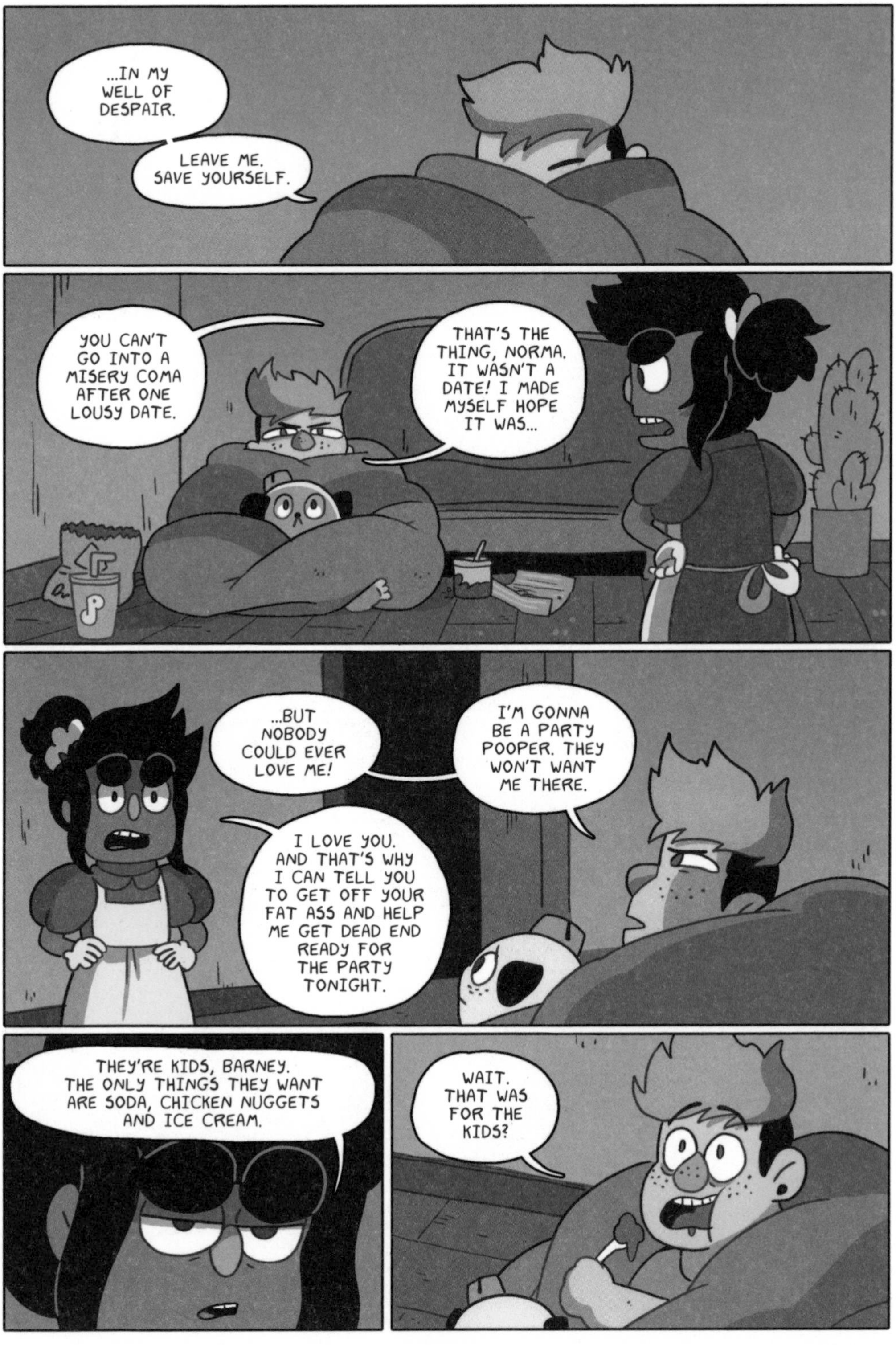
...IN MY WELL OF DESPAIR.
LEAVE ME. SAVE YOURSELF.
YOU CAN'T GO INTO A MISERY COMA AFTER ONE LOUSY DATE.
THAT'S THE THING, NORMA. IT WASN'T A DATE! I MADE MYSELF HOPE IT WAS...
...BUT NOBODY COULD EVER LOVE ME!
I'M GONNA BE A PARTY POOPER. THEY WON'T WANT ME THERE.
I LOVE YOU. AND THAT'S WHY I CAN TELL YOU TO GET OFF YOUR FAT ASS AND HELP ME GET DEAD END READY FOR THE PARTY TONIGHT.
THEY'RE KIDS, BARNEY. THE ONLY THINGS THEY WANT ARE SODA, CHICKEN NUGGETS AND ICE CREAM.
WAIT. THAT WAS FOR THE KIDS?

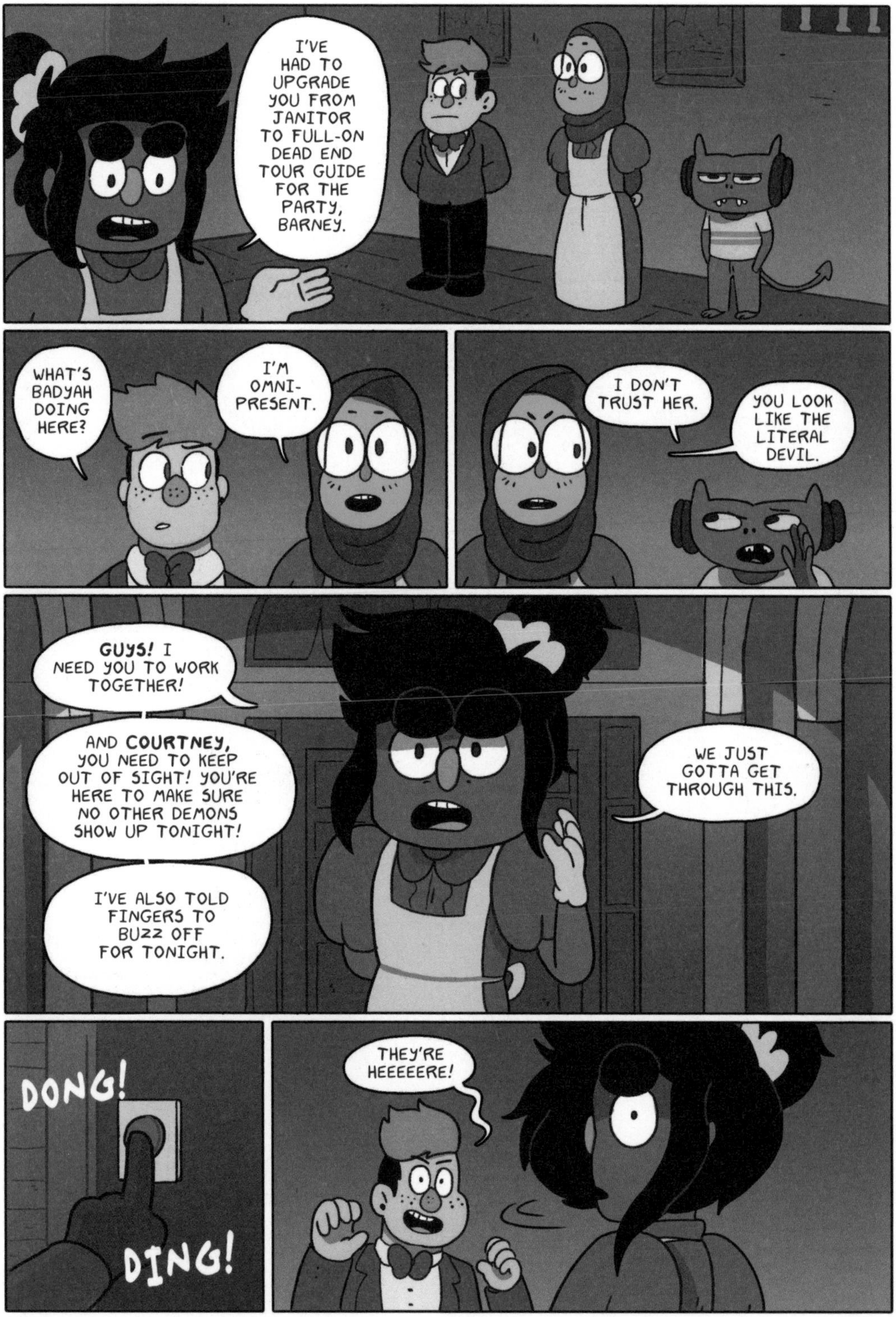
I'VE HAD TO UPGRADE YOU FROM JANITOR TO FULL-ON DEAD END TOUR GUIDE FOR THE PARTY, BARNEY.
WHAT'S BADYAH DOING HERE?
I'M OMNI-PRESENT.
I DON'T TRUST HER.
YOU LOOK LIKE THE LITERAL DEVIL.
GUYS! I NEED YOU TO WORK TOGETHER!
AND COURTNEY, YOU NEED TO KEEP OUT OF SIGHT! YOU'RE HERE TO MAKE SURE NO OTHER DEMONS SHOW UP TONIGHT!
I'VE ALSO TOLD FINGERS TO BUZZ OFF FOR TONIGHT.
WE JUST GOTTA GET THROUGH THIS.
DONG!
DING!
THEY'RE HEEEEERE!

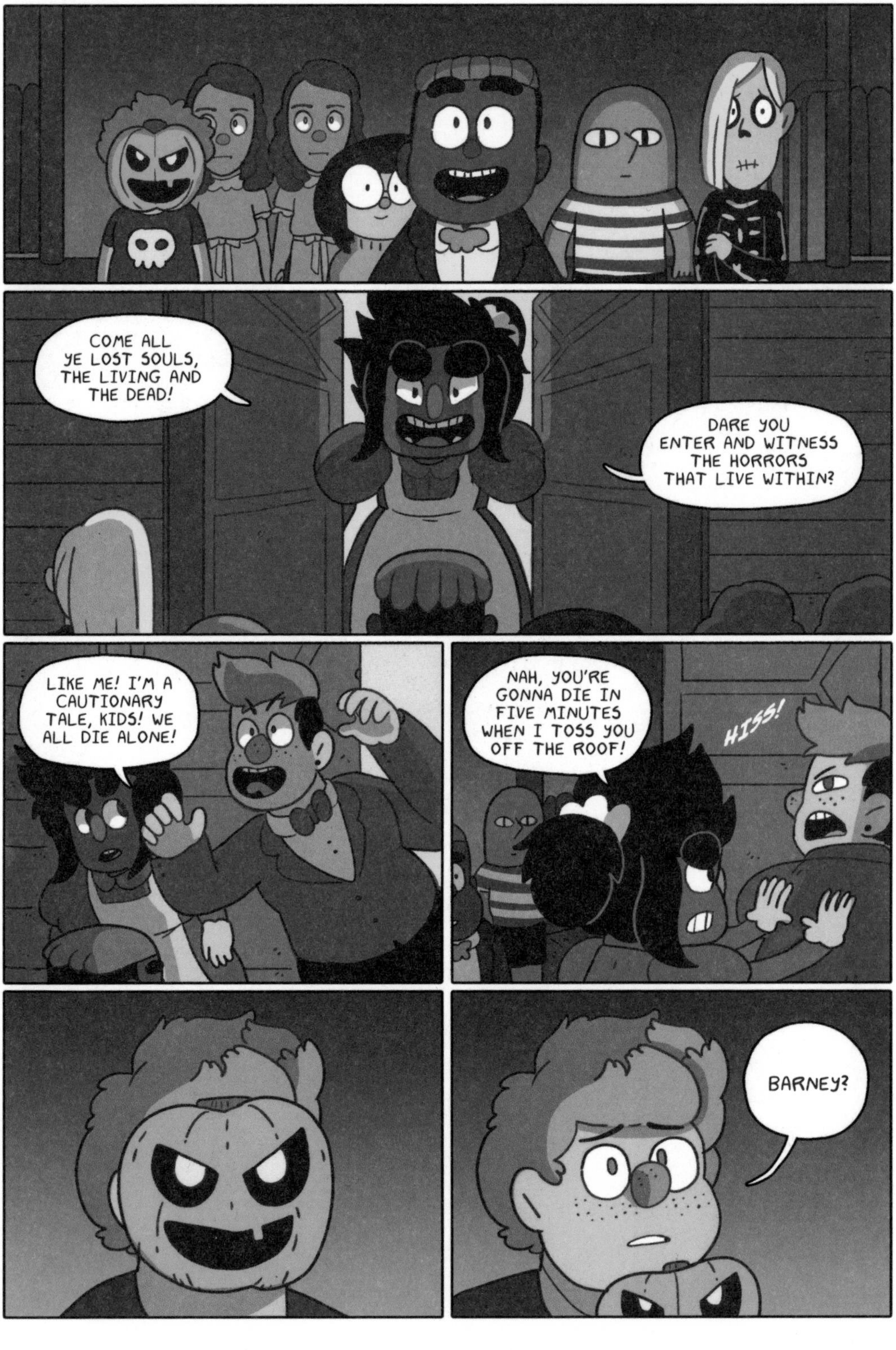
COME ALL YE LOST SOULS, THE LIVING AND THE DEAD!
DARE YOU ENTER AND WITNESS THE HORRORS THAT LIVE WITHIN?
LIKE ME! I'M A CAUTIONARY TALE, KIDS! WE ALL DIE ALONE!
NAH, YOU'RE GONNA DIE IN FIVE MINUTES WHEN I TOSS YOU OFF THE ROOF!
HISS!
BARNEY?

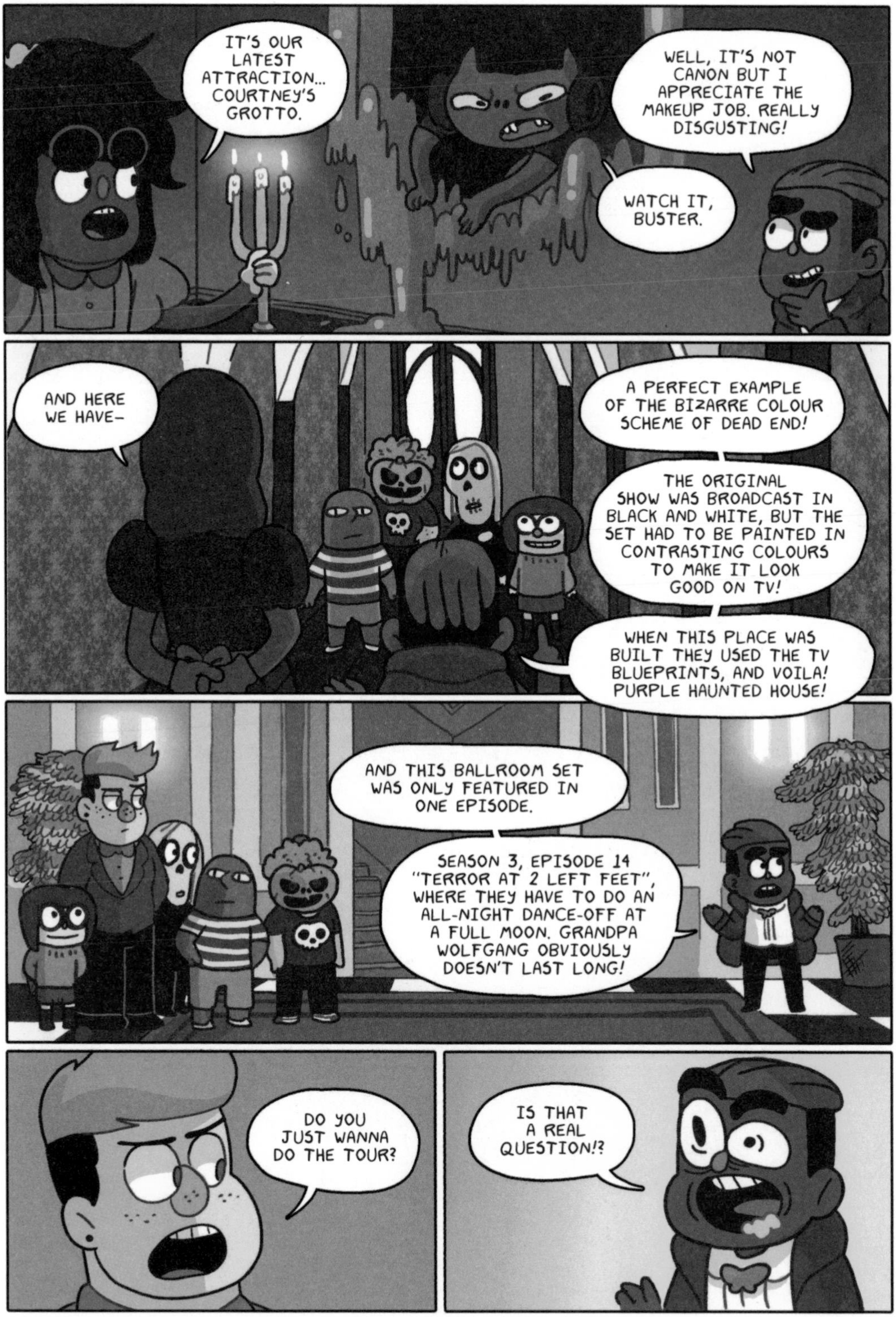
IT'S OUR LATEST ATTRACTION... COURTNEY'S GROTTO.
WELL, IT'S NOT CANON BUT I APPRECIATE THE MAKEUP JOB. REALLY DISGUSTING!
WATCH IT, BUSTER.
AND HERE WE HAVE–
A PERFECT EXAMPLE OF THE BIZARRE COLOUR SCHEME OF DEAD END!
THE ORIGINAL SHOW WAS BROADCAST IN BLACK AND WHITE, BUT THE SET HAD TO BE PAINTED IN CONTRASTING COLOURS TO MAKE IT LOOK GOOD ON TV!
WHEN THIS PLACE WAS BUILT THEY USED THE TV BLUEPRINTS, AND VOILA! PURPLE HAUNTED HOUSE!
AND THIS BALLROOM SET WAS ONLY FEATURED IN ONE EPISODE.
SEASON 3, EPISODE 14 "TERROR AT 2 LEFT FEET", WHERE THEY HAVE TO DO AN ALL-NIGHT DANCE-OFF AT A FULL MOON. GRANDPA WOLFGANG OBVIOUSLY DOESN'T LAST LONG!
DO YOU JUST WANNA DO THE TOUR?
IS THAT A REAL QUESTION!?

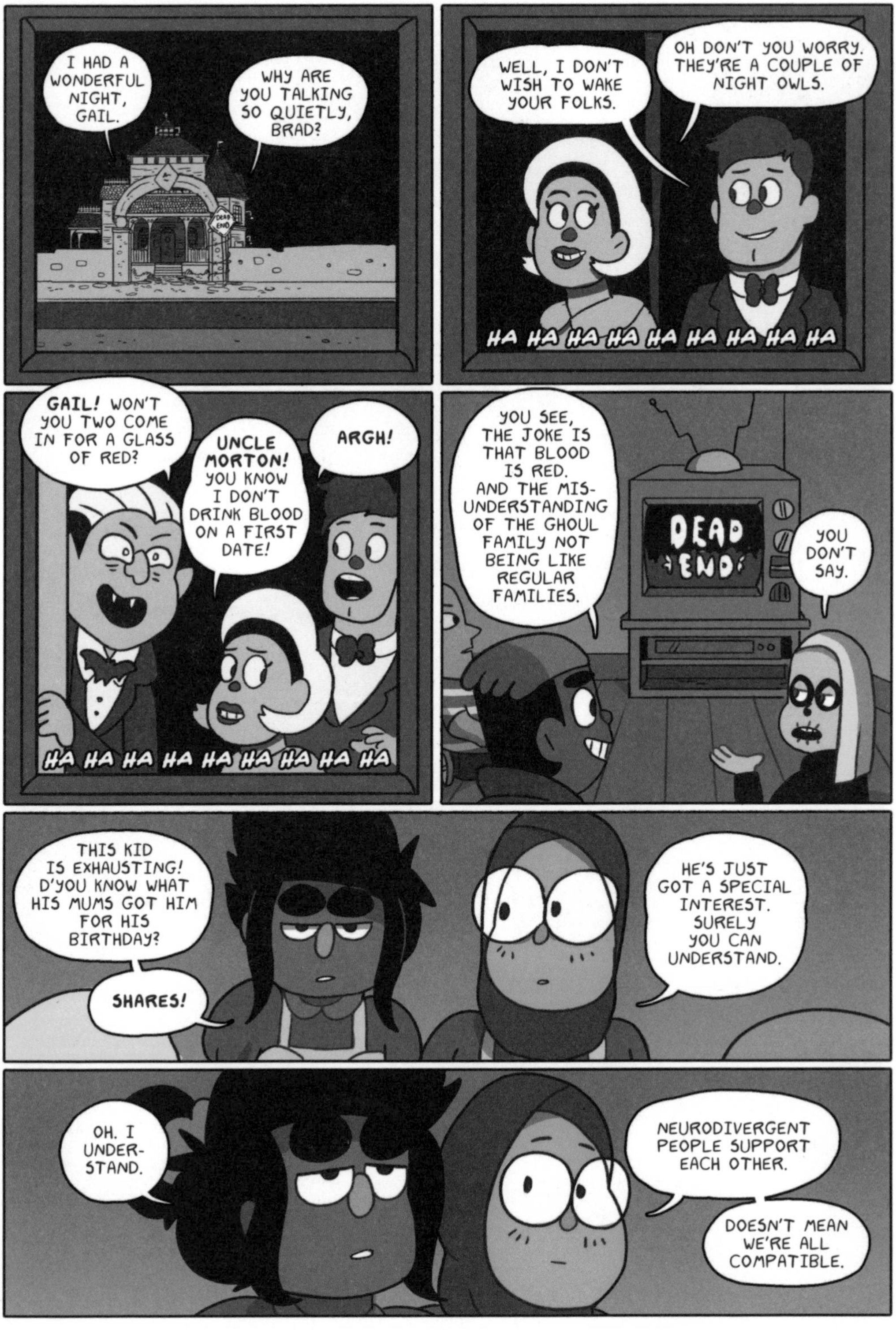
I HAD A WONDERFUL NIGHT, GAIL.
WHY ARE YOU TALKING SO QUIETLY, BRAD?
DEAD END
WELL, I DON'T WISH TO WAKE YOUR FOLKS.
OH DON'T YOU WORRY. THEY'RE A COUPLE OF NIGHT OWLS.
HA HA HA HA HA HA HA HA HA
GAIL! WON'T YOU TWO COME IN FOR A GLASS OF RED?
UNCLE MORTON! YOU KNOW I DON'T DRINK BLOOD ON A FIRST DATE!
ARGH!
HA HA HA HA HA HA HA HA HA
YOU SEE, THE JOKE IS THAT BLOOD IS RED. AND THE MIS-UNDERSTANDING OF THE GHOUL FAMILY NOT BEING LIKE REGULAR FAMILIES.
DEAD END
YOU DON'T SAY.
THIS KID IS EXHAUSTING! D'YOU KNOW WHAT HIS MUMS GOT HIM FOR HIS BIRTHDAY?
SHARES!
HE'S JUST GOT A SPECIAL INTEREST. SURELY YOU CAN UNDERSTAND.
OH. I UNDER-STAND.
NEURODIVERGENT PEOPLE SUPPORT EACH OTHER.
DOESN'T MEAN WE'RE ALL COMPATIBLE.

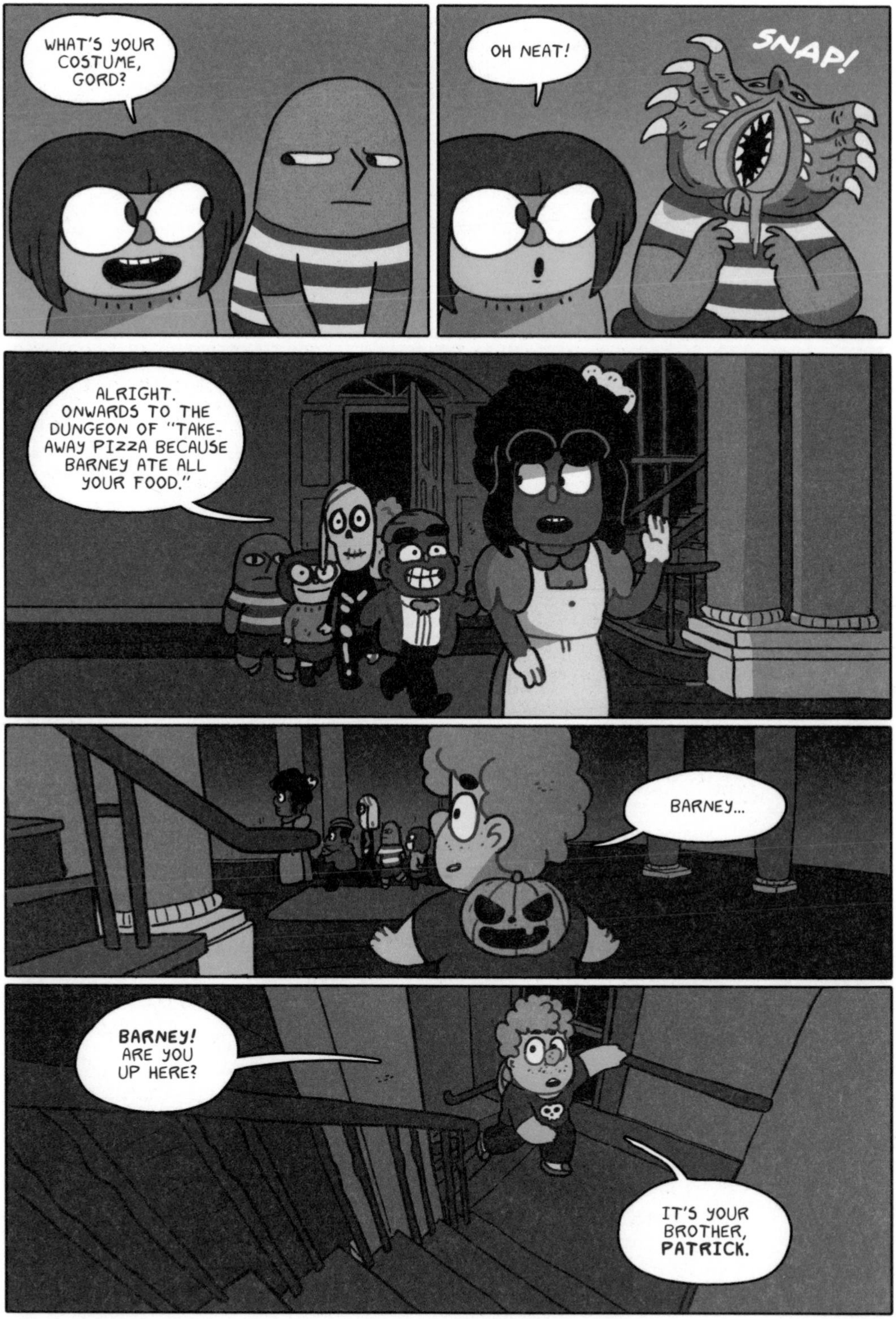
WHAT'S YOUR COSTUME, GORD?
OH NEAT!
SNAP!
ALRIGHT. ONWARDS TO THE DUNGEON OF "TAKE-AWAY PIZZA BECAUSE BARNEY ATE ALL YOUR FOOD."
BARNEY...
BARNEY! ARE YOU UP HERE?
IT'S YOUR BROTHER, PATRICK.

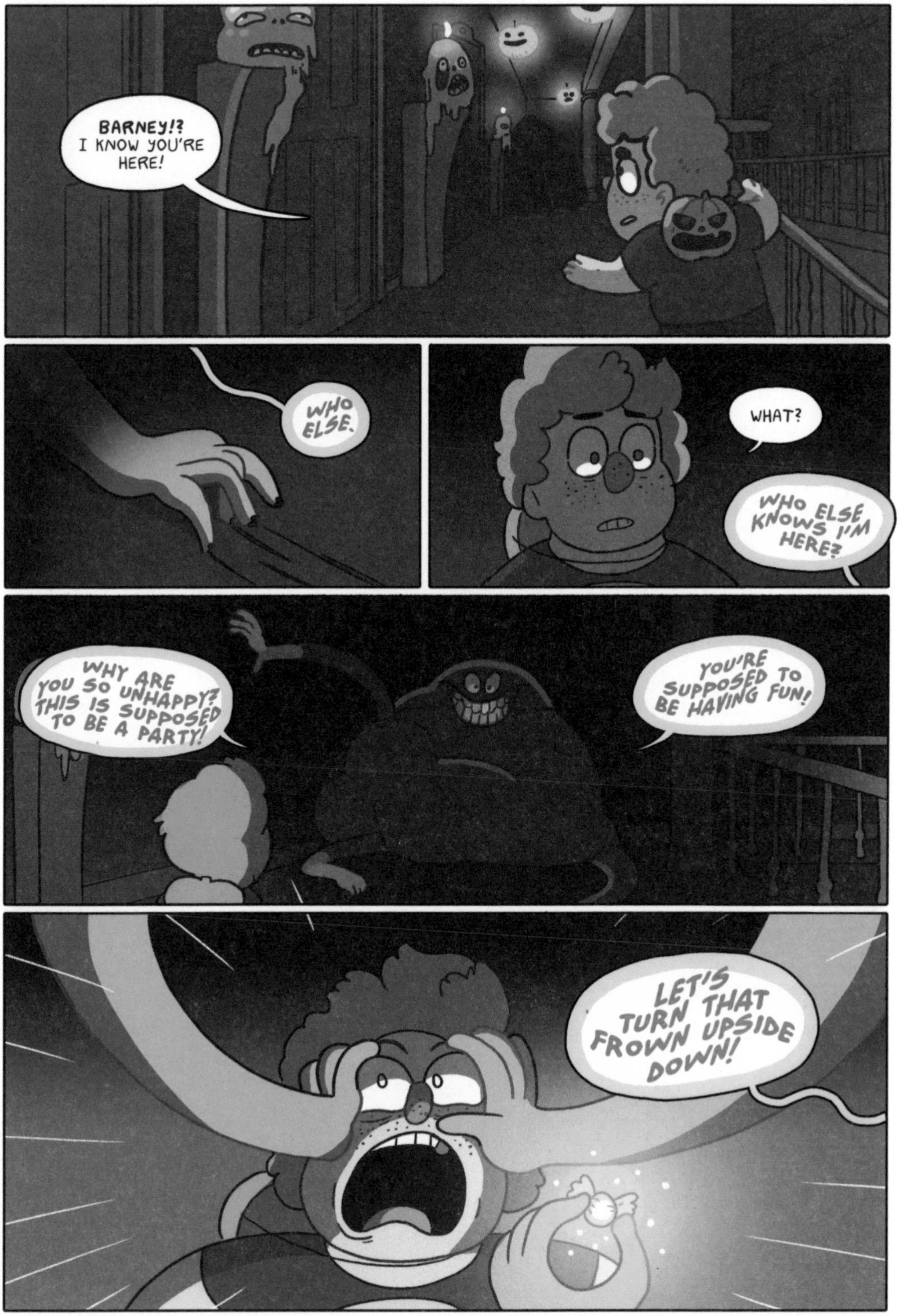

BARNEY!? I KNOW YOU'RE HERE!
WHO ELSE.
WHAT?
WHO ELSE KNOWS I'M HERE?
WHY ARE YOU SO UNHAPPY? THIS IS SUPPOSED TO BE A PARTY!
YOU'RE SUPPOSED TO BE HAVING FUN!
LET'S TURN THAT FROWN UPSIDE DOWN!

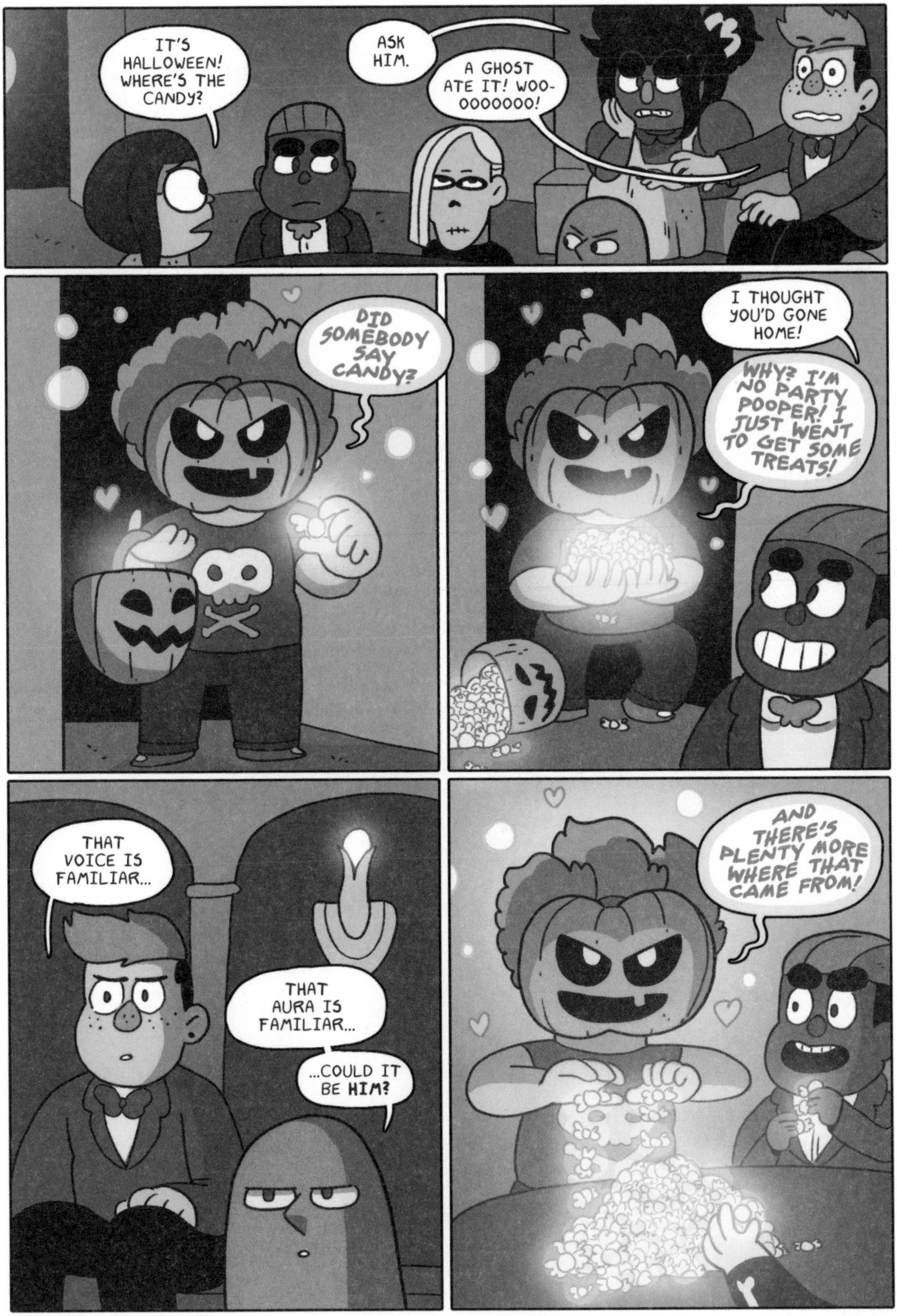
IT'S HALLOWEEN! WHERE'S THE CANDY?
ASK HIM.
A GHOST ATE IT! WOO-OOOOOOO!
DID SOMEBODY SAY CANDY?
I THOUGHT YOU'D GONE HOME!
WHY? I'M NO PARTY POOPER! I JUST WENT TO GET SOME TREATS!
THAT VOICE IS FAMILIAR...
THAT AURA IS FAMILIAR...
...COULD IT BE HIM?
AND THERE'S PLENTY MORE WHERE THAT CAME FROM!

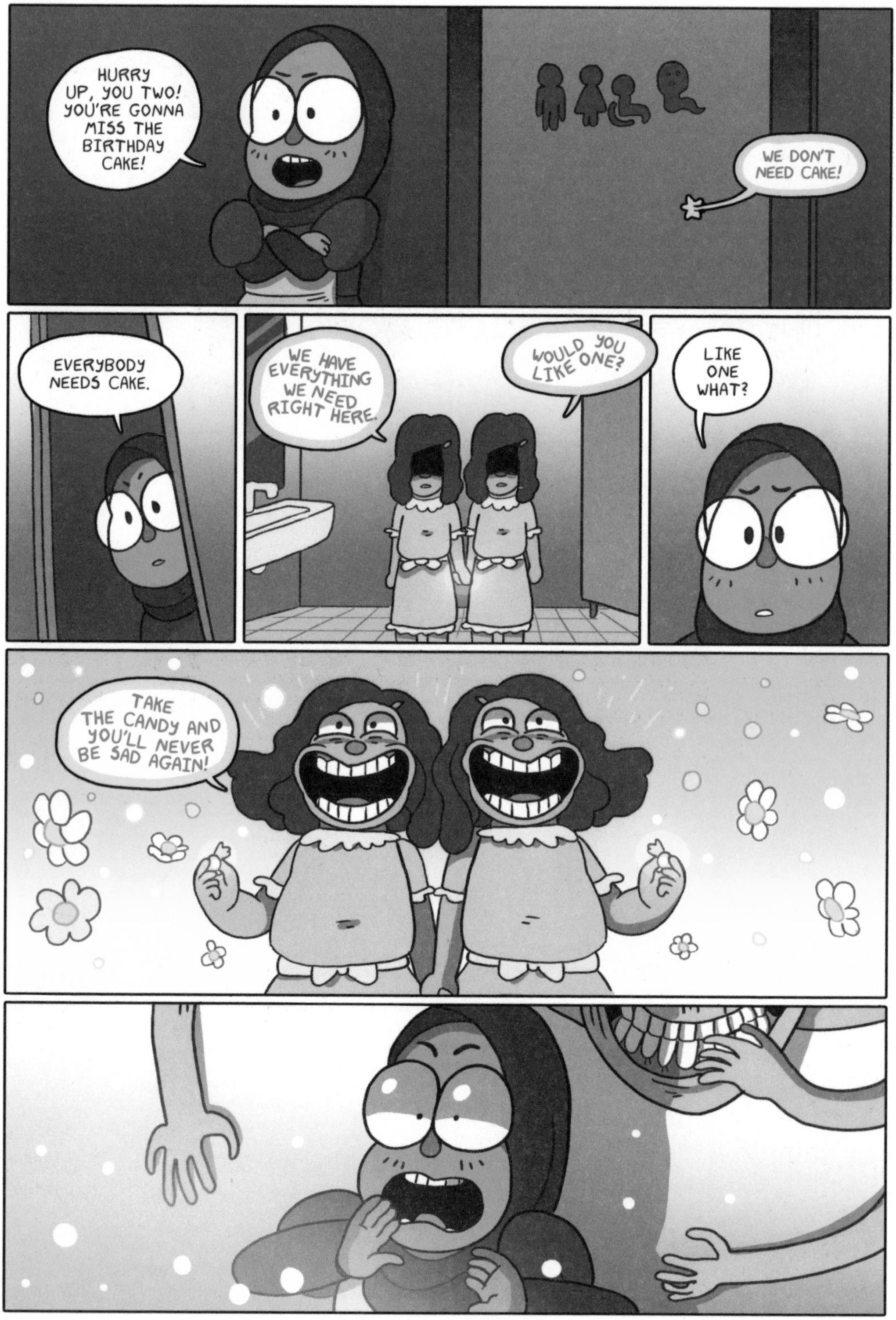
HURRY UP, YOU TWO! YOU'RE GONNA MISS THE BIRTHDAY CAKE!
WE DON'T NEED CAKE!
EVERYBODY NEEDS CAKE.
WE HAVE EVERYTHING WE NEED RIGHT HERE.
WOULD YOU LIKE ONE?
LIKE ONE WHAT?
TAKE THE CANDY AND YOU'LL NEVER BE SAD AGAIN!

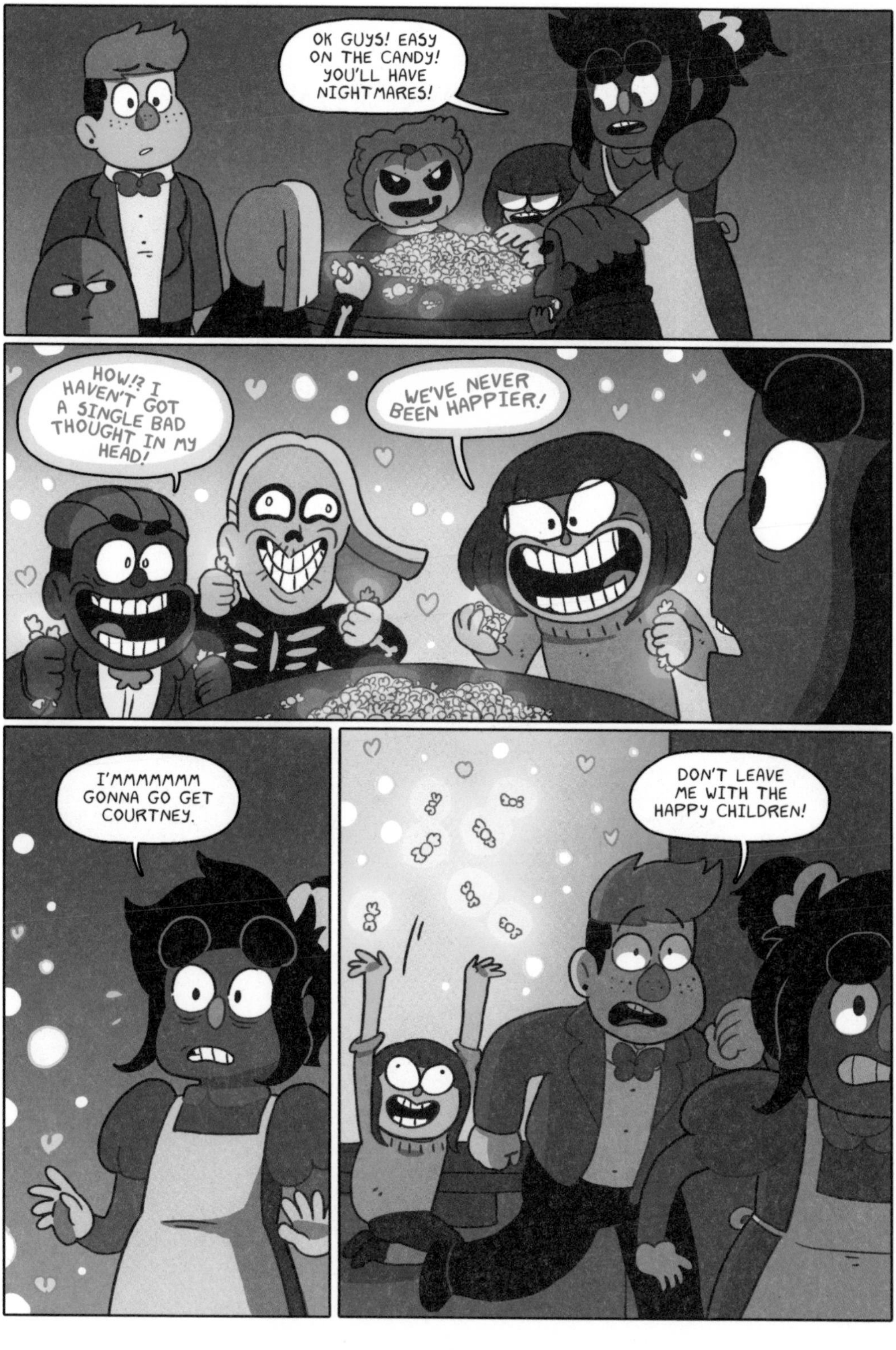
OK GUYS! EASY ON THE CANDY! YOU'LL HAVE NIGHTMARES!
HOW!? I HAVEN'T GOT A SINGLE BAD THOUGHT IN MY HEAD!
WE'VE NEVER BEEN HAPPIER!
I'MMMMMMM GONNA GO GET COURTNEY.
DON'T LEAVE ME WITH THE HAPPY CHILDREN!

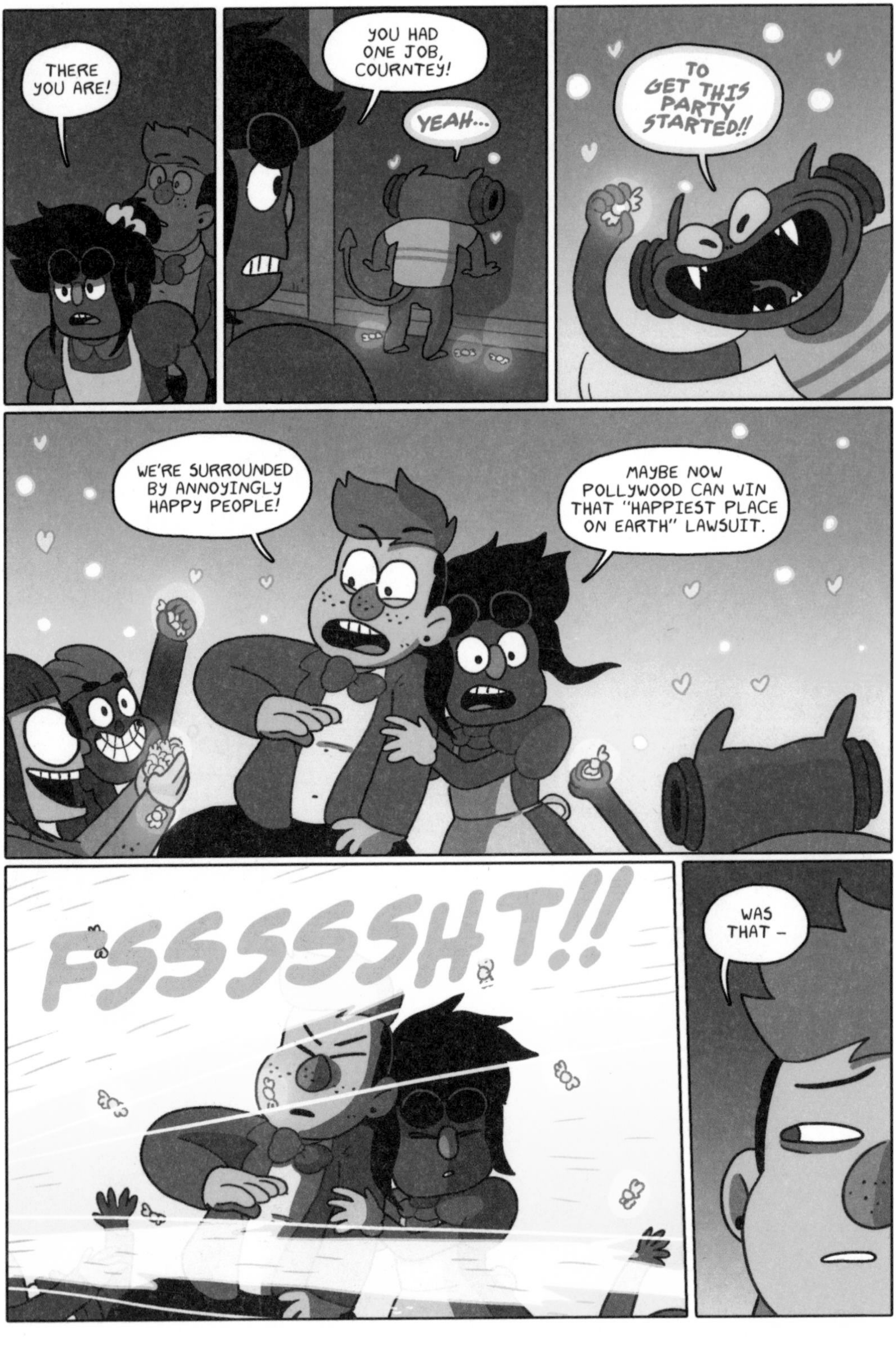
THERE YOU ARE!
YOU HAD ONE JOB, COURNTEY!
YEAH...
TO GET THIS PARTY STARTED!!
WE'RE SURROUNDED BY ANNOYINGLY HAPPY PEOPLE!
MAYBE NOW POLLYWOOD CAN WIN THAT "HAPPIEST PLACE ON EARTH" LAWSUIT.
FSSSSSHT!!
WAS THAT –

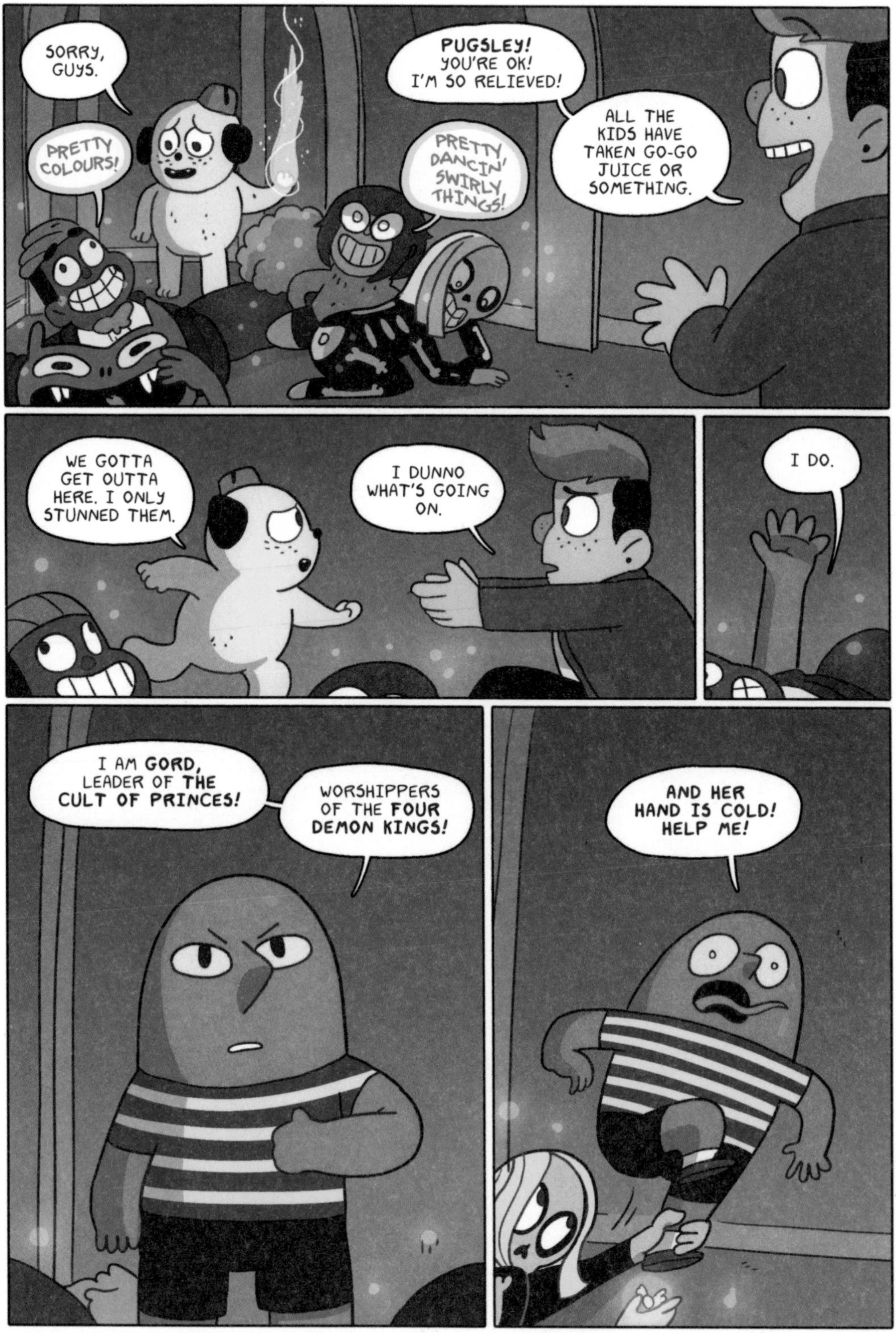

SORRY, GUYS.
PRETTY COLOURS!
PUGSLEY! YOU'RE OK! I'M SO RELIEVED!
PRETTY, DANCIN' SWIRLY THINGS!
ALL THE KIDS HAVE TAKEN GO-GO JUICE OR SOMETHING.
WE GOTTA GET OUTTA HERE. I ONLY STUNNED THEM.
I DUNNO WHAT'S GOING ON.
I DO.
I AM GORD, LEADER OF THE CULT OF PRINCES!
WORSHIPPERS OF THE FOUR DEMON KINGS!
AND HER HAND IS COLD! HELP ME!

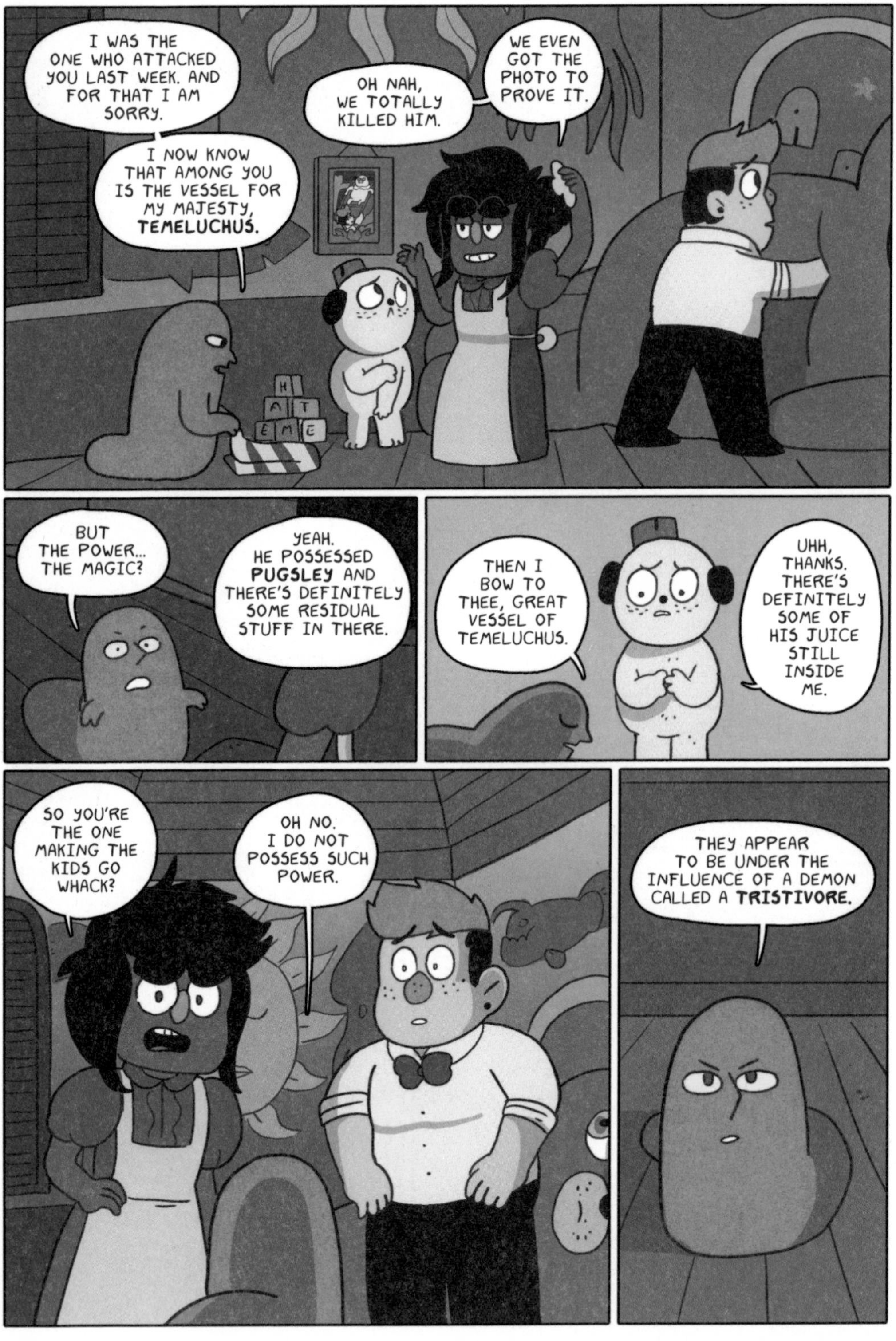
I WAS THE ONE WHO ATTACKED YOU LAST WEEK. AND FOR THAT I AM SORRY.
I NOW KNOW THAT AMONG YOU IS THE VESSEL FOR MY MAJESTY, TEMELUCHUS.
OH NAH, WE TOTALLY KILLED HIM.
WE EVEN GOT THE PHOTO TO PROVE IT.
BUT THE POWER... THE MAGIC?
YEAH. HE POSSESSED PUGSLEY AND THERE'S DEFINITELY SOME RESIDUAL STUFF IN THERE.
THEN I BOW TO THEE, GREAT VESSEL OF TEMELUCHUS.
UHH, THANKS. THERE'S DEFINITELY SOME OF HIS JUICE STILL INSIDE ME.
SO YOU'RE THE ONE MAKING THE KIDS GO WHACK?
OH NO. I DO NOT POSSESS SUCH POWER.
THEY APPEAR TO BE UNDER THE INFLUENCE OF A DEMON CALLED A TRISTIVORE.

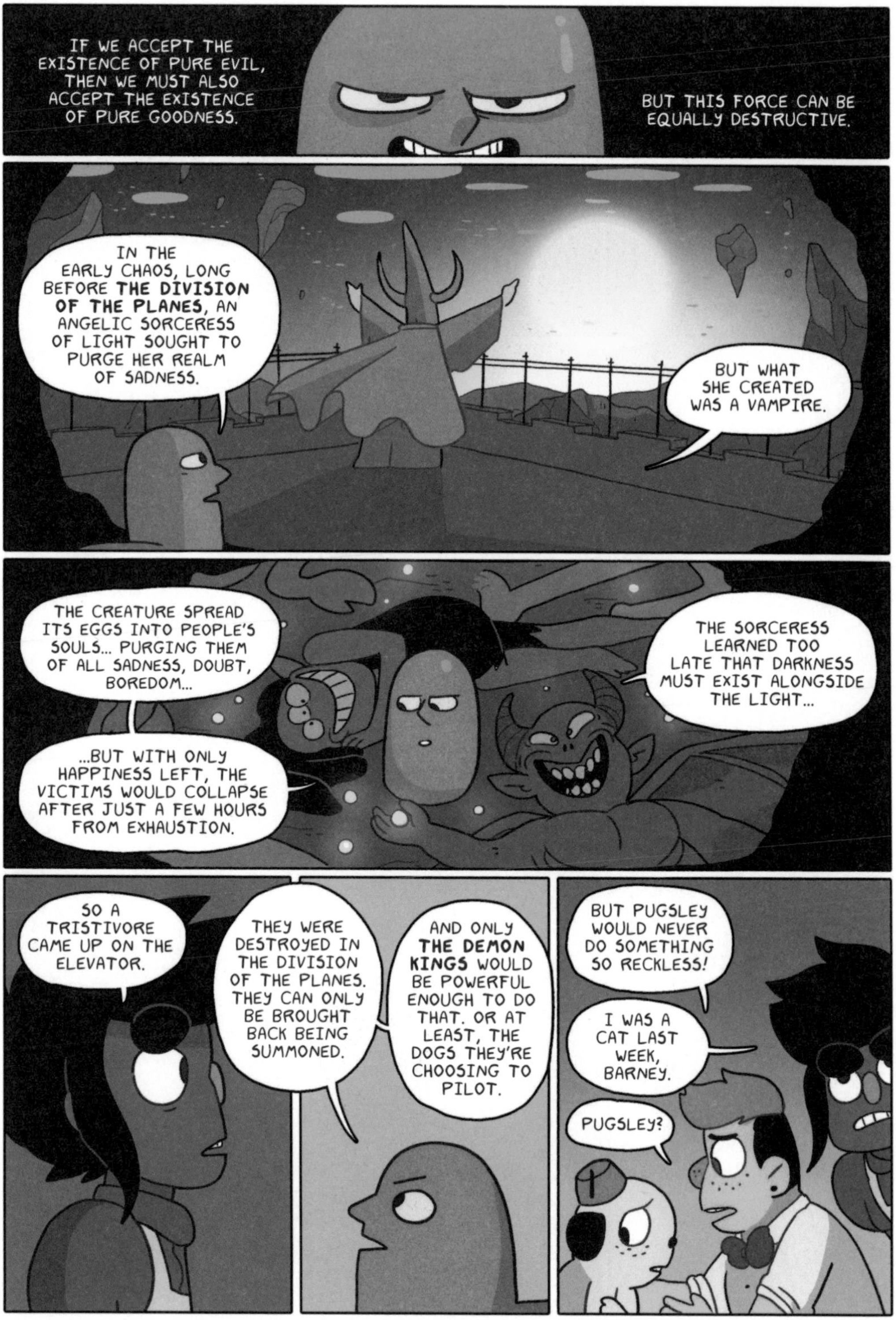
IF WE ACCEPT THE EXISTENCE OF PURE EVIL, THEN WE MUST ALSO ACCEPT THE EXISTENCE OF PURE GOODNESS.
BUT THIS FORCE CAN BE EQUALLY DESTRUCTIVE.
IN THE EARLY CHAOS, LONG BEFORE **THE DIVISION OF THE PLANES**, AN ANGELIC SORCERESS OF LIGHT SOUGHT TO PURGE HER REALM OF SADNESS.
BUT WHAT SHE CREATED WAS A VAMPIRE.
THE CREATURE SPREAD ITS EGGS INTO PEOPLE'S SOULS... PURGING THEM OF ALL SADNESS, DOUBT, BOREDOM...
...BUT WITH ONLY HAPPINESS LEFT, THE VICTIMS WOULD COLLAPSE AFTER JUST A FEW HOURS FROM EXHAUSTION.
THE SORCERESS LEARNED TOO LATE THAT DARKNESS MUST EXIST ALONGSIDE THE LIGHT...
SO A TRISTIVORE CAME UP ON THE ELEVATOR.
THEY WERE DESTROYED IN THE DIVISION OF THE PLANES. THEY CAN ONLY BE BROUGHT BACK BEING SUMMONED.
AND ONLY **THE DEMON KINGS** WOULD BE POWERFUL ENOUGH TO DO THAT. OR AT LEAST, THE DOGS THEY'RE CHOOSING TO PILOT.
BUT PUGSLEY WOULD NEVER DO SOMETHING SO RECKLESS!
I WAS A CAT LAST WEEK, BARNEY.
PUGSLEY?

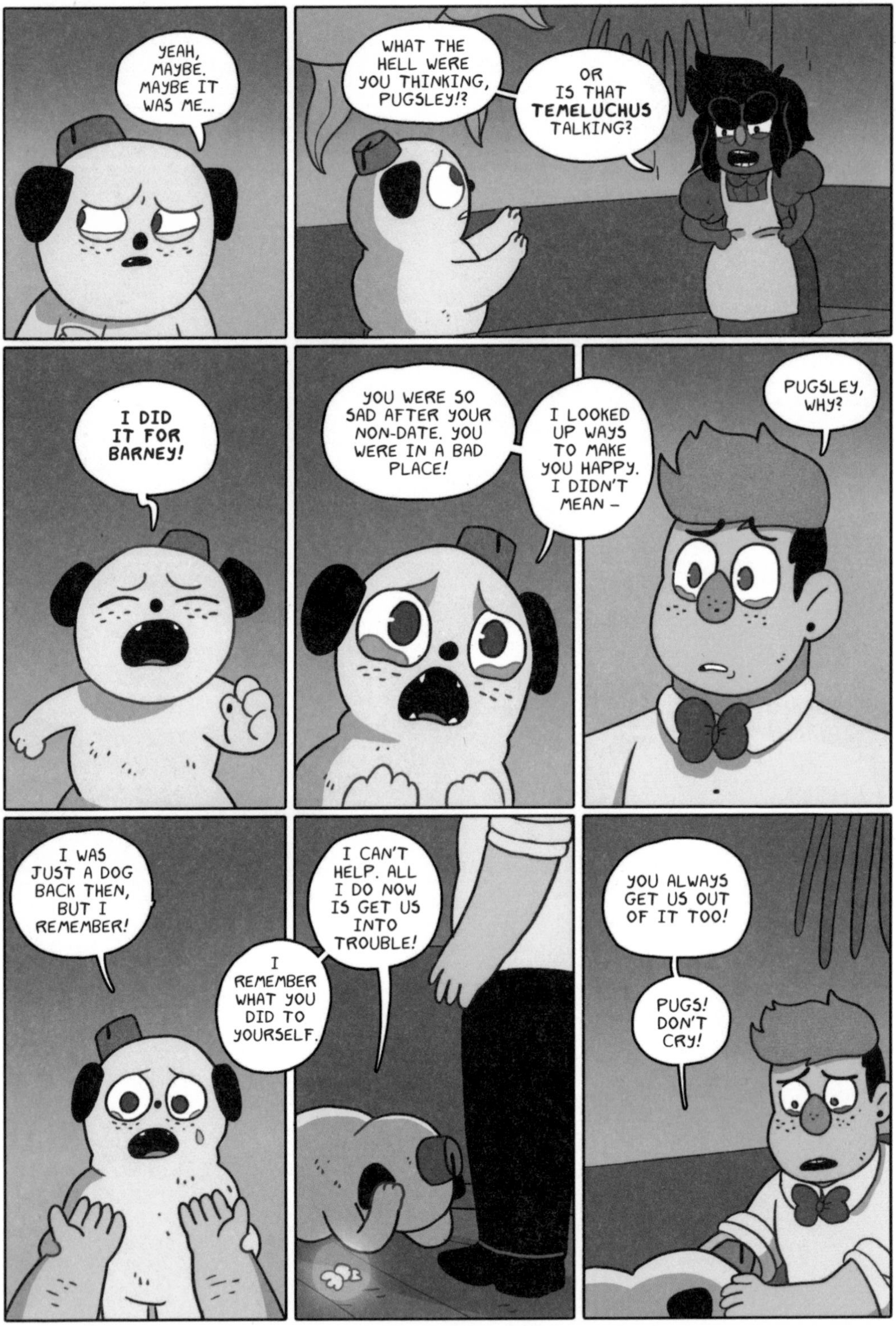
YEAH, MAYBE. MAYBE IT WAS ME...
WHAT THE HELL WERE YOU THINKING, PUGSLEY!?
OR IS THAT **TEMELUCHUS** TALKING?
I DID IT FOR BARNEY!
YOU WERE SO SAD AFTER YOUR NON-DATE. YOU WERE IN A BAD PLACE!
I LOOKED UP WAYS TO MAKE YOU HAPPY. I DIDN'T MEAN –
PUGSLEY, WHY?
I WAS JUST A DOG BACK THEN, BUT I REMEMBER!
I REMEMBER WHAT YOU DID TO YOURSELF.
I CAN'T HELP. ALL I DO NOW IS GET US INTO TROUBLE!
YOU ALWAYS GET US OUT OF IT TOO!
PUGS! DON'T CRY!

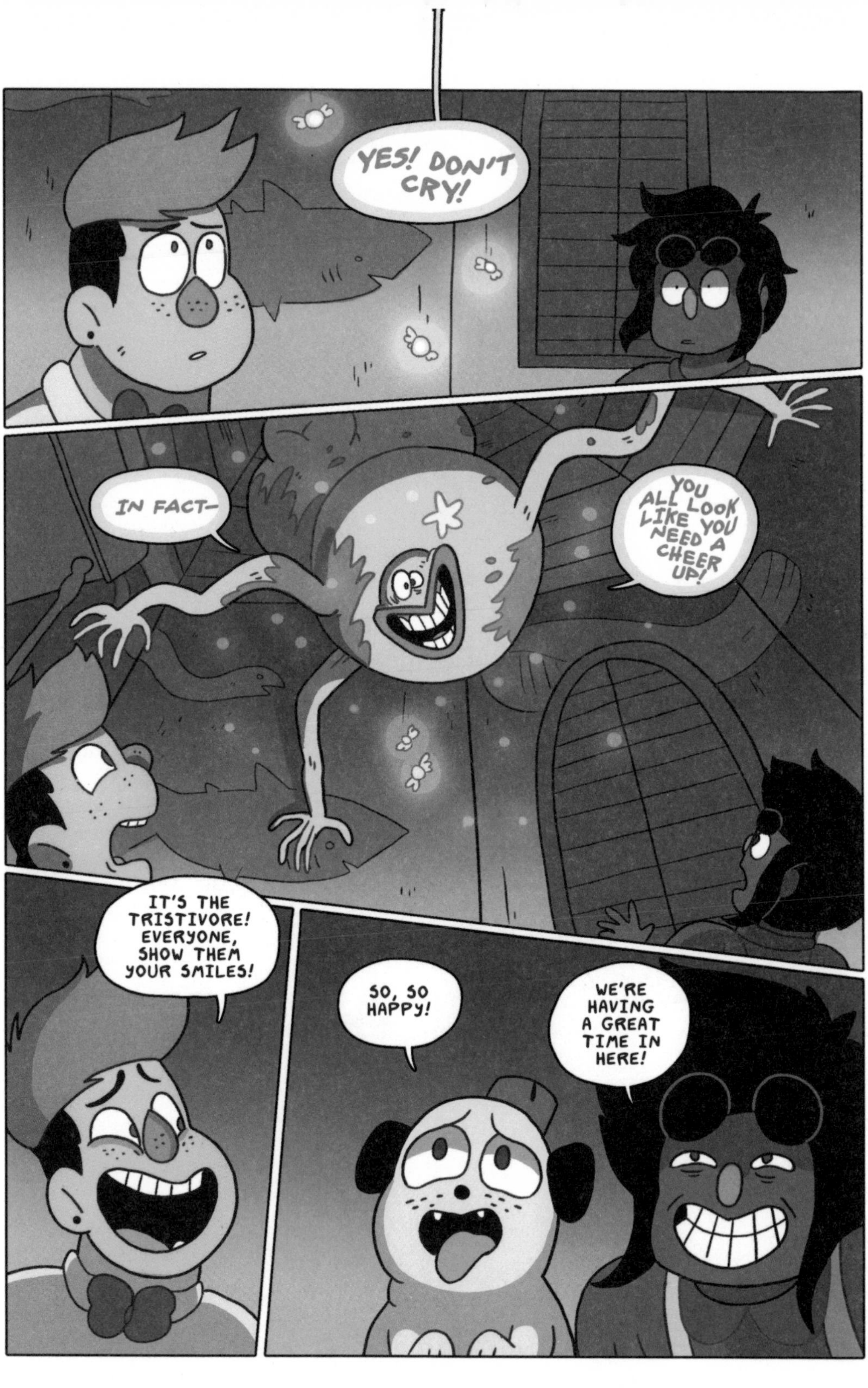
YES! DON'T CRY!
IN FACT—
YOU ALL LOOK LIKE YOU NEED A CHEER UP!
IT'S THE TRISTIVORE! EVERYONE, SHOW THEM YOUR SMILES!
SO, SO HAPPY!
WE'RE HAVING A GREAT TIME IN HERE!

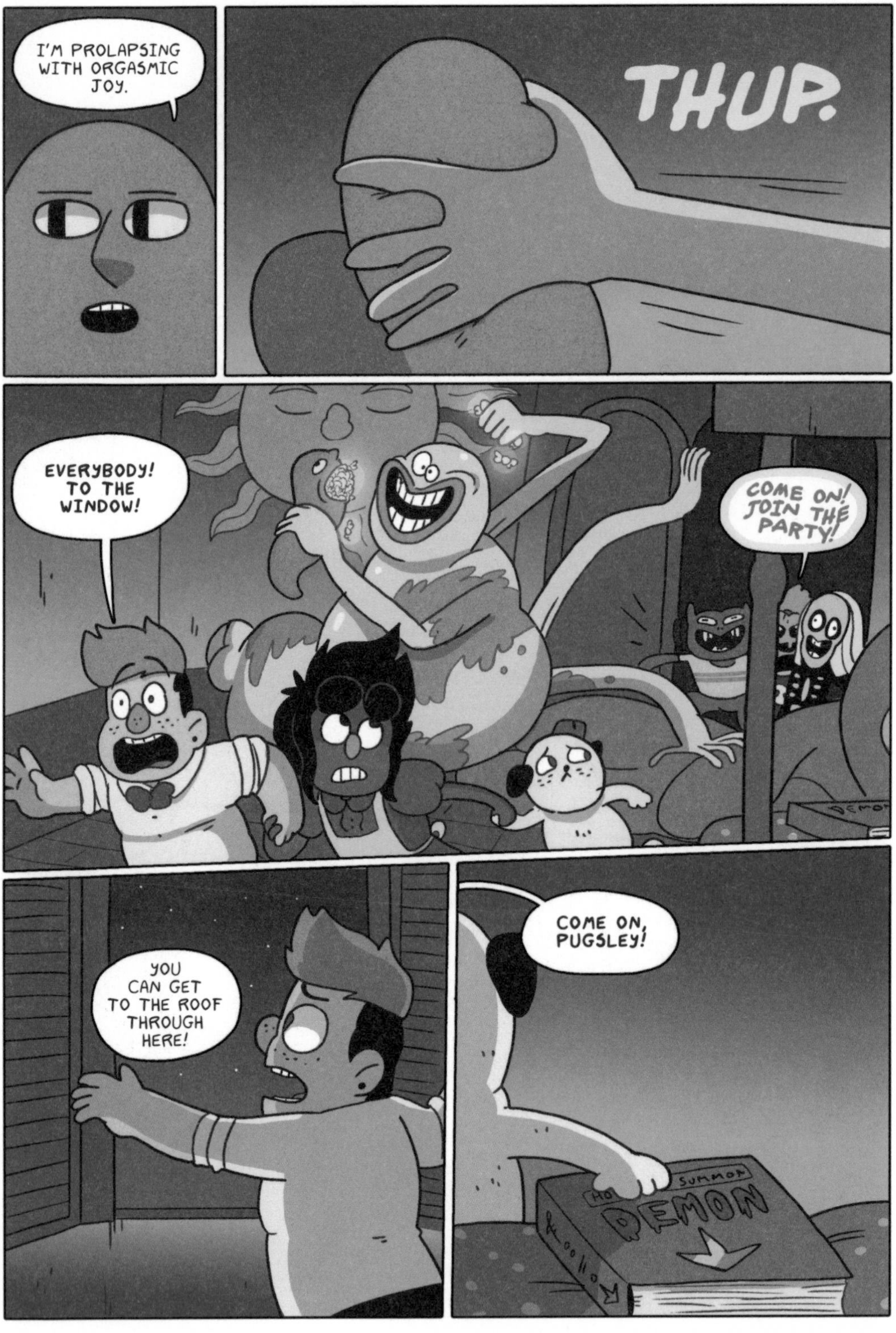
I'M PROLAPSING WITH ORGASMIC JOY.
THUP.
EVERYBODY! TO THE WINDOW!
COME ON! JOIN THE PARTY!
YOU CAN GET TO THE ROOF THROUGH HERE!
COME ON, PUGSLEY!
SUMMON
DEMON

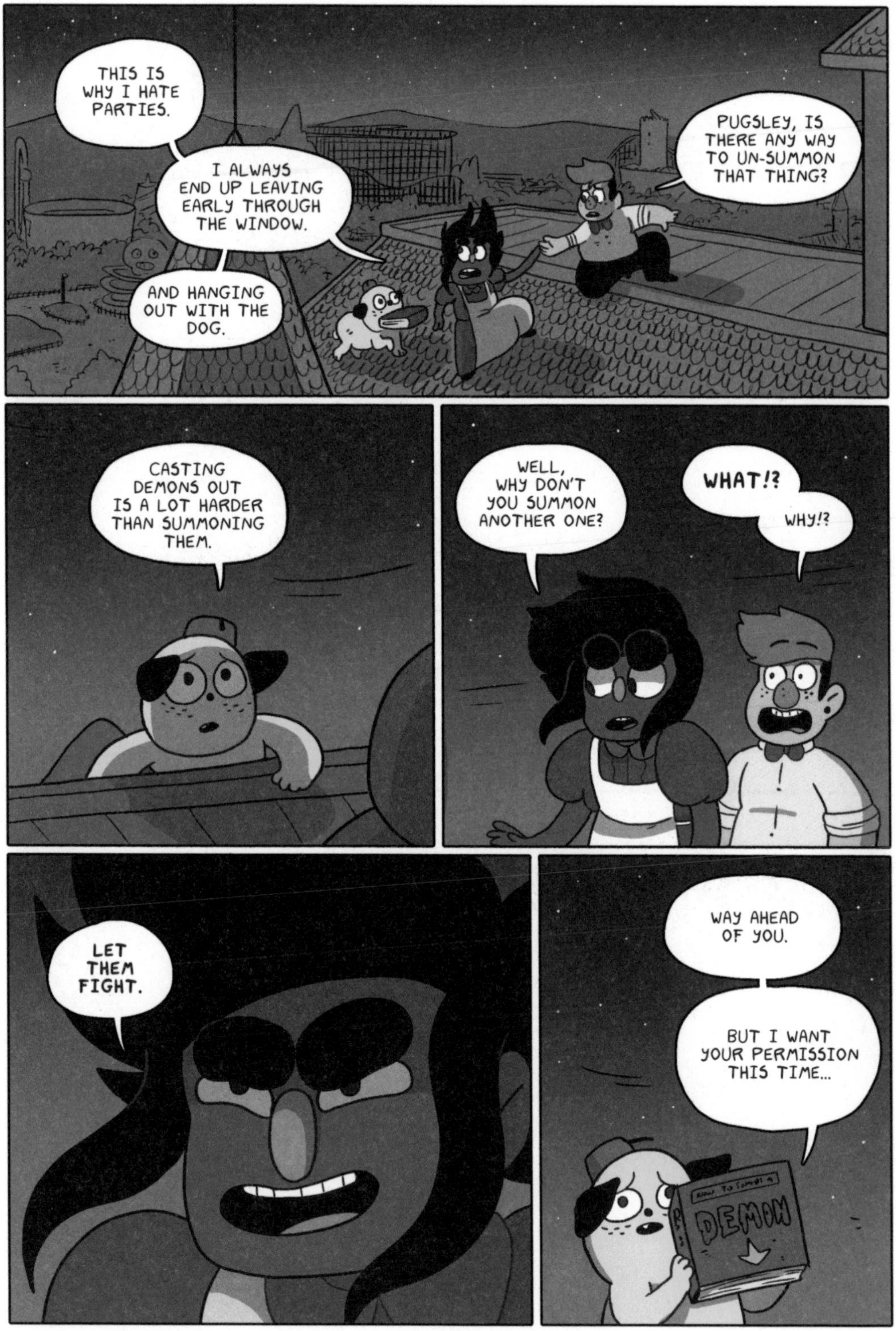
THIS IS WHY I HATE PARTIES.
I ALWAYS END UP LEAVING EARLY THROUGH THE WINDOW.
AND HANGING OUT WITH THE DOG.
PUGSLEY, IS THERE ANY WAY TO UN-SUMMON THAT THING?
CASTING DEMONS OUT IS A LOT HARDER THAN SUMMONING THEM.
WELL, WHY DON'T YOU SUMMON ANOTHER ONE?
WHAT!?
WHY!?
LET THEM FIGHT.
WAY AHEAD OF YOU.
BUT I WANT YOUR PERMISSION THIS TIME...
DEMON

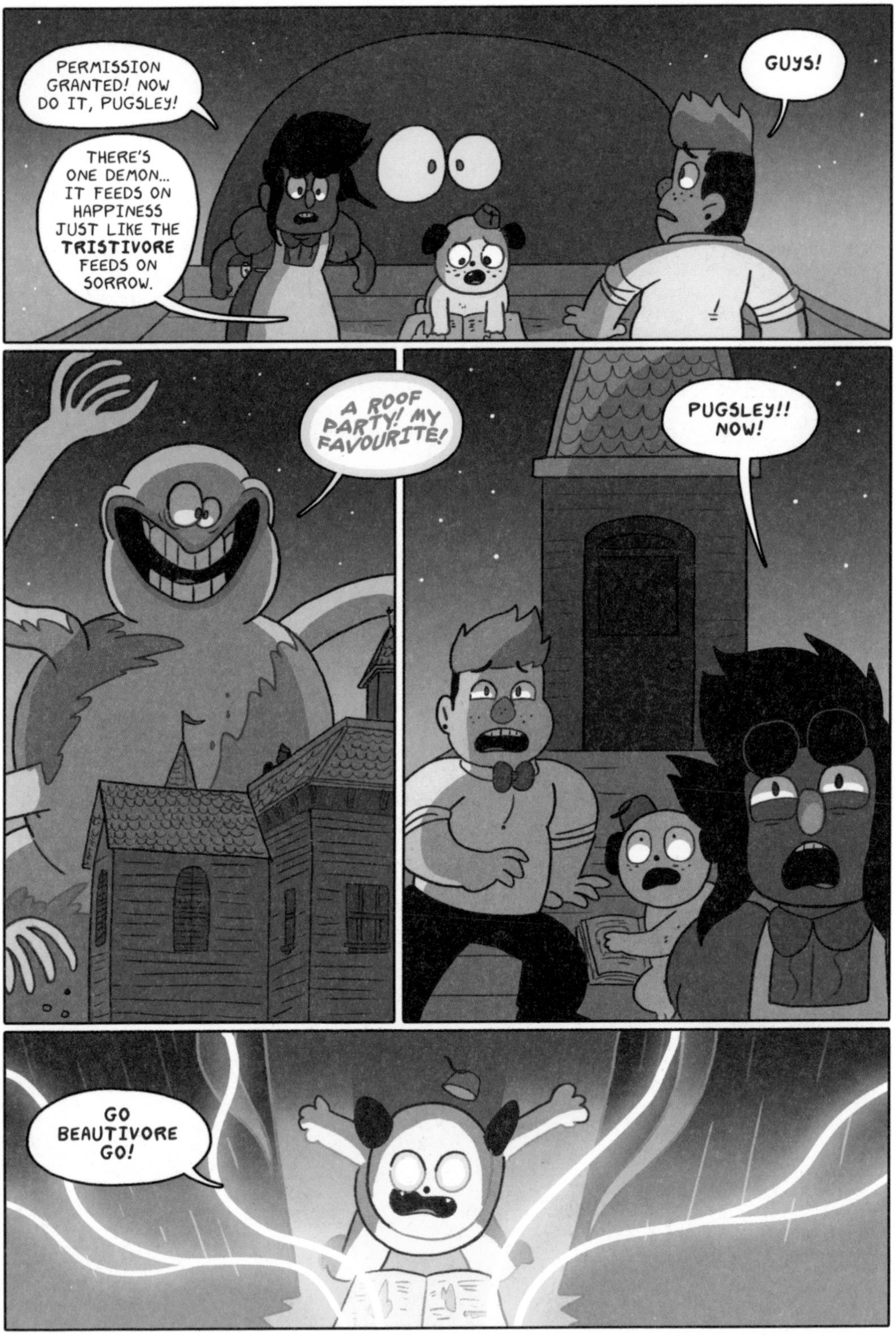
PERMISSION GRANTED! NOW DO IT, PUGSLEY!
THERE'S ONE DEMON... IT FEEDS ON HAPPINESS JUST LIKE THE **TRISTIVORE** FEEDS ON SORROW.
GUYS!
A ROOF PARTY! MY FAVOURITE!
PUGSLEY!! NOW!
GO BEAUTIVORE GO!

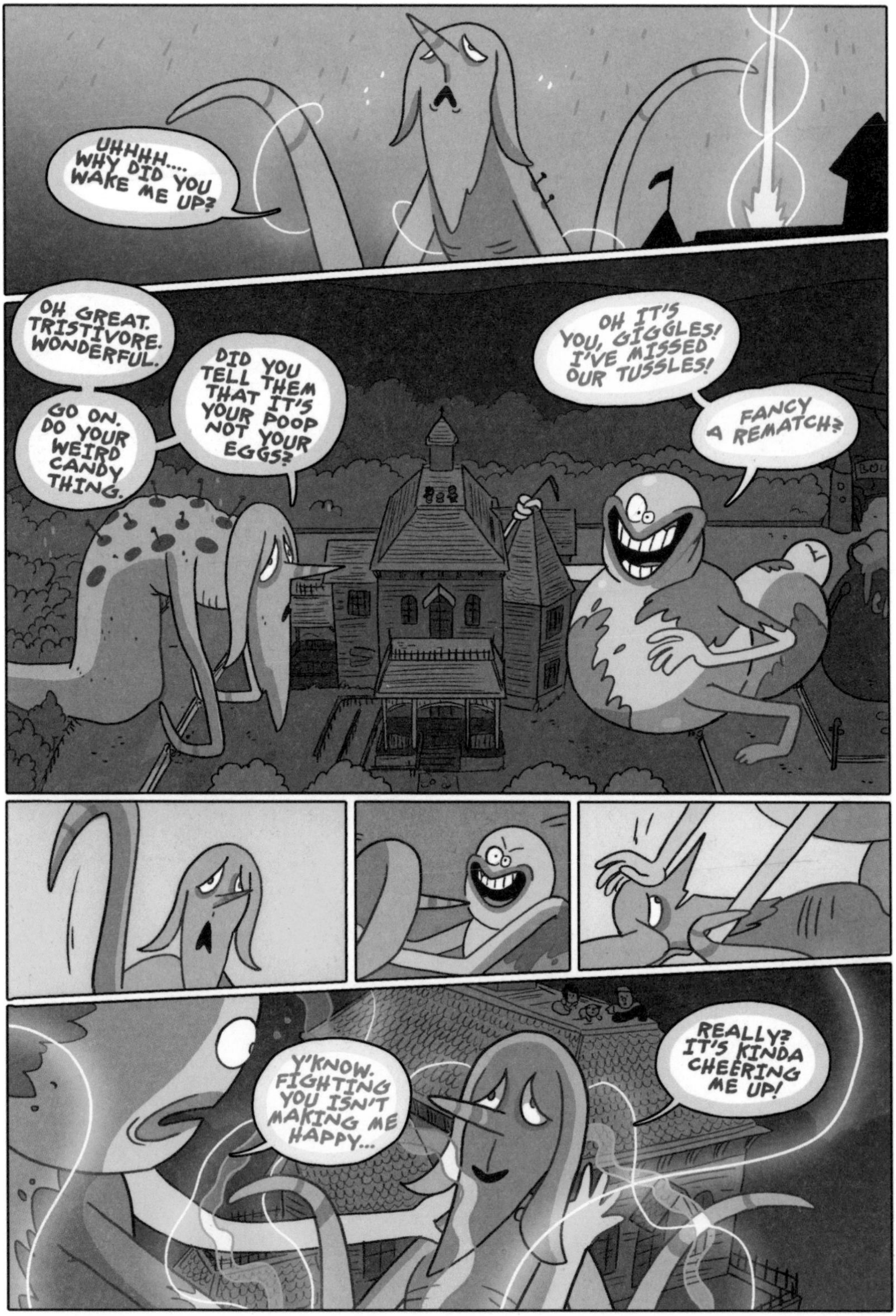
UHHHH....
WHY DID YOU
WAKE ME UP?
OH GREAT.
TRISTIVORE.
WONDERFUL.
GO ON.
DO YOUR
WEIRD
CANDY
THING.
DID YOU
TELL THEM
THAT IT'S
YOUR POOP
NOT YOUR
EGGS?
OH IT'S
YOU, GIGGLES!
I'VE MISSED
OUR TUSSLES!
FANCY
A REMATCH?
Y'KNOW.
FIGHTING
YOU ISN'T
MAKING ME
HAPPY...
REALLY?
IT'S KINDA
CHEERING
ME UP!

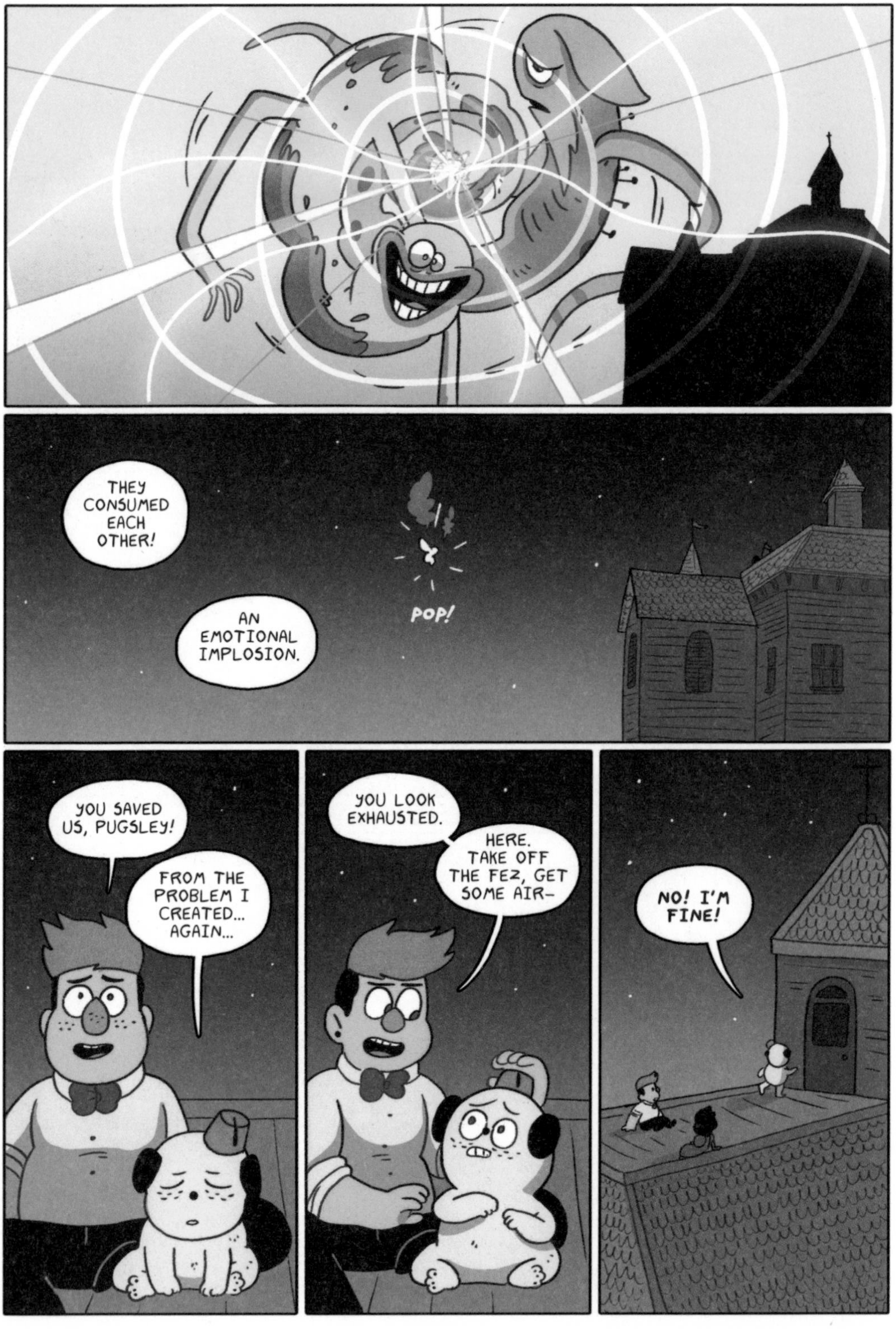
THEY CONSUMED EACH OTHER!
AN EMOTIONAL IMPLOSION.
POP!
YOU SAVED US, PUGSLEY!
FROM THE PROBLEM I CREATED... AGAIN...
YOU LOOK EXHAUSTED.
HERE. TAKE OFF THE FEZ, GET SOME AIR-
NO! I'M FINE!

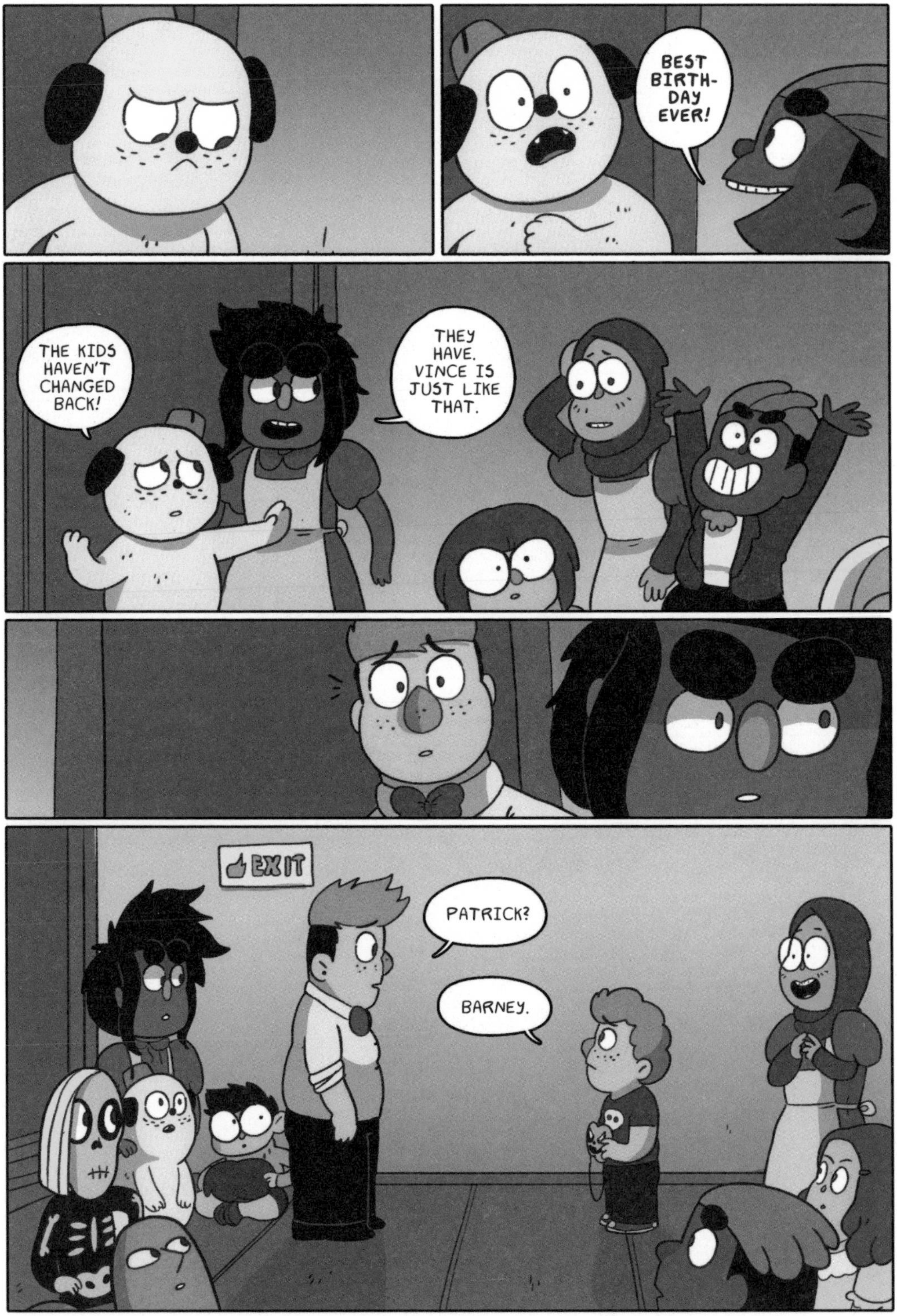
BEST BIRTH-DAY EVER!
THE KIDS HAVEN'T CHANGED BACK!
THEY HAVE. VINCE IS JUST LIKE THAT.
EXIT
PATRICK?
BARNEY.

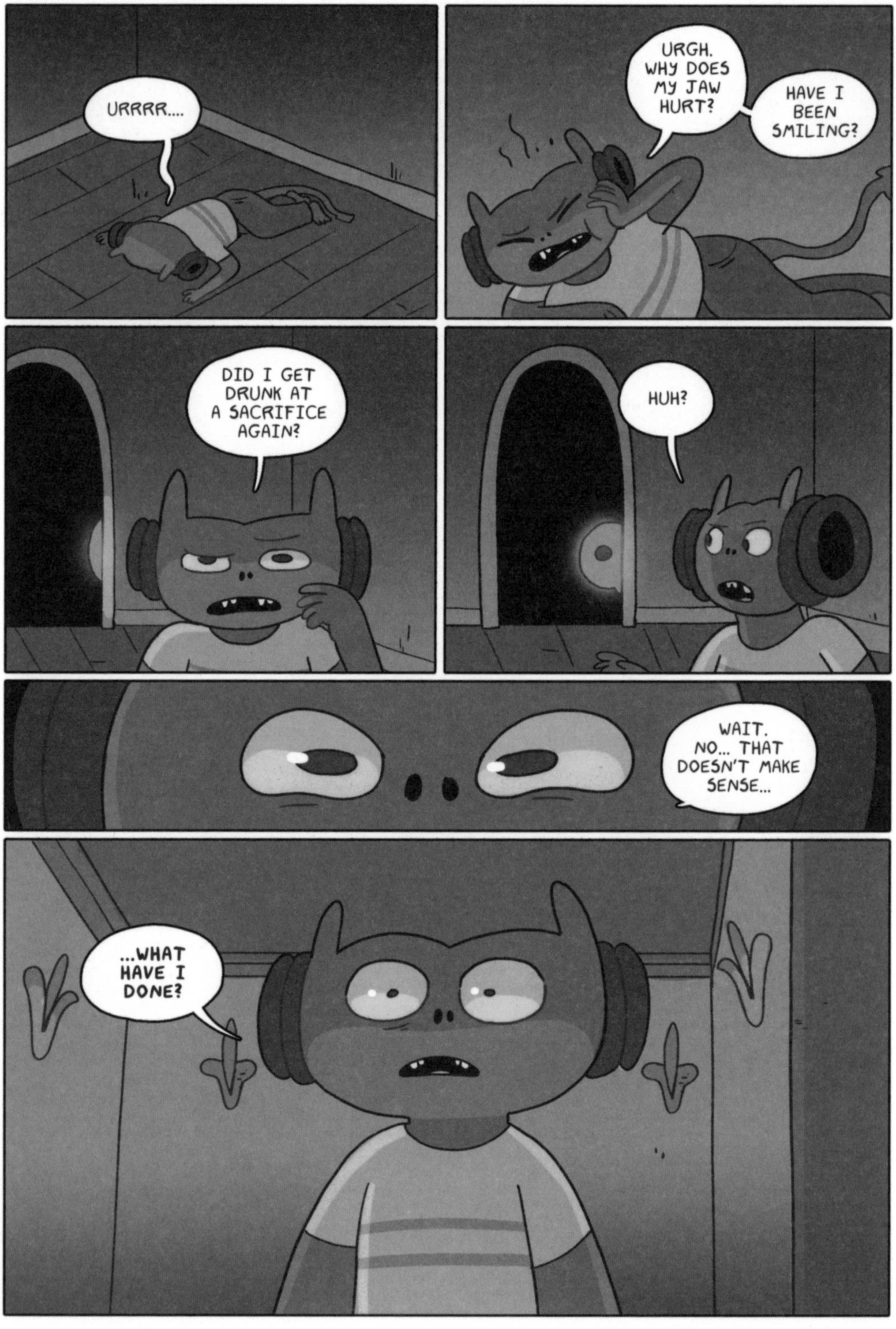
URRRR....
URGH. WHY DOES MY JAW HURT?
HAVE I BEEN SMILING?
DID I GET DRUNK AT A SACRIFICE AGAIN?
HUH?
WAIT. NO... THAT DOESN'T MAKE SENSE...
...WHAT HAVE I DONE?

CHAPTER 6

COVER ART BY TIFFANY BAXTER

SLAY BELLS

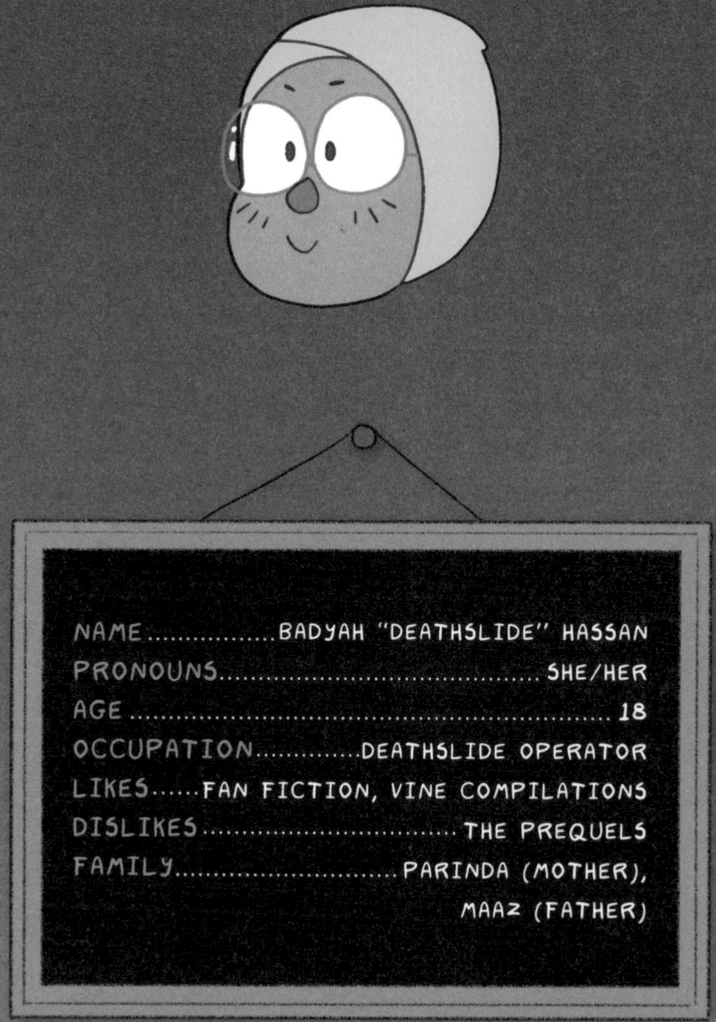

NAME.................BADYAH "DEATHSLIDE" HASSAN
PRONOUNS.............................SHE/HER
AGE 18
OCCUPATION............DEATHSLIDE OPERATOR
LIKES......FAN FICTION, VINE COMPILATIONS
DISLIKES.....................THE PREQUELS
FAMILY...................PARINDA (MOTHER),
                         MAAZ (FATHER)

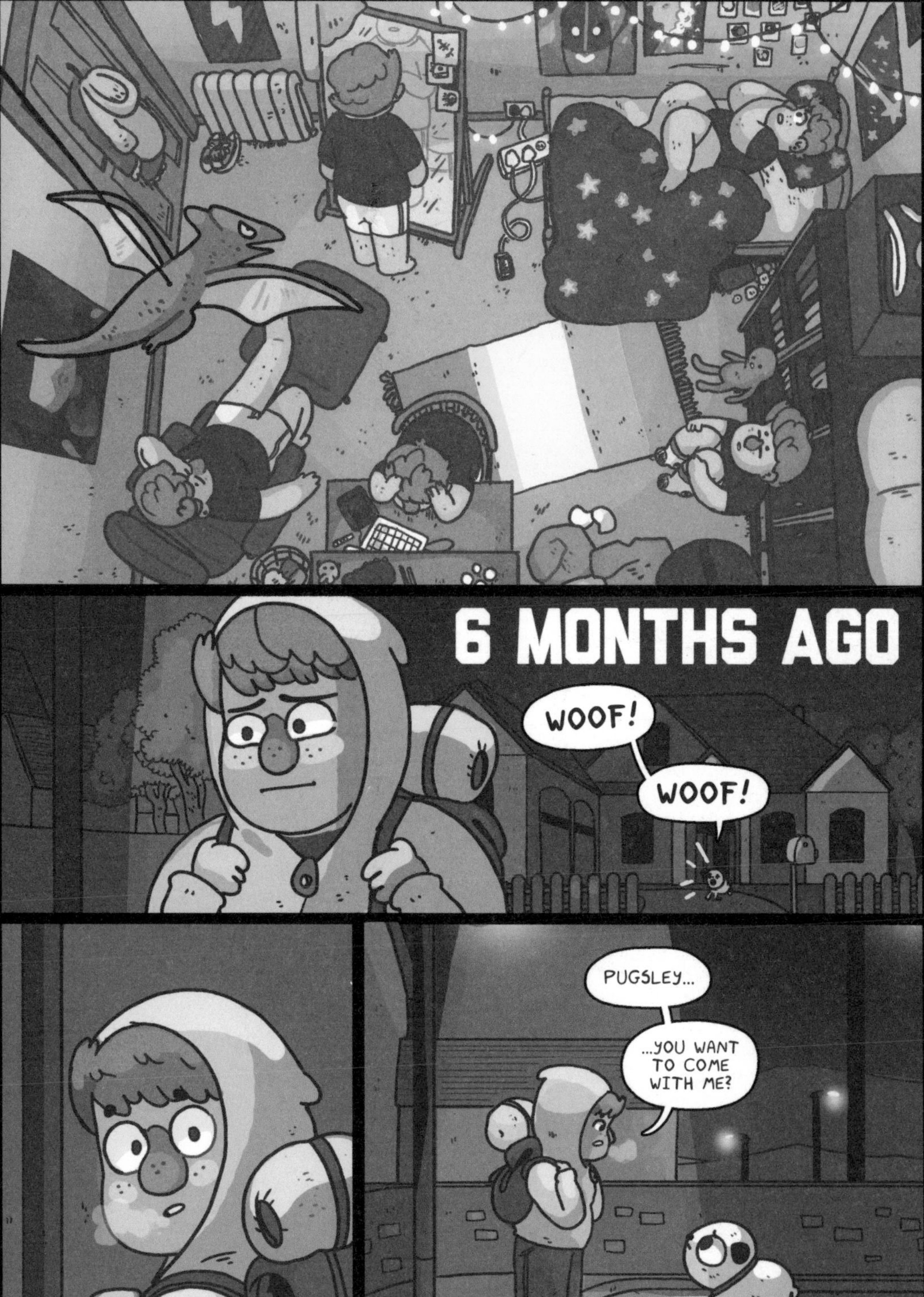
6 MONTHS AGO
WOOF!
WOOF!
PUGSLEY...
...YOU WANT TO COME WITH ME?

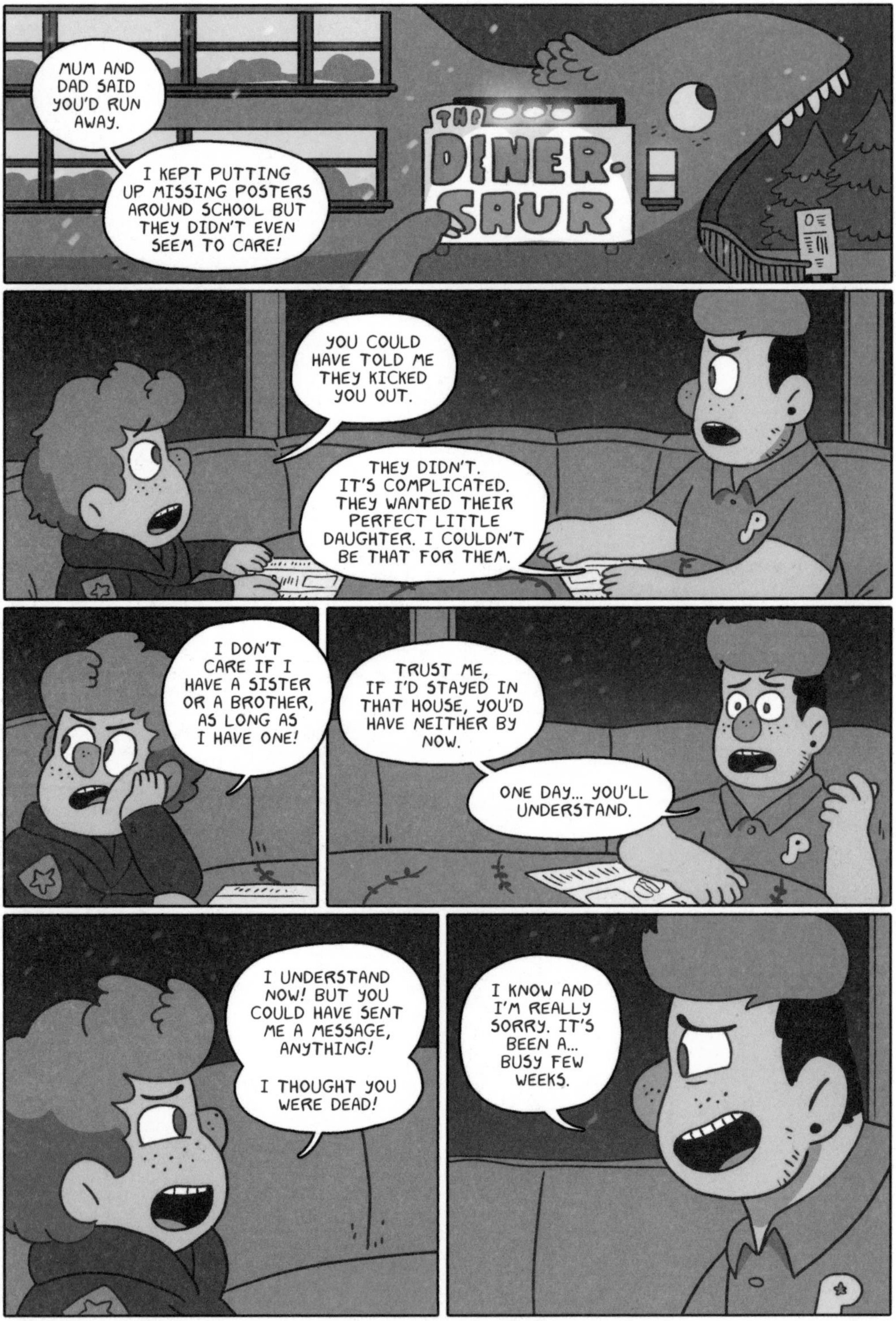
MUM AND DAD SAID YOU'D RUN AWAY.
I KEPT PUTTING UP MISSING POSTERS AROUND SCHOOL BUT THEY DIDN'T EVEN SEEM TO CARE!
THE DINER-SAUR
YOU COULD HAVE TOLD ME THEY KICKED YOU OUT.
THEY DIDN'T. IT'S COMPLICATED. THEY WANTED THEIR PERFECT LITTLE DAUGHTER. I COULDN'T BE THAT FOR THEM.
I DON'T CARE IF I HAVE A SISTER OR A BROTHER, AS LONG AS I HAVE ONE!
TRUST ME, IF I'D STAYED IN THAT HOUSE, YOU'D HAVE NEITHER BY NOW.
ONE DAY... YOU'LL UNDERSTAND.
I UNDERSTAND NOW! BUT YOU COULD HAVE SENT ME A MESSAGE, ANYTHING!
I THOUGHT YOU WERE DEAD!
I KNOW AND I'M REALLY SORRY. IT'S BEEN A... BUSY FEW WEEKS.

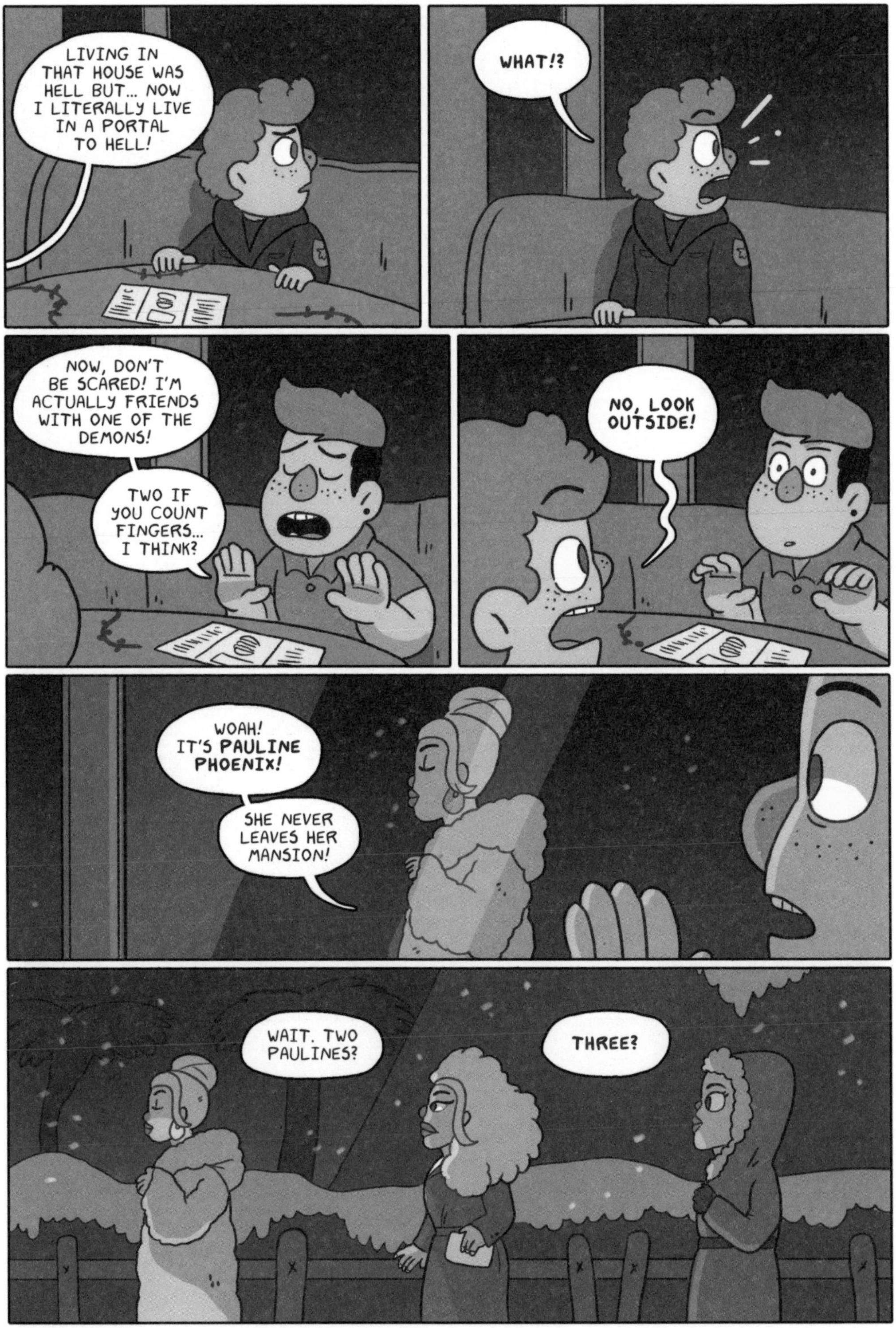
LIVING IN THAT HOUSE WAS HELL BUT... NOW I LITERALLY LIVE IN A PORTAL TO HELL!
WHAT!?
NOW, DON'T BE SCARED! I'M ACTUALLY FRIENDS WITH ONE OF THE DEMONS!
TWO IF YOU COUNT FINGERS... I THINK?
NO, LOOK OUTSIDE!
WOAH! IT'S PAULINE PHOENIX!
SHE NEVER LEAVES HER MANSION!
WAIT. TWO PAULINES?
THREE?

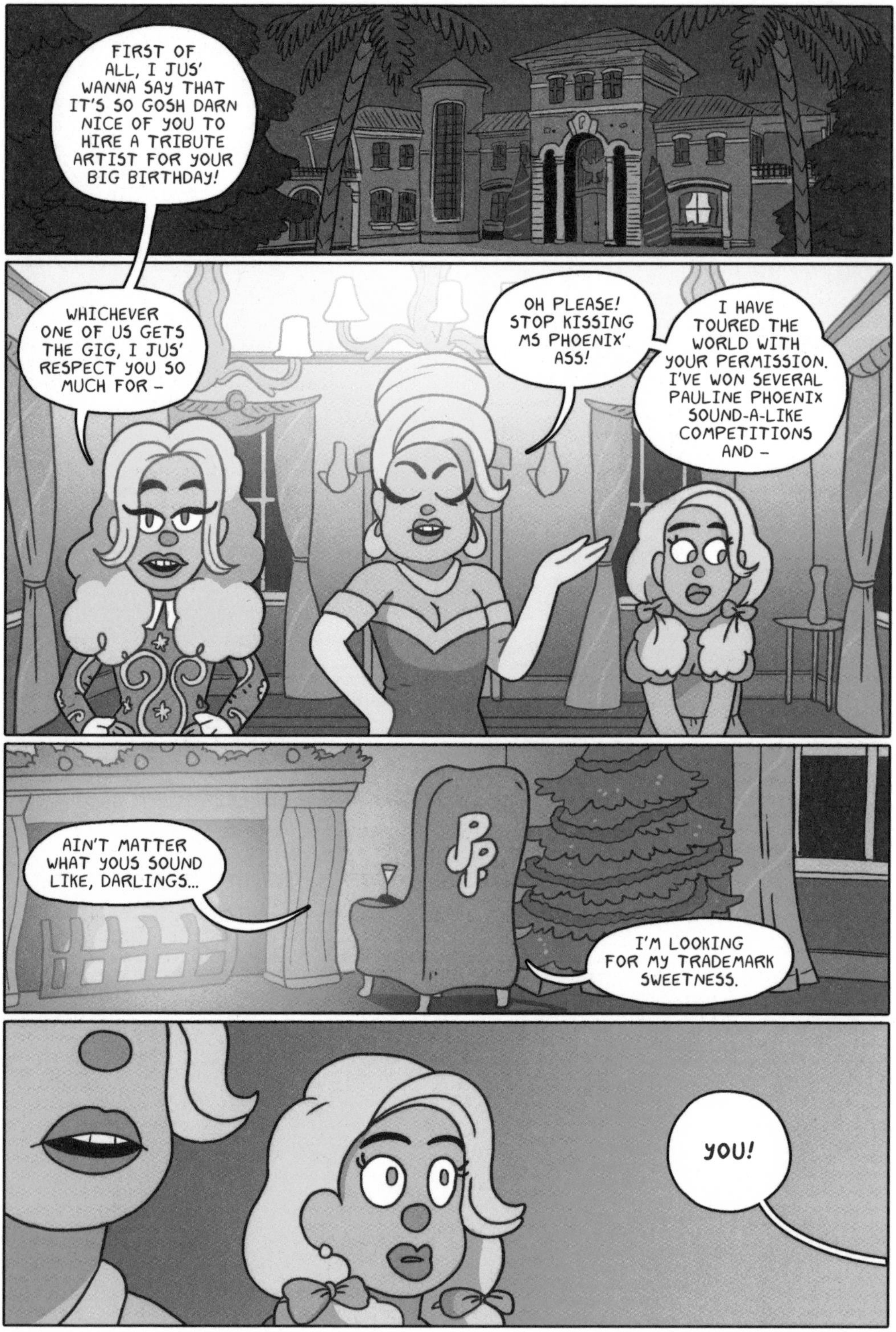
FIRST OF ALL, I JUS' WANNA SAY THAT IT'S SO GOSH DARN NICE OF YOU TO HIRE A TRIBUTE ARTIST FOR YOUR BIG BIRTHDAY!
WHICHEVER ONE OF US GETS THE GIG, I JUS' RESPECT YOU SO MUCH FOR –
OH PLEASE! STOP KISSING MS PHOENIX' ASS!
I HAVE TOURED THE WORLD WITH YOUR PERMISSION. I'VE WON SEVERAL PAULINE PHOENIX SOUND-A-LIKE COMPETITIONS AND –
PP
AIN'T MATTER WHAT YOUS SOUND LIKE, DARLINGS...
I'M LOOKING FOR MY TRADEMARK SWEETNESS.
YOU!

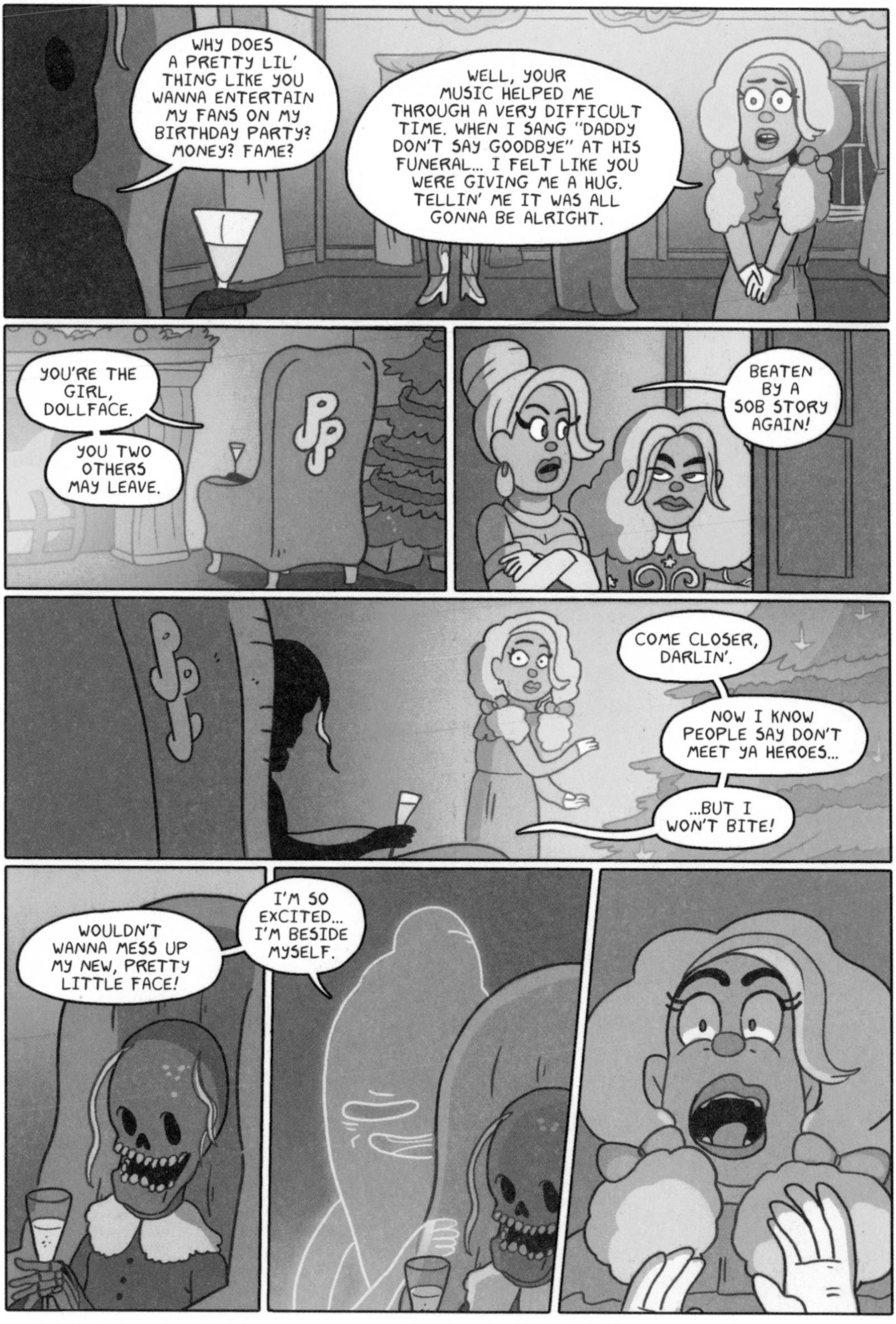
WHY DOES A PRETTY LIL' THING LIKE YOU WANNA ENTERTAIN MY FANS ON MY BIRTHDAY PARTY? MONEY? FAME?
WELL, YOUR MUSIC HELPED ME THROUGH A VERY DIFFICULT TIME. WHEN I SANG "DADDY DON'T SAY GOODBYE" AT HIS FUNERAL... I FELT LIKE YOU WERE GIVING ME A HUG. TELLIN' ME IT WAS ALL GONNA BE ALRIGHT.
YOU'RE THE GIRL, DOLLFACE.
YOU TWO OTHERS MAY LEAVE.
BEATEN BY A SOB STORY AGAIN!
COME CLOSER, DARLIN'.
NOW I KNOW PEOPLE SAY DON'T MEET YA HEROES...
...BUT I WON'T BITE!
WOULDN'T WANNA MESS UP MY NEW, PRETTY LITTLE FACE!
I'M SO EXCITED... I'M BESIDE MYSELF.

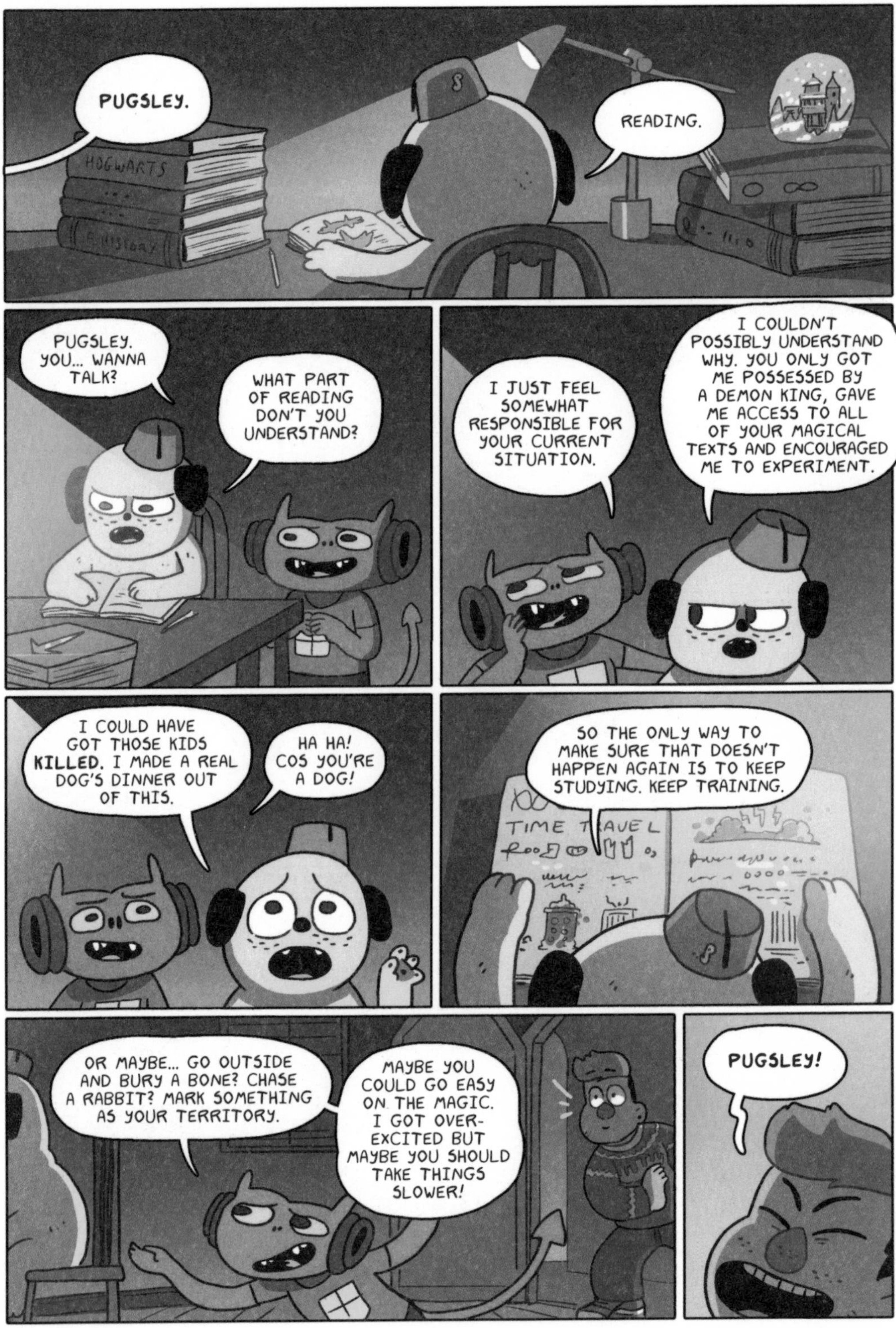
PUGSLEY.
READING.
HOGWARTS
PUGSLEY. YOU... WANNA TALK?
WHAT PART OF READING DON'T YOU UNDERSTAND?
I JUST FEEL SOMEWHAT RESPONSIBLE FOR YOUR CURRENT SITUATION.
I COULDN'T POSSIBLY UNDERSTAND WHY. YOU ONLY GOT ME POSSESSED BY A DEMON KING, GAVE ME ACCESS TO ALL OF YOUR MAGICAL TEXTS AND ENCOURAGED ME TO EXPERIMENT.
I COULD HAVE GOT THOSE KIDS **KILLED.** I MADE A REAL DOG'S DINNER OUT OF THIS.
HA HA! COS YOU'RE A DOG!
SO THE ONLY WAY TO MAKE SURE THAT DOESN'T HAPPEN AGAIN IS TO KEEP STUDYING. KEEP TRAINING.
TIME TRAVEL
OR MAYBE... GO OUTSIDE AND BURY A BONE? CHASE A RABBIT? MARK SOMETHING AS YOUR TERRITORY.
MAYBE YOU COULD GO EASY ON THE MAGIC. I GOT OVER-EXCITED BUT MAYBE YOU SHOULD TAKE THINGS SLOWER!
PUGSLEY!

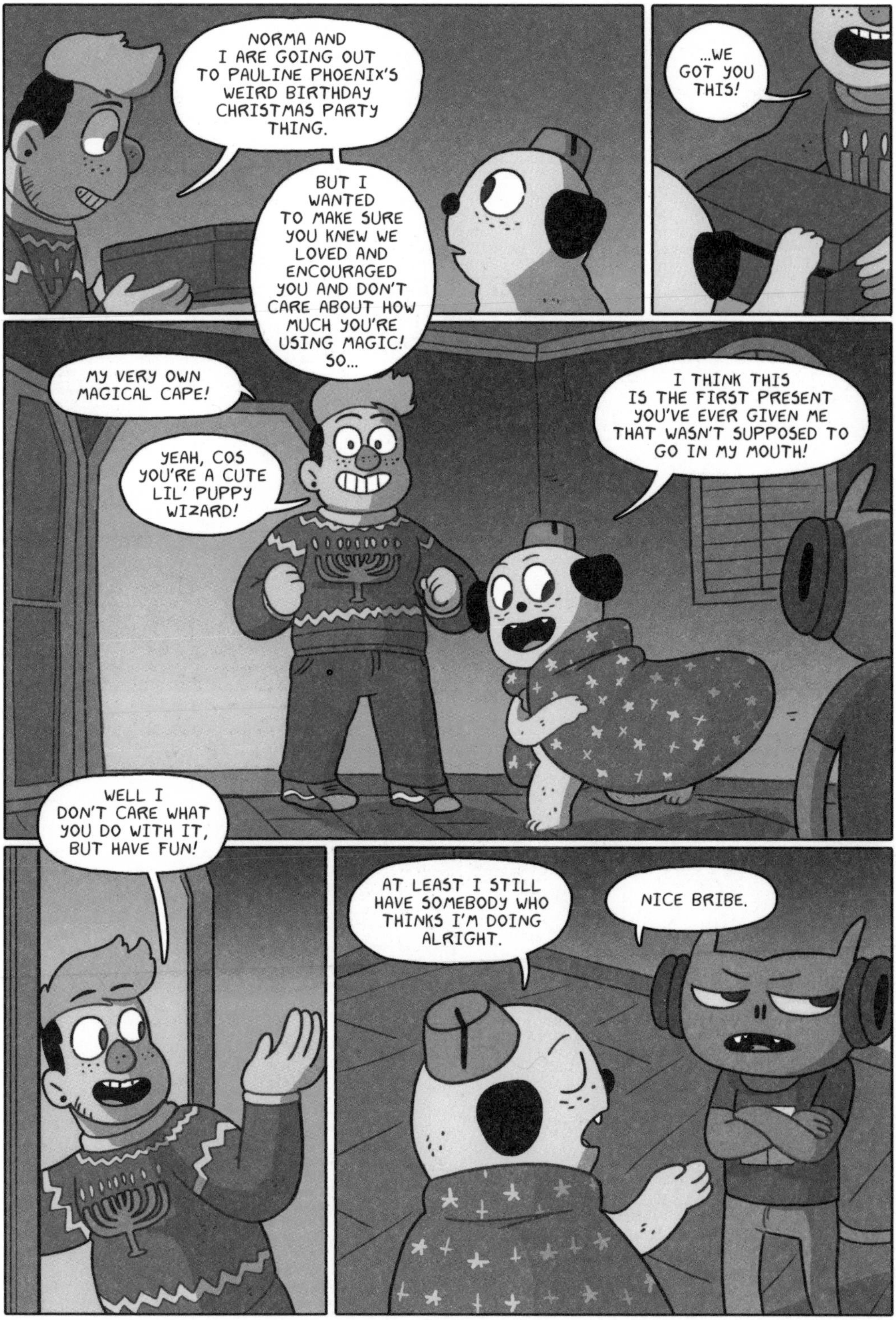
NORMA AND I ARE GOING OUT TO PAULINE PHOENIX'S WEIRD BIRTHDAY CHRISTMAS PARTY THING.
BUT I WANTED TO MAKE SURE YOU KNEW WE LOVED AND ENCOURAGED YOU AND DON'T CARE ABOUT HOW MUCH YOU'RE USING MAGIC! SO...
...WE GOT YOU THIS!
MY VERY OWN MAGICAL CAPE!
YEAH, COS YOU'RE A CUTE LIL' PUPPY WIZARD!
I THINK THIS IS THE FIRST PRESENT YOU'VE EVER GIVEN ME THAT WASN'T SUPPOSED TO GO IN MY MOUTH!
WELL I DON'T CARE WHAT YOU DO WITH IT, BUT HAVE FUN!
AT LEAST I STILL HAVE SOMEBODY WHO THINKS I'M DOING ALRIGHT.
NICE BRIBE.

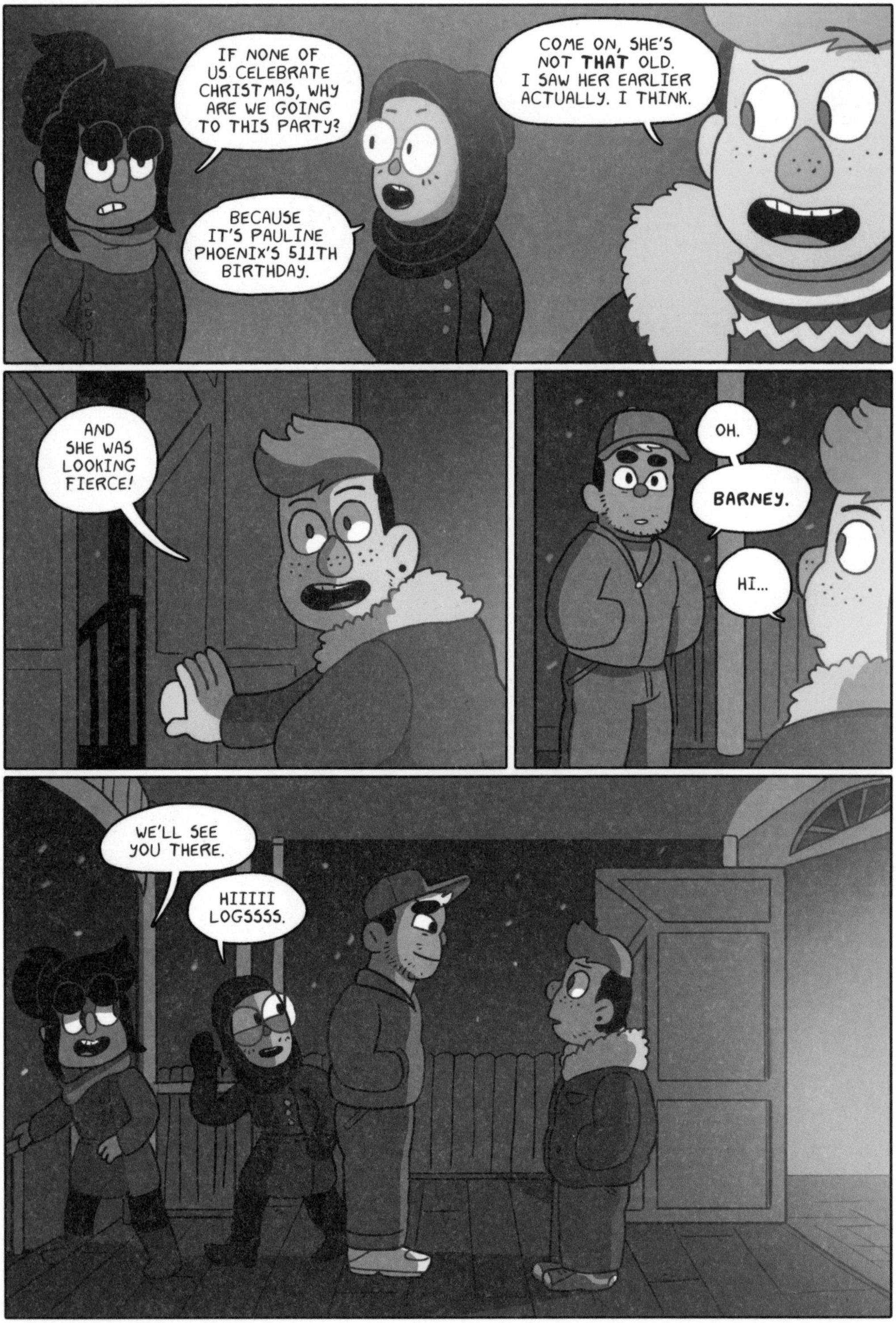
IF NONE OF US CELEBRATE CHRISTMAS, WHY ARE WE GOING TO THIS PARTY?
BECAUSE IT'S PAULINE PHOENIX'S 511TH BIRTHDAY.
COME ON, SHE'S NOT THAT OLD. I SAW HER EARLIER ACTUALLY. I THINK.
AND SHE WAS LOOKING FIERCE!
OH.
BARNEY.
HI...
WE'LL SEE YOU THERE.
HIIIII LOGSSSS.

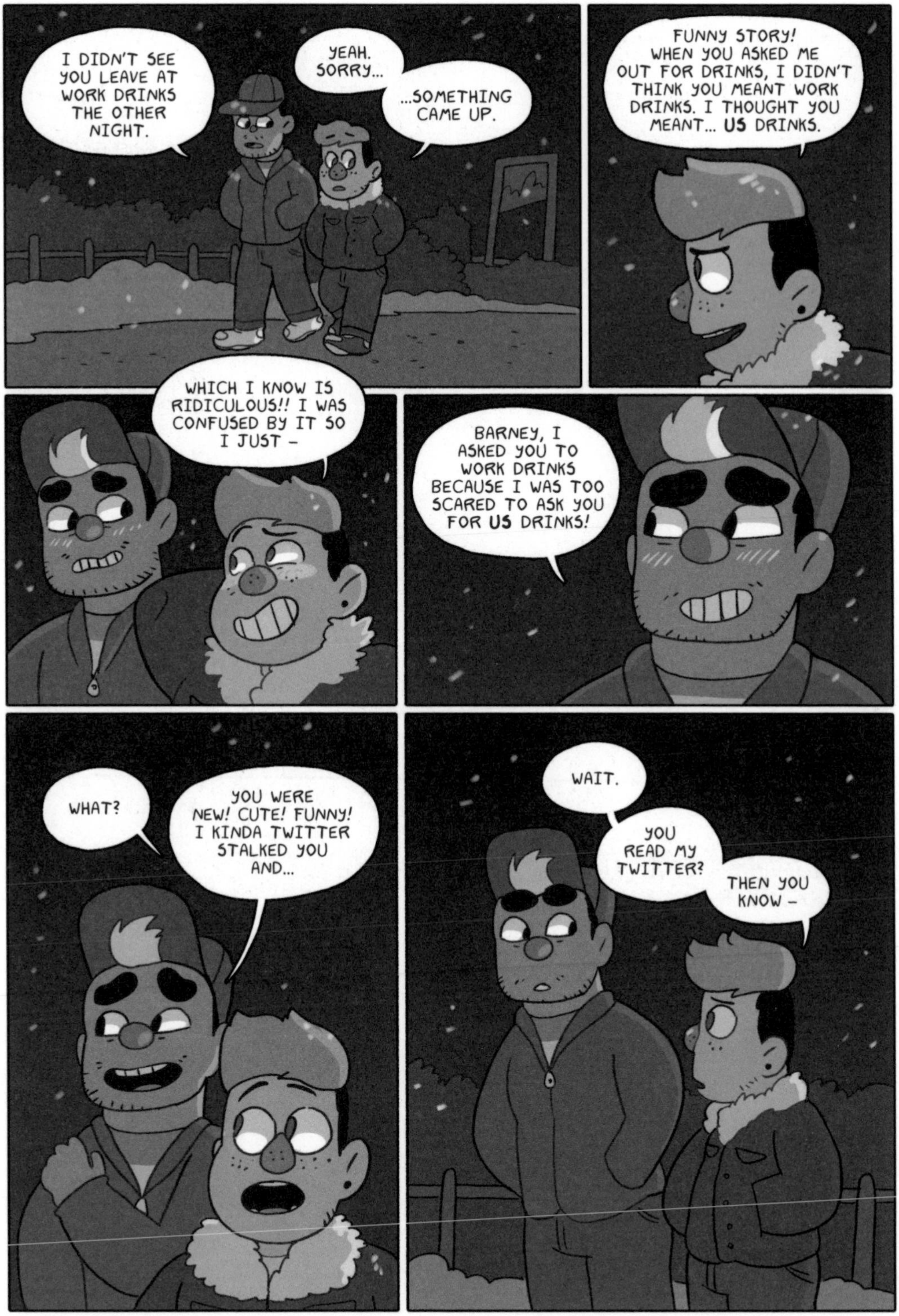
I DIDN'T SEE YOU LEAVE AT WORK DRINKS THE OTHER NIGHT.
YEAH. SORRY...
...SOMETHING CAME UP.
FUNNY STORY! WHEN YOU ASKED ME OUT FOR DRINKS, I DIDN'T THINK YOU MEANT WORK DRINKS. I THOUGHT YOU MEANT... US DRINKS.
WHICH I KNOW IS RIDICULOUS!! I WAS CONFUSED BY IT SO I JUST –
BARNEY, I ASKED YOU TO WORK DRINKS BECAUSE I WAS TOO SCARED TO ASK YOU FOR US DRINKS!
WHAT?
YOU WERE NEW! CUTE! FUNNY! I KINDA TWITTER STALKED YOU AND...
WAIT.
YOU READ MY TWITTER?
THEN YOU KNOW –

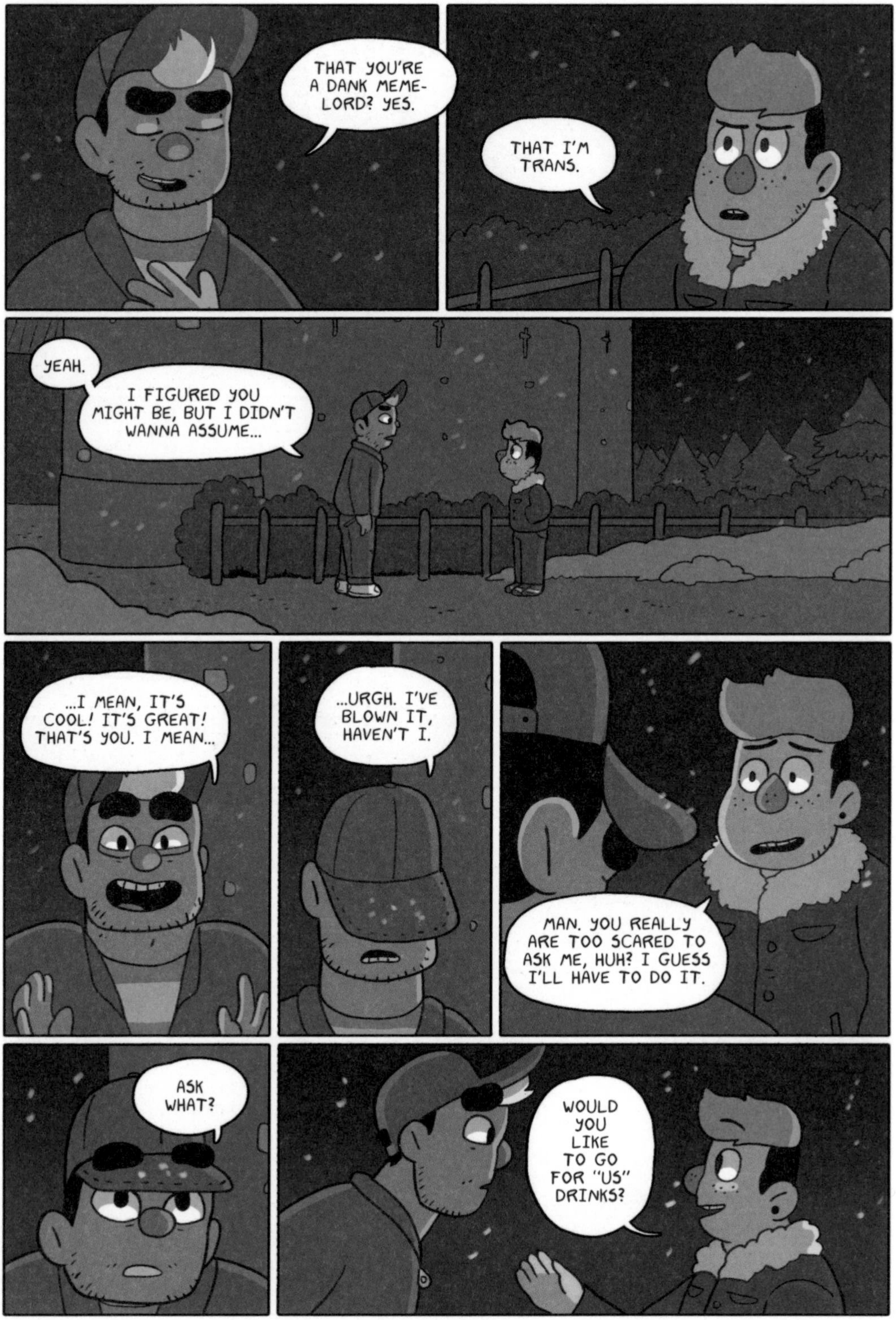
THAT YOU'RE A DANK MEME-LORD? YES.
THAT I'M TRANS.
YEAH.
I FIGURED YOU MIGHT BE, BUT I DIDN'T WANNA ASSUME...
...I MEAN, IT'S COOL! IT'S GREAT! THAT'S YOU. I MEAN...
...URGH. I'VE BLOWN IT, HAVEN'T I.
MAN. YOU REALLY ARE TOO SCARED TO ASK ME, HUH? I GUESS I'LL HAVE TO DO IT.
ASK WHAT?
WOULD YOU LIKE TO GO FOR "US" DRINKS?

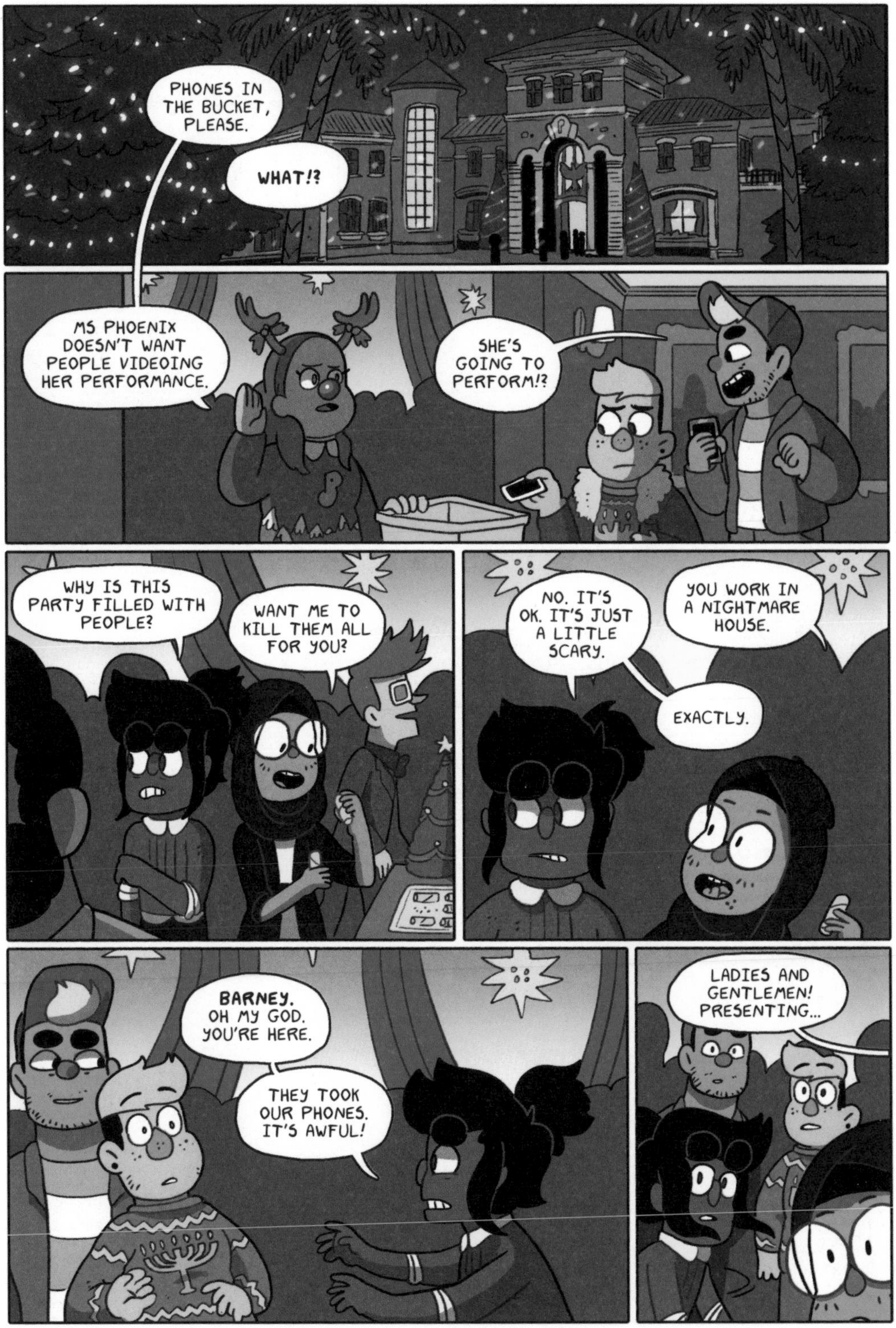
PHONES IN THE BUCKET, PLEASE.
WHAT!?
MS PHOENIX DOESN'T WANT PEOPLE VIDEOING HER PERFORMANCE.
SHE'S GOING TO PERFORM!?
WHY IS THIS PARTY FILLED WITH PEOPLE?
WANT ME TO KILL THEM ALL FOR YOU?
NO. IT'S OK. IT'S JUST A LITTLE SCARY.
YOU WORK IN A NIGHTMARE HOUSE.
EXACTLY.
BARNEY. OH MY GOD. YOU'RE HERE.
THEY TOOK OUR PHONES. IT'S AWFUL!
LADIES AND GENTLEMEN! PRESENTING...

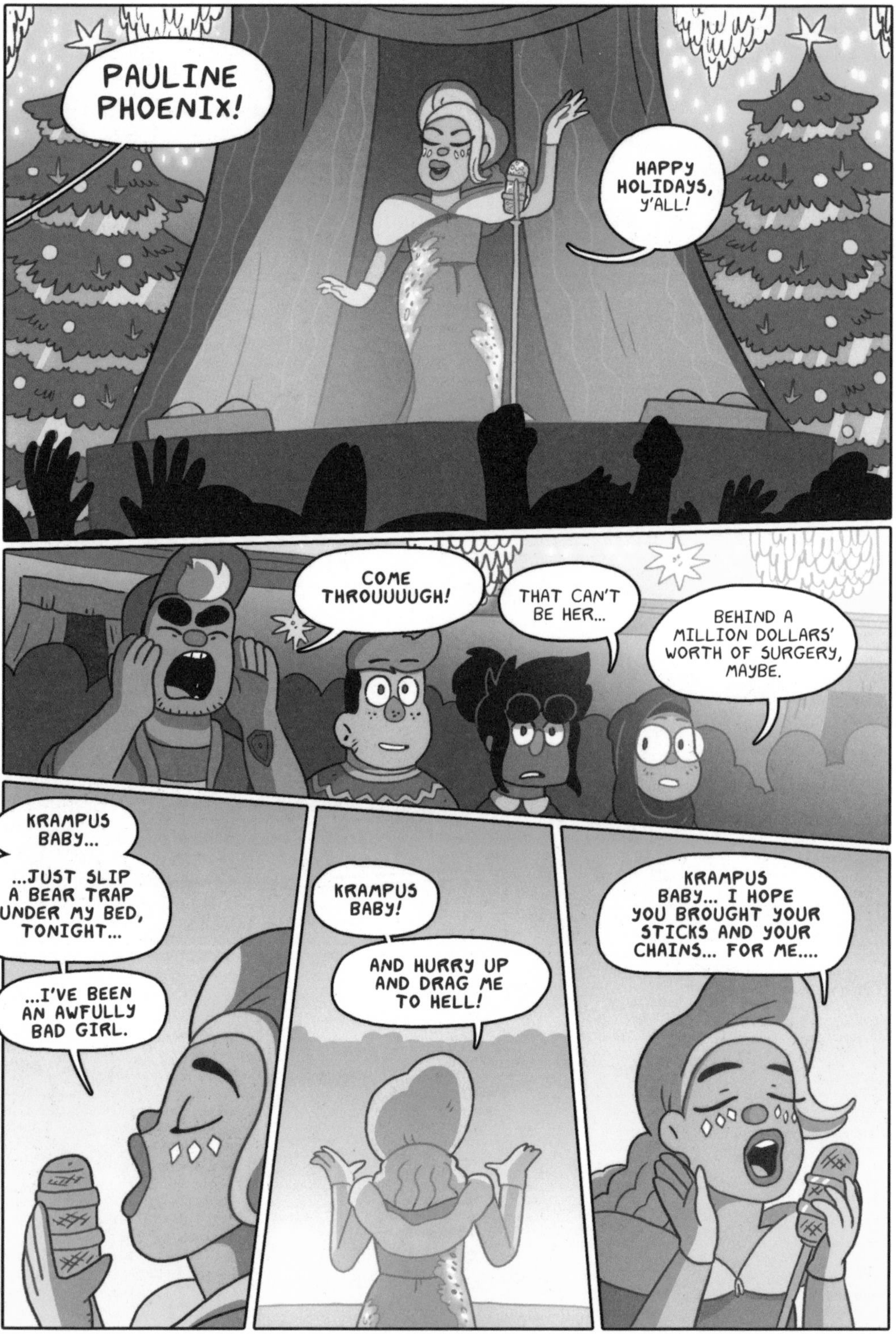
PAULINE PHOENIX!
HAPPY HOLIDAYS, Y'ALL!
COME THROUUUUGH!
THAT CAN'T BE HER...
BEHIND A MILLION DOLLARS' WORTH OF SURGERY, MAYBE.
KRAMPUS BABY...
...JUST SLIP A BEAR TRAP UNDER MY BED, TONIGHT...
...I'VE BEEN AN AWFULLY BAD GIRL.
KRAMPUS BABY!
AND HURRY UP AND DRAG ME TO HELL!
KRAMPUS BABY... I HOPE YOU BROUGHT YOUR STICKS AND YOUR CHAINS... FOR ME....

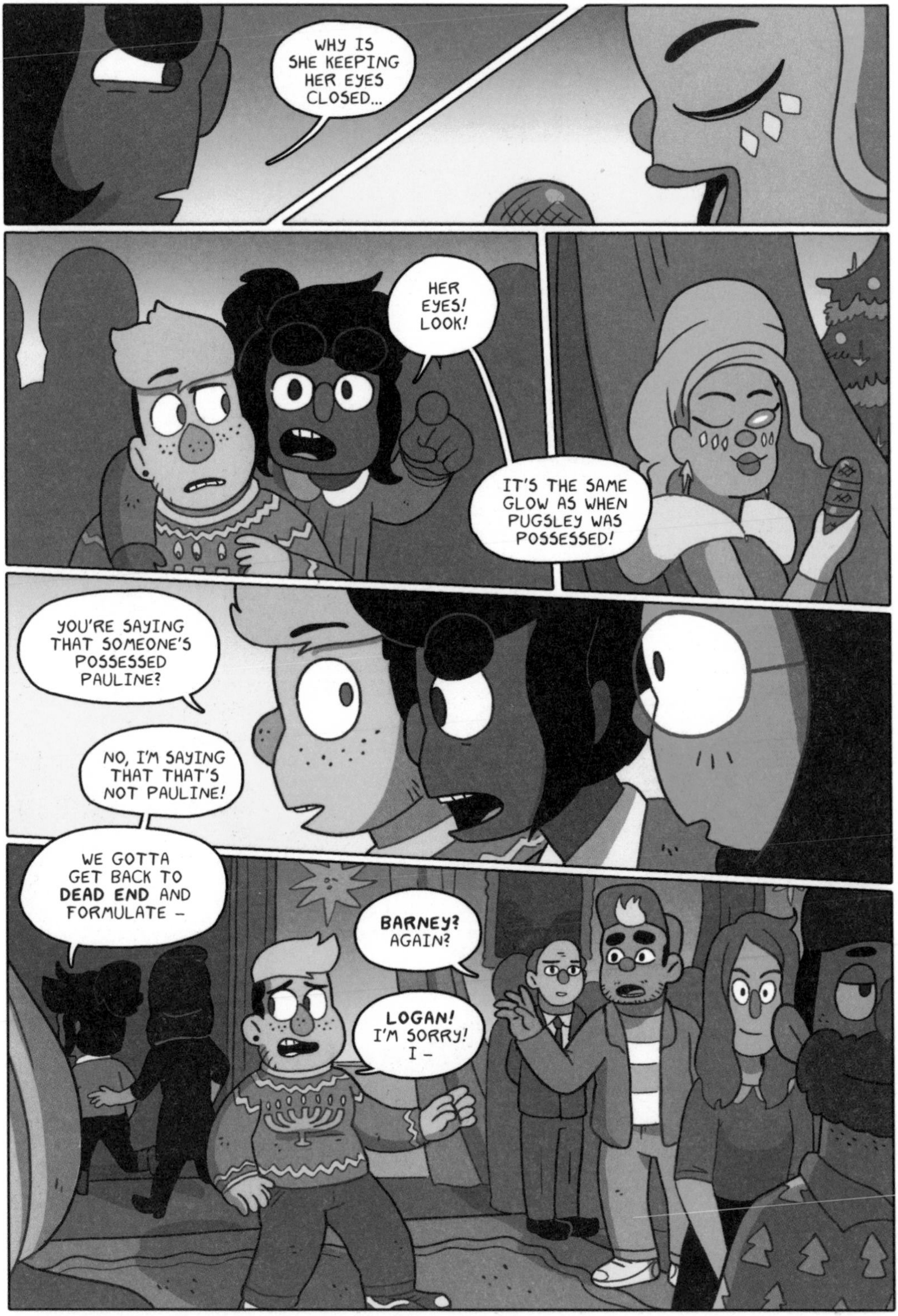
WHY IS SHE KEEPING HER EYES CLOSED...
HER EYES! LOOK!
IT'S THE SAME GLOW AS WHEN PUGSLEY WAS POSSESSED!
YOU'RE SAYING THAT SOMEONE'S POSSESSED PAULINE?
NO, I'M SAYING THAT THAT'S NOT PAULINE!
WE GOTTA GET BACK TO **DEAD END** AND FORMULATE –
BARNEY? AGAIN?
LOGAN! I'M SORRY! I –

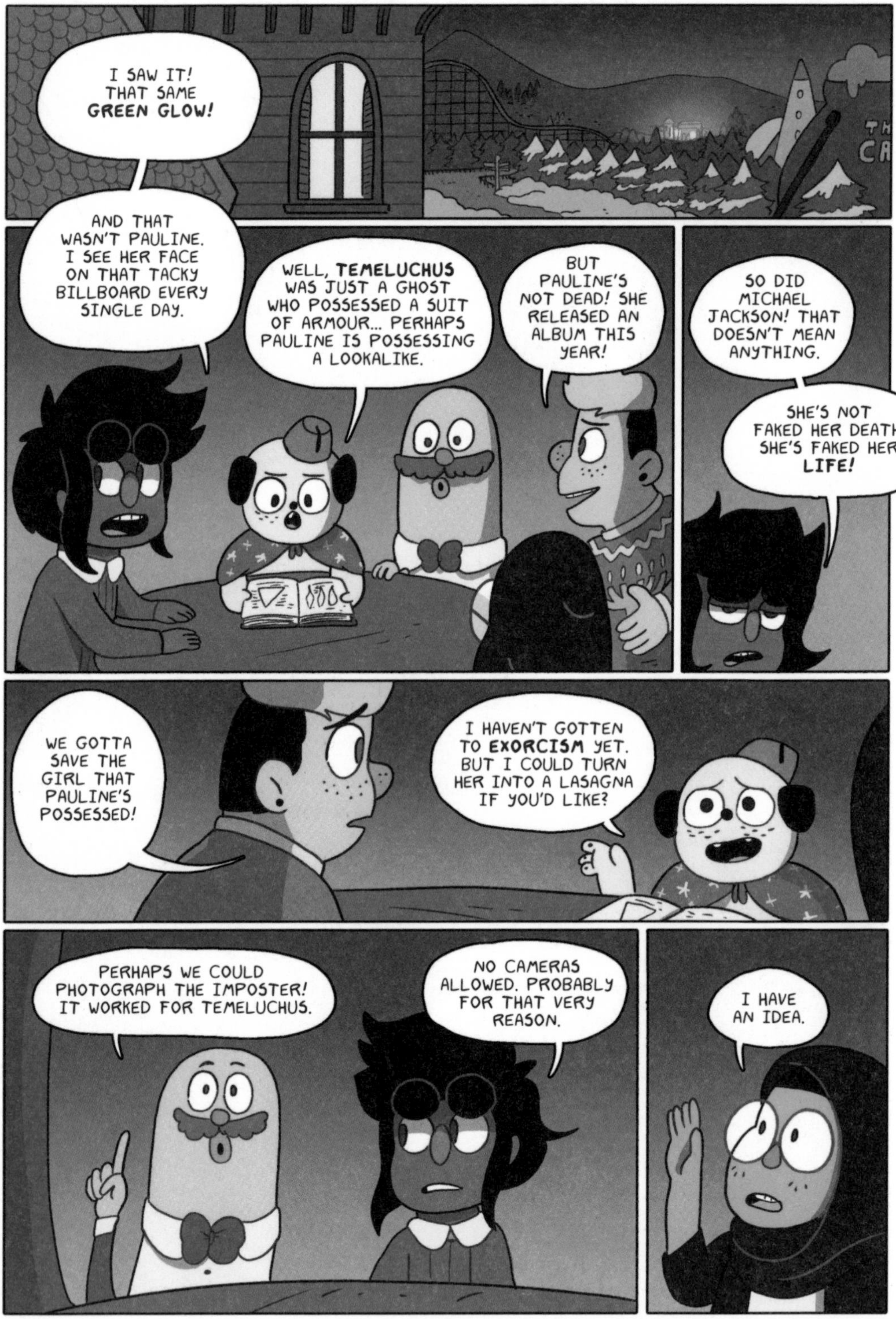
I SAW IT! THAT SAME GREEN GLOW!
AND THAT WASN'T PAULINE. I SEE HER FACE ON THAT TACKY BILLBOARD EVERY SINGLE DAY.
WELL, TEMELUCHUS WAS JUST A GHOST WHO POSSESSED A SUIT OF ARMOUR... PERHAPS PAULINE IS POSSESSING A LOOKALIKE.
BUT PAULINE'S NOT DEAD! SHE RELEASED AN ALBUM THIS YEAR!
SO DID MICHAEL JACKSON! THAT DOESN'T MEAN ANYTHING.
SHE'S NOT FAKED HER DEATH. SHE'S FAKED HER LIFE!
WE GOTTA SAVE THE GIRL THAT PAULINE'S POSSESSED!
I HAVEN'T GOTTEN TO EXORCISM YET. BUT I COULD TURN HER INTO A LASAGNA IF YOU'D LIKE?
PERHAPS WE COULD PHOTOGRAPH THE IMPOSTER! IT WORKED FOR TEMELUCHUS.
NO CAMERAS ALLOWED. PROBABLY FOR THAT VERY REASON.
I HAVE AN IDEA.

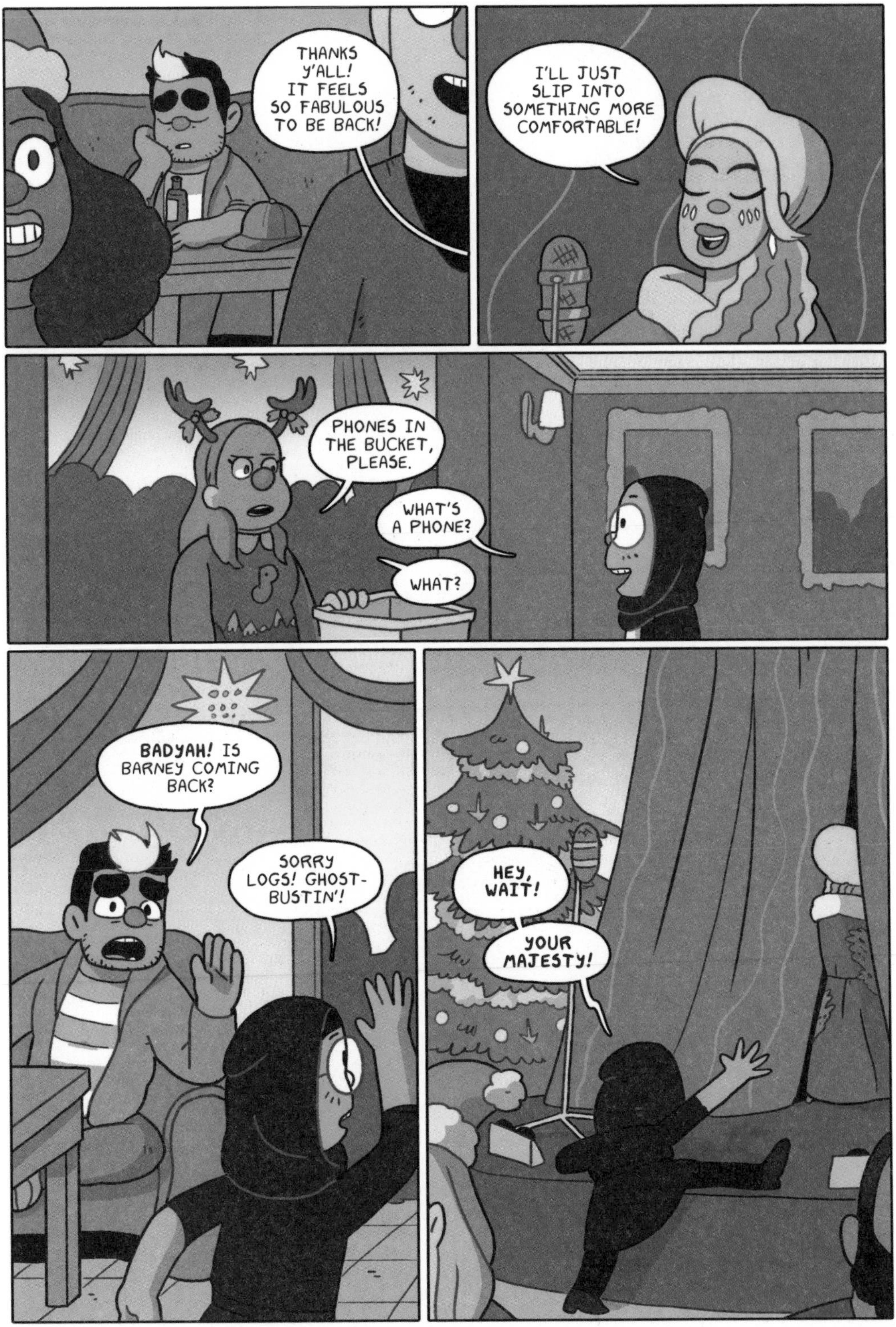
THANKS Y'ALL! IT FEELS SO FABULOUS TO BE BACK!
I'LL JUST SLIP INTO SOMETHING MORE COMFORTABLE!
PHONES IN THE BUCKET, PLEASE.
WHAT'S A PHONE?
WHAT?
BADYAH! IS BARNEY COMING BACK?
SORRY LOGS! GHOST-BUSTIN'!
HEY, WAIT!
YOUR MAJESTY!

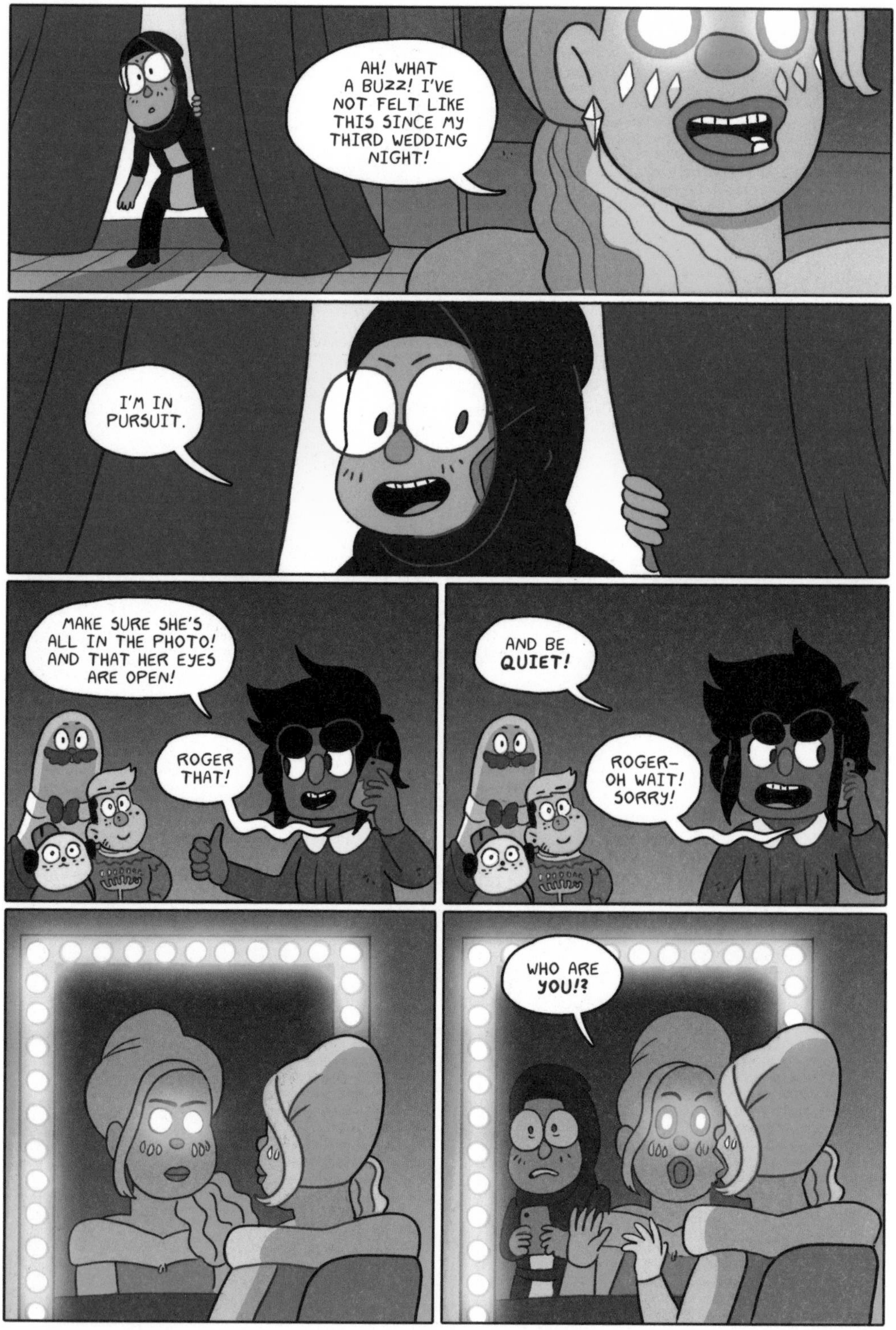
AH! WHAT A BUZZ! I'VE NOT FELT LIKE THIS SINCE MY THIRD WEDDING NIGHT!
I'M IN PURSUIT.
MAKE SURE SHE'S ALL IN THE PHOTO! AND THAT HER EYES ARE OPEN!
ROGER THAT!
AND BE **QUIET!**
ROGER— OH WAIT! SORRY!
WHO ARE **YOU!?**

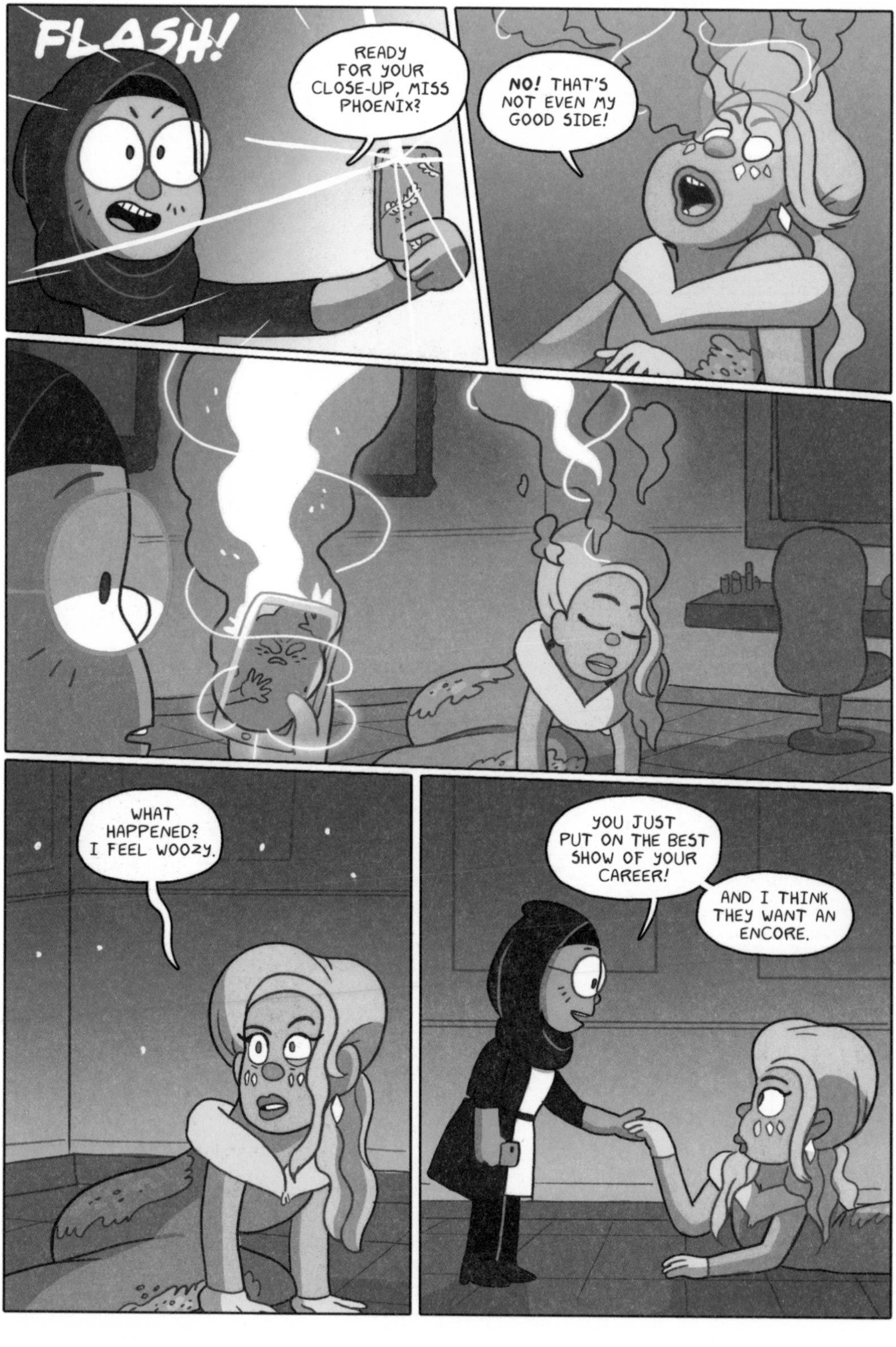
FLASH!
READY FOR YOUR CLOSE-UP, MISS PHOENIX?
NO! THAT'S NOT EVEN MY GOOD SIDE!
WHAT HAPPENED? I FEEL WOOZY.
YOU JUST PUT ON THE BEST SHOW OF YOUR CAREER!
AND I THINK THEY WANT AN ENCORE.

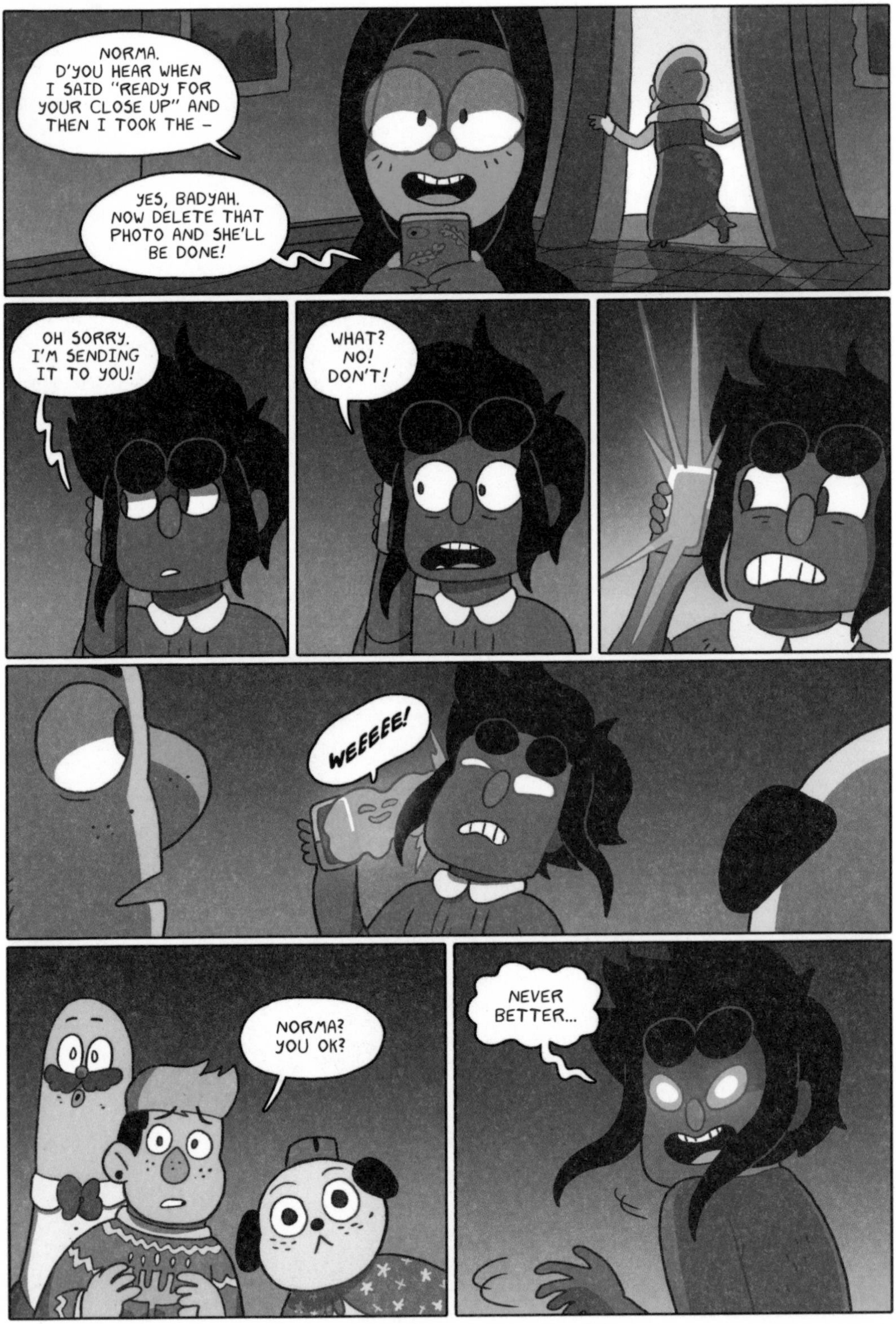
NORMA. D'YOU HEAR WHEN I SAID "READY FOR YOUR CLOSE UP" AND THEN I TOOK THE –
YES, BADYAH. NOW DELETE THAT PHOTO AND SHE'LL BE DONE!
OH SORRY. I'M SENDING IT TO YOU!
WHAT? NO! DON'T!
WEEEEE!
NORMA? YOU OK?
NEVER BETTER...

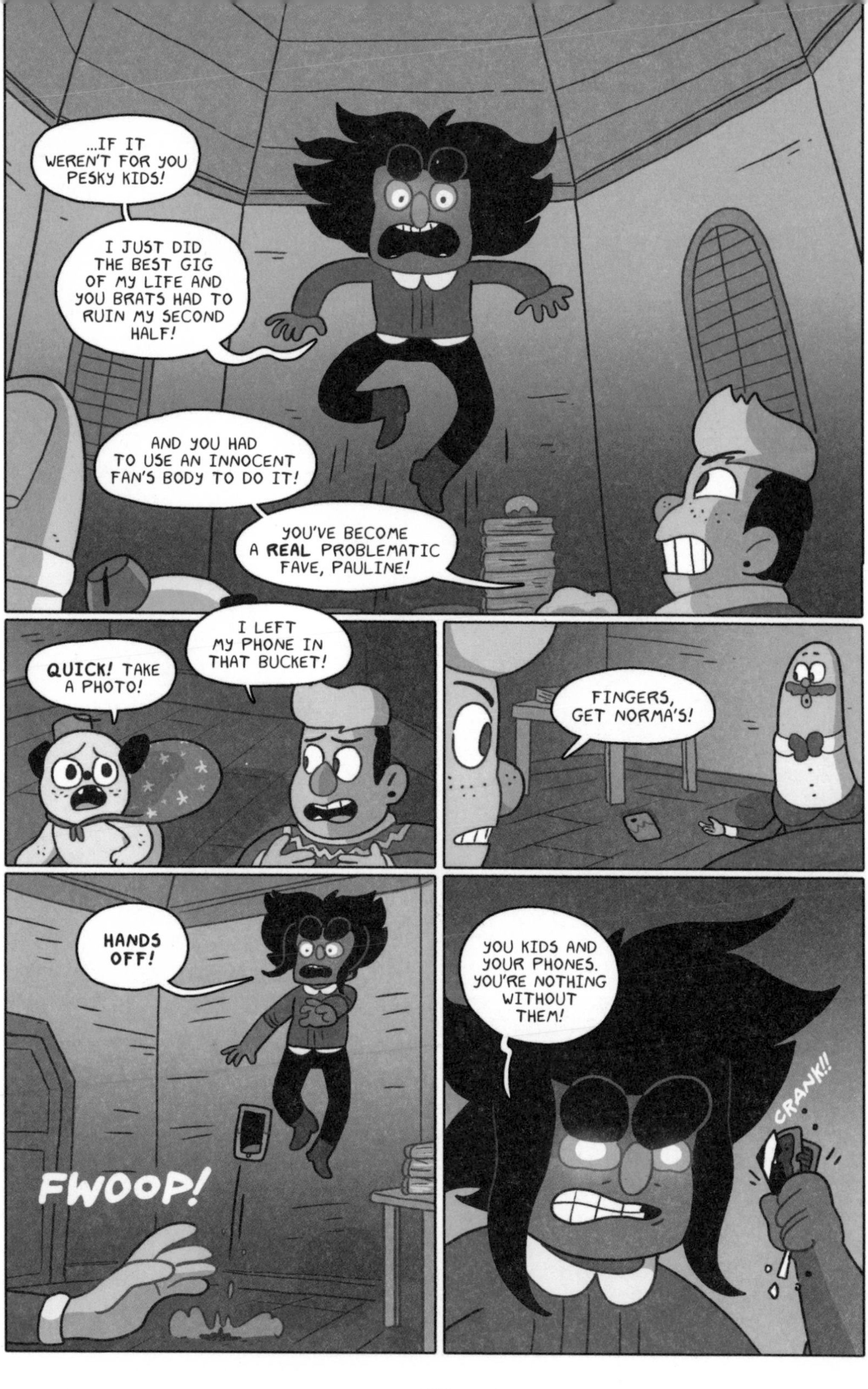
...IF IT WEREN'T FOR YOU PESKY KIDS!
I JUST DID THE BEST GIG OF MY LIFE AND YOU BRATS HAD TO RUIN MY SECOND HALF!
AND YOU HAD TO USE AN INNOCENT FAN'S BODY TO DO IT!
YOU'VE BECOME A **REAL** PROBLEMATIC FAVE, PAULINE!
QUICK! TAKE A PHOTO!
I LEFT MY PHONE IN THAT BUCKET!
FINGERS, GET NORMA'S!
HANDS OFF!
FWOOP!
YOU KIDS AND YOUR PHONES. YOU'RE NOTHING WITHOUT THEM!
CRANK!!

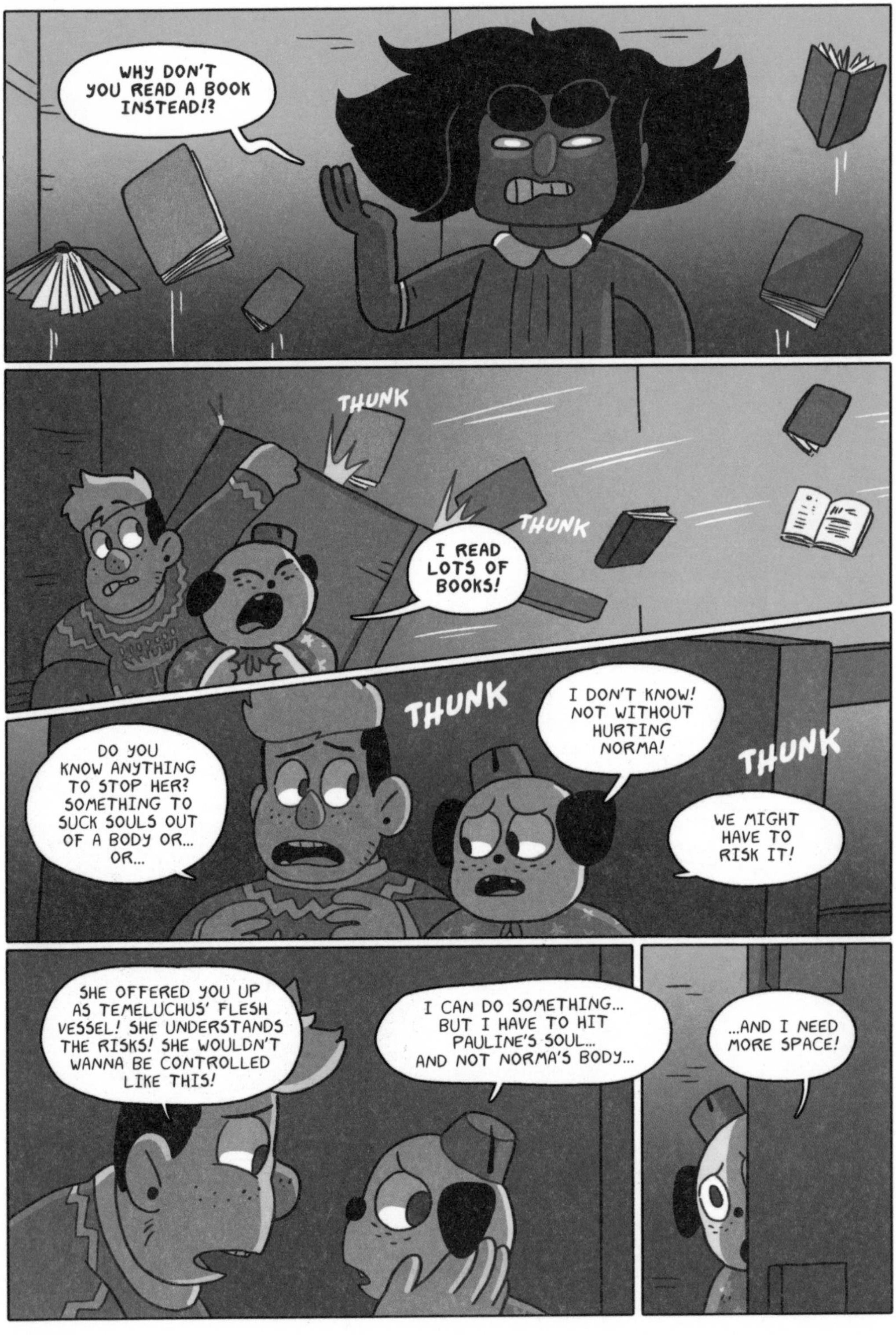
WHY DON'T YOU READ A BOOK INSTEAD!?
THUNK
THUNK
I READ LOTS OF BOOKS!
THUNK
THUNK
DO YOU KNOW ANYTHING TO STOP HER? SOMETHING TO SUCK SOULS OUT OF A BODY OR... OR...
I DON'T KNOW! NOT WITHOUT HURTING NORMA!
WE MIGHT HAVE TO RISK IT!
SHE OFFERED YOU UP AS TEMELUCHUS' FLESH VESSEL! SHE UNDERSTANDS THE RISKS! SHE WOULDN'T WANNA BE CONTROLLED LIKE THIS!
I CAN DO SOMETHING... BUT I HAVE TO HIT PAULINE'S SOUL... AND NOT NORMA'S BODY...
...AND I NEED MORE SPACE!

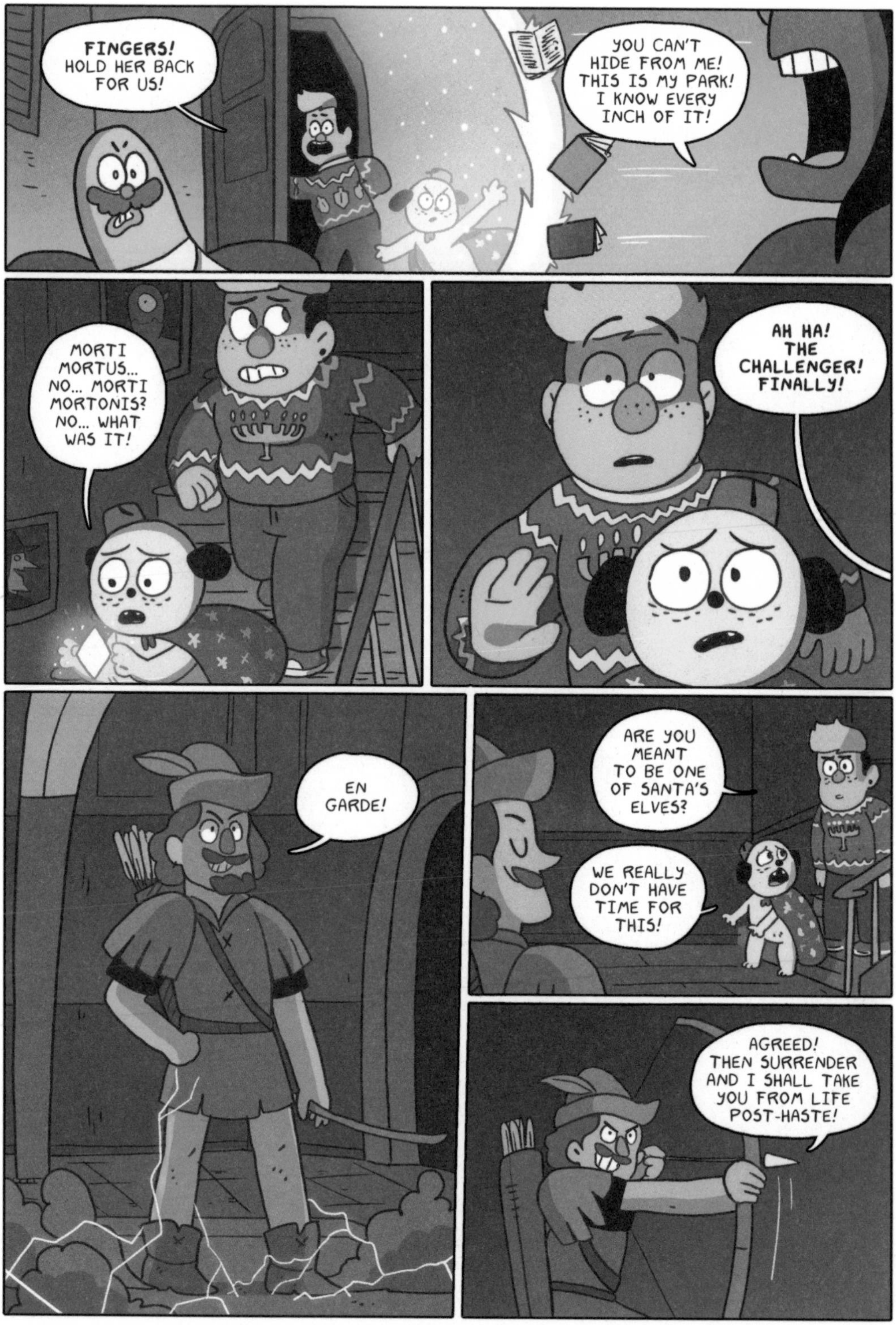
FINGERS! HOLD HER BACK FOR US!
YOU CAN'T HIDE FROM ME! THIS IS MY PARK! I KNOW EVERY INCH OF IT!
MORTI MORTUS... NO... MORTI MORTONIS? NO... WHAT WAS IT!
AH HA! THE CHALLENGER! FINALLY!
EN GARDE!
ARE YOU MEANT TO BE ONE OF SANTA'S ELVES?
WE REALLY DON'T HAVE TIME FOR THIS!
AGREED! THEN SURRENDER AND I SHALL TAKE YOU FROM LIFE POST-HASTE!

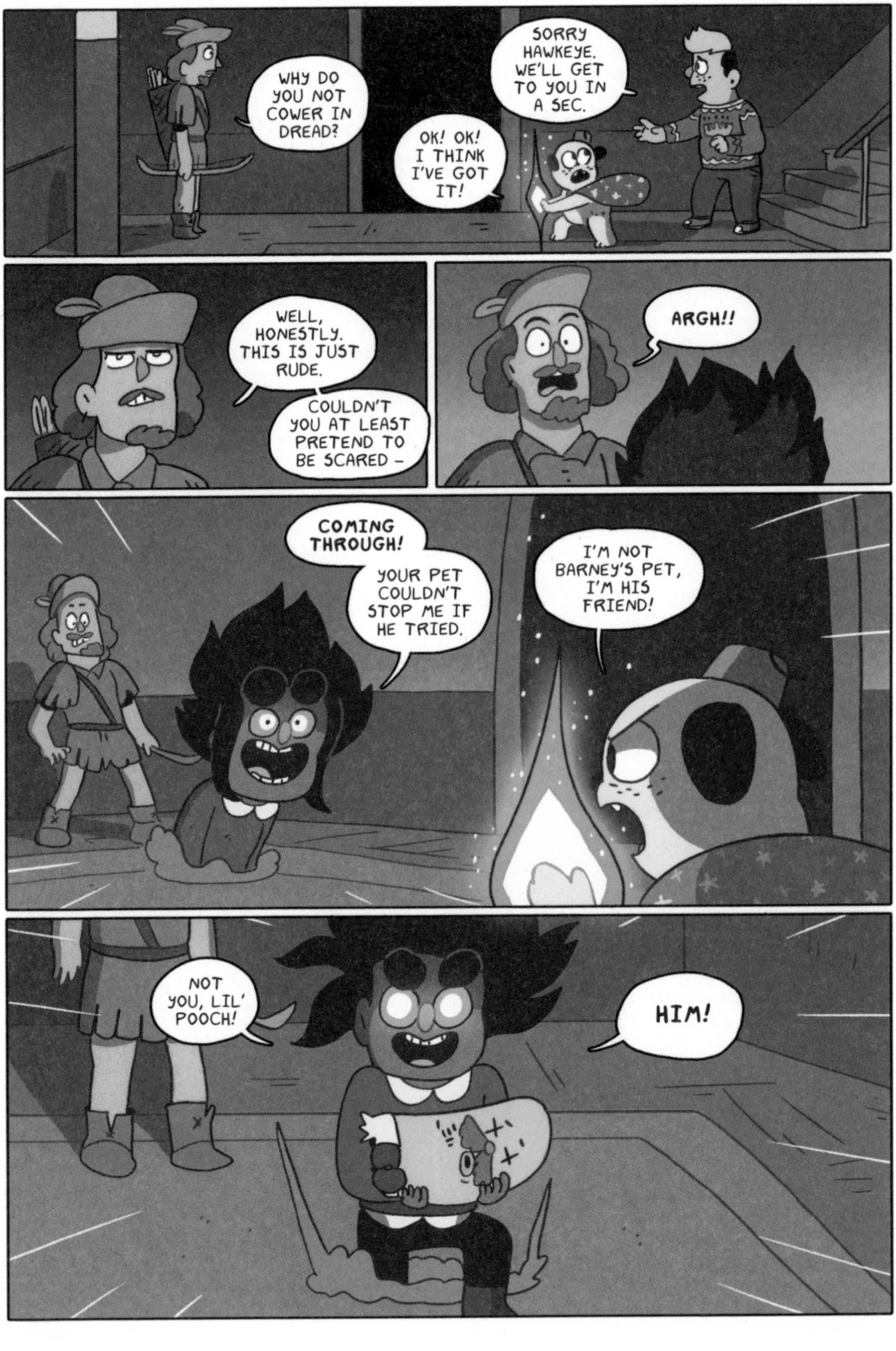

WHY DO YOU NOT COWER IN DREAD?
SORRY HAWKEYE. WE'LL GET TO YOU IN A SEC.
OK! OK! I THINK I'VE GOT IT!
WELL, HONESTLY. THIS IS JUST RUDE.
COULDN'T YOU AT LEAST PRETEND TO BE SCARED -
ARGH!!
COMING THROUGH!
YOUR PET COULDN'T STOP ME IF HE TRIED.
I'M NOT BARNEY'S PET, I'M HIS FRIEND!
NOT YOU, LIL' POOCH!
HIM!

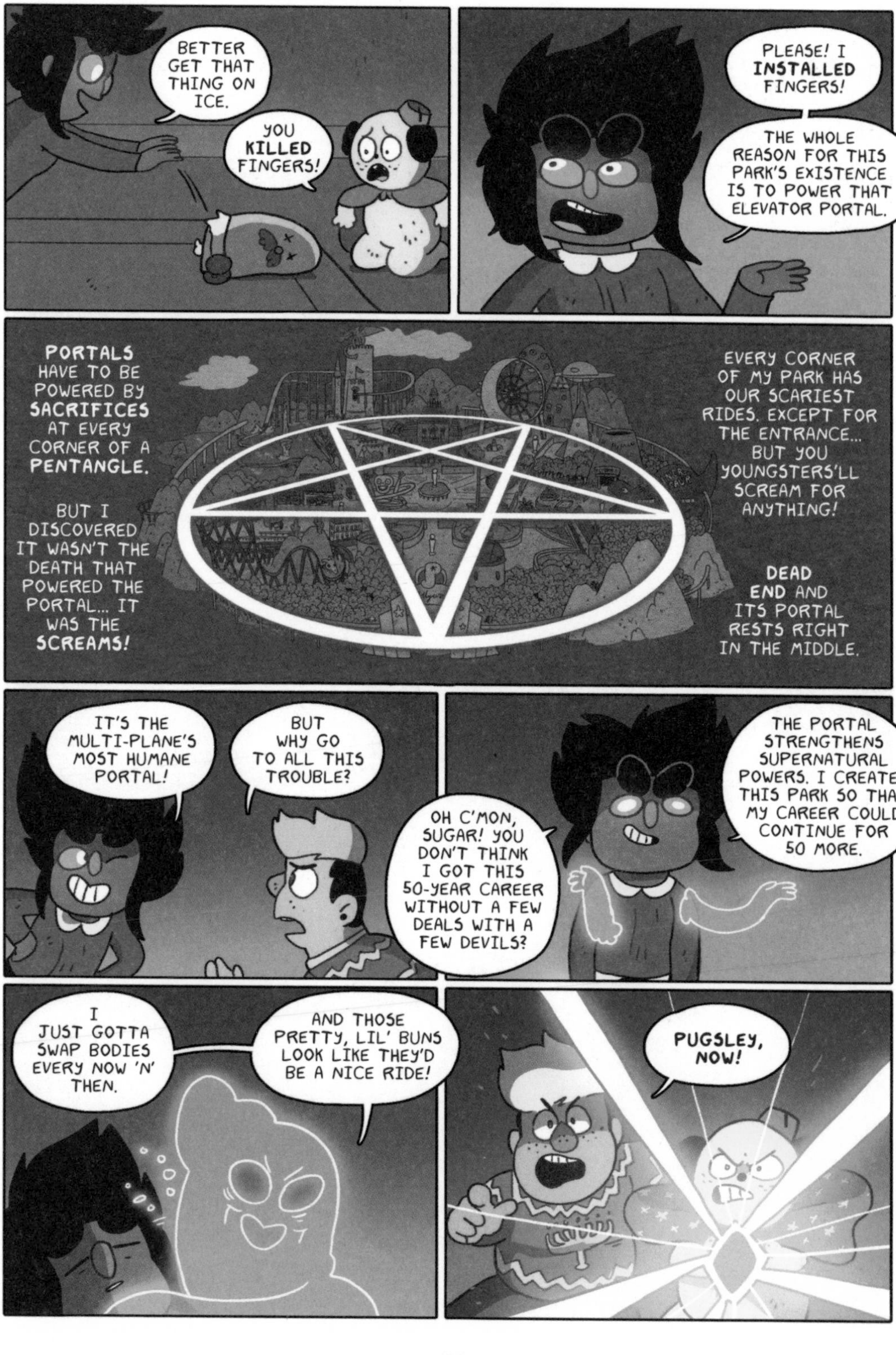
BETTER GET THAT THING ON ICE.
YOU KILLED FINGERS!
PLEASE! I INSTALLED FINGERS!
THE WHOLE REASON FOR THIS PARK'S EXISTENCE IS TO POWER THAT ELEVATOR PORTAL.
PORTALS HAVE TO BE POWERED BY SACRIFICES AT EVERY CORNER OF A PENTANGLE.
BUT I DISCOVERED IT WASN'T THE DEATH THAT POWERED THE PORTAL... IT WAS THE SCREAMS!
EVERY CORNER OF MY PARK HAS OUR SCARIEST RIDES. EXCEPT FOR THE ENTRANCE... BUT YOU YOUNGSTERS'LL SCREAM FOR ANYTHING!
DEAD END AND ITS PORTAL RESTS RIGHT IN THE MIDDLE.
IT'S THE MULTI-PLANE'S MOST HUMANE PORTAL!
BUT WHY GO TO ALL THIS TROUBLE?
OH C'MON, SUGAR! YOU DON'T THINK I GOT THIS 50-YEAR CAREER WITHOUT A FEW DEALS WITH A FEW DEVILS?
THE PORTAL STRENGTHENS SUPERNATURAL POWERS. I CREATED THIS PARK SO THAT MY CAREER COULD CONTINUE FOR 50 MORE.
I JUST GOTTA SWAP BODIES EVERY NOW 'N' THEN.
AND THOSE PRETTY, LIL' BUNS LOOK LIKE THEY'D BE A NICE RIDE!
PUGSLEY, NOW!

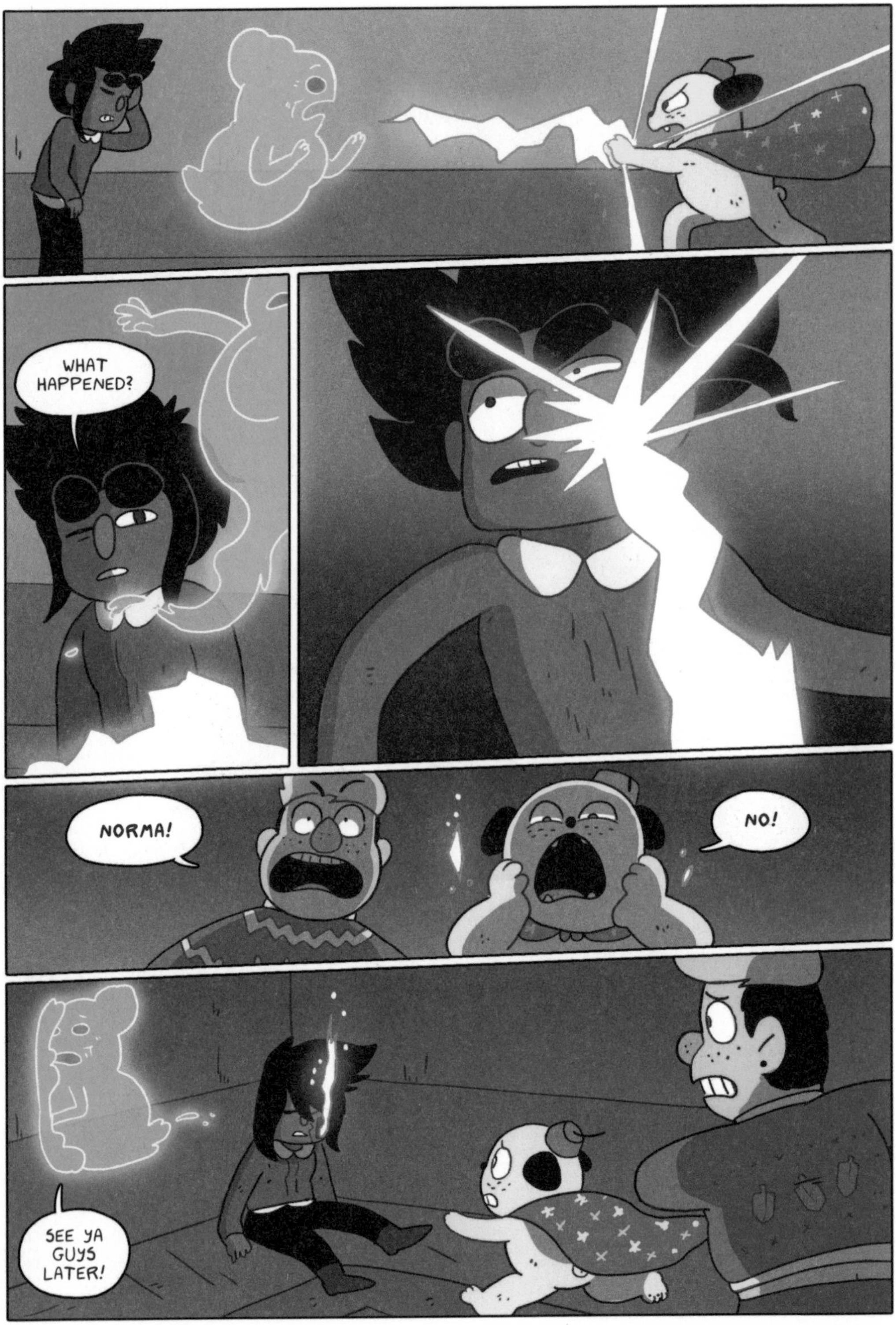
WHAT HAPPENED?
NORMA!
NO!
SEE YA GUYS LATER!

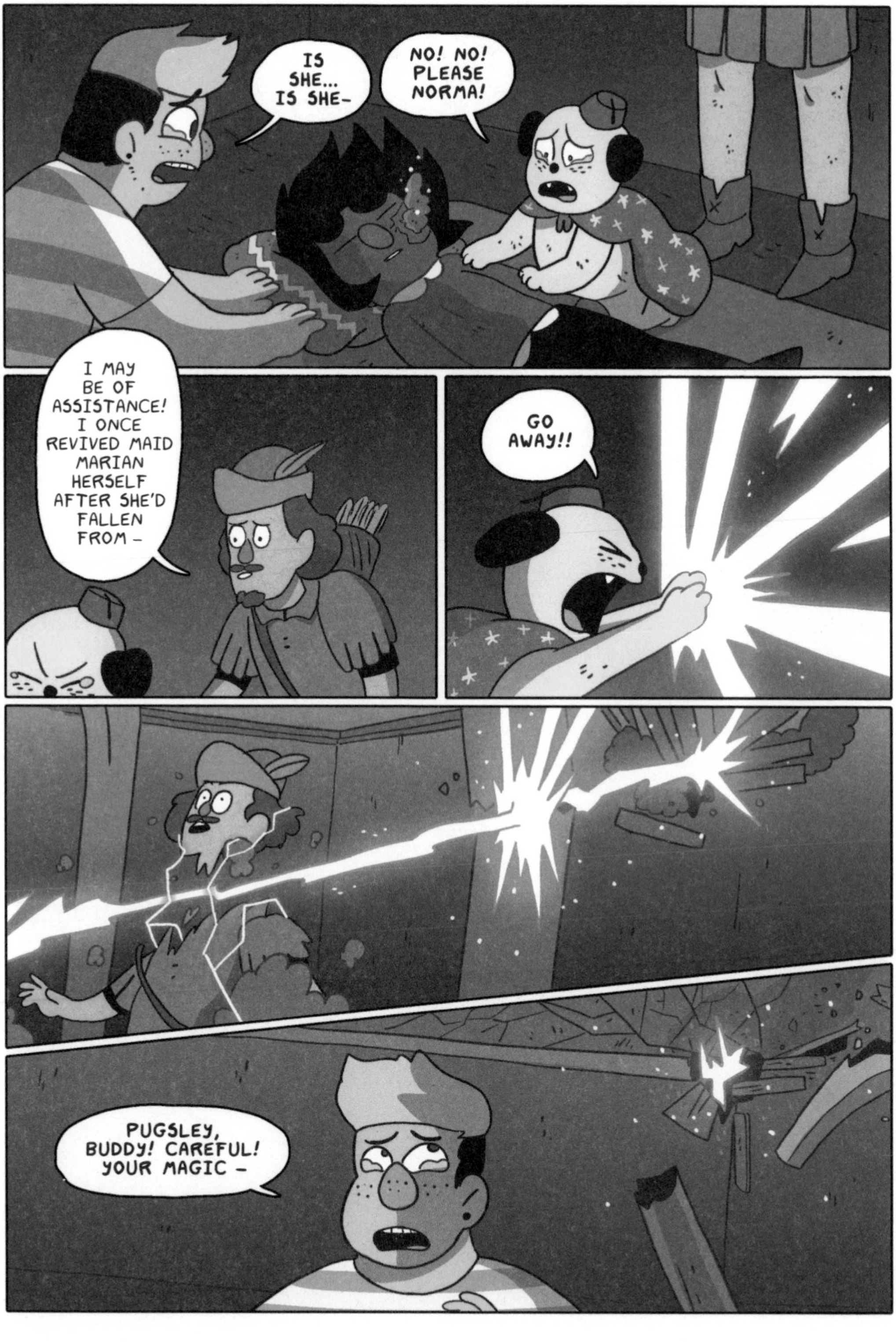
IS SHE... IS SHE-
NO! NO! PLEASE NORMA!
I MAY BE OF ASSISTANCE! I ONCE REVIVED MAID MARIAN HERSELF AFTER SHE'D FALLEN FROM -
GO AWAY!!
PUGSLEY, BUDDY! CAREFUL! YOUR MAGIC -

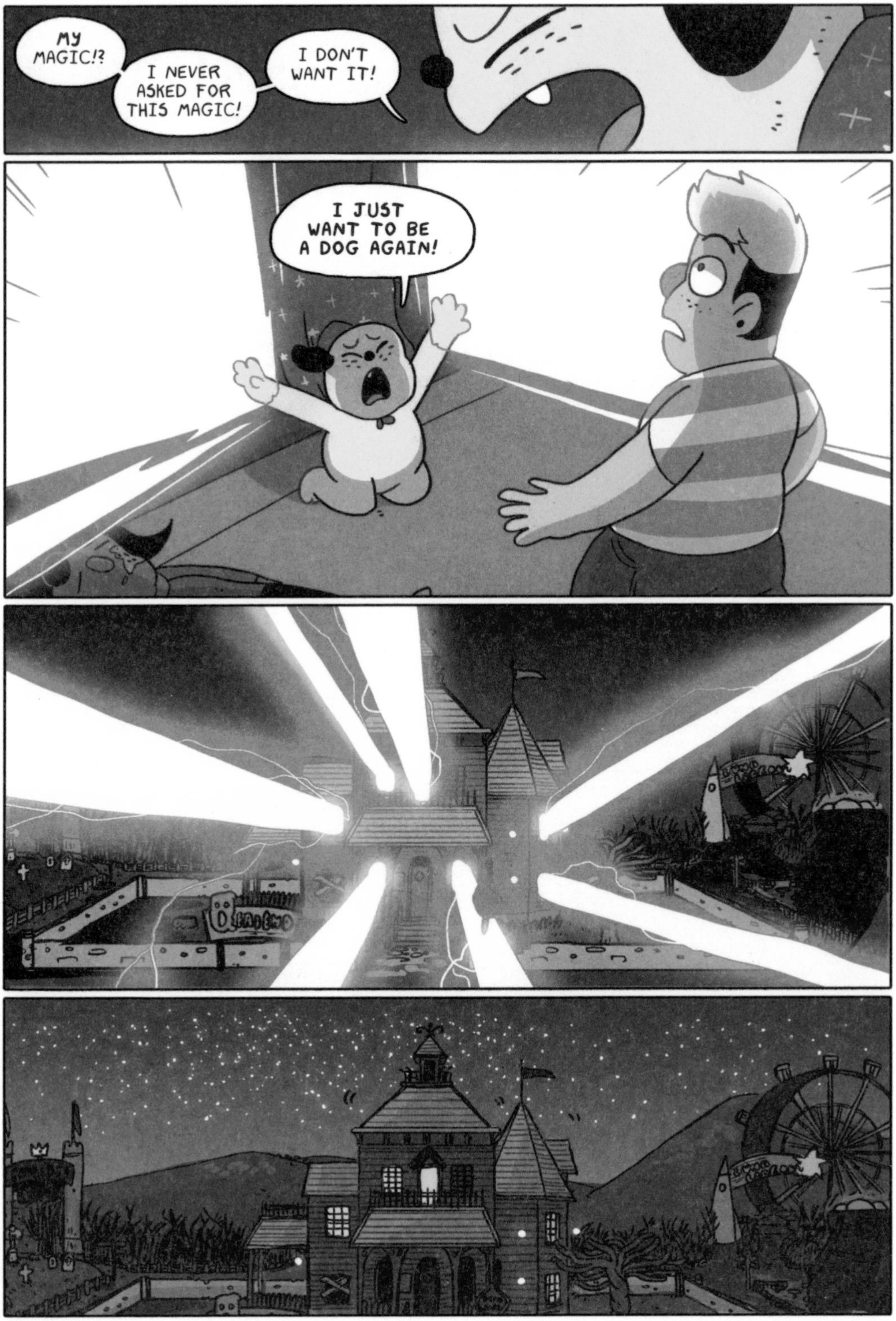
MY MAGIC!?
I NEVER ASKED FOR THIS MAGIC!
I DON'T WANT IT!
I JUST WANT TO BE A DOG AGAIN!

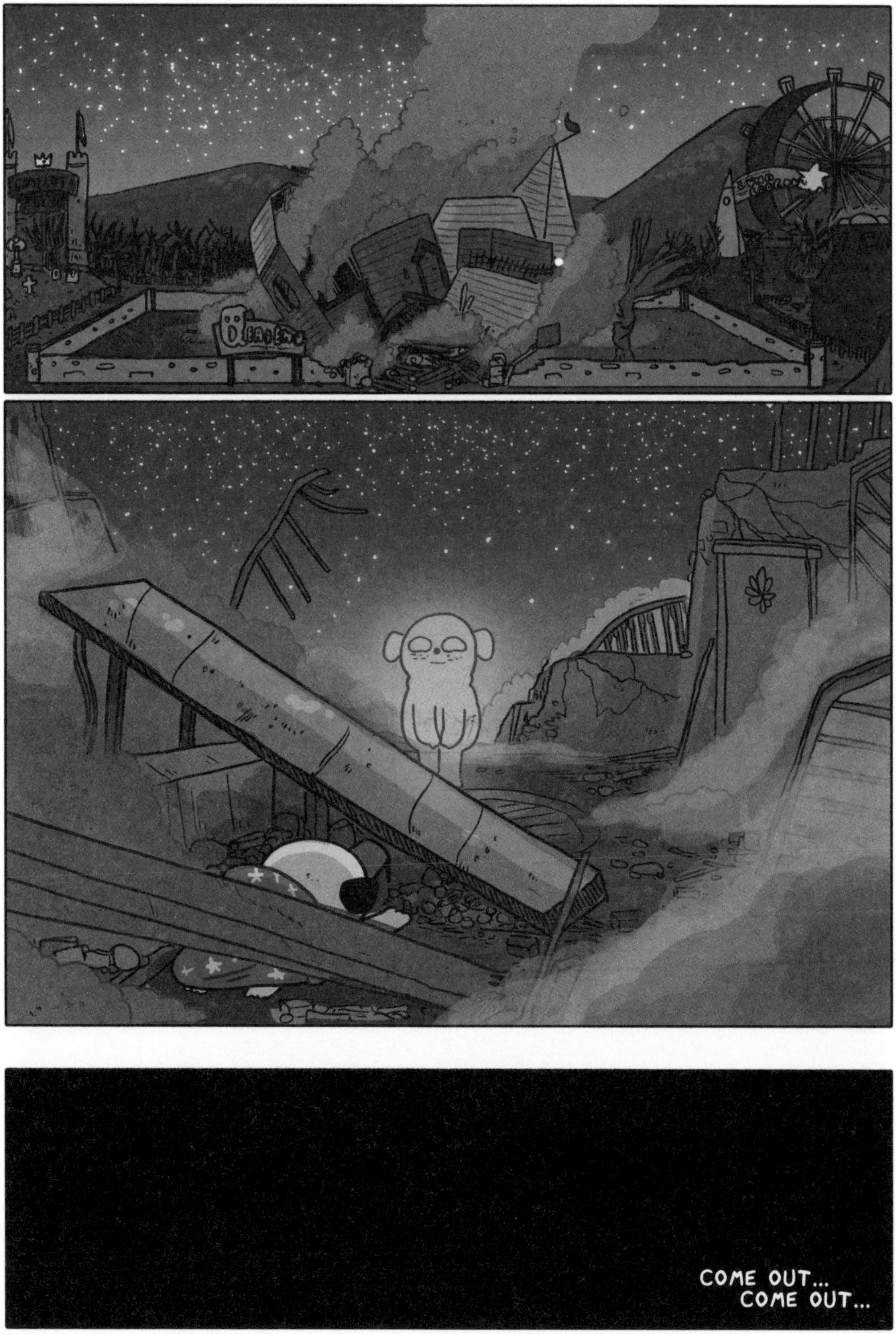
COME OUT...
COME OUT...

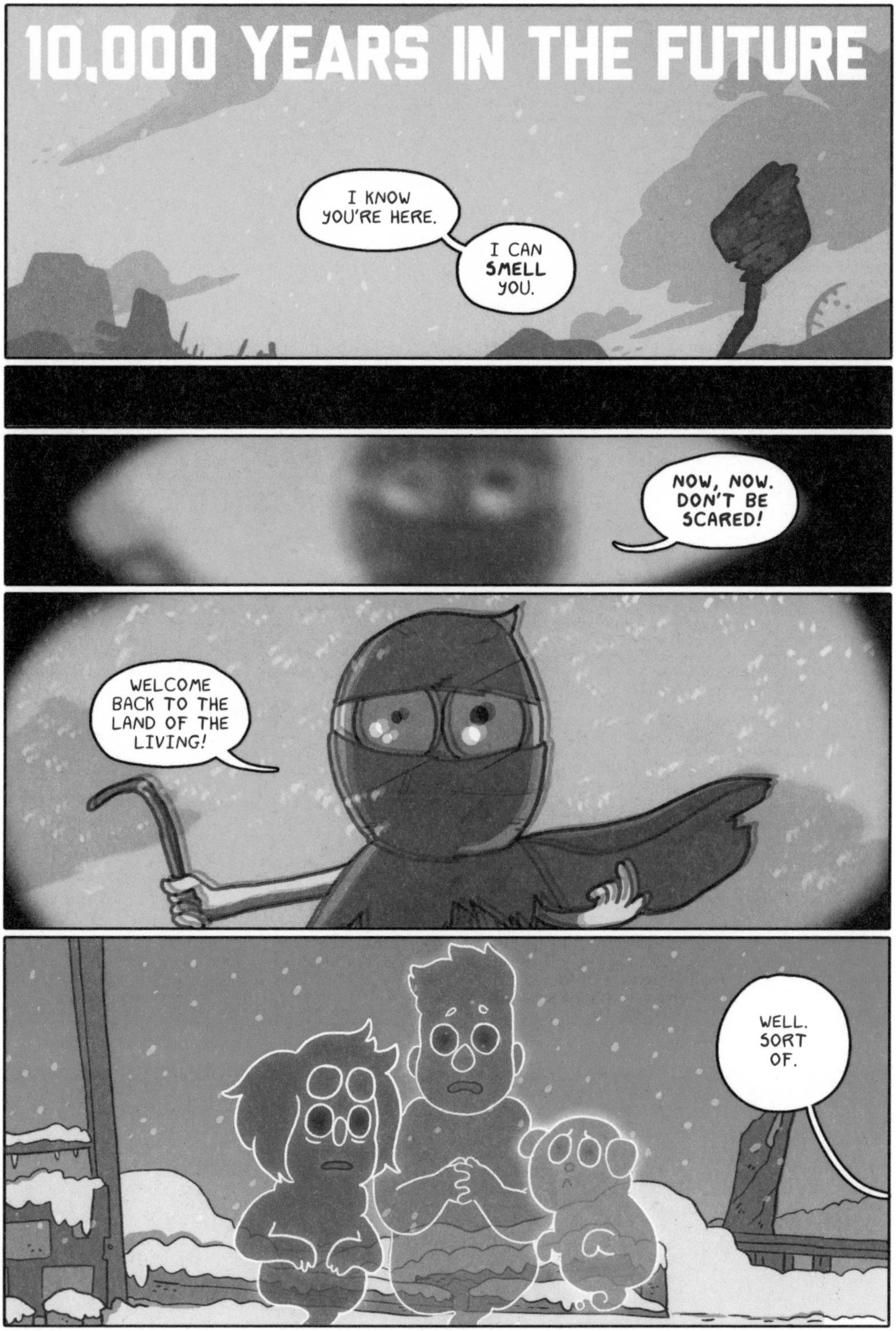
10,000 YEARS IN THE FUTURE
I KNOW YOU'RE HERE.
I CAN **SMELL** YOU.
NOW, NOW. DON'T BE SCARED!
WELCOME BACK TO THE LAND OF THE LIVING!
WELL. SORT OF.

CHAPTER 7

COVER ART BY TIFFANY BAXTER

THE WATCHER'S TEST

```
NAME .............................................."FINGERS"
PRONOUNS.........................................HE/HIM
AGE .............................................................31
OCCUPATION......................PORTAL PORTER
LIKES......................READING, WORKING HARD
DISLIKES........... GETTING CAUGHT IN DOORS
FAMILY .........................................IMPOSSIBLE
```

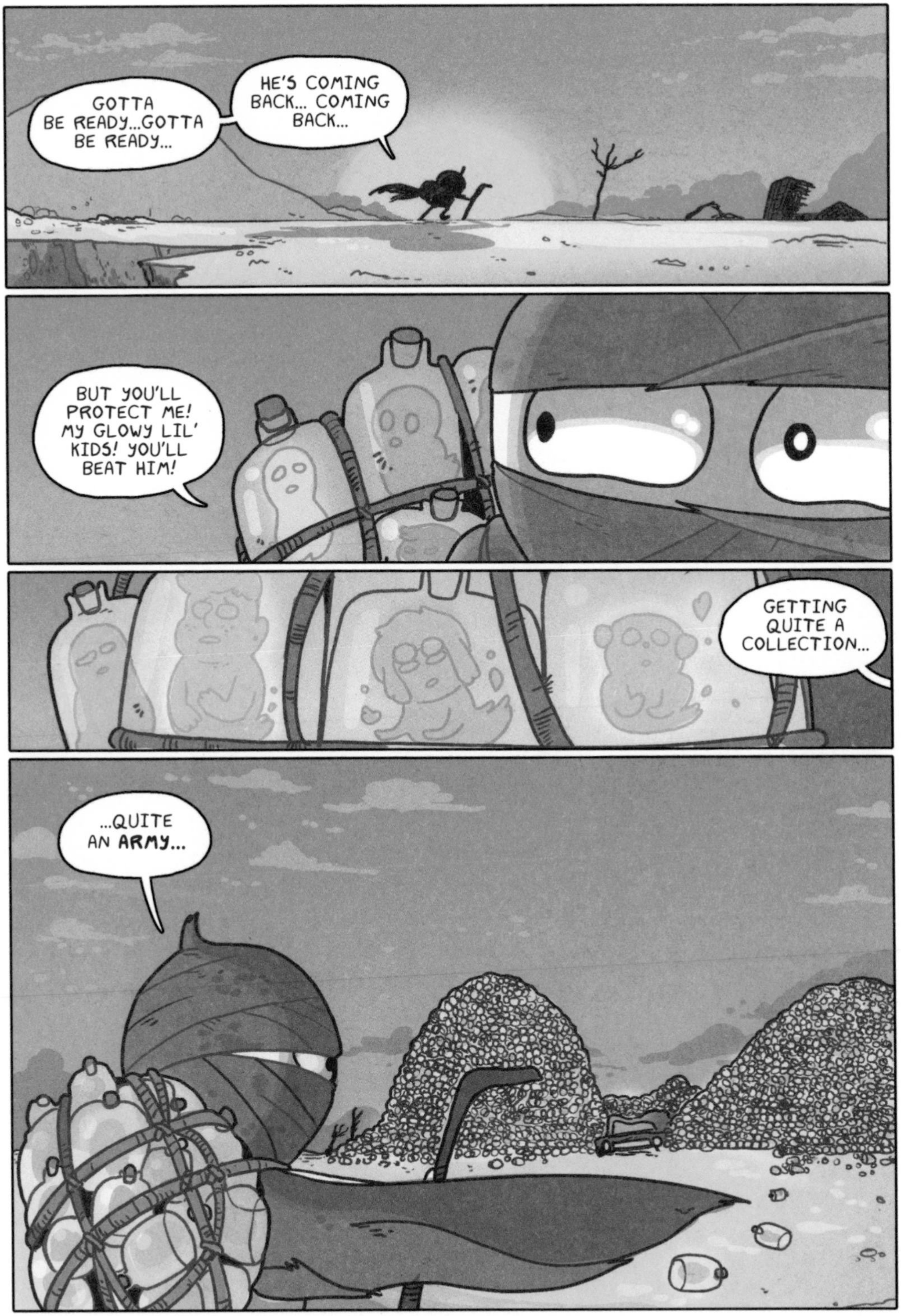
GOTTA BE READY...GOTTA BE READY...
HE'S COMING BACK... COMING BACK...
BUT YOU'LL PROTECT ME! MY GLOWY LIL' KIDS! YOU'LL BEAT HIM!
GETTING QUITE A COLLECTION...
...QUITE AN **ARMY**...

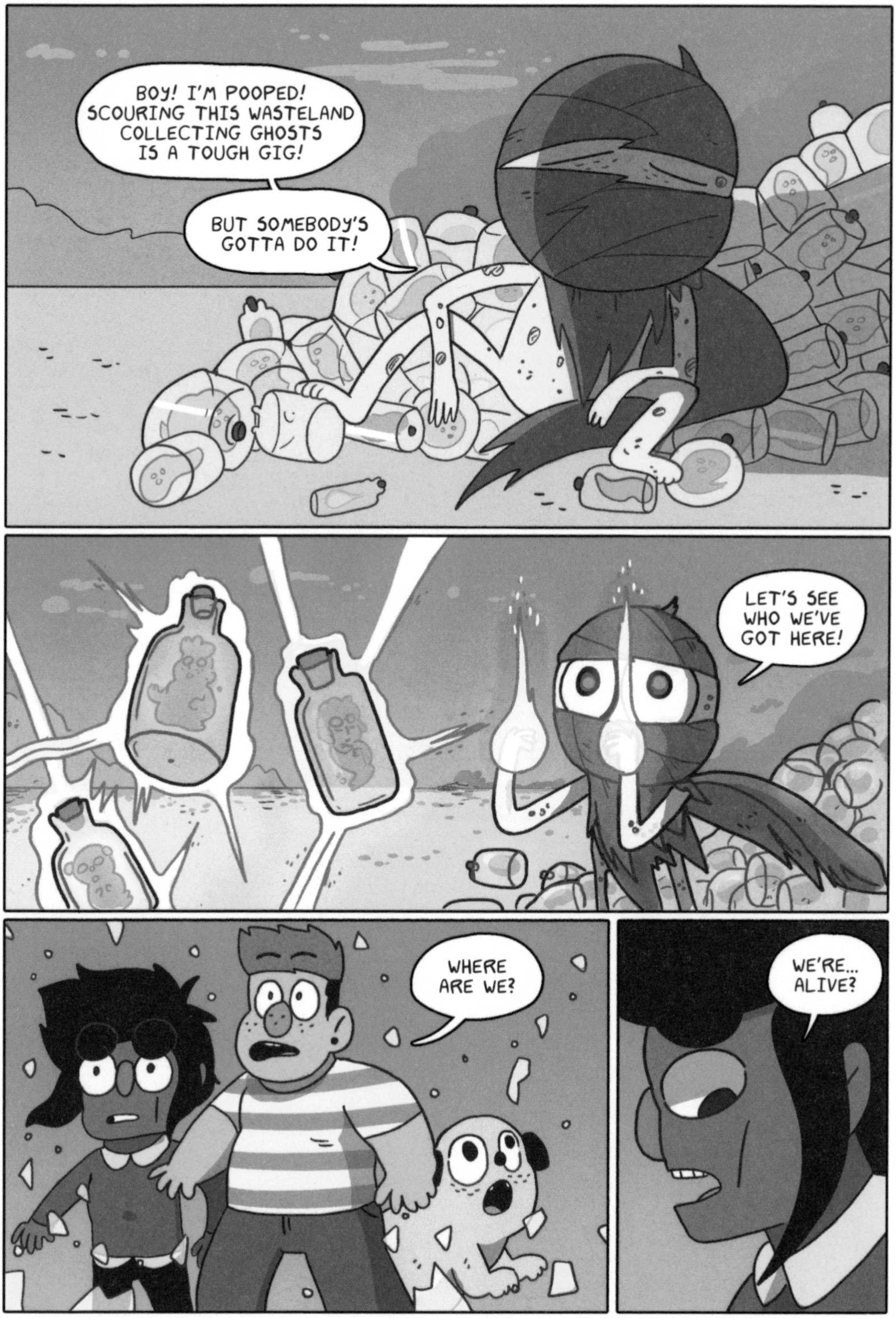
BOY! I'M POOPED! SCOURING THIS WASTELAND COLLECTING GHOSTS IS A TOUGH GIG!
BUT SOMEBODY'S GOTTA DO IT!
LET'S SEE WHO WE'VE GOT HERE!
WHERE ARE WE?
WE'RE... ALIVE?

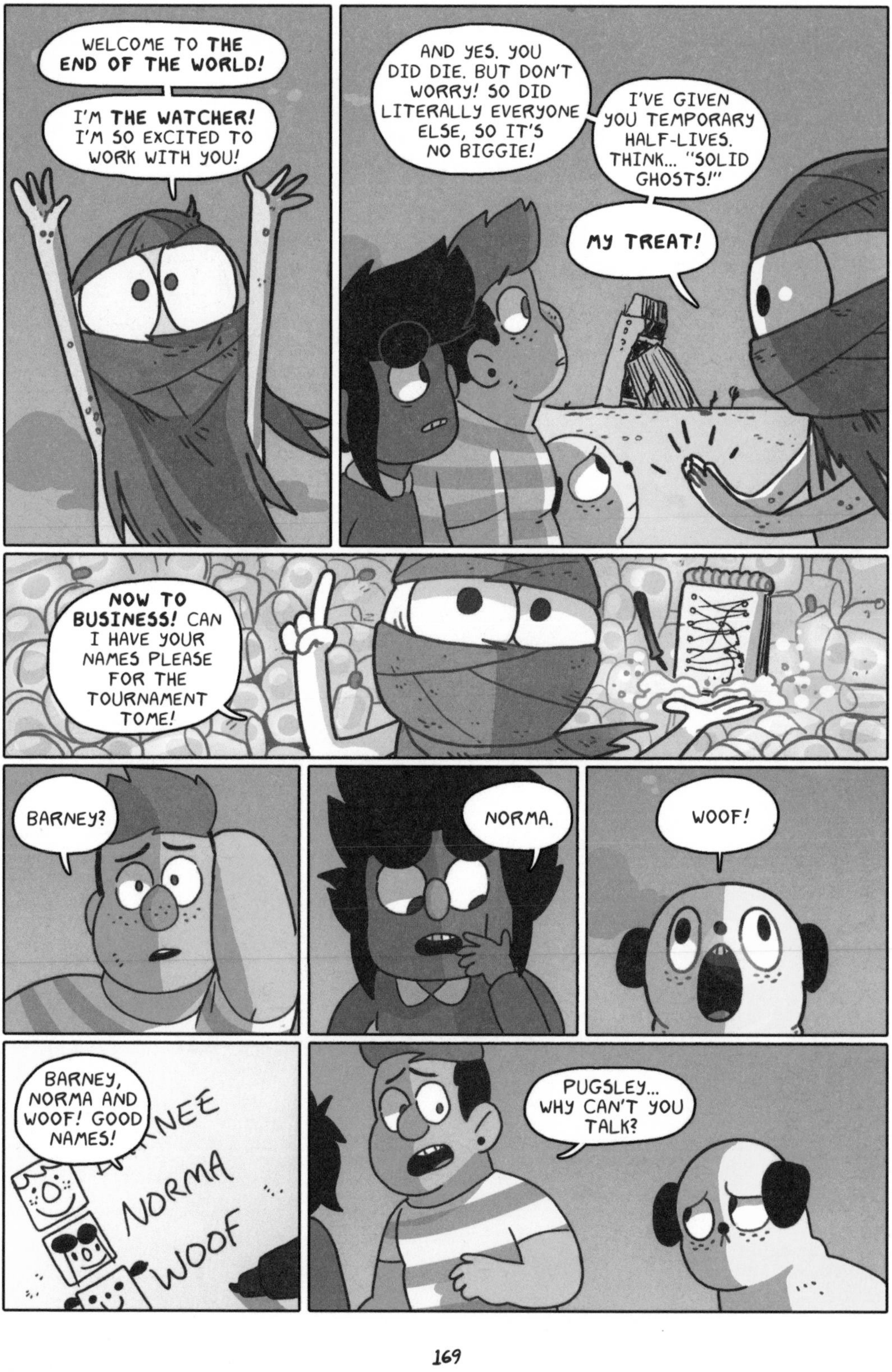
WELCOME TO THE END OF THE WORLD!
I'M THE WATCHER! I'M SO EXCITED TO WORK WITH YOU!
AND YES. YOU DID DIE. BUT DON'T WORRY! SO DID LITERALLY EVERYONE ELSE, SO IT'S NO BIGGIE!
I'VE GIVEN YOU TEMPORARY HALF-LIVES. THINK... "SOLID GHOSTS!"
MY TREAT!
NOW TO BUSINESS! CAN I HAVE YOUR NAMES PLEASE FOR THE TOURNAMENT TOME!
BARNEY?
NORMA.
WOOF!
BARNEY, NORMA AND WOOF! GOOD NAMES!
NORMA
WOOF
PUGSLEY... WHY CAN'T YOU TALK?

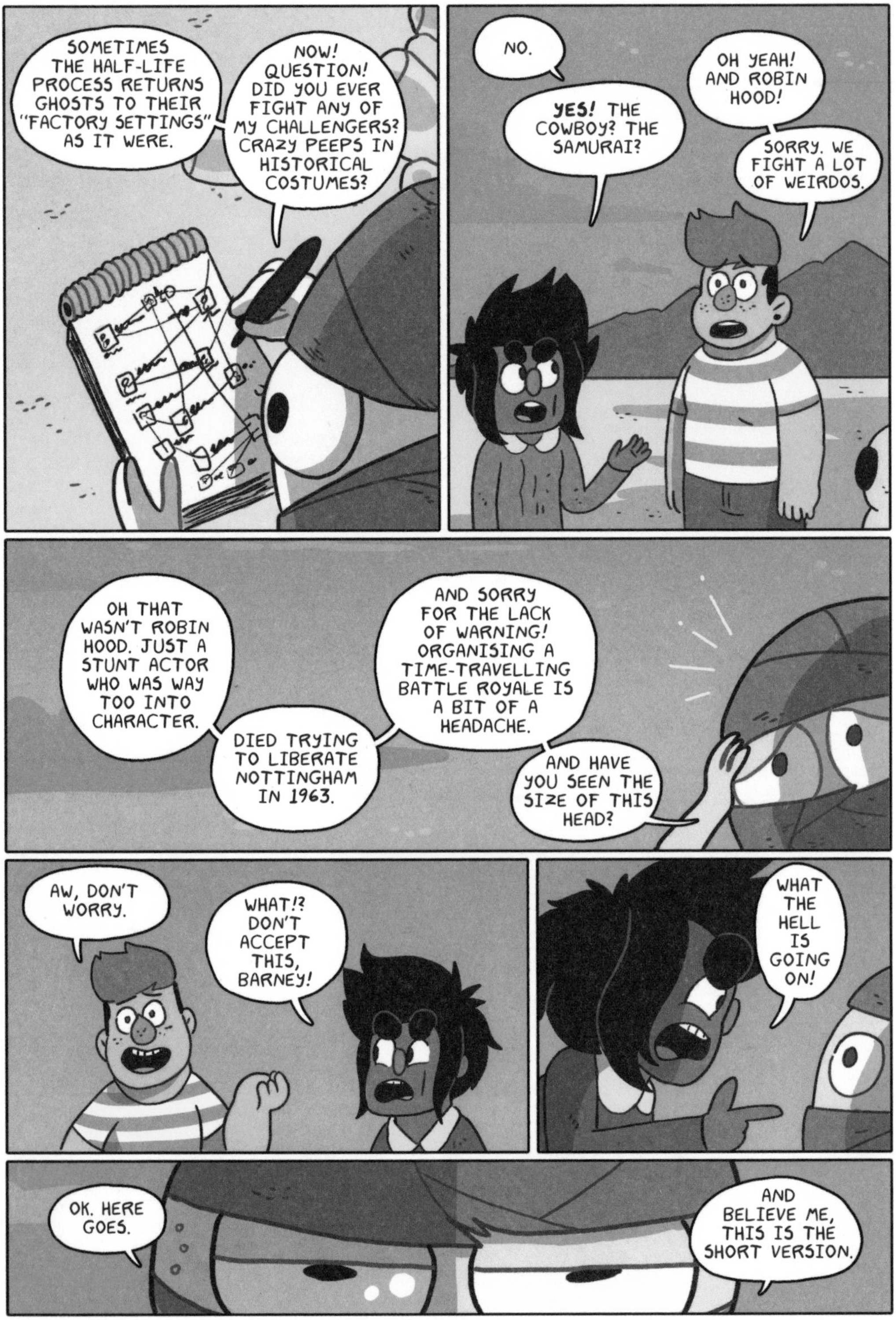
SOMETIMES THE HALF-LIFE PROCESS RETURNS GHOSTS TO THEIR "FACTORY SETTINGS" AS IT WERE.
NOW! QUESTION! DID YOU EVER FIGHT ANY OF MY CHALLENGERS? CRAZY PEEPS IN HISTORICAL COSTUMES?
NO.
YES! THE COWBOY? THE SAMURAI?
OH YEAH! AND ROBIN HOOD!
SORRY. WE FIGHT A LOT OF WEIRDOS.
OH THAT WASN'T ROBIN HOOD. JUST A STUNT ACTOR WHO WAS WAY TOO INTO CHARACTER.
DIED TRYING TO LIBERATE NOTTINGHAM IN 1963.
AND SORRY FOR THE LACK OF WARNING! ORGANISING A TIME-TRAVELLING BATTLE ROYALE IS A BIT OF A HEADACHE.
AND HAVE YOU SEEN THE SIZE OF THIS HEAD?
AW, DON'T WORRY.
WHAT!? DON'T ACCEPT THIS, BARNEY!
WHAT THE HELL IS GOING ON!
OK. HERE GOES.
AND BELIEVE ME, THIS IS THE SHORT VERSION.

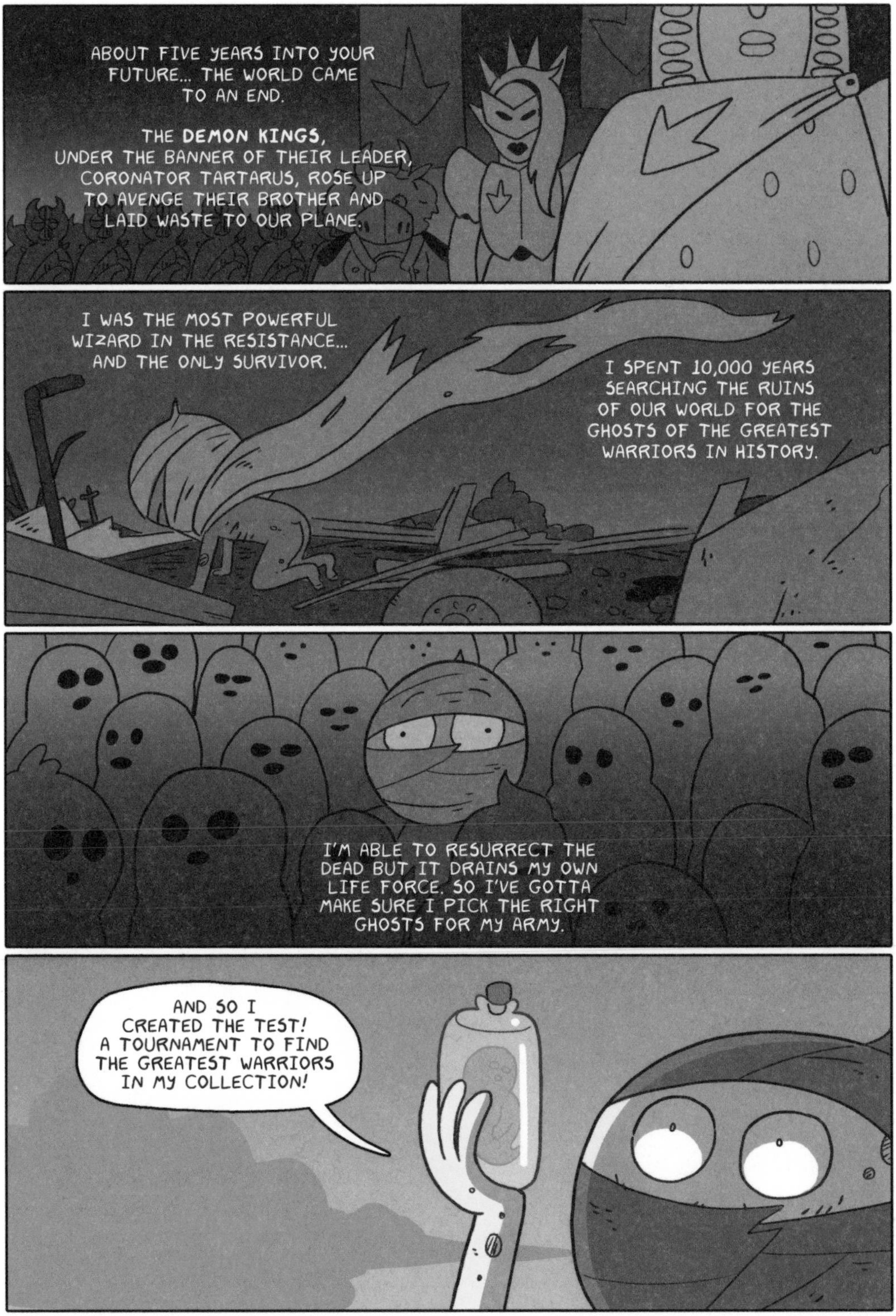
ABOUT FIVE YEARS INTO YOUR FUTURE... THE WORLD CAME TO AN END.
THE **DEMON KINGS**, UNDER THE BANNER OF THEIR LEADER, CORONATOR TARTARUS, ROSE UP TO AVENGE THEIR BROTHER AND LAID WASTE TO OUR PLANE.
I WAS THE MOST POWERFUL WIZARD IN THE RESISTANCE... AND THE ONLY SURVIVOR.
I SPENT 10,000 YEARS SEARCHING THE RUINS OF OUR WORLD FOR THE GHOSTS OF THE GREATEST WARRIORS IN HISTORY.
I'M ABLE TO RESURRECT THE DEAD BUT IT DRAINS MY OWN LIFE FORCE. SO I'VE GOTTA MAKE SURE I PICK THE RIGHT GHOSTS FOR MY ARMY.
AND SO I CREATED THE TEST! A TOURNAMENT TO FIND THE GREATEST WARRIORS IN MY COLLECTION!

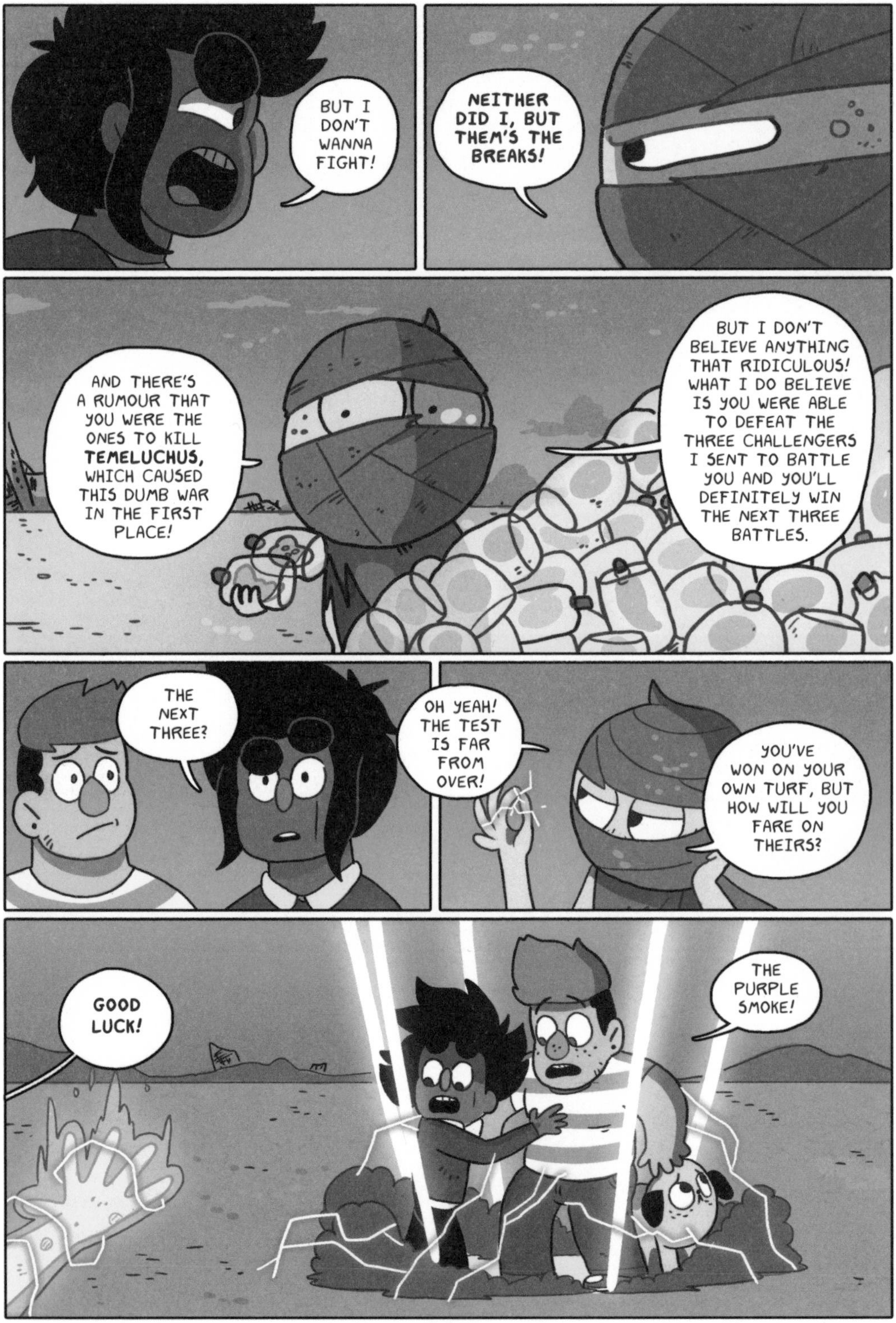
BUT I DON'T WANNA FIGHT!
NEITHER DID I, BUT THEM'S THE BREAKS!
AND THERE'S A RUMOUR THAT YOU WERE THE ONES TO KILL **TEMELUCHUS,** WHICH CAUSED THIS DUMB WAR IN THE FIRST PLACE!
BUT I DON'T BELIEVE ANYTHING THAT RIDICULOUS! WHAT I DO BELIEVE IS YOU WERE ABLE TO DEFEAT THE THREE CHALLENGERS I SENT TO BATTLE YOU AND YOU'LL DEFINITELY WIN THE NEXT THREE BATTLES.
THE NEXT THREE?
OH YEAH! THE TEST IS FAR FROM OVER!
YOU'VE WON ON YOUR OWN TURF, BUT HOW WILL YOU FARE ON THEIRS?
GOOD LUCK!
THE PURPLE SMOKE!

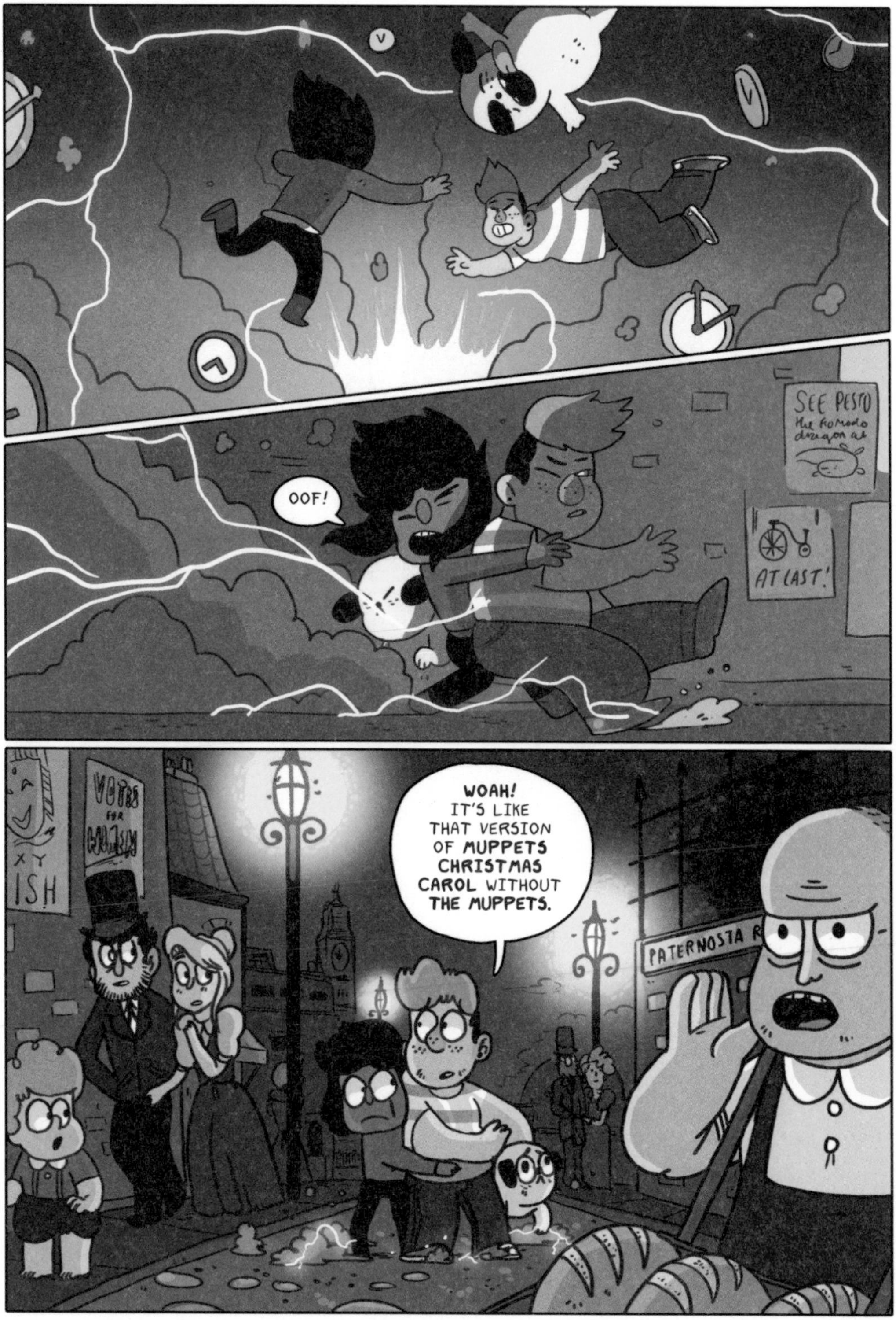
SEE PESTO
the Komodo dragon at
AT LAST!
OOF!
WOAH! IT'S LIKE THAT VERSION OF **MUPPETS CHRISTMAS CAROL** WITHOUT **THE MUPPETS**.
PATERNOSTA

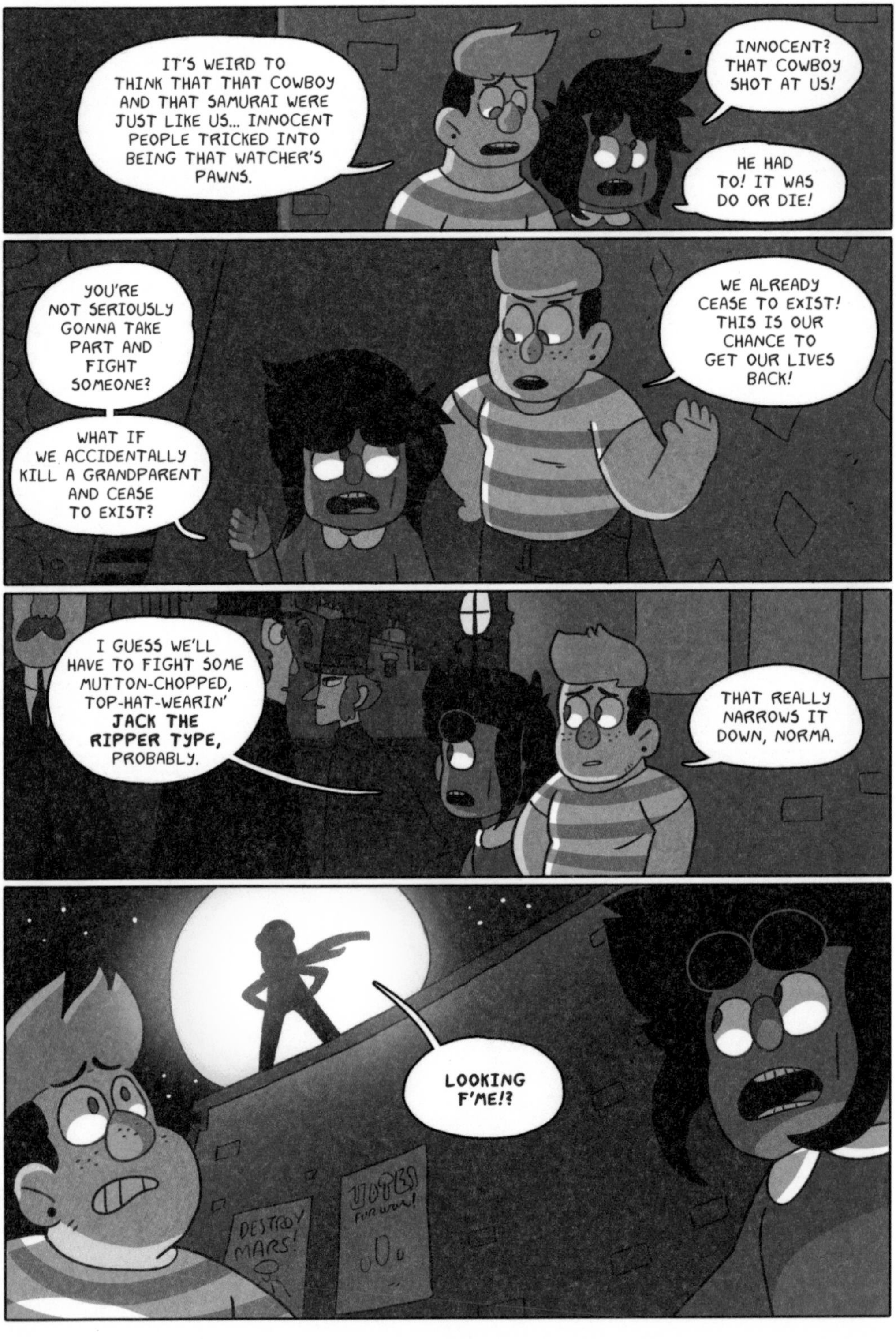
IT'S WEIRD TO THINK THAT THAT COWBOY AND THAT SAMURAI WERE JUST LIKE US... INNOCENT PEOPLE TRICKED INTO BEING THAT WATCHER'S PAWNS.
INNOCENT? THAT COWBOY SHOT AT US!
HE HAD TO! IT WAS DO OR DIE!
YOU'RE NOT SERIOUSLY GONNA TAKE PART AND FIGHT SOMEONE?
WHAT IF WE ACCIDENTALLY KILL A GRANDPARENT AND CEASE TO EXIST?
WE ALREADY CEASE TO EXIST! THIS IS OUR CHANCE TO GET OUR LIVES BACK!
I GUESS WE'LL HAVE TO FIGHT SOME MUTTON-CHOPPED, TOP-HAT-WEARIN' **JACK THE RIPPER TYPE,** PROBABLY.
THAT REALLY NARROWS IT DOWN, NORMA.
LOOKING F'ME!?
DESTROY MARS!

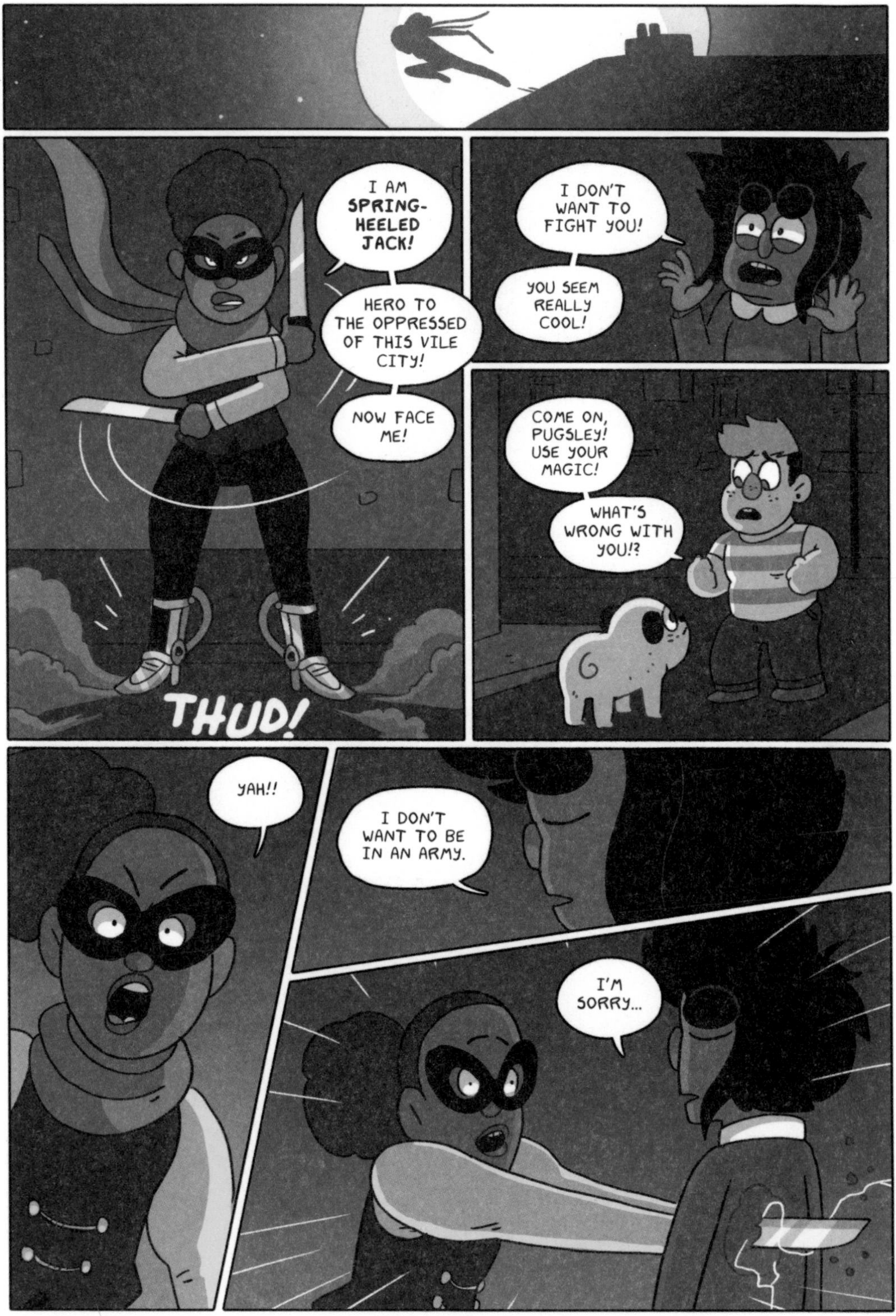
I AM **SPRING-HEELED JACK!**
HERO TO THE OPPRESSED OF THIS VILE CITY!
NOW FACE ME!
THUD!
I DON'T WANT TO FIGHT YOU!
YOU SEEM REALLY COOL!
COME ON, PUGSLEY! USE YOUR MAGIC!
WHAT'S WRONG WITH YOU!?
YAH!!
I DON'T WANT TO BE IN AN ARMY.
I'M SORRY...

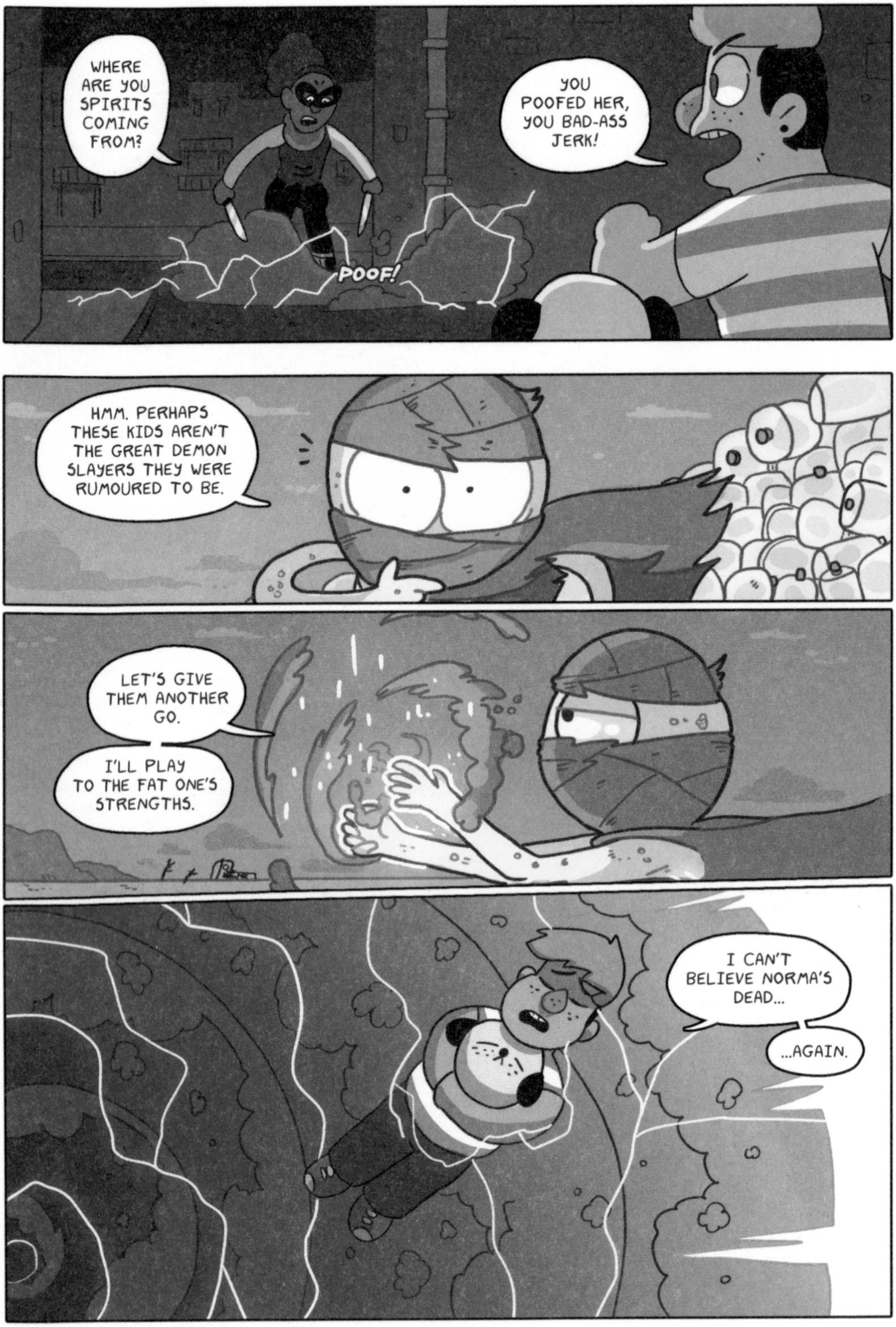
WHERE ARE YOU SPIRITS COMING FROM?
YOU POOFED HER, YOU BAD-ASS JERK!
POOF!
HMM. PERHAPS THESE KIDS AREN'T THE GREAT DEMON SLAYERS THEY WERE RUMOURED TO BE.
LET'S GIVE THEM ANOTHER GO.
I'LL PLAY TO THE FAT ONE'S STRENGTHS.
I CAN'T BELIEVE NORMA'S DEAD...
...AGAIN.

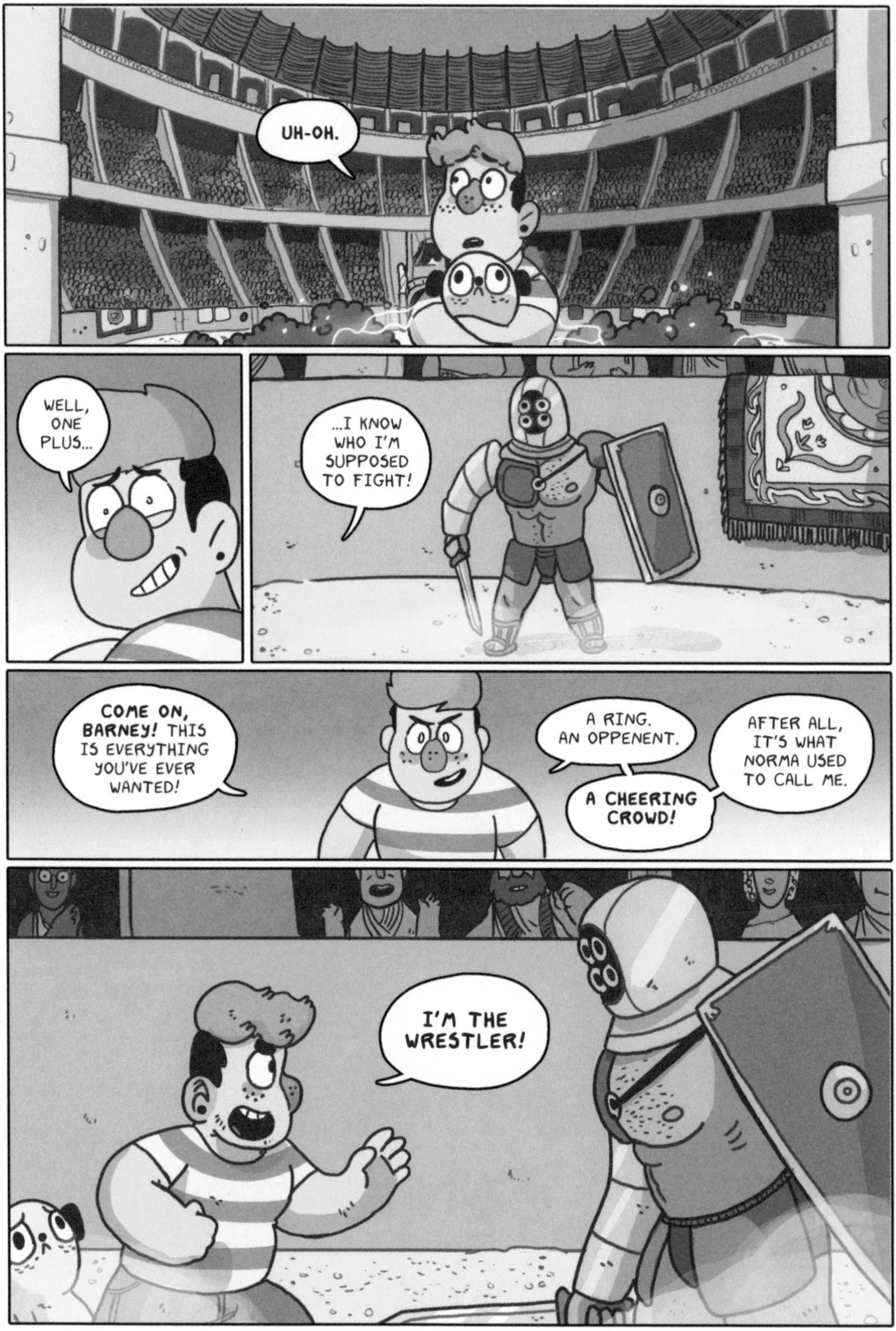
UH-OH.
WELL, ONE PLUS...
...I KNOW WHO I'M SUPPOSED TO FIGHT!
COME ON, BARNEY! THIS IS EVERYTHING YOU'VE EVER WANTED!
A RING. AN OPPENENT.
A CHEERING CROWD!
AFTER ALL, IT'S WHAT NORMA USED TO CALL ME.
I'M THE WRESTLER!

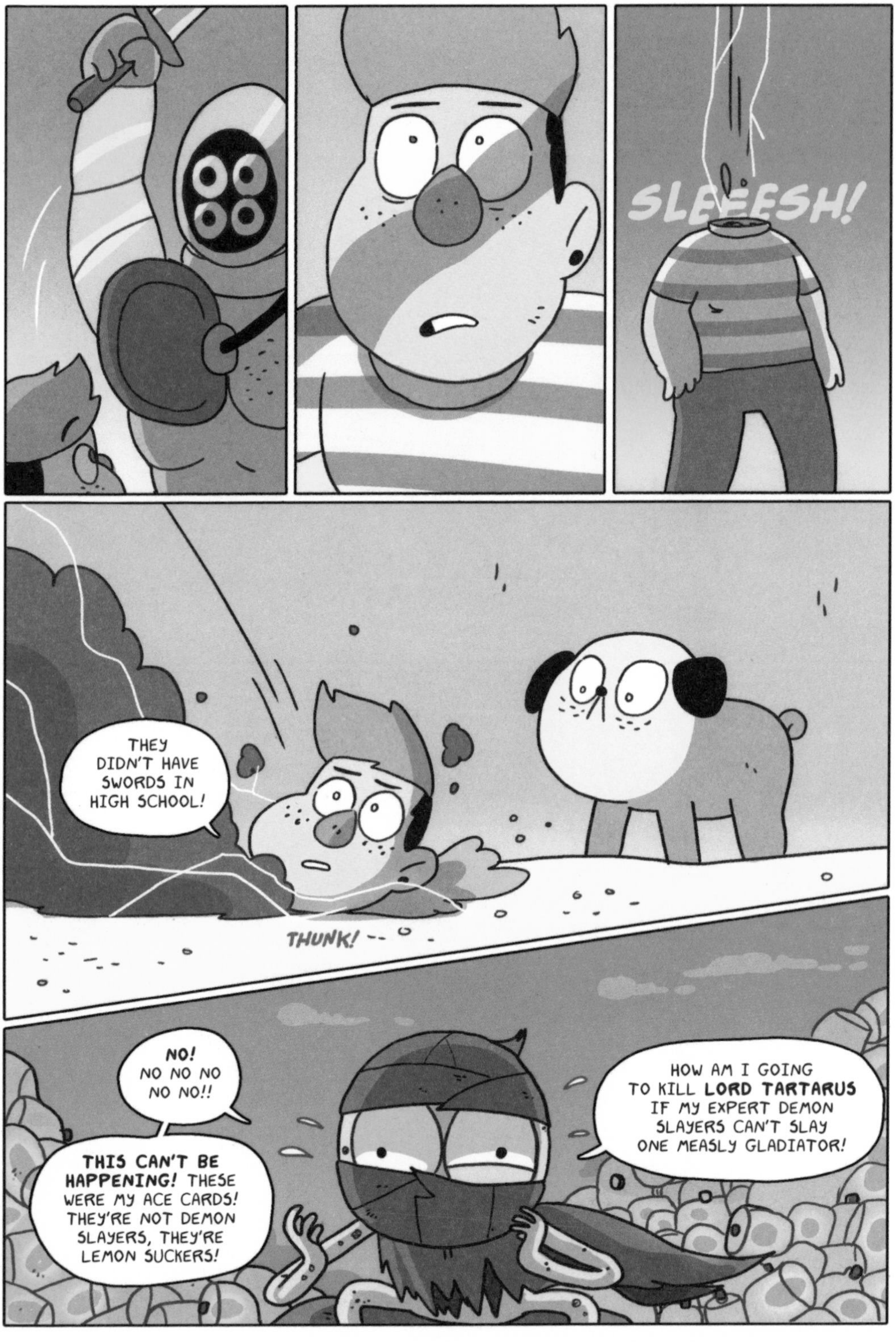
SLEEESH!
THEY DIDN'T HAVE SWORDS IN HIGH SCHOOL!
THUNK!
NO! NO NO NO NO NO!!
THIS CAN'T BE HAPPENING! THESE WERE MY ACE CARDS! THEY'RE NOT DEMON SLAYERS, THEY'RE LEMON SUCKERS!
HOW AM I GOING TO KILL LORD TARTARUS IF MY EXPERT DEMON SLAYERS CAN'T SLAY ONE MEASLY GLADIATOR!

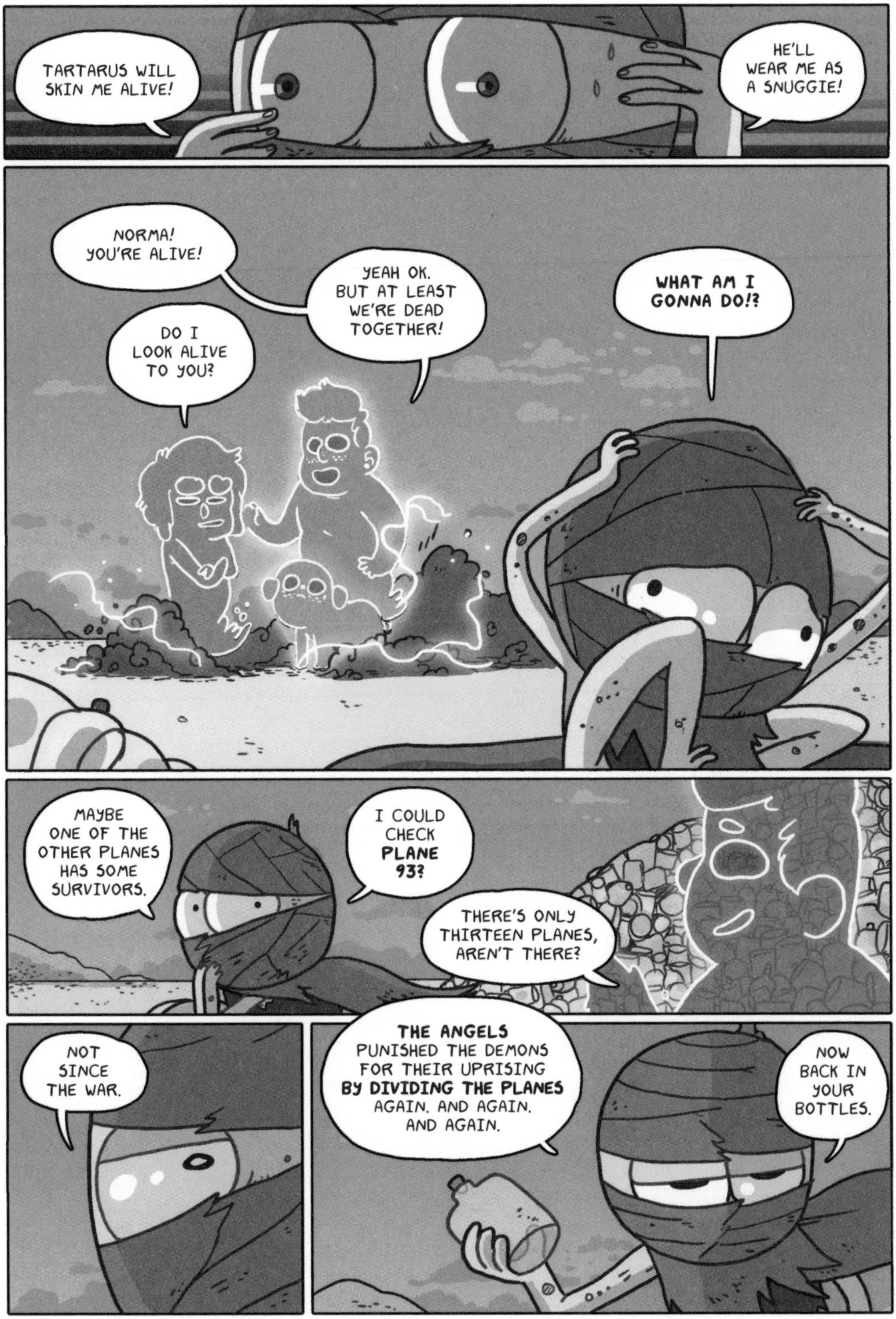
TARTARUS WILL SKIN ME ALIVE!
HE'LL WEAR ME AS A SNUGGIE!
NORMA! YOU'RE ALIVE!
DO I LOOK ALIVE TO YOU?
YEAH OK. BUT AT LEAST WE'RE DEAD TOGETHER!
WHAT AM I GONNA DO!?
MAYBE ONE OF THE OTHER PLANES HAS SOME SURVIVORS.
I COULD CHECK PLANE 93?
THERE'S ONLY THIRTEEN PLANES, AREN'T THERE?
NOT SINCE THE WAR.
THE ANGELS PUNISHED THE DEMONS FOR THEIR UPRISING BY DIVIDING THE PLANES AGAIN. AND AGAIN. AND AGAIN.
NOW BACK IN YOUR BOTTLES.

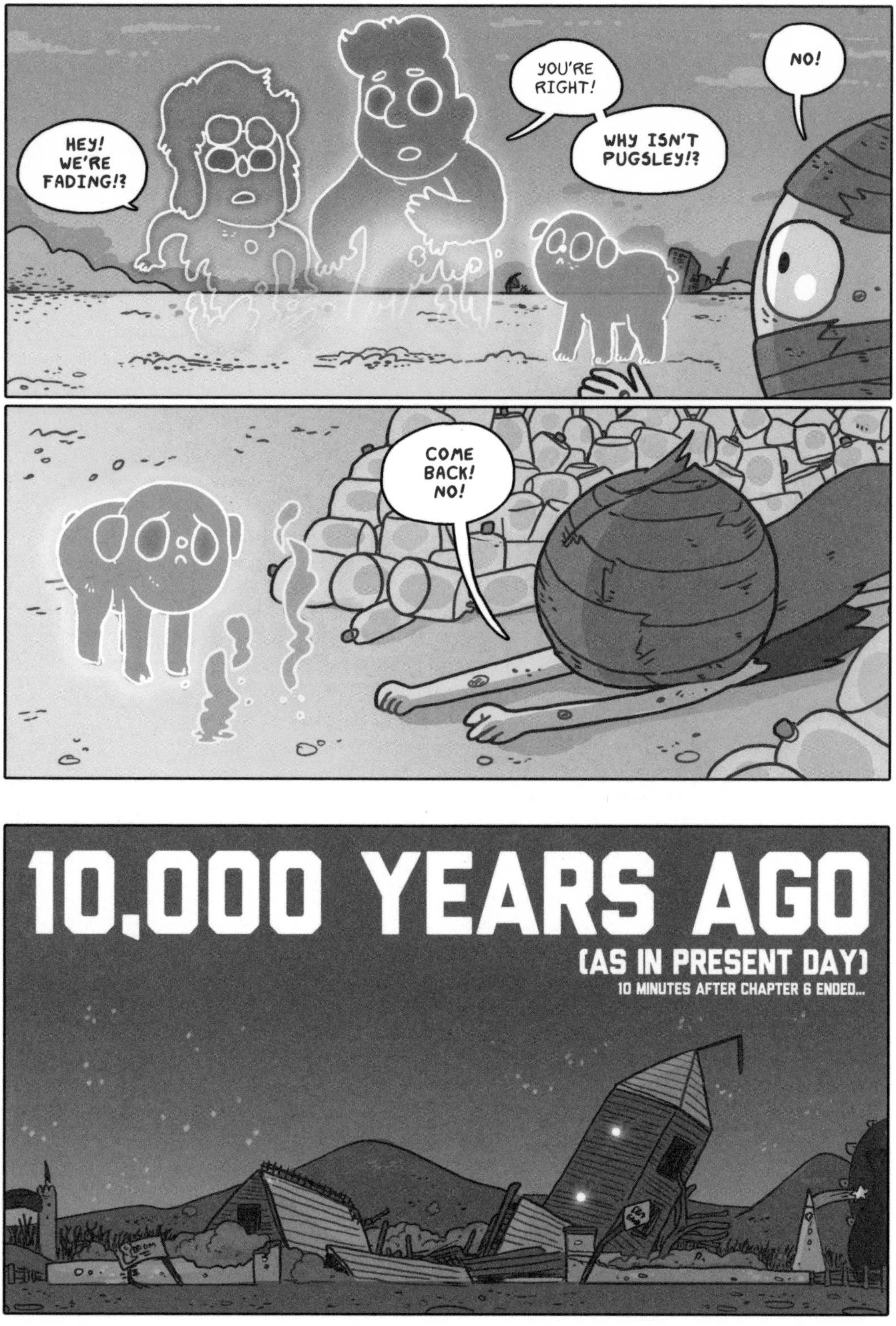
HEY! WE'RE FADING!?
YOU'RE RIGHT!
WHY ISN'T PUGSLEY!?
NO!
COME BACK! NO!
10,000 YEARS AGO
(AS IN PRESENT DAY)
10 MINUTES AFTER CHAPTER 6 ENDED...

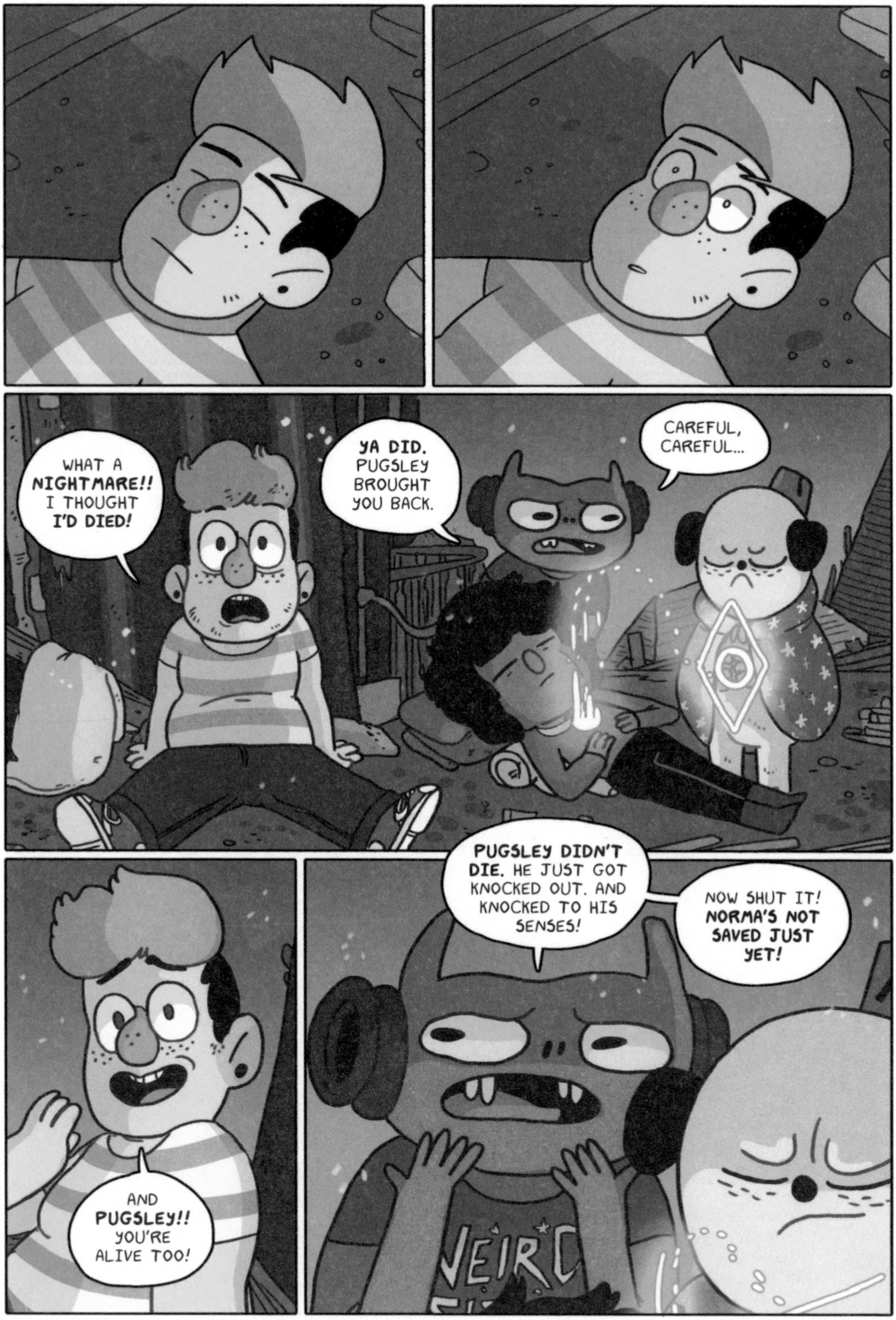
WHAT A **NIGHTMARE!!** I THOUGHT **I'D DIED!**
YA DID. PUGSLEY BROUGHT YOU BACK.
CAREFUL, CAREFUL...
AND **PUGSLEY!!** YOU'RE ALIVE TOO!
PUGSLEY DIDN'T DIE. HE JUST GOT KNOCKED OUT. AND KNOCKED TO HIS SENSES!
NOW SHUT IT! **NORMA'S NOT SAVED JUST YET!**
WEIRD

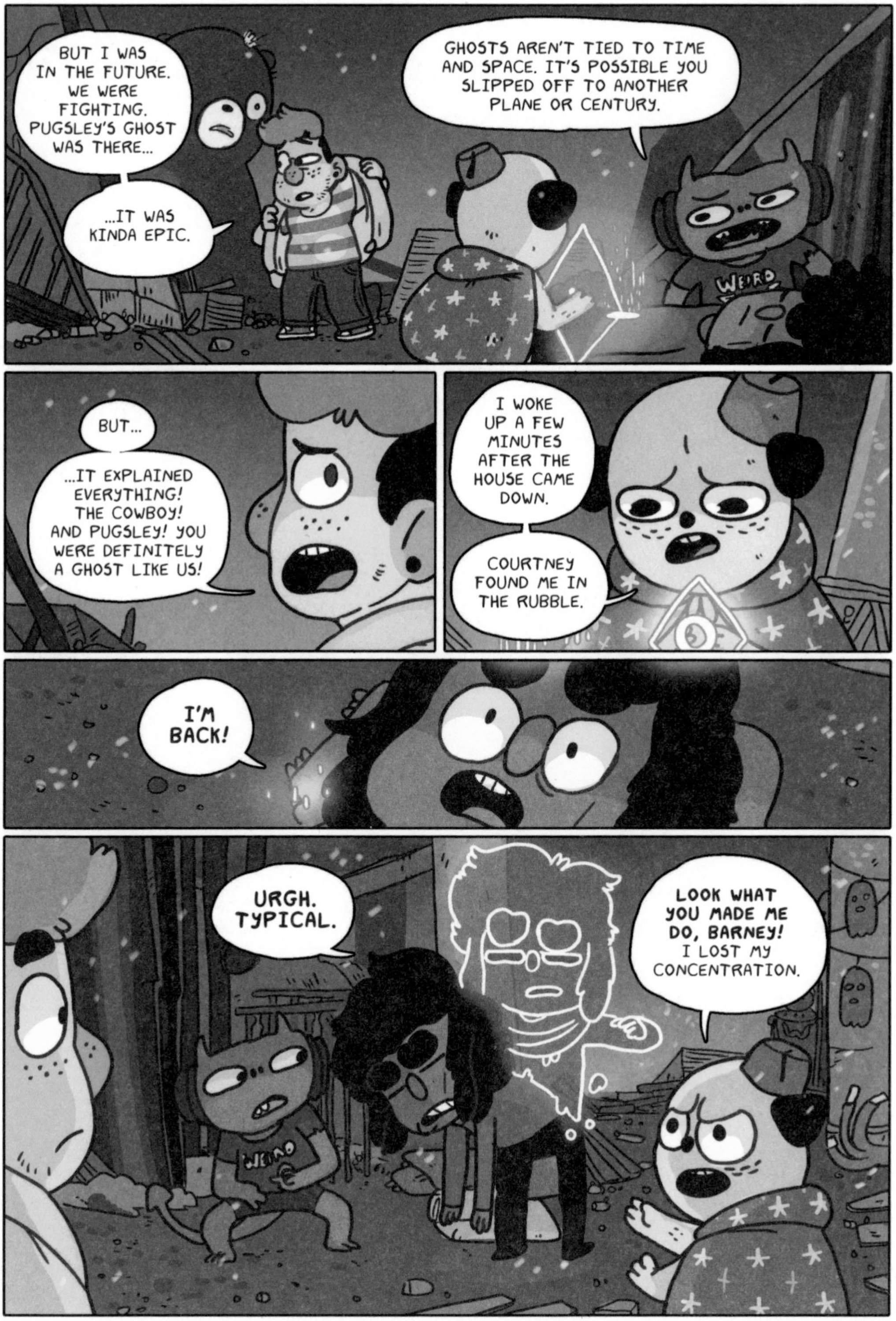
BUT I WAS IN THE FUTURE. WE WERE FIGHTING. PUGSLEY'S GHOST WAS THERE...
...IT WAS KINDA EPIC.
GHOSTS AREN'T TIED TO TIME AND SPACE. IT'S POSSIBLE YOU SLIPPED OFF TO ANOTHER PLANE OR CENTURY.
WEIRD
BUT...
...IT EXPLAINED EVERYTHING! THE COWBOY! AND PUGSLEY! YOU WERE DEFINITELY A GHOST LIKE US!
I WOKE UP A FEW MINUTES AFTER THE HOUSE CAME DOWN.
COURTNEY FOUND ME IN THE RUBBLE.
I'M BACK!
URGH. TYPICAL.
LOOK WHAT YOU MADE ME DO, BARNEY! I LOST MY CONCENTRATION.
WEIRD

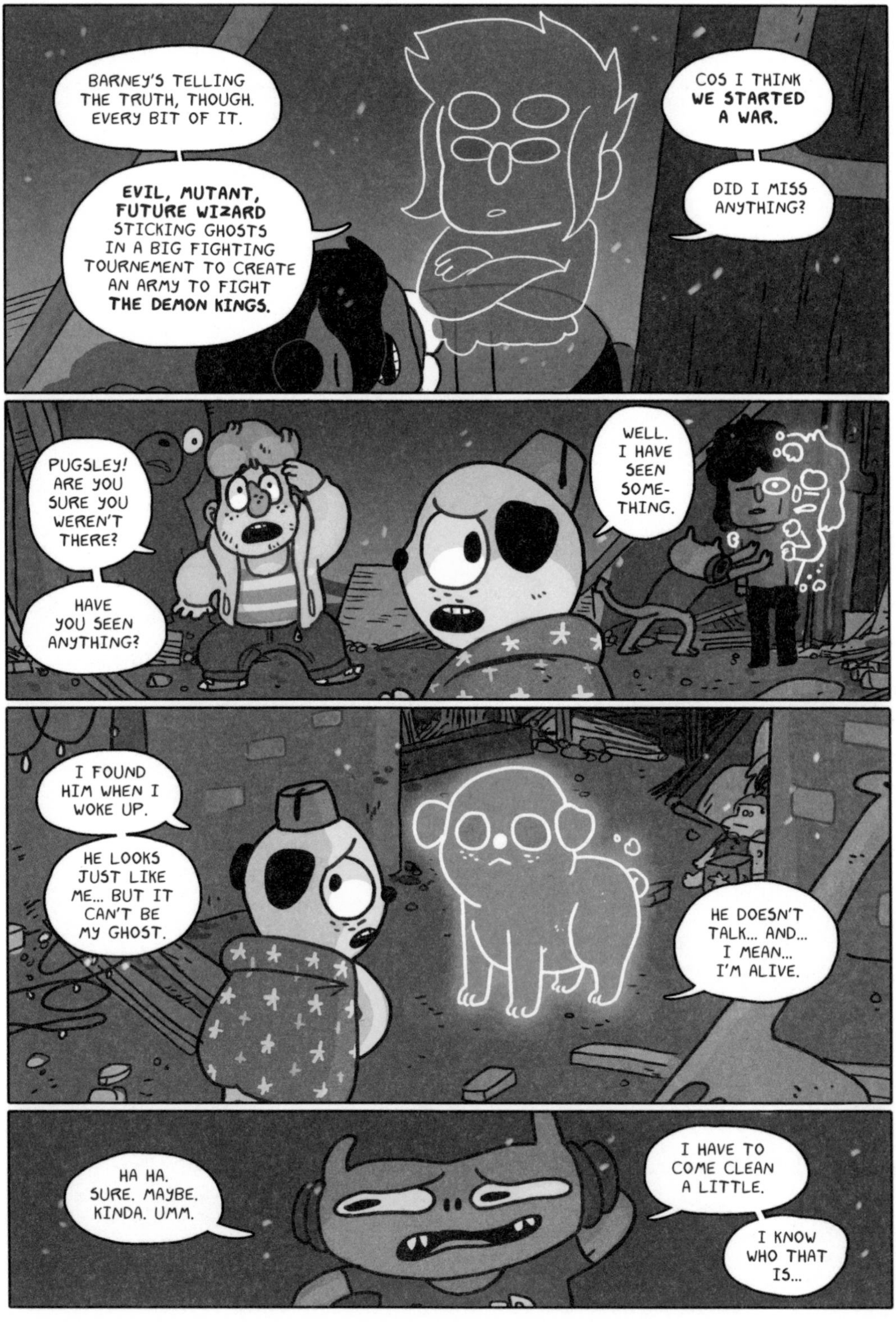
BARNEY'S TELLING THE TRUTH, THOUGH. EVERY BIT OF IT.
EVIL, MUTANT, FUTURE WIZARD STICKING GHOSTS IN A BIG FIGHTING TOURNEMENT TO CREATE AN ARMY TO FIGHT **THE DEMON KINGS.**
COS I THINK **WE STARTED A WAR.**
DID I MISS ANYTHING?
PUGSLEY! ARE YOU SURE YOU WEREN'T THERE?
HAVE YOU SEEN ANYTHING?
WELL. I HAVE SEEN SOME-THING.
I FOUND HIM WHEN I WOKE UP.
HE LOOKS JUST LIKE ME... BUT IT CAN'T BE MY GHOST.
HE DOESN'T TALK... AND... I MEAN... I'M ALIVE.
HA HA. SURE. MAYBE. KINDA. UMM.
I HAVE TO COME CLEAN A LITTLE.
I KNOW WHO THAT IS...

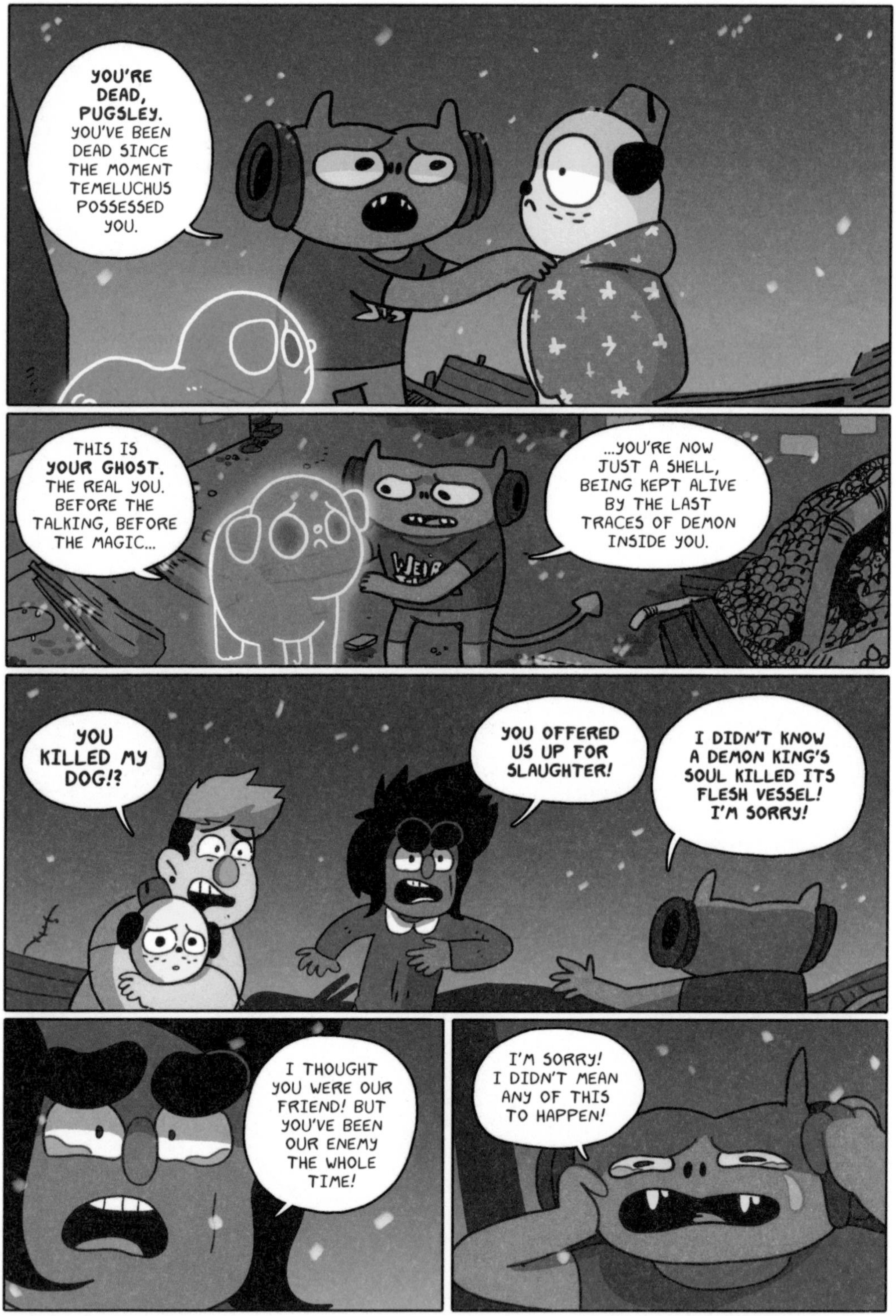
YOU'RE DEAD, PUGSLEY. YOU'VE BEEN DEAD SINCE THE MOMENT TEMELUCHUS POSSESSED YOU.
THIS IS YOUR GHOST. THE REAL YOU. BEFORE THE TALKING, BEFORE THE MAGIC...
...YOU'RE NOW JUST A SHELL, BEING KEPT ALIVE BY THE LAST TRACES OF DEMON INSIDE YOU.
YOU KILLED MY DOG!?
YOU OFFERED US UP FOR SLAUGHTER!
I DIDN'T KNOW A DEMON KING'S SOUL KILLED ITS FLESH VESSEL! I'M SORRY!
I THOUGHT YOU WERE OUR FRIEND! BUT YOU'VE BEEN OUR ENEMY THE WHOLE TIME!
I'M SORRY! I DIDN'T MEAN ANY OF THIS TO HAPPEN!

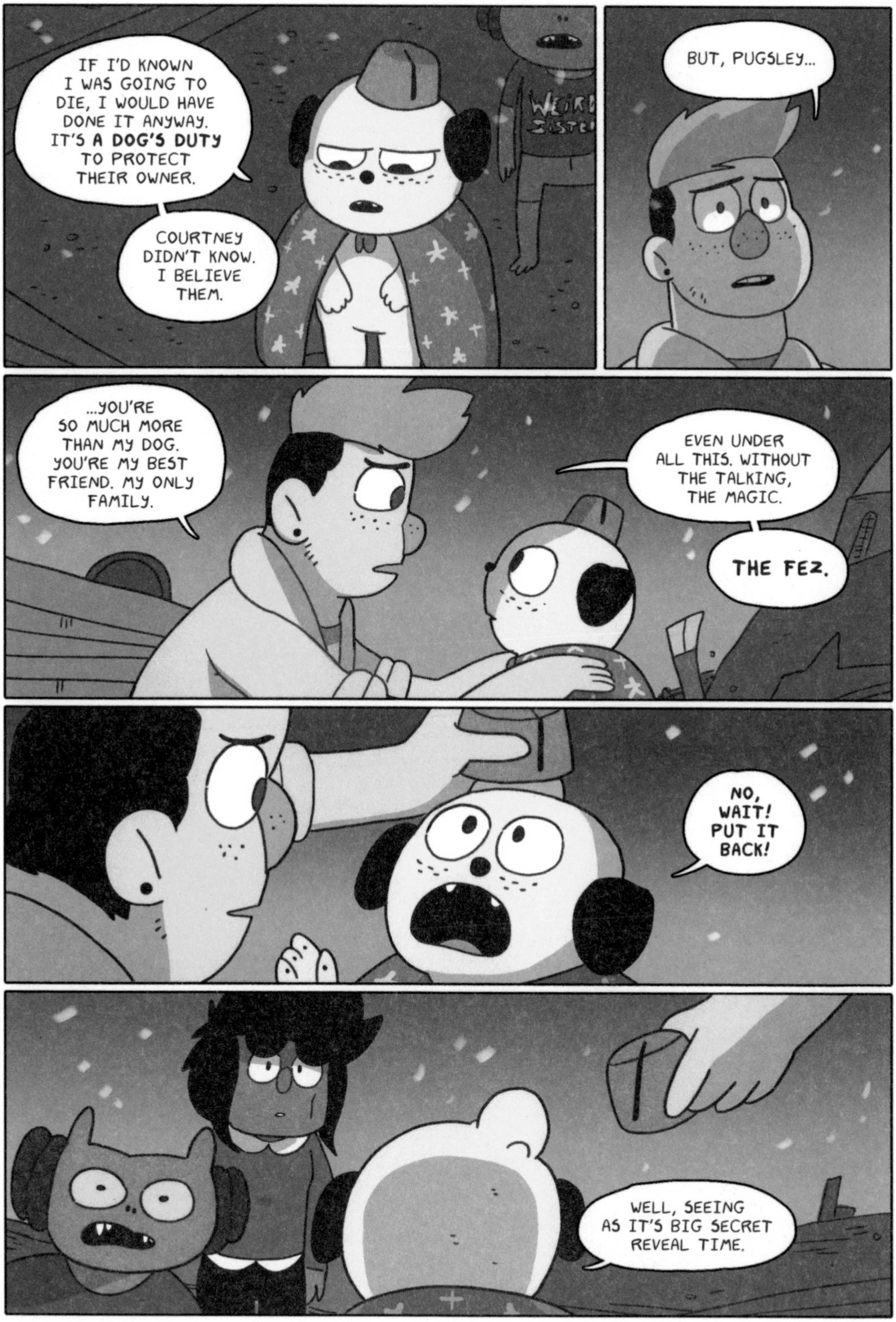
IF I'D KNOWN I WAS GOING TO DIE, I WOULD HAVE DONE IT ANYWAY. IT'S **A DOG'S DUTY** TO PROTECT THEIR OWNER.
COURTNEY DIDN'T KNOW. I BELIEVE THEM.
BUT, PUGSLEY...
...YOU'RE SO MUCH MORE THAN MY DOG. YOU'RE MY BEST FRIEND. MY ONLY FAMILY.
EVEN UNDER ALL THIS. WITHOUT THE TALKING, THE MAGIC.
THE FEZ.
NO, WAIT! PUT IT BACK!
WELL, SEEING AS IT'S BIG SECRET REVEAL TIME.

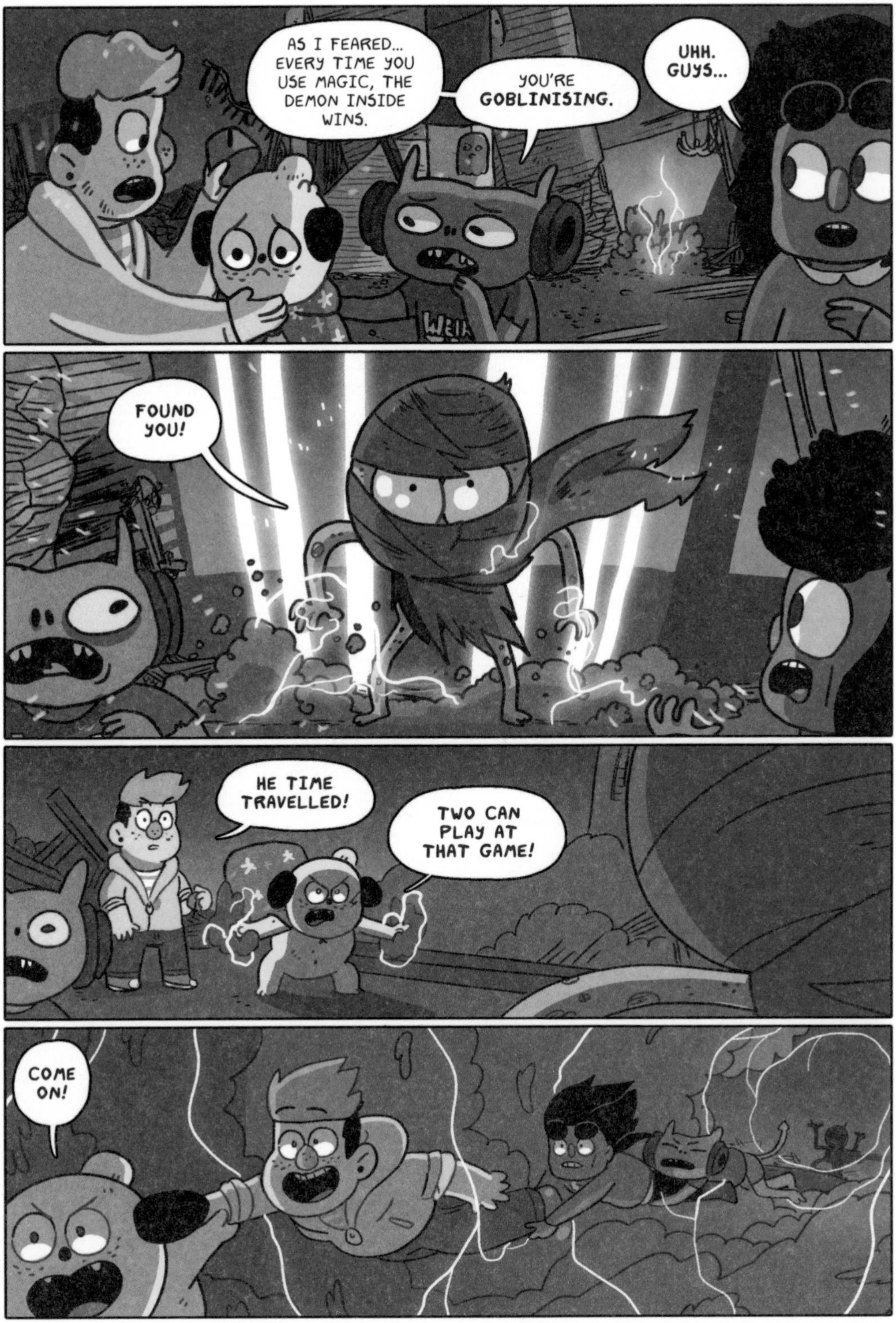

AS I FEARED... EVERY TIME YOU USE MAGIC, THE DEMON INSIDE WINS.
YOU'RE **GOBLINISING.**
UHH. GUYS...
FOUND YOU!
HE TIME TRAVELLED!
TWO CAN PLAY AT THAT GAME!
COME ON!

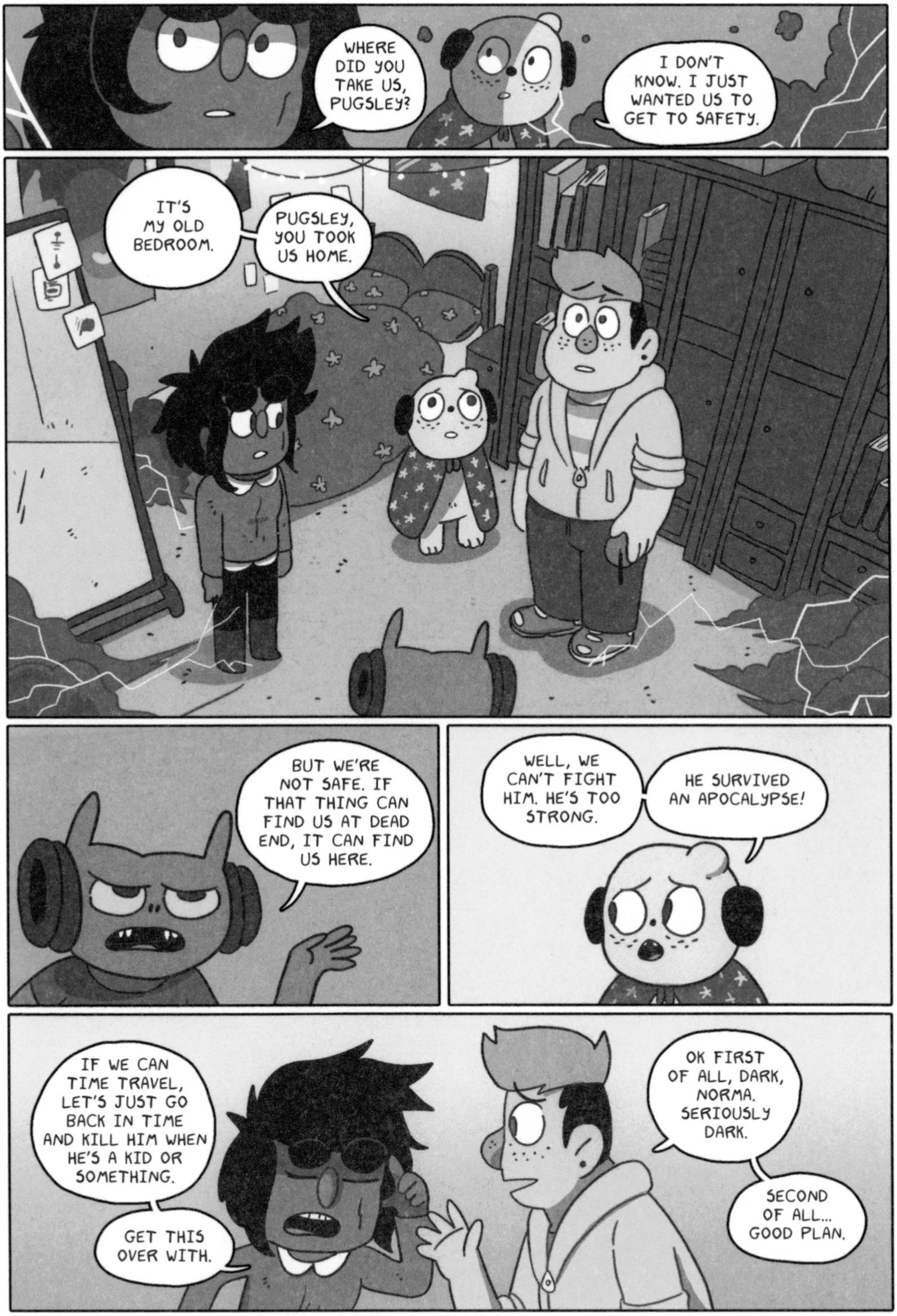
WHERE DID YOU TAKE US, PUGSLEY?
I DON'T KNOW. I JUST WANTED US TO GET TO SAFETY.
IT'S MY OLD BEDROOM.
PUGSLEY, YOU TOOK US HOME.
BUT WE'RE NOT SAFE. IF THAT THING CAN FIND US AT DEAD END, IT CAN FIND US HERE.
WELL, WE CAN'T FIGHT HIM. HE'S TOO STRONG.
HE SURVIVED AN APOCALYPSE!
IF WE CAN TIME TRAVEL, LET'S JUST GO BACK IN TIME AND KILL HIM WHEN HE'S A KID OR SOMETHING.
GET THIS OVER WITH.
OK FIRST OF ALL, DARK, NORMA. SERIOUSLY DARK.
SECOND OF ALL... GOOD PLAN.

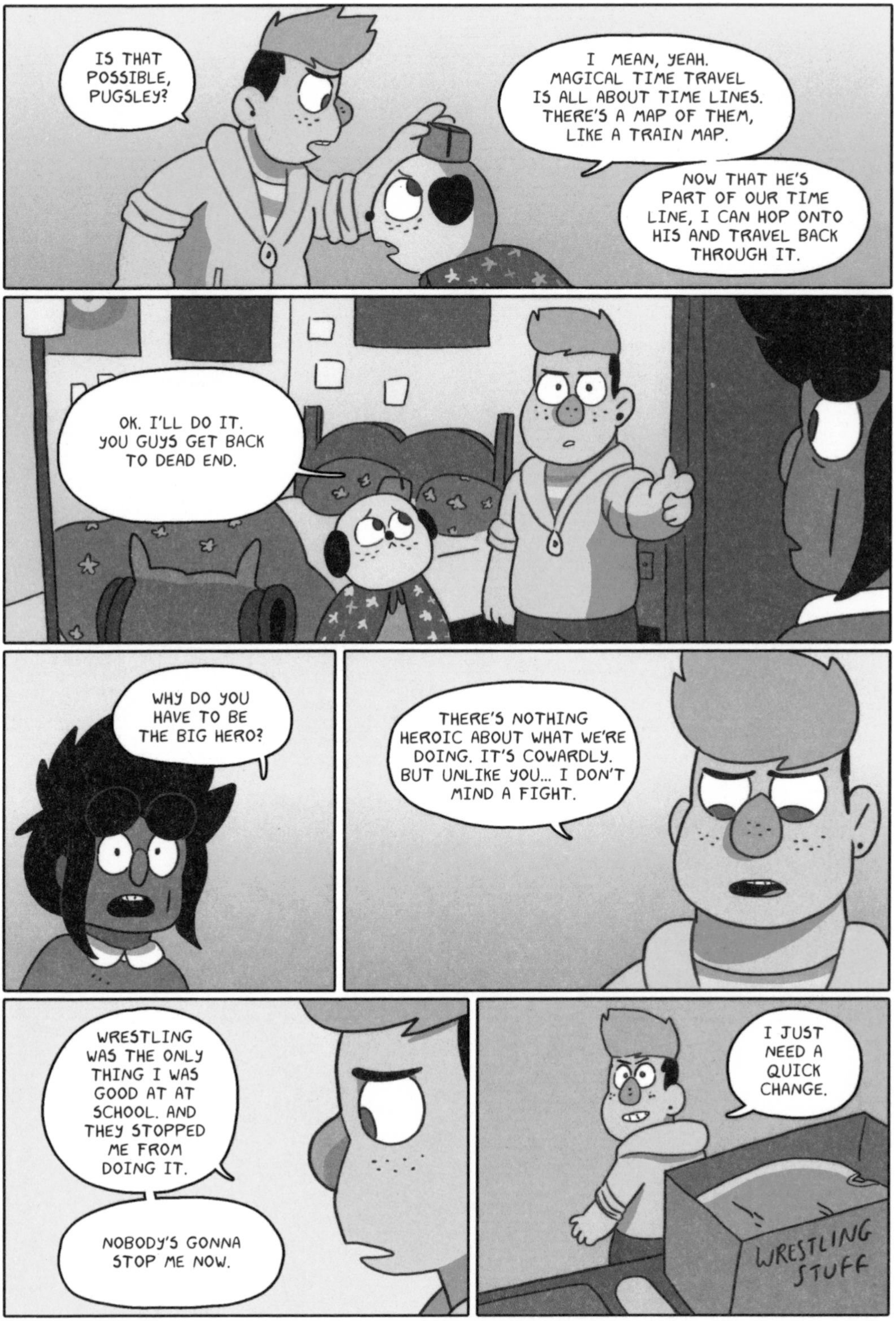
IS THAT POSSIBLE, PUGSLEY?
I MEAN, YEAH. MAGICAL TIME TRAVEL IS ALL ABOUT TIME LINES. THERE'S A MAP OF THEM, LIKE A TRAIN MAP.
NOW THAT HE'S PART OF OUR TIME LINE, I CAN HOP ONTO HIS AND TRAVEL BACK THROUGH IT.
OK. I'LL DO IT. YOU GUYS GET BACK TO DEAD END.
WHY DO YOU HAVE TO BE THE BIG HERO?
THERE'S NOTHING HEROIC ABOUT WHAT WE'RE DOING. IT'S COWARDLY. BUT UNLIKE YOU... I DON'T MIND A FIGHT.
WRESTLING WAS THE ONLY THING I WAS GOOD AT AT SCHOOL. AND THEY STOPPED ME FROM DOING IT.
NOBODY'S GONNA STOP ME NOW.
I JUST NEED A QUICK CHANGE.
WRESTLING STUFF

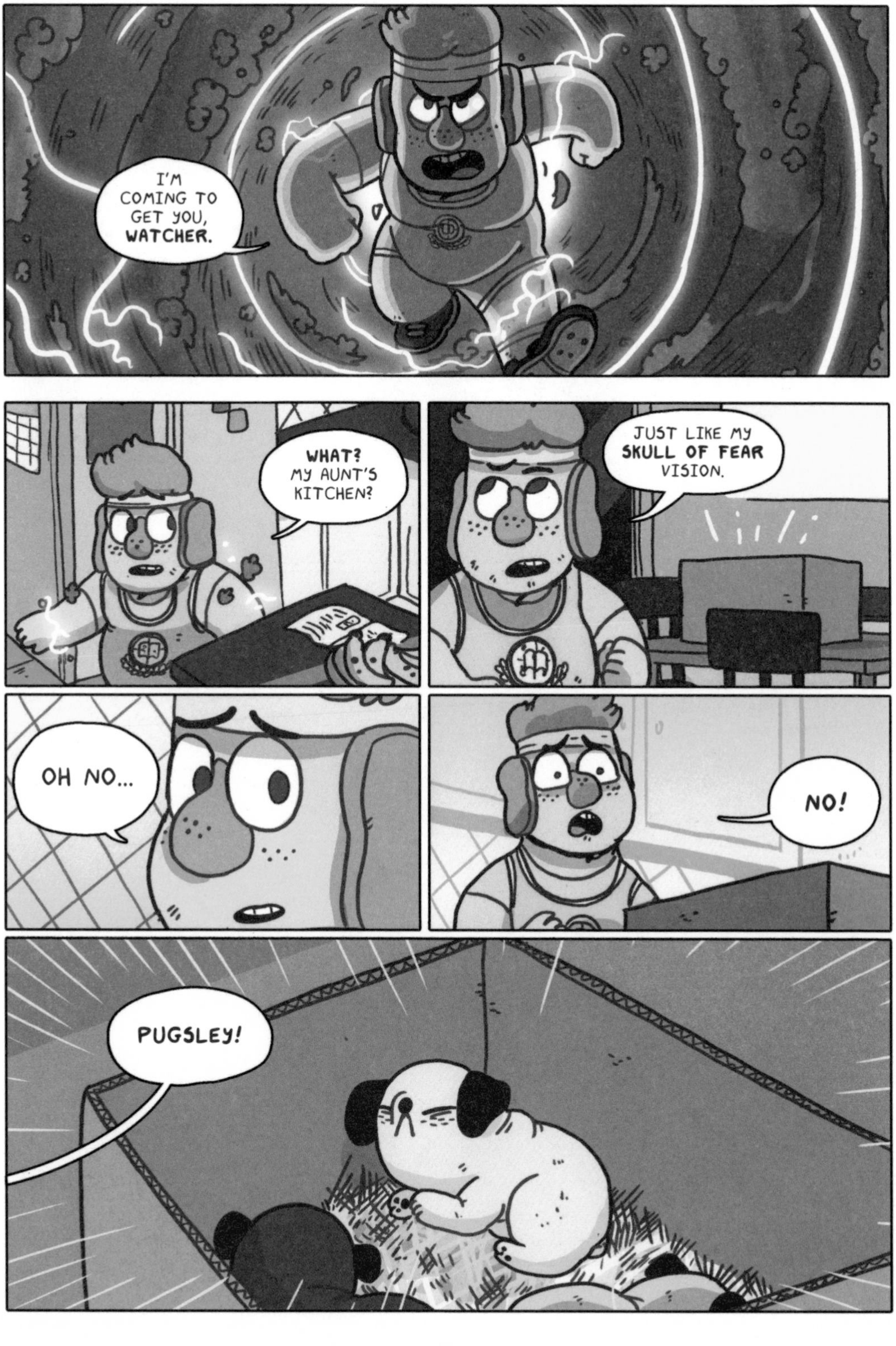

I'M COMING TO GET YOU, WATCHER.
WHAT? MY AUNT'S KITCHEN?
JUST LIKE MY SKULL OF FEAR VISION.
OH NO...
NO!
PUGSLEY!

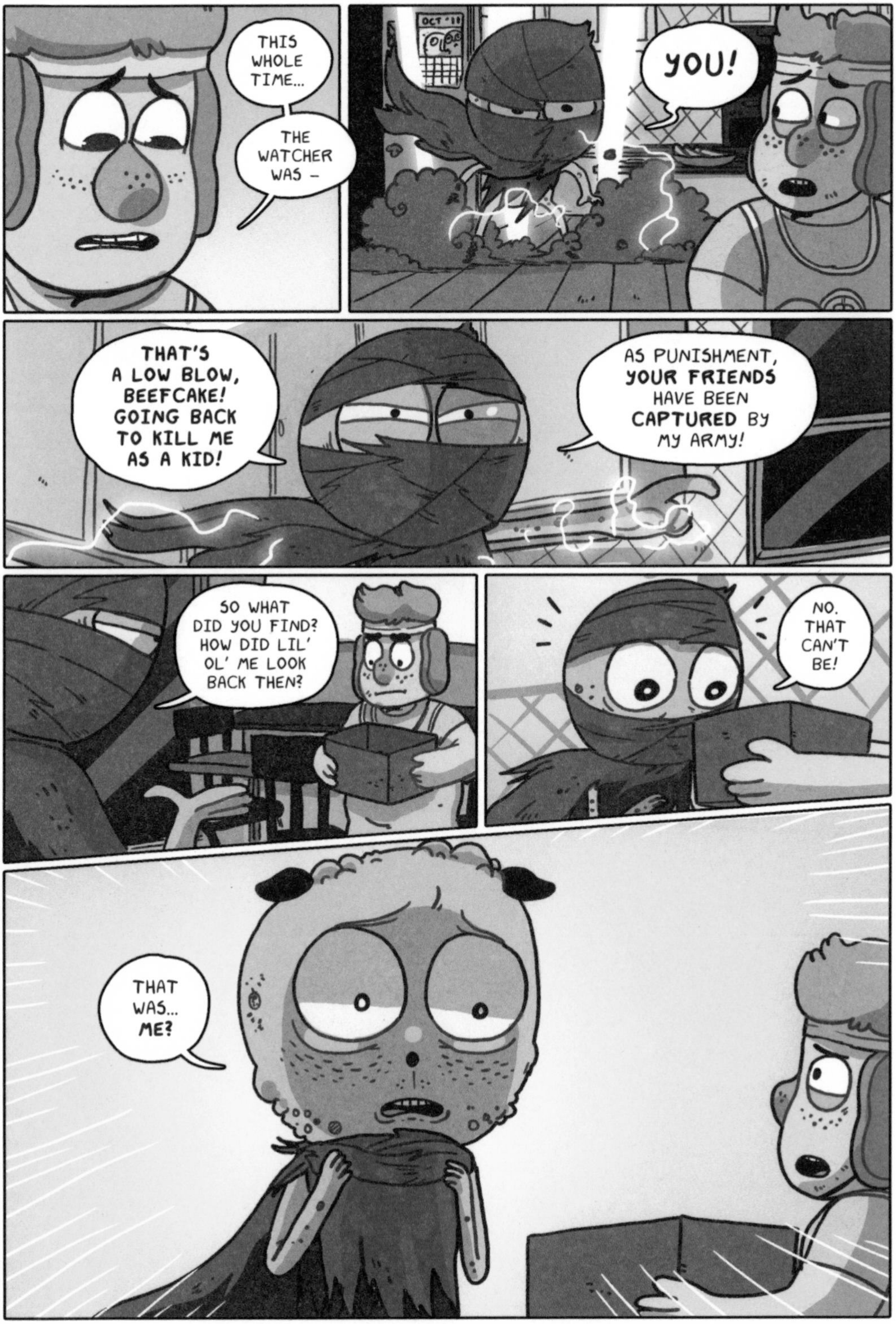
THIS WHOLE TIME...
THE WATCHER WAS –
YOU!
THAT'S A LOW BLOW, BEEFCAKE! GOING BACK TO KILL ME AS A KID!
AS PUNISHMENT, YOUR FRIENDS HAVE BEEN CAPTURED BY MY ARMY!
SO WHAT DID YOU FIND? HOW DID LIL' OL' ME LOOK BACK THEN?
NO. THAT CAN'T BE!
THAT WAS... ME?

CHAPTER 8

COVER ART BY DARYL TOH

THE BALLAD OF PUGSLEY

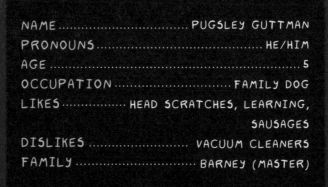

NAME .... PUGSLEY GUTTMAN
PRONOUNS .... HE/HIM
AGE 5
OCCUPATION .... FAMILY DOG
LIKES .... HEAD SCRATCHES, LEARNING,
SAUSAGES
DISLIKES .... VACUUM CLEANERS
FAMILY .... BARNEY (MASTER)

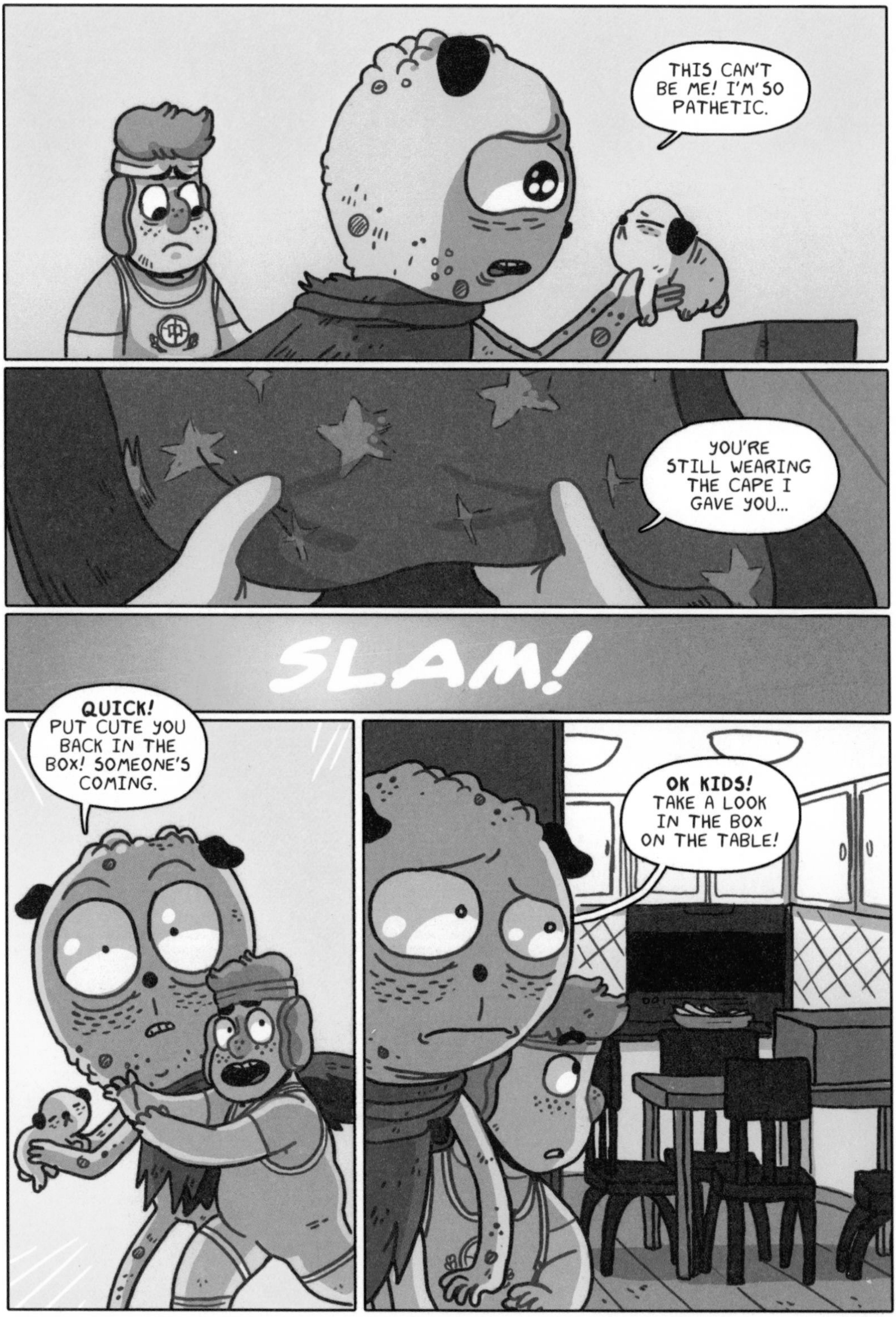
THIS CAN'T BE ME! I'M SO PATHETIC.
YOU'RE STILL WEARING THE CAPE I GAVE YOU...
SLAM!
QUICK! PUT CUTE YOU BACK IN THE BOX! SOMEONE'S COMING.
OK KIDS! TAKE A LOOK IN THE BOX ON THE TABLE!

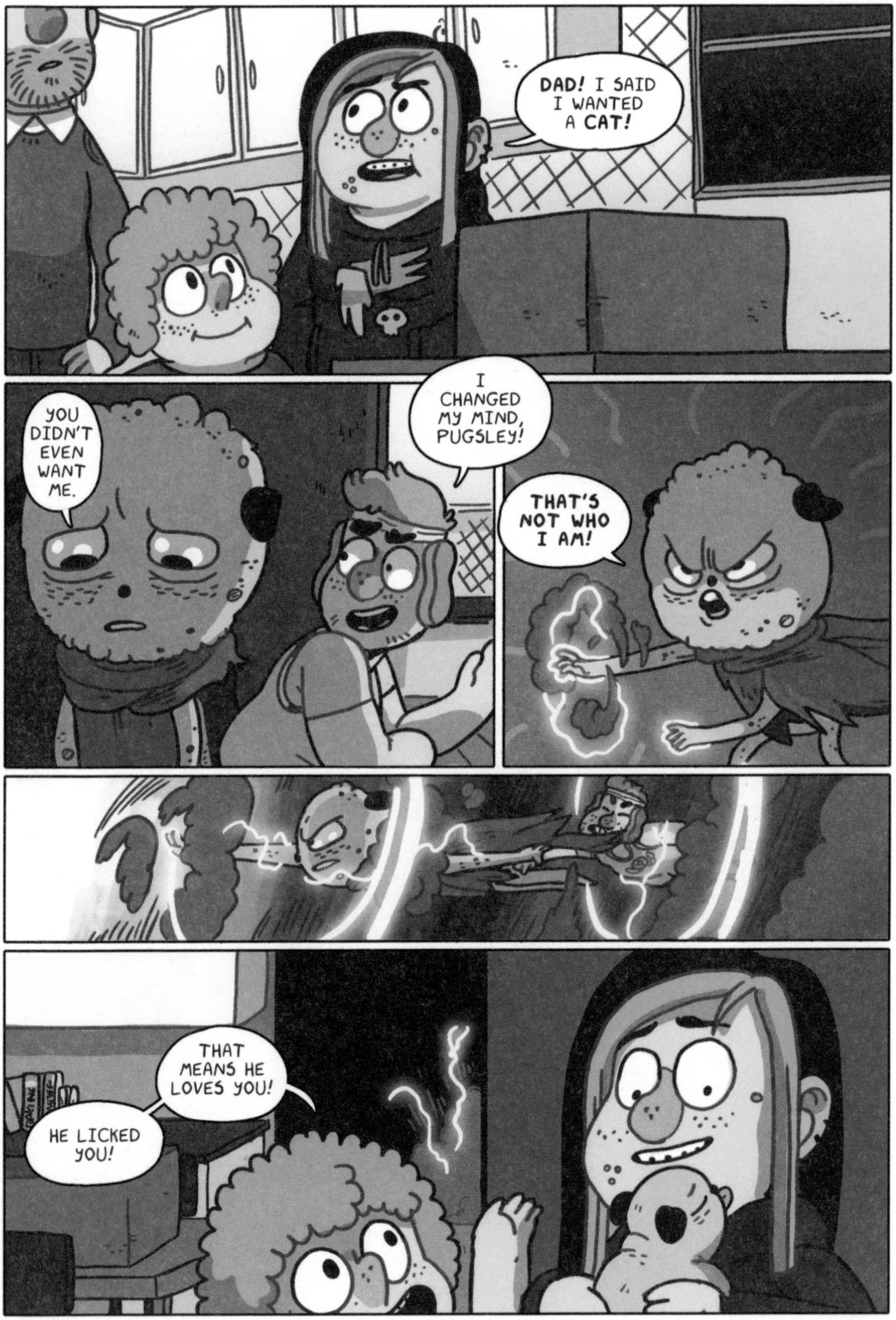
DAD! I SAID I WANTED A CAT!
YOU DIDN'T EVEN WANT ME.
I CHANGED MY MIND, PUGSLEY!
THAT'S NOT WHO I AM!
HE LICKED YOU!
THAT MEANS HE LOVES YOU!

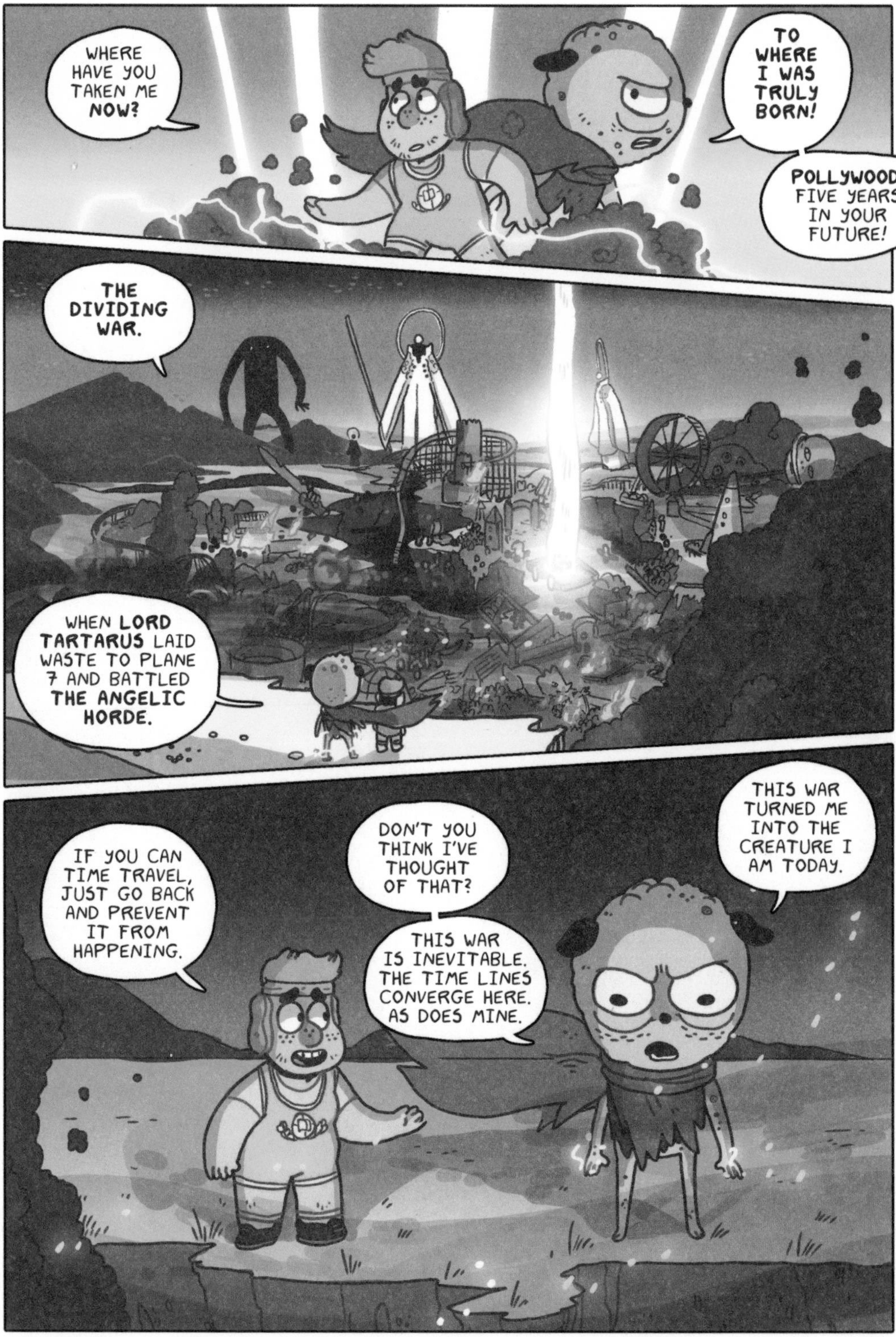
WHERE HAVE YOU TAKEN ME NOW?
TO WHERE I WAS TRULY BORN!
POLLYWOOD. FIVE YEARS IN YOUR FUTURE!
THE DIVIDING WAR.
WHEN LORD TARTARUS LAID WASTE TO PLANE 7 AND BATTLED THE ANGELIC HORDE.
IF YOU CAN TIME TRAVEL, JUST GO BACK AND PREVENT IT FROM HAPPENING.
DON'T YOU THINK I'VE THOUGHT OF THAT?
THIS WAR IS INEVITABLE. THE TIME LINES CONVERGE HERE. AS DOES MINE.
THIS WAR TURNED ME INTO THE CREATURE I AM TODAY.

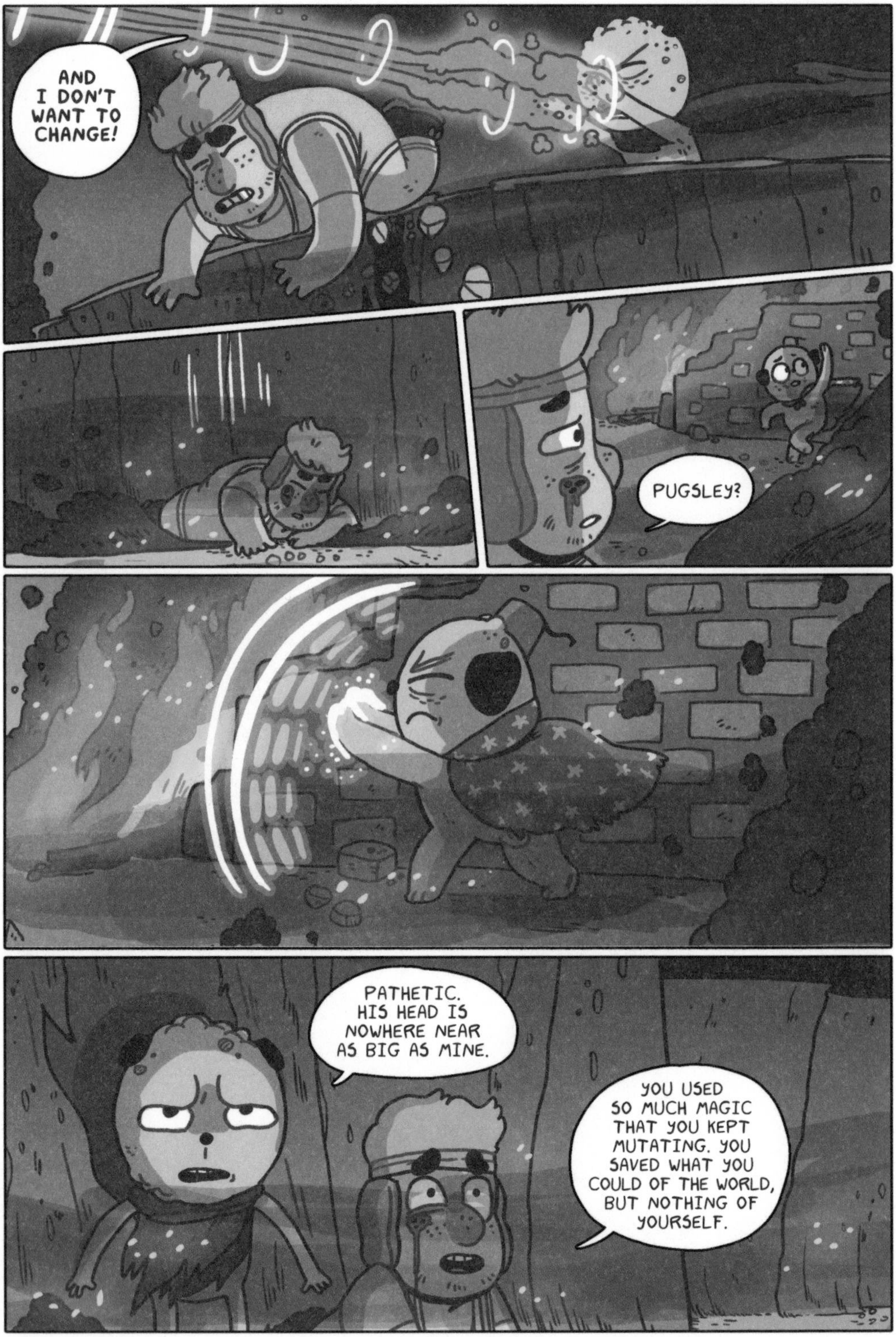
AND I DON'T WANT TO CHANGE!
PUGSLEY?
PATHETIC. HIS HEAD IS NOWHERE NEAR AS BIG AS MINE.
YOU USED SO MUCH MAGIC THAT YOU KEPT MUTATING. YOU SAVED WHAT YOU COULD OF THE WORLD, BUT NOTHING OF YOURSELF.

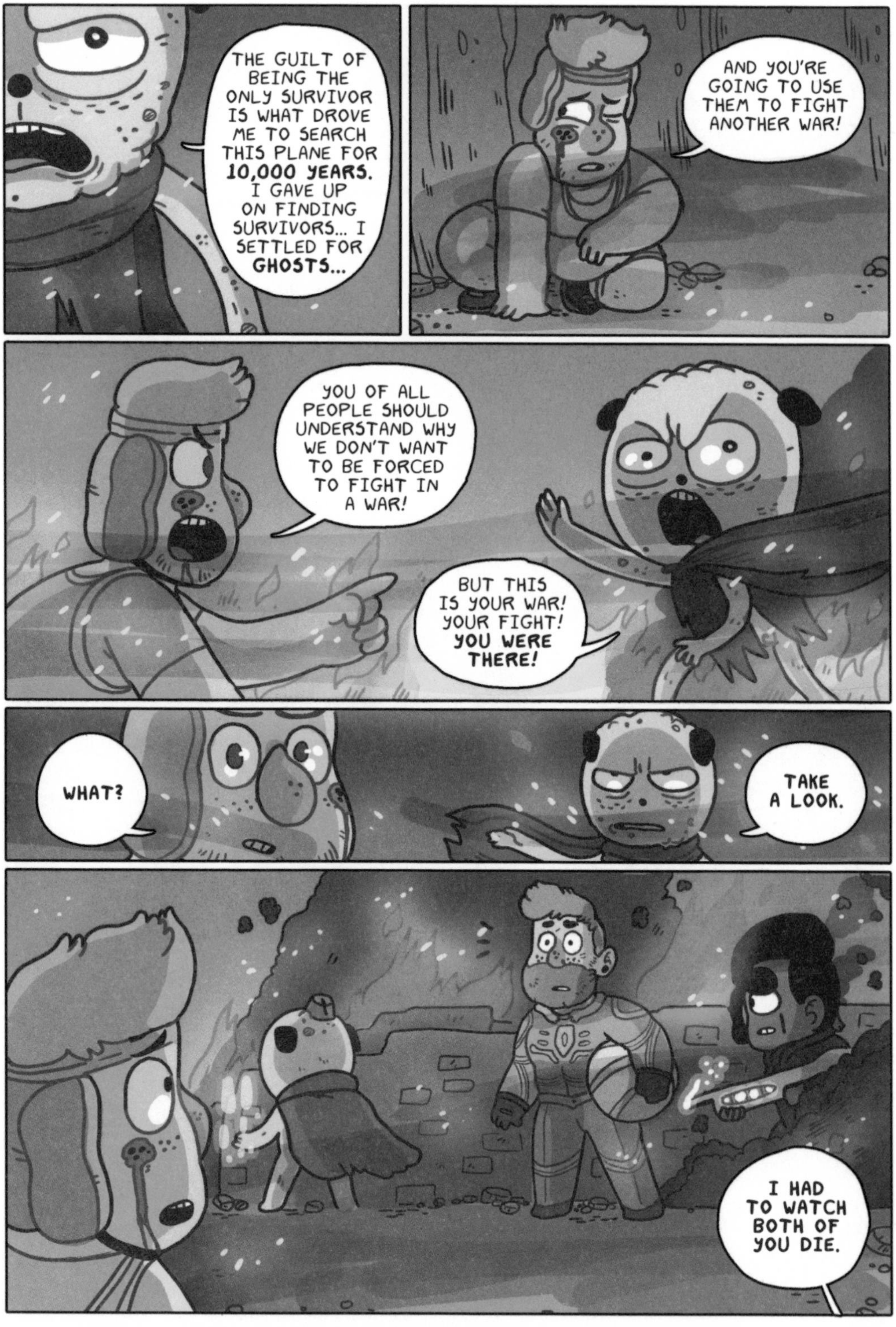
THE GUILT OF BEING THE ONLY SURVIVOR IS WHAT DROVE ME TO SEARCH THIS PLANE FOR **10,000 YEARS.** I GAVE UP ON FINDING SURVIVORS... I SETTLED FOR **GHOSTS...**
AND YOU'RE GOING TO USE THEM TO FIGHT ANOTHER WAR!
YOU OF ALL PEOPLE SHOULD UNDERSTAND WHY WE DON'T WANT TO BE FORCED TO FIGHT IN A WAR!
BUT THIS IS YOUR WAR! YOUR FIGHT! **YOU WERE THERE!**
WHAT?
TAKE A LOOK.
I HAD TO WATCH BOTH OF YOU DIE.

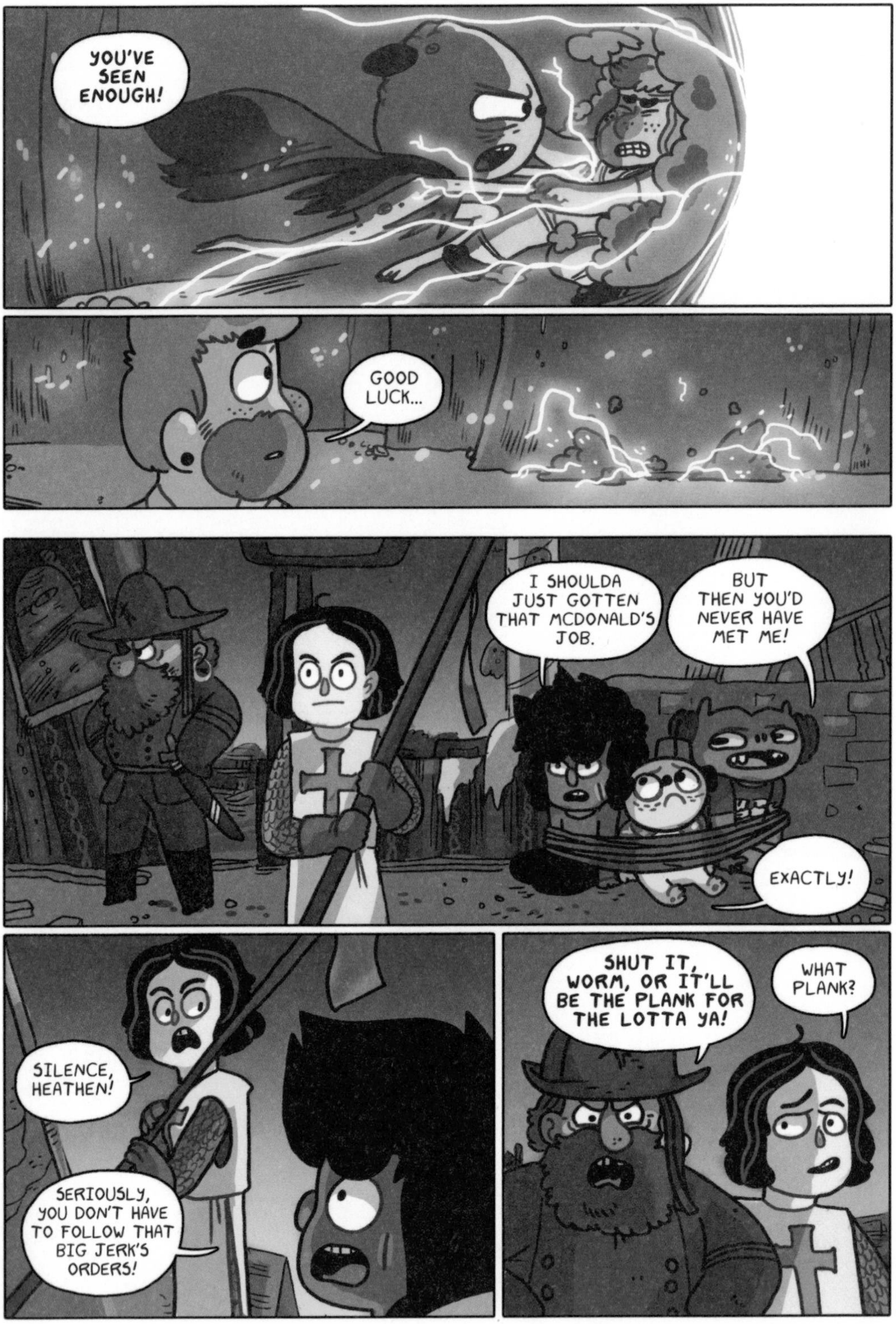
YOU'VE SEEN ENOUGH!
GOOD LUCK...
I SHOULDA JUST GOTTEN THAT MCDONALD'S JOB.
BUT THEN YOU'D NEVER HAVE MET ME!
EXACTLY!
SILENCE, HEATHEN!
SERIOUSLY, YOU DON'T HAVE TO FOLLOW THAT BIG JERK'S ORDERS!
SHUT IT, WORM, OR IT'LL BE THE PLANK FOR THE LOTTA YA!
WHAT PLANK?

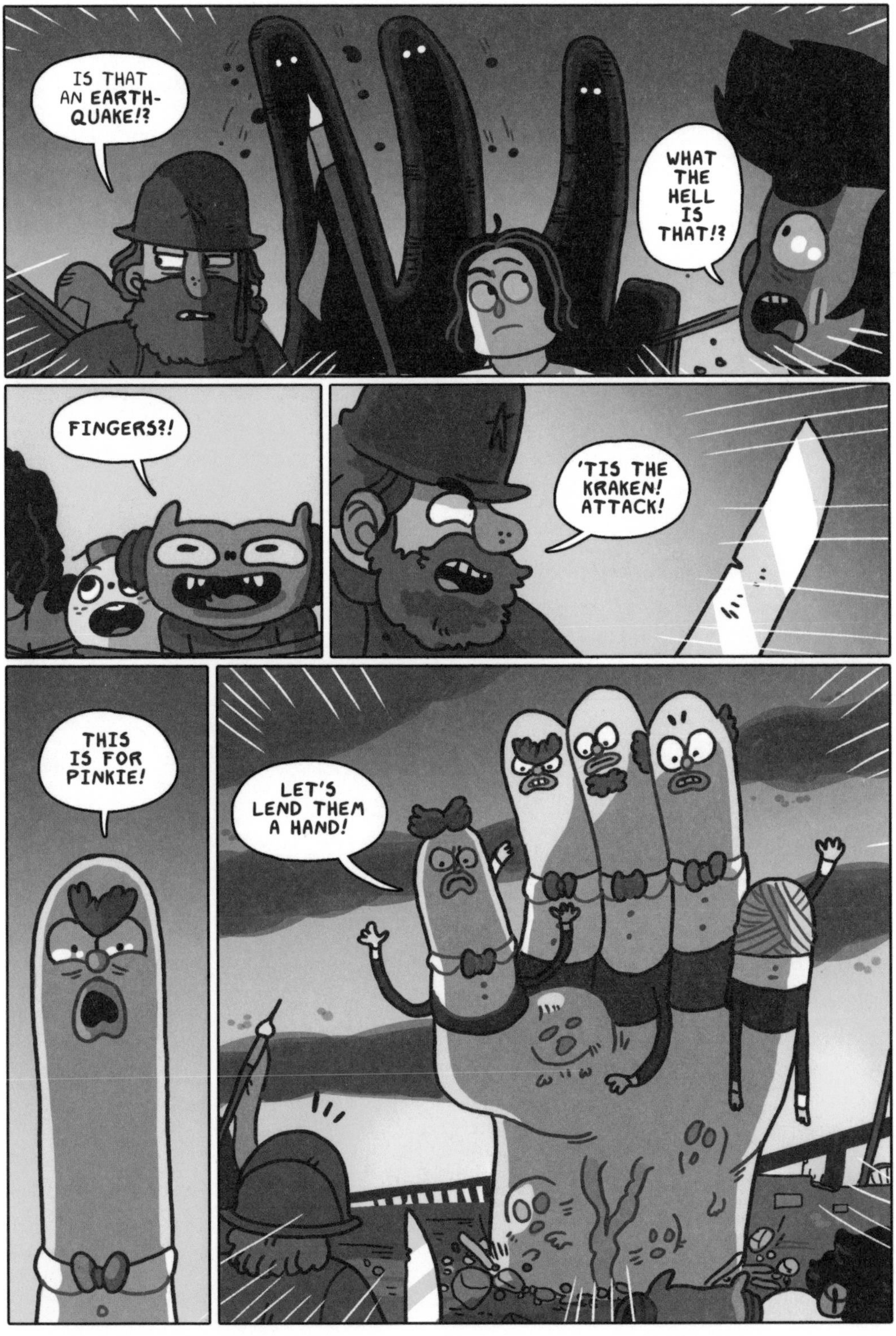
IS THAT AN EARTH-QUAKE!?
WHAT THE HELL IS THAT!?
FINGERS?!
'TIS THE KRAKEN! ATTACK!
THIS IS FOR PINKIE!
LET'S LEND THEM A HAND!

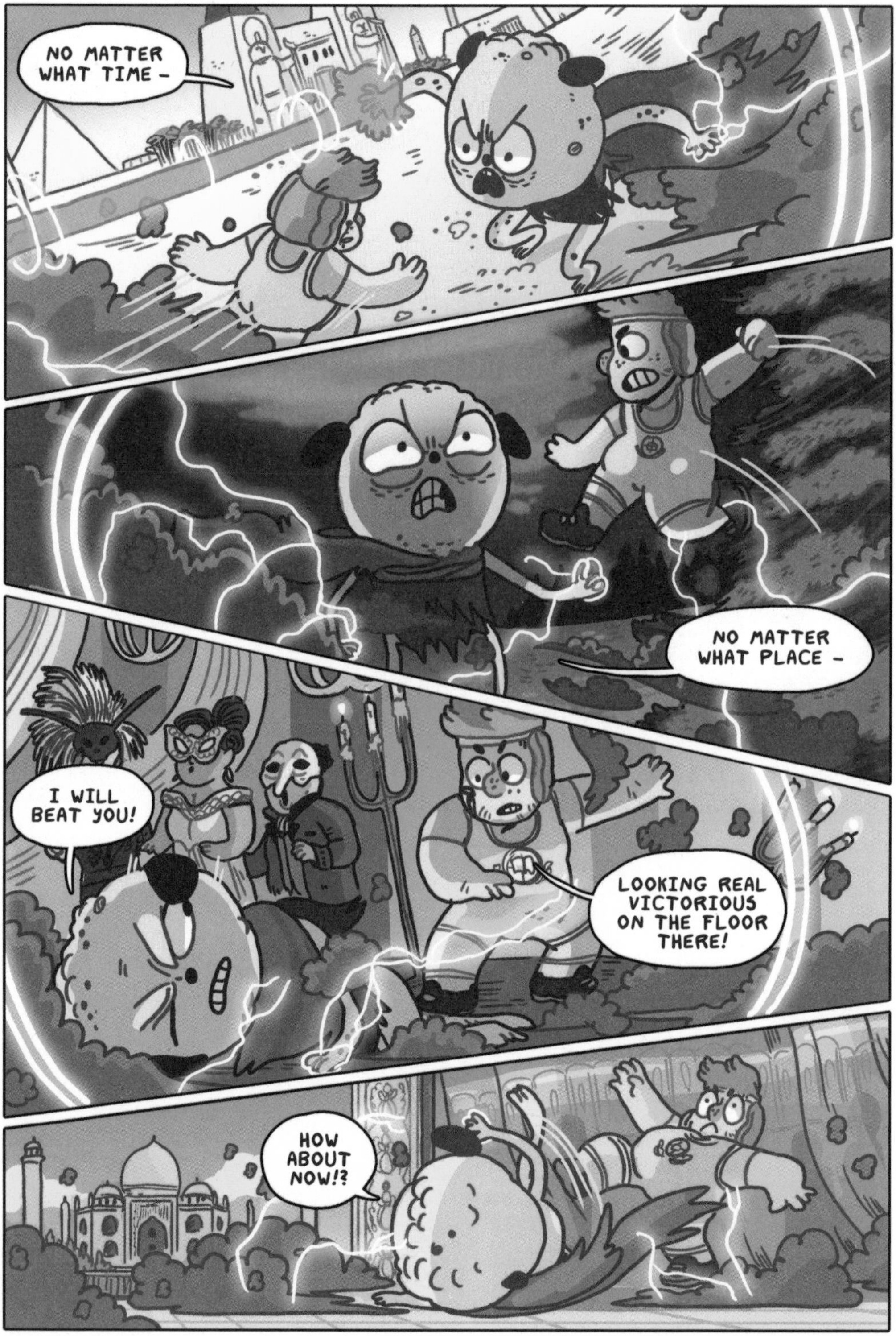
NO MATTER WHAT TIME -
NO MATTER WHAT PLACE -
I WILL BEAT YOU!
LOOKING REAL VICTORIOUS ON THE FLOOR THERE!
HOW ABOUT NOW!?

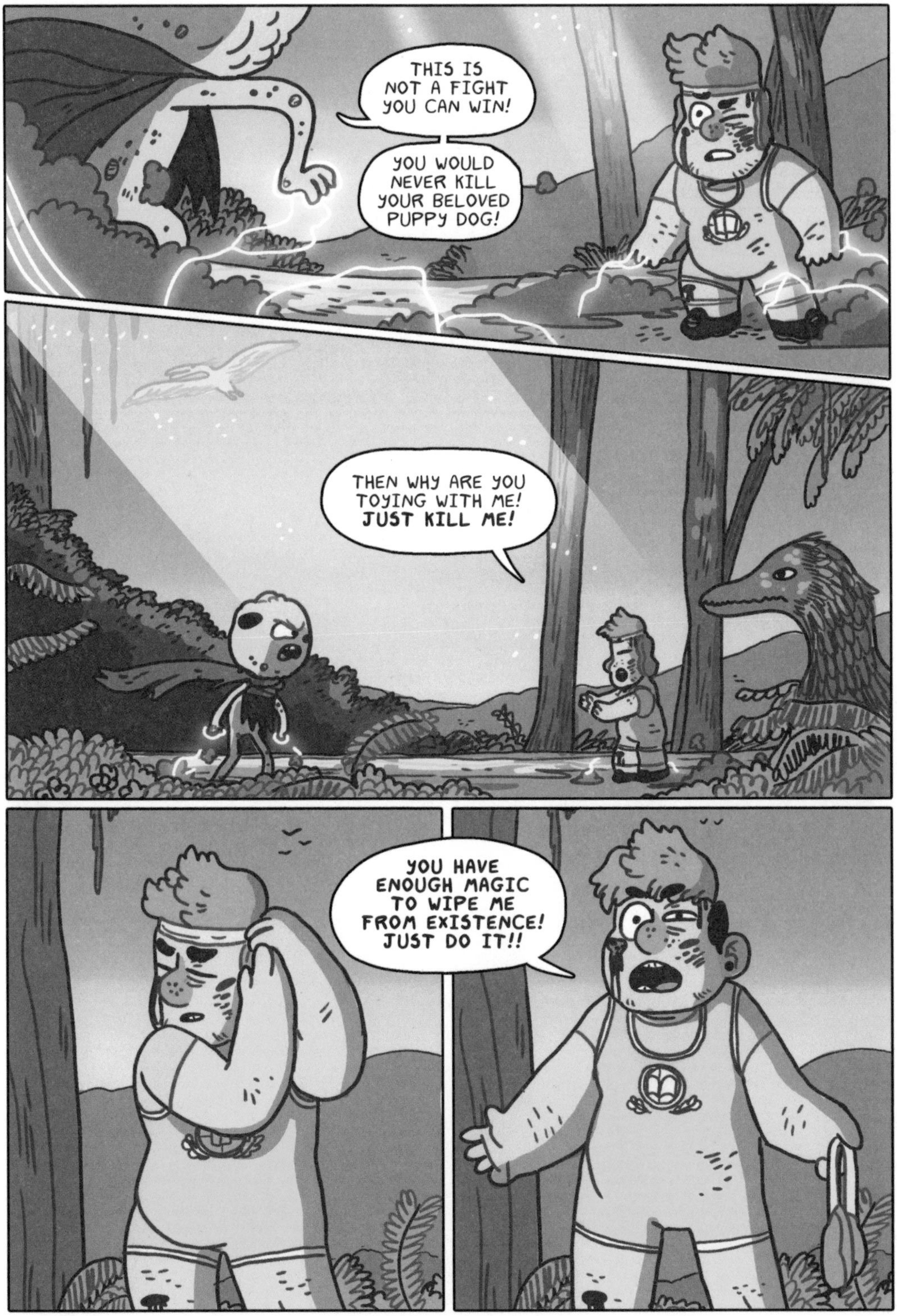
THIS IS NOT A FIGHT YOU CAN WIN!
YOU WOULD NEVER KILL YOUR BELOVED PUPPY DOG!
THEN WHY ARE YOU TOYING WITH ME! JUST KILL ME!
YOU HAVE ENOUGH MAGIC TO WIPE ME FROM EXISTENCE! JUST DO IT!!

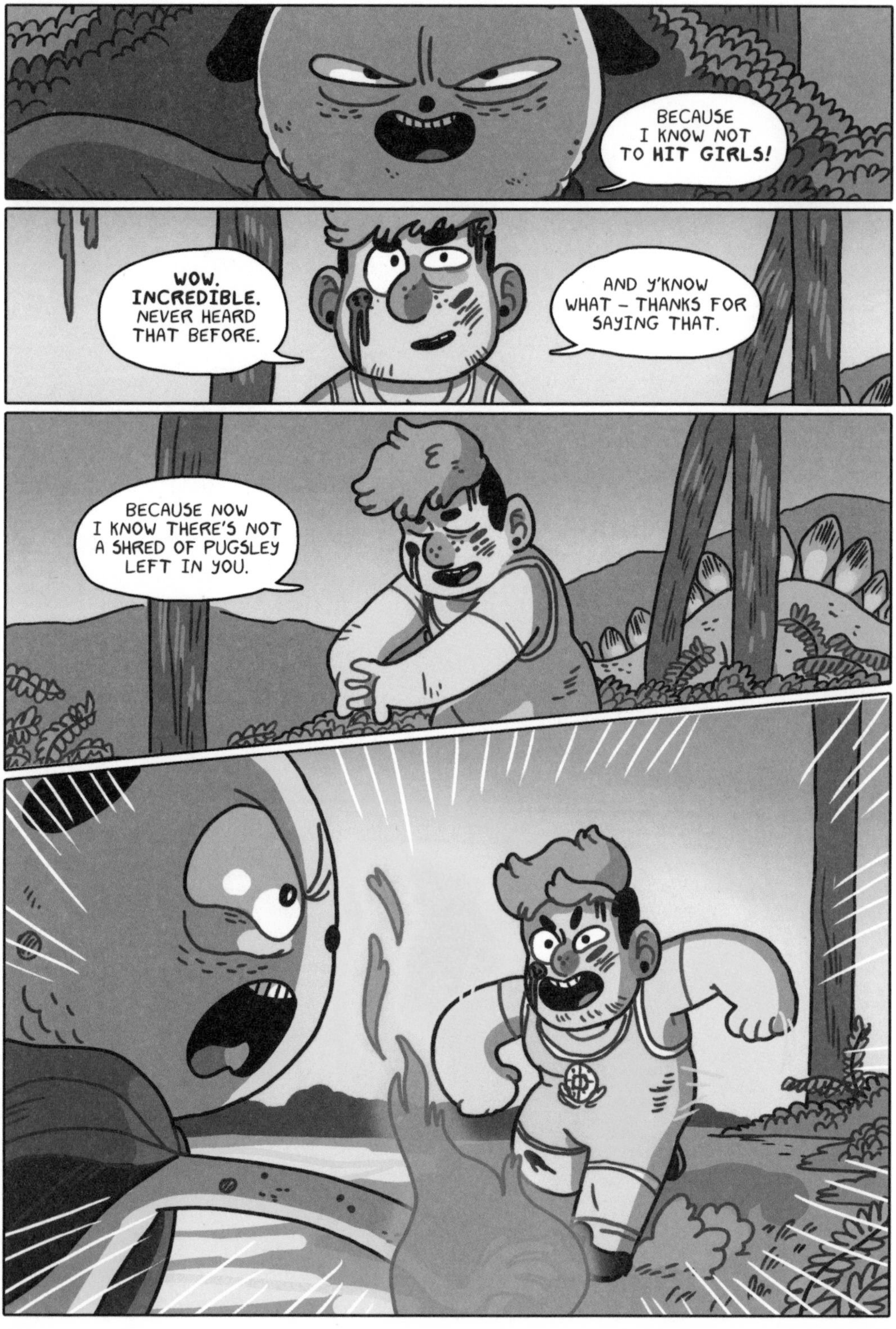

BECAUSE I KNOW NOT TO **HIT GIRLS!**
WOW. INCREDIBLE. NEVER HEARD THAT BEFORE.
AND Y'KNOW WHAT – THANKS FOR SAYING THAT.
BECAUSE NOW I KNOW THERE'S NOT A SHRED OF PUGSLEY LEFT IN YOU.

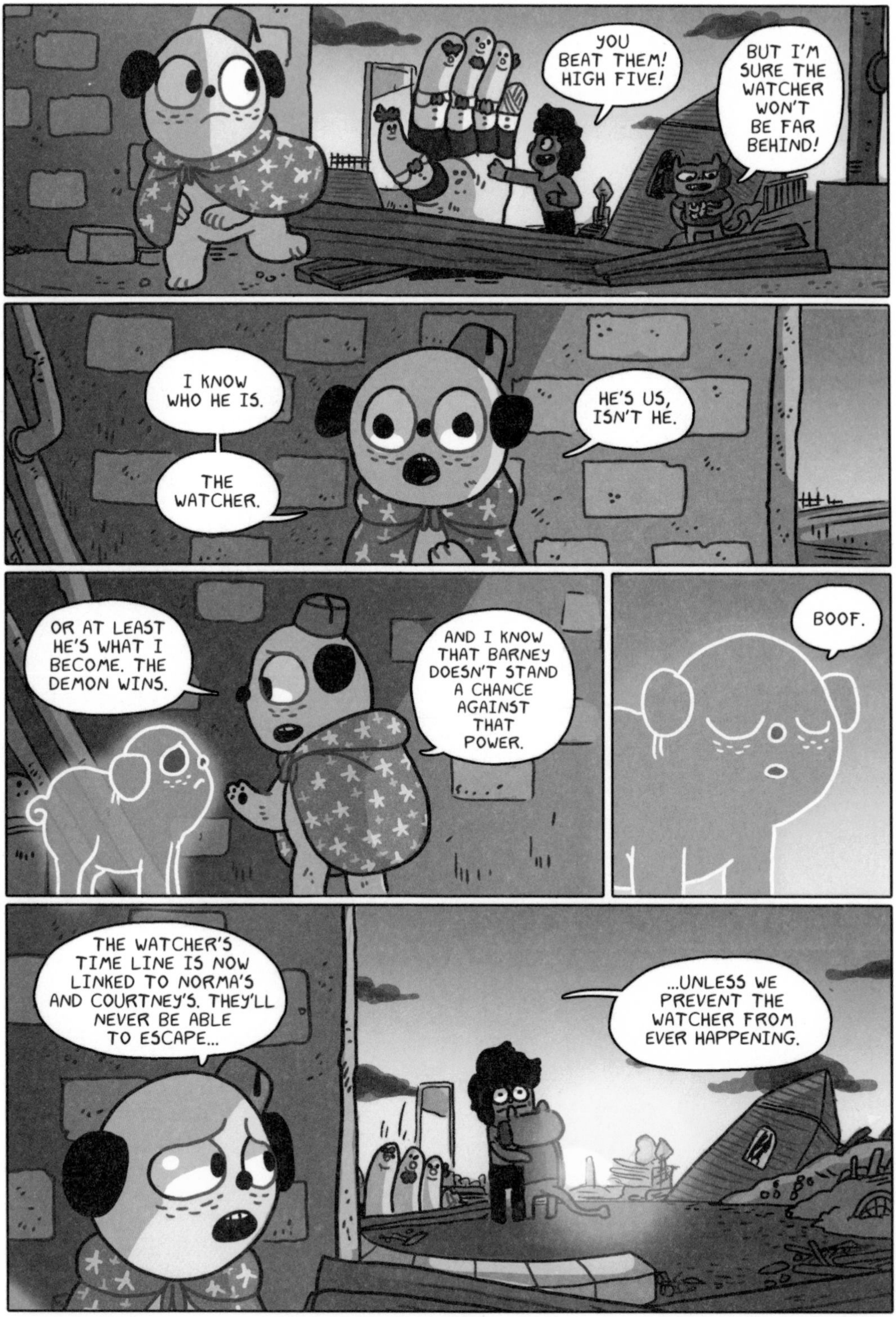

YOU BEAT THEM! HIGH FIVE!
BUT I'M SURE THE WATCHER WON'T BE FAR BEHIND!
I KNOW WHO HE IS.
THE WATCHER.
HE'S US, ISN'T HE.
OR AT LEAST HE'S WHAT I BECOME. THE DEMON WINS.
AND I KNOW THAT BARNEY DOESN'T STAND A CHANCE AGAINST THAT POWER.
BOOF.
THE WATCHER'S TIME LINE IS NOW LINKED TO NORMA'S AND COURTNEY'S. THEY'LL NEVER BE ABLE TO ESCAPE...
...UNLESS WE PREVENT THE WATCHER FROM EVER HAPPENING.

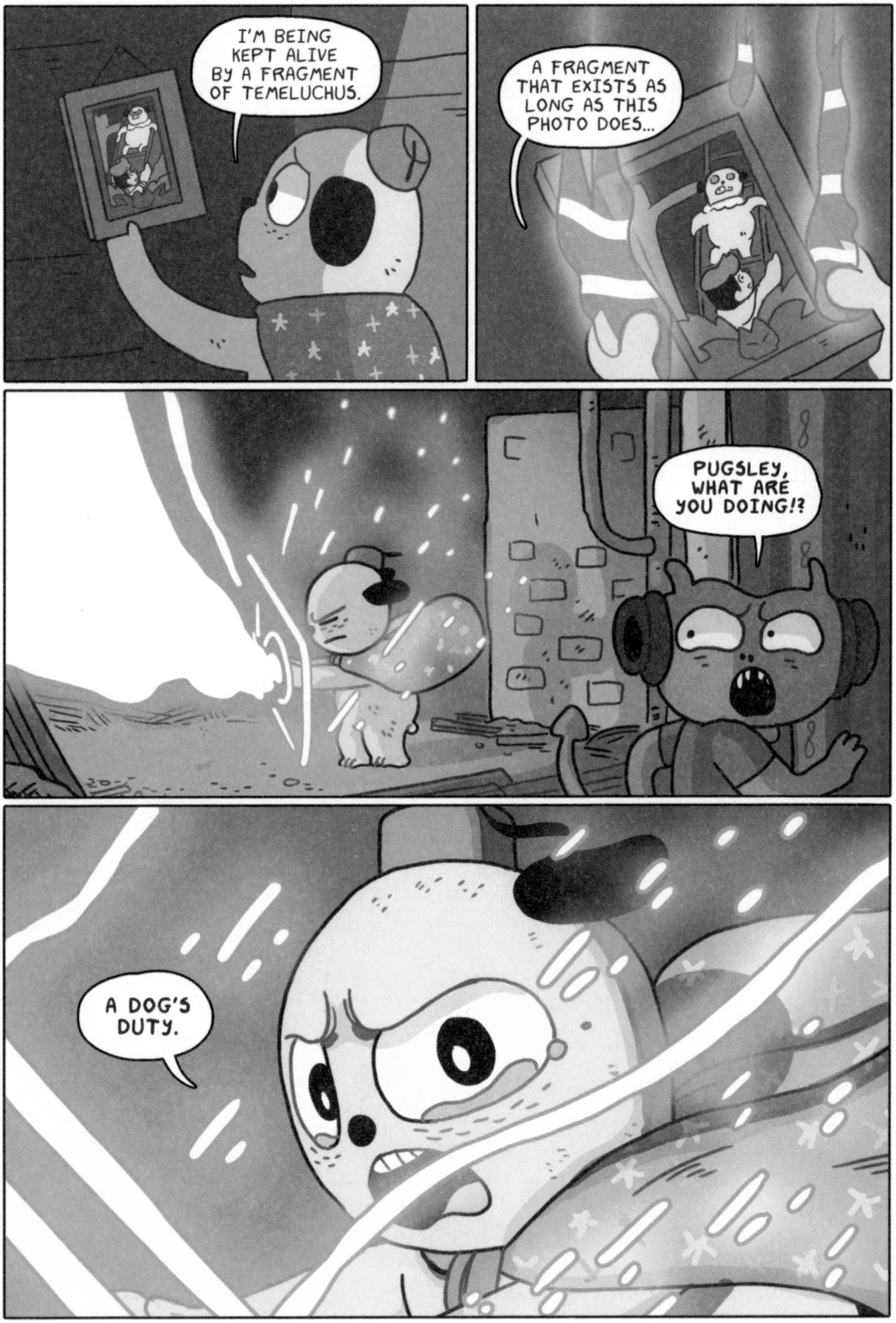
I'M BEING KEPT ALIVE BY A FRAGMENT OF TEMELUCHUS.
A FRAGMENT THAT EXISTS AS LONG AS THIS PHOTO DOES...
PUGSLEY, WHAT ARE YOU DOING!?
A DOG'S DUTY.

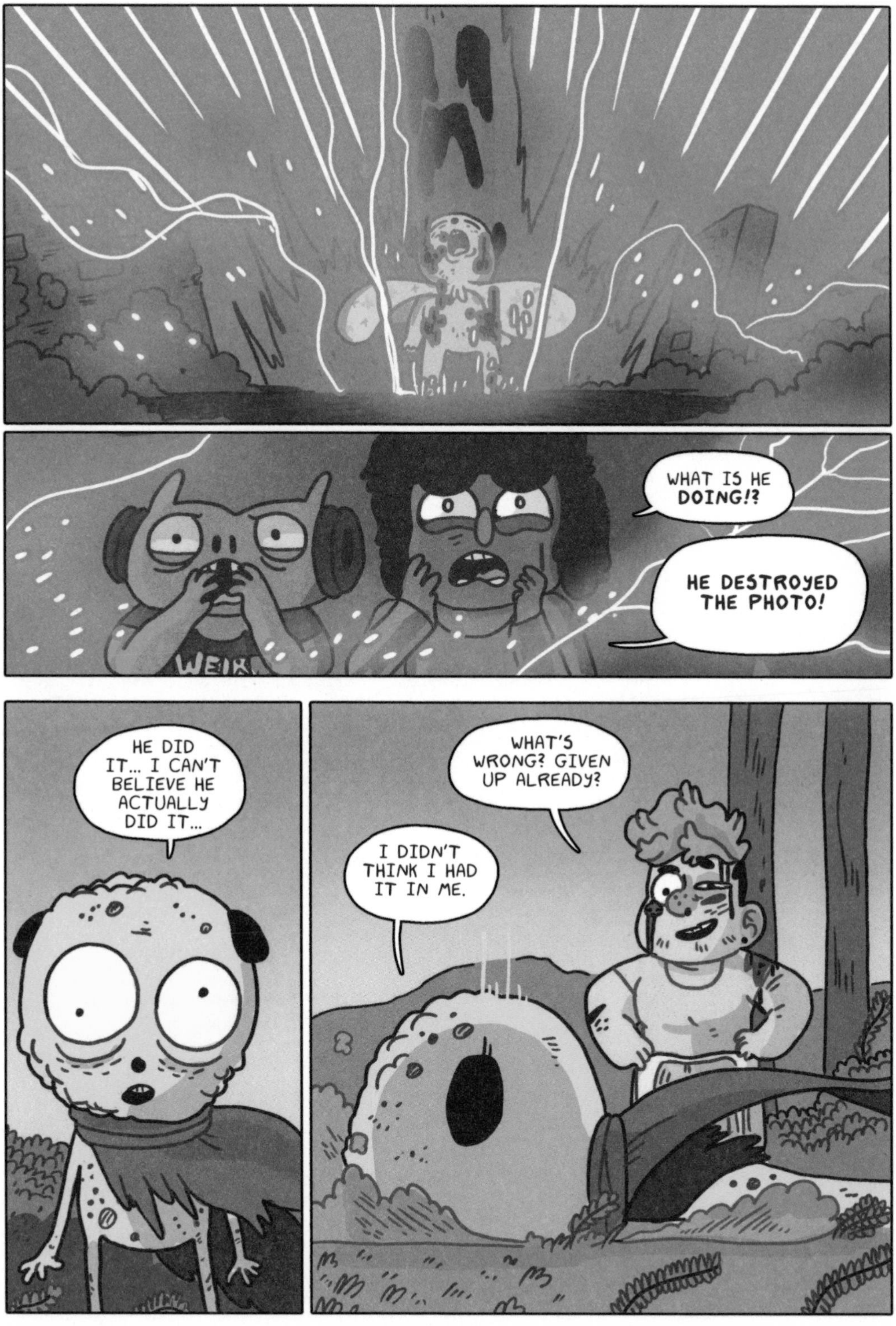
WHAT IS HE DOING!?
HE DESTROYED THE PHOTO!
HE DID IT... I CAN'T BELIEVE HE ACTUALLY DID IT...
WHAT'S WRONG? GIVEN UP ALREADY?
I DIDN'T THINK I HAD IT IN ME.

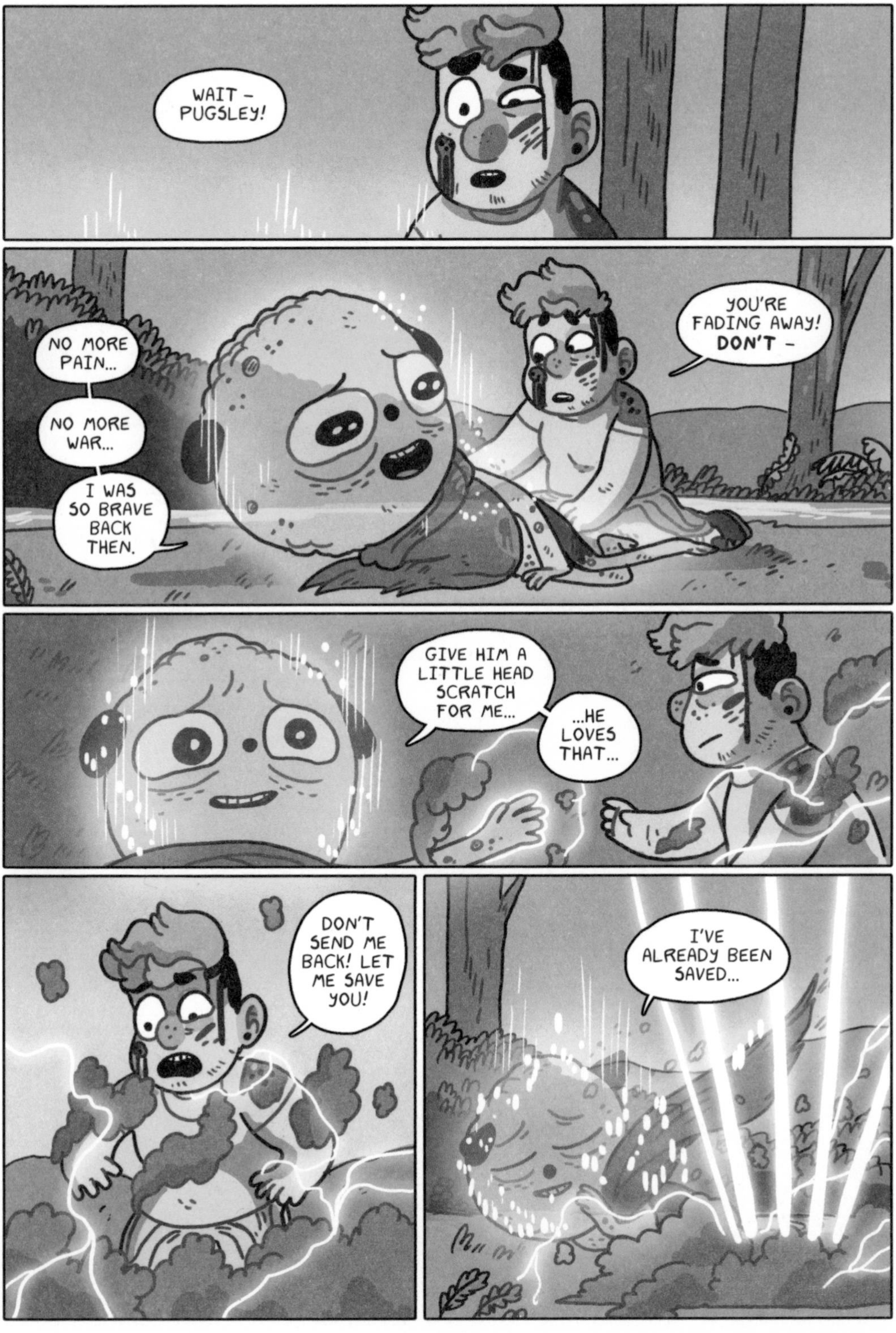
WAIT - PUGSLEY!
NO MORE PAIN...
NO MORE WAR...
I WAS SO BRAVE BACK THEN.
YOU'RE FADING AWAY! **DON'T** -
GIVE HIM A LITTLE HEAD SCRATCH FOR ME...
...HE LOVES THAT...
DON'T SEND ME BACK! LET ME SAVE YOU!
I'VE ALREADY BEEN SAVED...

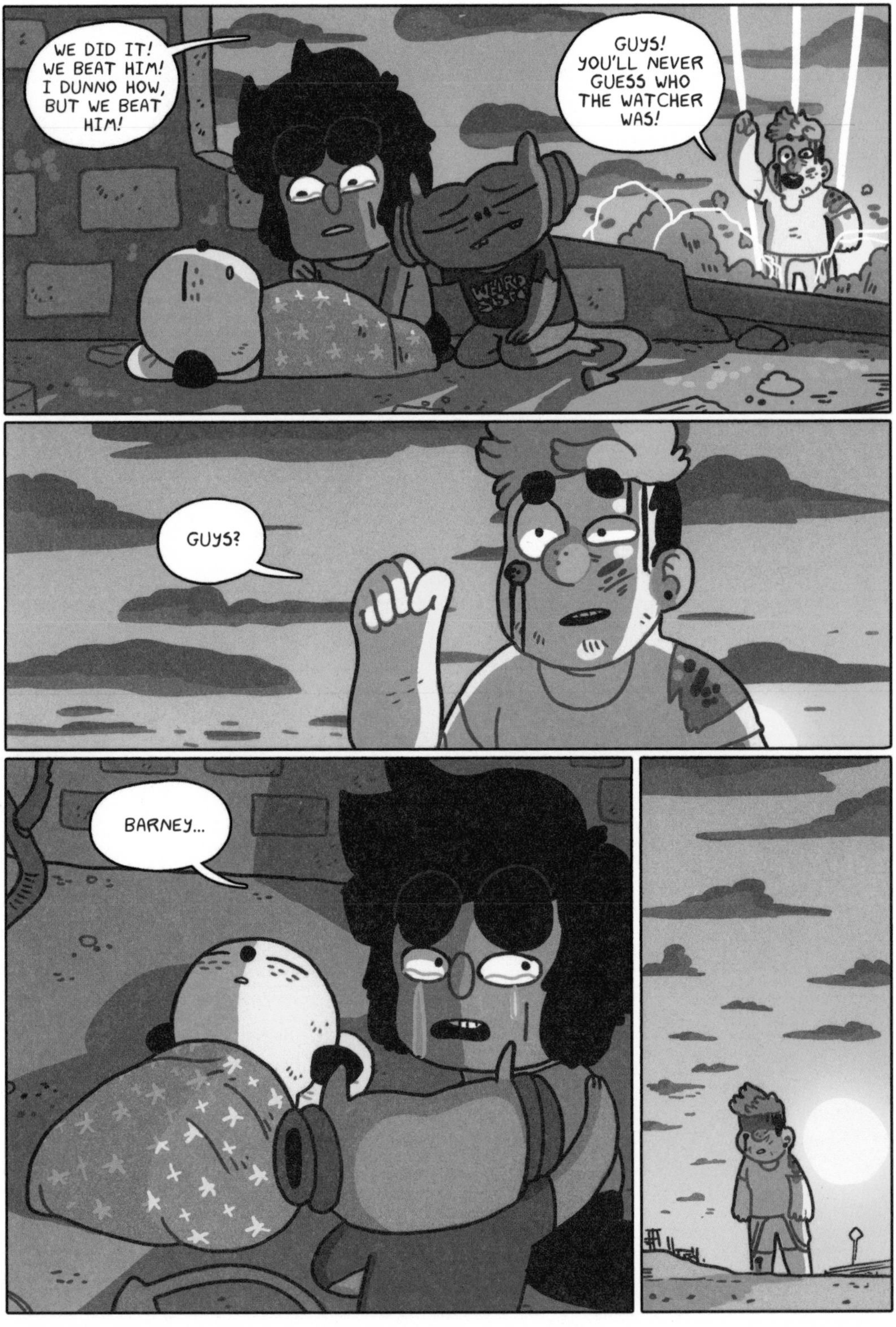
WE DID IT! WE BEAT HIM! I DUNNO HOW, BUT WE BEAT HIM!
GUYS! YOU'LL NEVER GUESS WHO THE WATCHER WAS!
GUYS?
BARNEY...

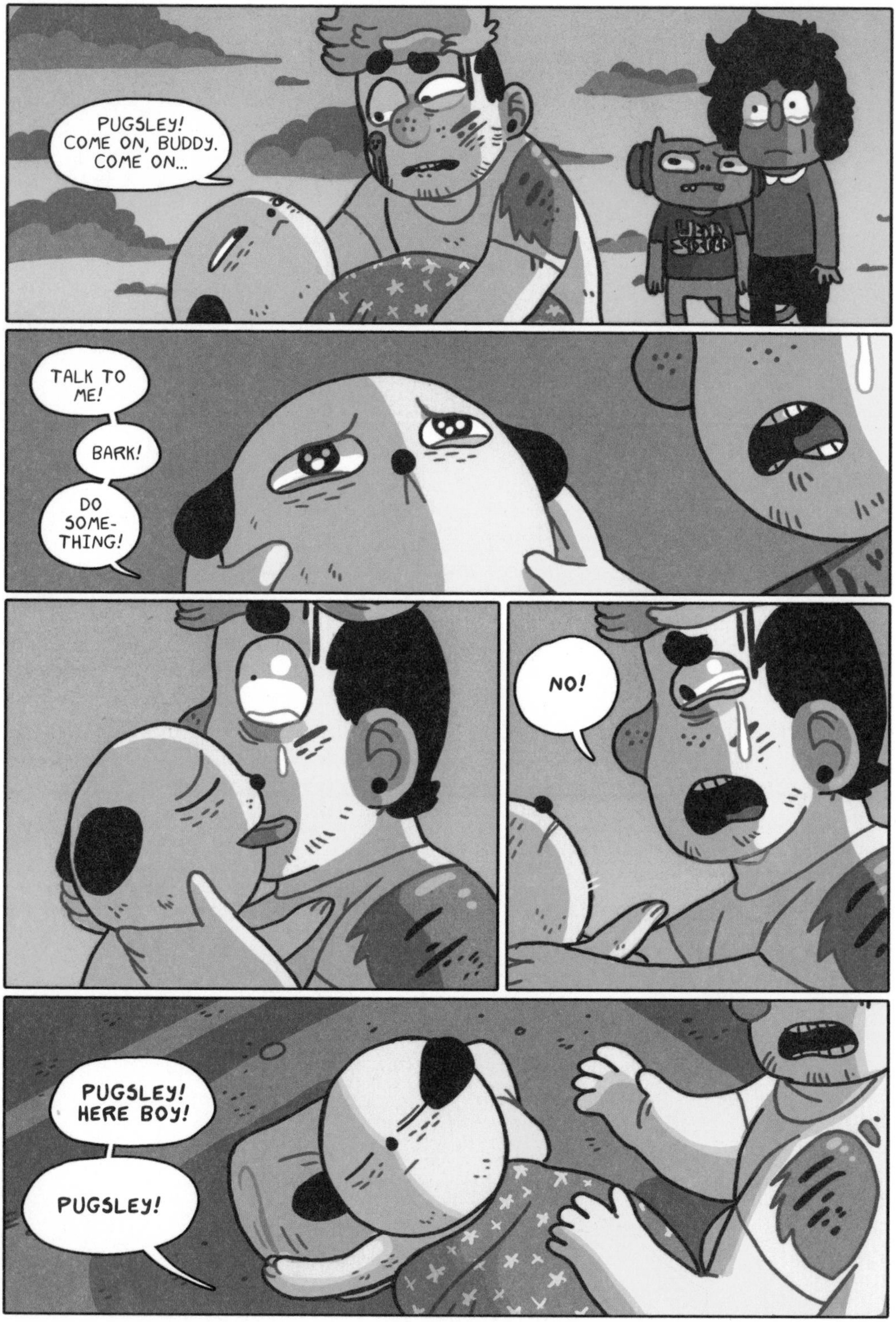
PUGSLEY! COME ON, BUDDY. COME ON...
TALK TO ME!
BARK!
DO SOME-THING!
NO!
PUGSLEY! HERE BOY!
PUGSLEY!

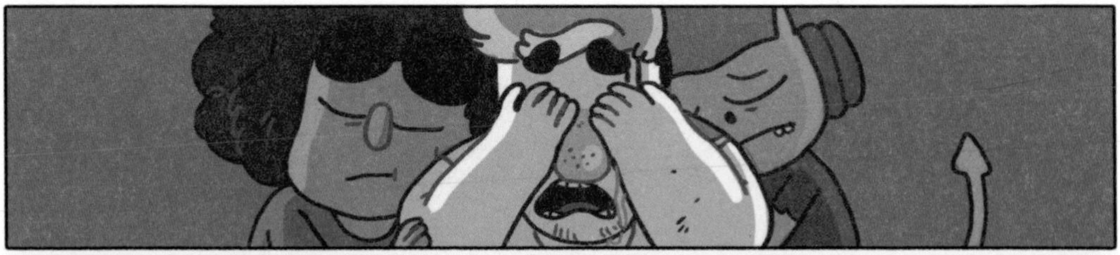

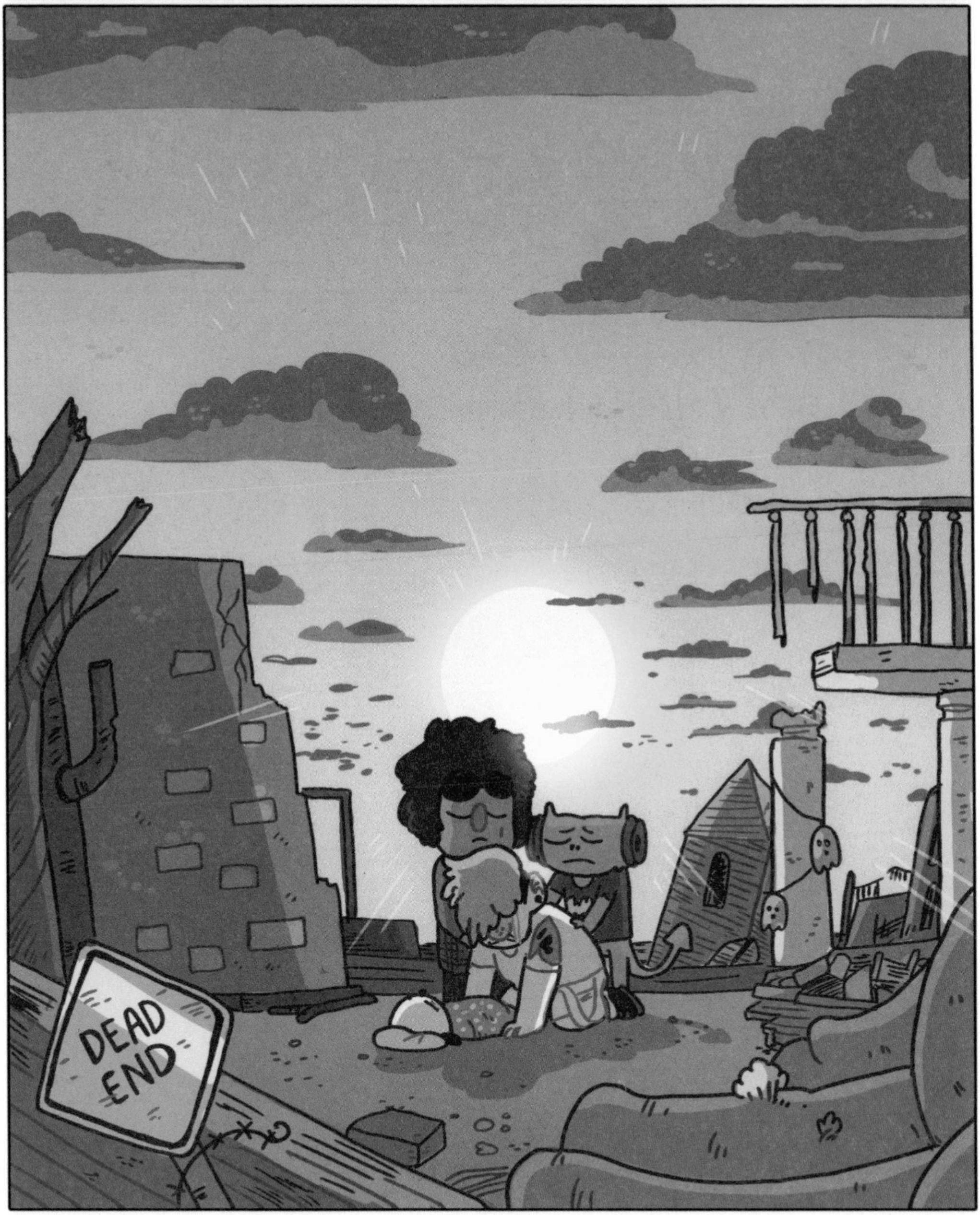
DEAD END

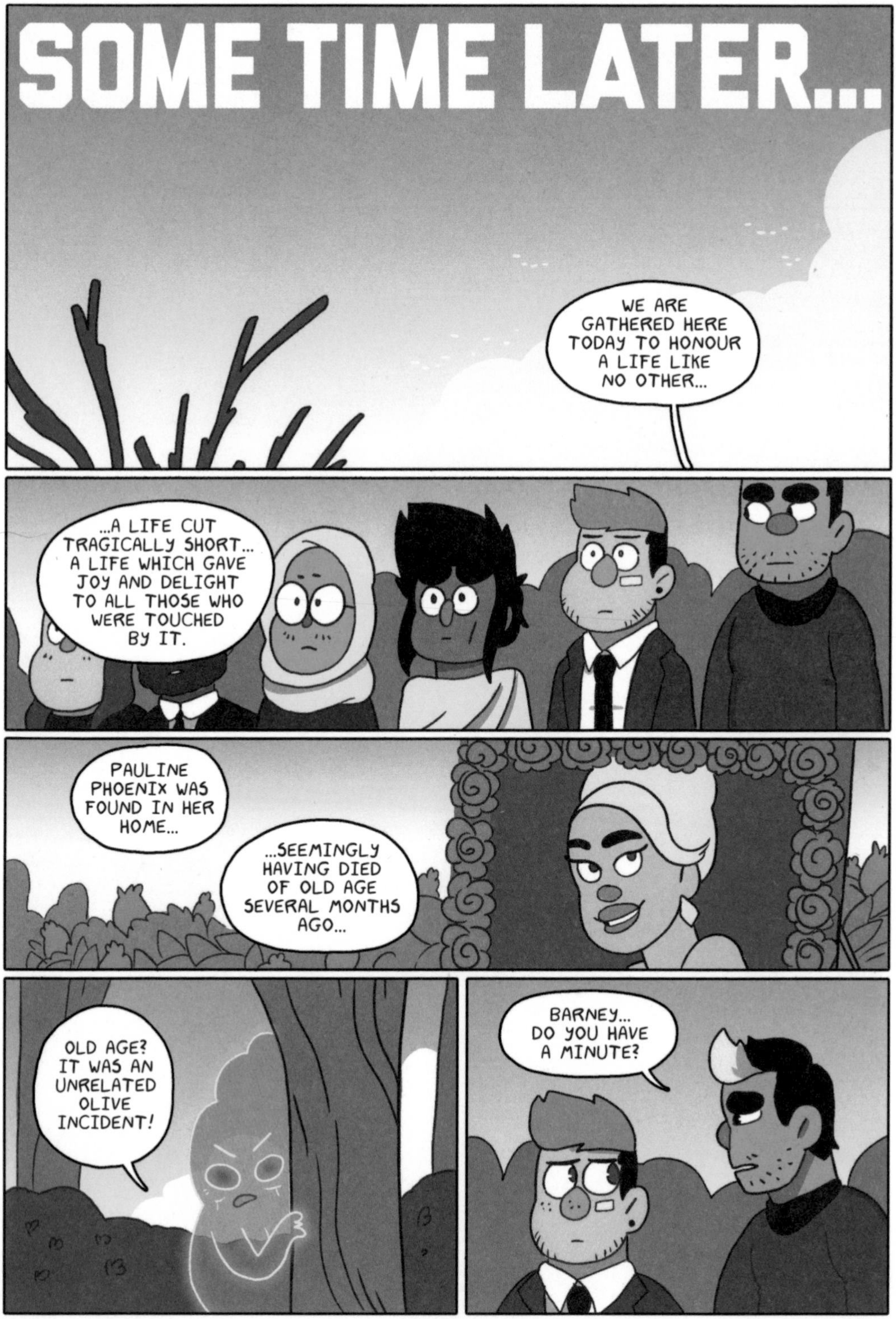
SOME TIME LATER...
WE ARE GATHERED HERE TODAY TO HONOUR A LIFE LIKE NO OTHER...
...A LIFE CUT TRAGICALLY SHORT... A LIFE WHICH GAVE JOY AND DELIGHT TO ALL THOSE WHO WERE TOUCHED BY IT.
PAULINE PHOENIX WAS FOUND IN HER HOME...
...SEEMINGLY HAVING DIED OF OLD AGE SEVERAL MONTHS AGO...
OLD AGE? IT WAS AN UNRELATED OLIVE INCIDENT!
BARNEY... DO YOU HAVE A MINUTE?

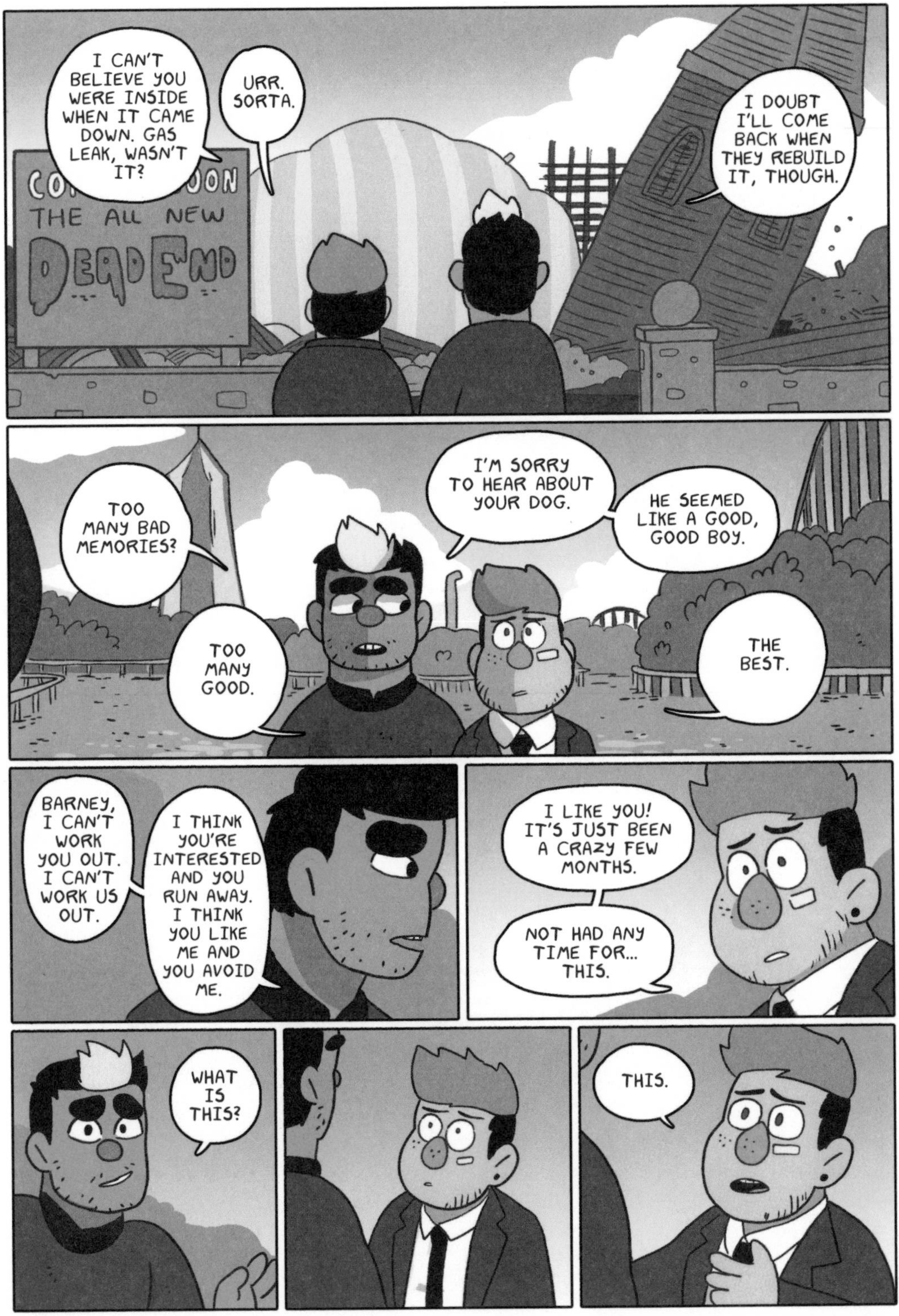
I CAN'T BELIEVE YOU WERE INSIDE WHEN IT CAME DOWN. GAS LEAK, WASN'T IT?
URR. SORTA.
I DOUBT I'LL COME BACK WHEN THEY REBUILD IT, THOUGH.
THE ALL NEW
DEAD END
TOO MANY BAD MEMORIES?
TOO MANY GOOD.
I'M SORRY TO HEAR ABOUT YOUR DOG.
HE SEEMED LIKE A GOOD, GOOD BOY.
THE BEST.
BARNEY, I CAN'T WORK YOU OUT. I CAN'T WORK US OUT.
I THINK YOU'RE INTERESTED AND YOU RUN AWAY. I THINK YOU LIKE ME AND YOU AVOID ME.
I LIKE YOU! IT'S JUST BEEN A CRAZY FEW MONTHS.
NOT HAD ANY TIME FOR... THIS.
WHAT IS THIS?
THIS.

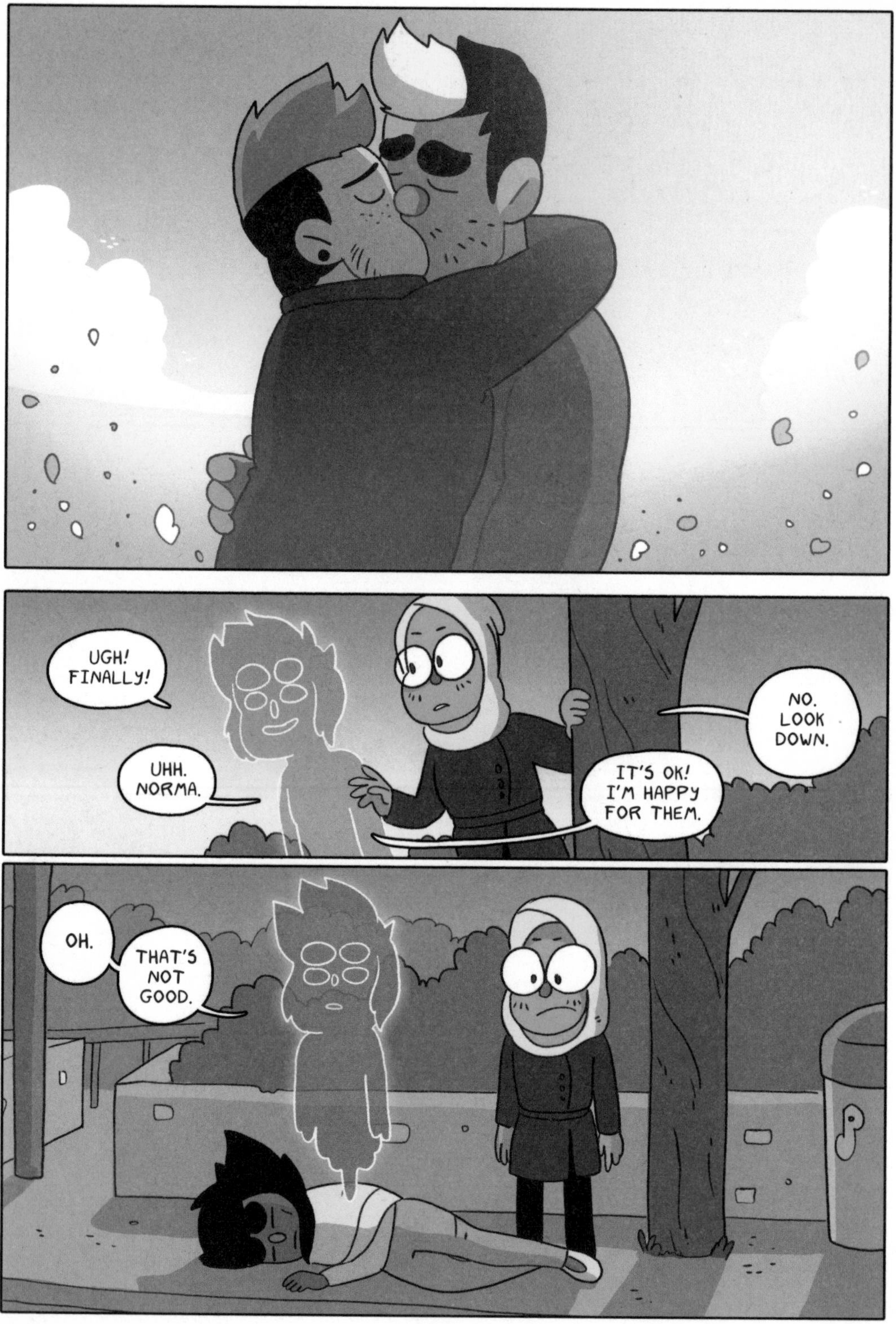
UGH! FINALLY!
UHH. NORMA.
IT'S OK! I'M HAPPY FOR THEM.
NO. LOOK DOWN.
OH.
THAT'S NOT GOOD.

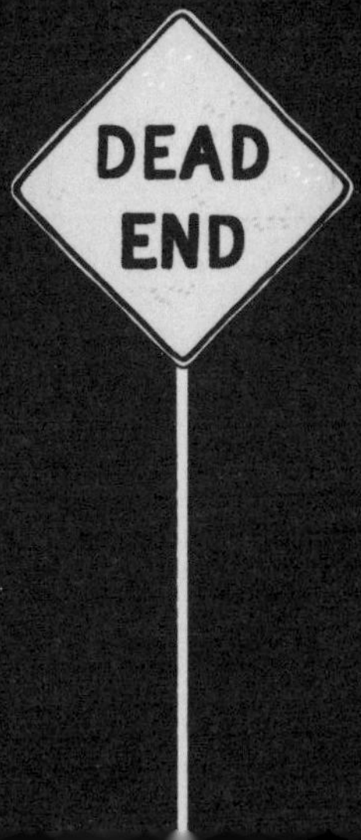
DEAD
END

WHAT
BRINGS YOU HERE,
ANGEL?

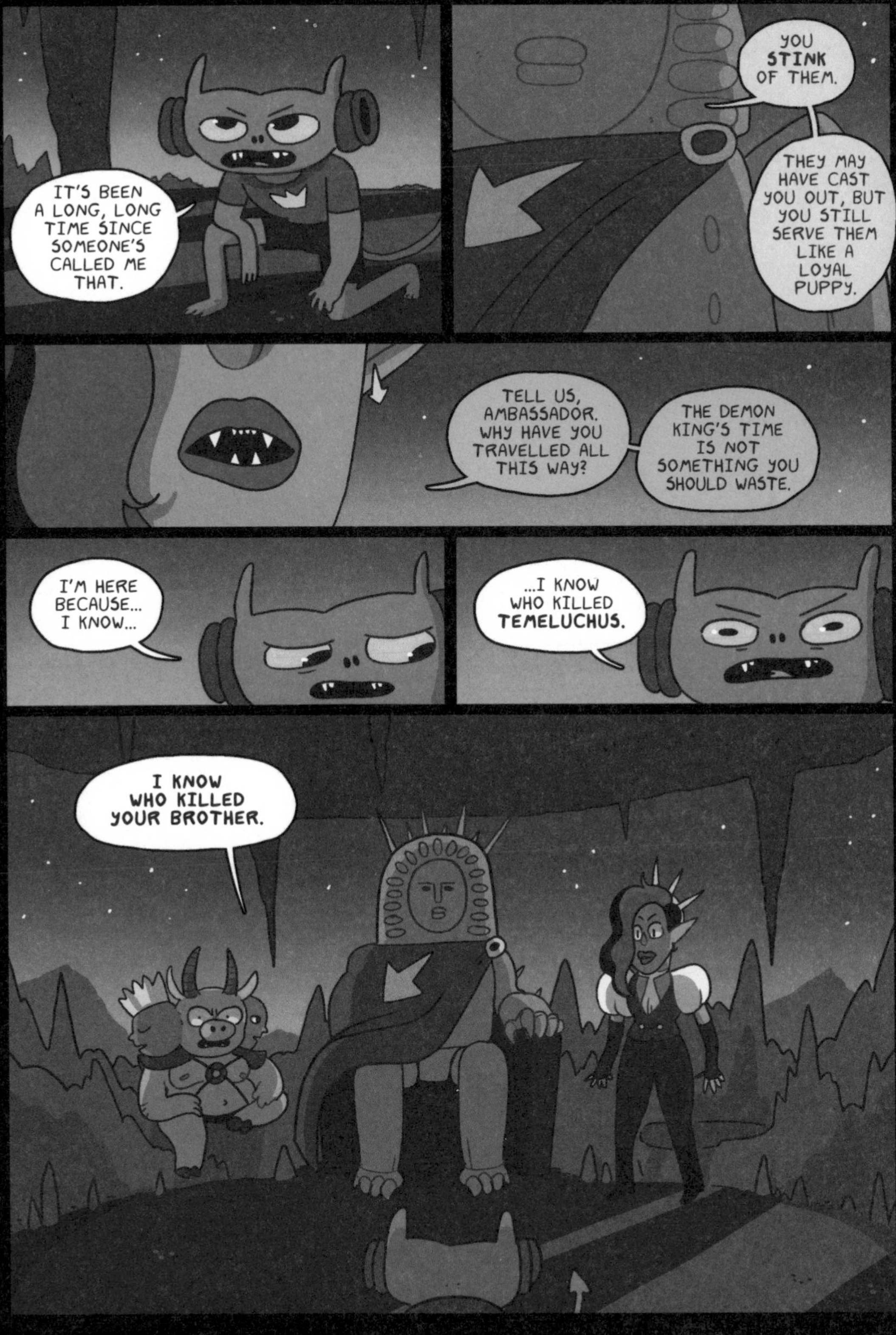
IT'S BEEN A LONG, LONG TIME SINCE SOMEONE'S CALLED ME THAT.
YOU **STINK** OF THEM.
THEY MAY HAVE CAST YOU OUT, BUT YOU STILL SERVE THEM LIKE A LOYAL PUPPY.
TELL US, AMBASSADOR. WHY HAVE YOU TRAVELLED ALL THIS WAY?
THE DEMON KING'S TIME IS NOT SOMETHING YOU SHOULD WASTE.
I'M HERE BECAUSE... I KNOW...
...I KNOW WHO KILLED **TEMELUCHUS.**
I KNOW WHO KILLED YOUR BROTHER.